Then They Came for Harry

Gary A. Campbell

Dear Reader;

The names, characters, organizations, and many of the locales in this story are products of the author's imagination. However, many of the incidents that occur in the story are based on true events, and the accounts that the Main Character reads on the Internet concerning the p.c./cancel culture/ woke movement(s) are all based in fact.

Thank you to my developmental editor, Barbara Sissel,
for all of your help along the way.
It is truly and deeply appreciated.

Thank you to my copy editor, Betsy Head,
Your help was appreciated.

Thank you to my friend, Robert M. Haig,
a fellow author, for all of your help.

Thank you to my friend, Angel Chavez,
for your help as a consultant.

Thank you, Zachary Binroth,
for your artwork.

First, they came for the socialists,
and I did not speak out—because I was not a socialist.

Then they came for the trade unionists,
and I did not speak out—because I was not a trade unionist.

Then they came for the Jews,
and I did not speak out—because I was not a Jew.

Then they came for me—
and there was no one left to speak for me.

Martin Niemoller

When bad men combine, the good must associate;
else they will fall, one by one,
an unpitied sacrifice in a contemptible struggle.

Edmund Burke:
Thoughts on the Cause of the Present Discontents

1

Albrecht, South Dakota was flanked by the Black Hills Mountains on the town's west side, and rolling hills, ravines, and buttes surrounded it to the north and south. After conquering the Cheyenne in 1776, the Lakota people took the territory of the Black Hills, which became their new homeland. The U.S. government signed the Fort Laramie Treaty of 1868, establishing the Great Sioux Reservation west of the Missouri River, and exempting the Black Hills from all white settlement forever.

But General Custer's Black Hills Expedition of 1874 changed everything. While Custer scouted the area for a suitable location for a future fort, civilians on the expedition searched for gold. Soon after, the area was overrun by miners seeking their fortune. The US government then reneged on the treaty, taking back the Black Hills and forcibly relocating the Lakota following the Great Sioux War of 1876, to five smaller reservations in western South Dakota, selling off nine million acres of their former land.

A sea of ponderosa pine lined nearly every hillside of the Black Hills, making the mountains look dark from a distance, an attribute that gave the mountain chain its moniker. Albrecht was nearly impenetrable on three sides, and many of the town's residents believed this was one of its greatest selling points. Access to the town was east, where Highway 79 fed into Maverick Junction.

The town was named after Friedrich Albrecht, a German farmer and amateur geologist who, fearing Adolph Hitler's gradual ascent to power in his homeland, emigrated, along with many other Germans, to America in the late 1920's and settled in the area before the town even had a name. A staunch capitalist at heart, Albrecht started several successful businesses, most notably a mining company that employed hundreds of people from the area and paid them well above industry standards in wages, benefits and bonuses. The company made Albrecht a rich man, and his business prowess and wealth enabled him to enter politics. At the age of forty, he became the first mayor of the newly incorporated municipality. In his later years, philanthropy became his passion. He founded several charities, including the county's first orphanage, and a year after his death in 1955, the town erected a bronze statue of the man in the town square and officially became Albrecht, South Dakota.

The residents of Albrecht took life slow and easy. Tourists and strangers were welcomed in town, as long as they respected the town's laws and ordinances. News traveled quickly through Albrecht, and the news of late concerned the new organizations that were gaining a foothold in town. And they seemed to be appearing out of nowhere. *They* weren't coming, the townsfolk murmured; *they* were already here.

2

In 1967, the conflict in Viet Nam was intensifying. Like his father and grandfather before him, Harry Blake Jr. joined the Marines after graduating from Albrecht High. He knew he wasn't college material, even though he excelled in math, and he was proficient with any tool that he could get his hands on. After completing basic training, Private Blake was in country, trudging through hilly, rocky terrain near Khe Sahn, south of the DMZ. Harry's platoon was on a recon mission, trying to assess enemy positions and strength near the soon-to-be besieged Marine base. Earl Decker, a gangly, good old boy from Texas, pulled up next to Harry. They were just weeks into their first tour, but it felt to Private Blake like they had been friends forever.

"Got a light, ya pole smoker?" Earl said.

Private Blake chuckled as he dug into a pocket and pulled out a lighter. "Speaking of pole smokers, you written your mama lately?"

"Tonight, after chow," replied Earl. As he took a drag on his smoke, Earl scanned the surrounding terrain. His body stiffened as he came to a stop. "Got a feeling Charlie's close, buddy. Real close."

"Command says the NVA's moving heavy artillery and personnel into the area," Private Blake said, continuing down the trail.

Earl yanked on his crotch. "I got some heavy artillery for Charlie right here," he said, grinning.

Blake chuckled as he walked on. "Sure, ya do. Keep up, pencil dick."

Earl started to trot. Two steps later, he tripped up a Bouncing Betty. The mine sprung into the air, spraying ball bearings in every direction. Shrapnel ripped through Earl's midsection, and he collapsed to the ground, screaming in agony.

"Oh, Jesus…" Blake gasped more than he said. He ran to Earl and ripped away his shredded fatigues. Blood gushed from a gaping laceration in Earl's midsection. Blake dug frantically into his pack and pulled out a field dressing. He pressed it hard against what was left of Earl's torso. "Corpsman!" he yelled.

Earl's breathing became labored as his eyes darted from side to side. He tried to smile through his sheer panic. "Charlie's clever, huh, buddy?" Blake pressed harder on the dressing. "Look at me, Earl. Look at me." he said. Then he looked over his shoulder for help. "Corpsman!"

Earl's breathing shallowed. Soaked up to his elbows in his friend's blood, Private Blake pressed still harder on the dressing trying to stanch the bleeding. "Earl, you hold on now, you hear! Help's coming!"

Earl clutched Blake's arm. "Tell Ma I love her, buddy."

"You tell her yourself, buddy. Hold on. Help's coming." Earl's breathing grew erratic.

Moments later, he was gone. "Earl? Earl?" Blake gazed into his friend's lifeless eyes. His head sagged into Earl's chest, and the tears gushed freely. "Corpsman…" he whimpered.

***

Nearly fifty years removed from his service in Vietnam, Harry Blake Jr. was still haunted by his friend's death, even in his sleep. He bolted upright in a cold sweat, his chest heaving as he gasped for air, and he clutched at drenched bed sheets, then quickly flung them aside. He lay down again. His breathing steadied and he closed his eyes. Just moments after he nodded off, a blinding light filled his bedroom, and Harry was jarred awake again. He cursed under his breath as he hoisted his two-hundred and ninety- pound frame off his bed. He already knew the source of the glare. He looked at the clock on the wall: three thirty a.m. "Son of a bitch…" he muttered as he stomped down the stairs and peered through the living room's bay window. The room went dark momentarily, then, it lit up again, like the Vegas strip at midnight. Harry averted his eyes from the intense light, and a few seconds later, the room fell into darkness again. *I'm gonna get that little prick.*

Harry stomped out the front door and down the steps as quickly as his old, battered body could carry him. He stopped at the curb, locking his gaze on the driveway across the street and what sat in it.

Harry couldn't pry his eyes away from the Detroit-made metal monster sitting in Crash's driveway: a 1970 jet black, Chevelle SS 454. From its hood to the deck lid, the car oozed power. *God, its beautiful,* Harry thought.

Crash Lamont, a nineteen- year- old, scrawny, long-haired ne'er-do-well, sat behind the wheel of the Chevelle, grinning. The Chevelle's engine idled in a low purr as if it could go airborne at any moment, but Crash seemed in no hurry to put the car in drive. He flipped on the car's high beams, rendering Harry momentarily blind.

"Turn 'em off, idiot!" Harry yelled.

"Eat it, fat man!" Crash yelled. He revved the Chevelle's engine. Its purr became a roar as the car rocked from side to side on it's chassis.

"I'm warning you, punk!" Harry stepped into the street, defiantly planting his feet into the concrete. Crash slammed the Chevelle into drive. The car's tires screeched as it rocketed down the driveway and fishtailed into the street. Harry's eyes widened when the Chevelle's ass end swerved toward him. He jumped out of the way and landed on his meaty rear end near the curb. The Chevelle regained its footing as its Mickey Thompson performance tires dug into the concrete like a bird of prey's talons digging into soft flesh.

"Get outta the road, Harry!" Crash yelled as he flipped Harry the finger.

Harry grabbed a rock as he hoisted himself off of the pavement. He took aim and fired. The rock shattered a taillight on the Chevelle. Hearing glass hit the pavement, Crash slammed on the brakes, then shifted into reverse. Harry stood his ground. "C'mon, punk!"

Before hitting the gas, Crash did some quick math. The boy realized that Harry had one- hundred pounds on him, easily. And he had seen Harry handle heavy tools like they were toys. Crash added one more factor into the equation as the Chevelle slowed to a near crawl; Harry was really, really pissed at that moment. Crash shifted into drive. As he tore off down the street, he flipped Harry the finger one more time.

Harry did a slow burn as he went back inside his house. He plodded toward the staircase, looked to the top of the stairwell, and sighed. Slowly, he ascended the stairs. And after tossing and turning for almost three hours, he finally managed to sleep.

3

The next morning, Harry sat at the kitchen table, yawning. He hadn't been awake for ten minutes yet, but he was already debating going back to bed. Today was a day he didn't want to face. His rear end still ached from the incident the night before, and pain shot through his bad knee. His grandson, Joey, walked into the kitchen, and, like most teenagers, he went right to the refrigerator. Harry's daughter, Melissa, had died at the tender age of thirty, after a short fight with cancer. Joey's biological father, a jobless slacker who never showed any interest in the boy, signed away his parental rights just two days after Melissa's death. Joey was barely out of diapers when Harry and Patsy adopted him. They were more than happy to give their grandson a good home.

Harry winced when he looked Joey over. The boy was all Emo. His hair was dyed jet black with long bangs, and he was dressed in skinny jeans, a tight t-shirt and a studded belt. Joey rifled through the refrigerator. "Did you and Crash go at it again last night?"

"He always starts it, Joey. You know that. Today's not the day to give Grandpa a hard time."

"Oh, right. Today's Gram's birthday," he said.

"You wanna go with me? We can see your mom, too."

"I've got school."

"I can wait until you get home."

"I've got soccer practice after school."

"That's a sissy-ass sport. You playing with dolls, too?"

"Sure am. Wanna see my collection?" Joey walked out of the kitchen without looking back.

"Joey, I didn't mean anything by that. Joey…" Harry hung his head low and ran his fingers through his thinning hair. *Way to go, Harry.* He reached for a trio of prescription medications staring at him from across the table.

He downed three pills, one for an oncoming migraine, one for the pain that was shooting through his knee, and one more to help him through this day: an anti-depressant. As he washed them down with a glass of water, he thought: *why don't they make a pill for stupidity?*

*****

Harry drove north on Highway 385. As he neared his exit, he saw a billboard that read: *Be Less White, Albrecht.* He tried to decipher the meaning of the message as he drove on, but his curiosity ceased when he passed the front gate of Our Lady of Hope Cemetery. Harry felt an ominous weight suddenly impose itself on him. This cemetery, or any cemetery, reminded him of his own mortality, and of the friends and family he had already lost. He parked his truck, grabbed his cane and a bouquet of flowers, and made his way along a path that led to his wife and daughter's graves.

When he reached their plots, he knelt down and placed a nosegay of irises at the base of both headstones. They were Patsy's favorite flower, and his daughter loved them as well. He slowly arose and stared at his wife's headstone. It read: Patsy Blake. Beloved wife and mother. *I miss you, Pats. Jesus, I miss you so much. And you, too, Melissa, my darling little girl.* The tears started to flow.

4

Colonial Drive North resembled a Norman Rockwell painting. The street was lined with oak trees on many of the front lawns, and Cape Cod-styled homes dominated the avenue. The neighborhood, one of the oldest in Albrecht, had small town charm oozing from it in every picket fence and porch swing that dotted the street.

It was a warm, sunny, mid-spring day that drew Harry out of the house. He stood on his front lawn, looking his home over. He knew the house needed a new coat of paint, and the gutters replacing as well. Patsy would have prodded him to get the projects done, but since she was no longer around, he just didn't give a damn whether or not the improvements got done any time soon, if ever.

Charlie Sloan, a slightly-built elderly man with gray, wispy hair, stepped out his front door and into the awaiting sunshine. He craned his neck skyward to bask in the warm glow of the sun. He spun his cane around, then tapped it on each of the steps that led him from his porch down to the sidewalk. As he approached his mailbox at the end of his front walkway, he stopped and sniffed the air. "Morning, Harry."

"How'd you know I was here, Sloan?"

"Your after shave could stop a charging rhino."

Harry smiled, knowing Charlie couldn't see his grin. "Five more steps and you'll be at the mailbox, Sloan."

"Five more steps would put me in the street, you ape."

"Let's find out," Harry said.

Charlie dug into his mailbox and pulled out the day's mail. "Any plans today, Harry?" But Harry didn't hear him. His gaze was locked on the Chevelle across the street. "Harry?"

When he still got no response from Harry, Charlie sniffed the air, got his bearings, and approached Harry. He brandished his cane once again and swung it. It clipped Harry's head. "Dammit, Sloan, what the hell's wrong with you?"

"Snap out of it, son. There's no law that says you have to be stupid and rude."

Harry rubbed his head as he scowled at the old man. "I oughta knock you into last week, old man."

Charlie chuckled as he reached for Harry's arm. "You're all talk, big fella. Anytime you want a good ass whipping, you know where to find me." Harry led the old man back to his front steps. They grabbed a seat on the bottom step.

"I heard you last night," Charlie said. "You woke me out of a sound sleep."

"The boy idiot was at it again. He nearly ran me over, but I got him."

"How so?"

"Knocked out one his taillights."

"You must be really proud."

"That sarcasm, old man?"

"Nothing gets past you, Harry. I heard the boy tear ass down the street. Where do you suppose he goes that time of the morning?"

"No idea."

"Any plans for the day?" Sloan said.

"Nope."

"You and free time, Harry? That's like a monkey and a handful of feces. It's bound to end up badly for someone."

"Die already, old man."

"After you," Charlie responded.

A grin stretched across Harry's face. After his visit to the cemetery earlier in the day, he really needed to smile. Across the street, a stunning, young girl came out the front door of Crash's house. She skipped down the steps, jiggling all the way. Harry perked up, and he tapped Sloan on the leg.

"What?" Charlie said.

"There's a hot, young girl across the street."

"Is she coming from the idiot's house?"

"Yeah. I hope her next stop is a clinic."

"What's she wearing?" Charlie said.

"Halter top, short shorts, and a smile," Harry said, waving to the girl.

"Is she walking this way?" Sloan said.

Harry looked over his shoulder. He saw his mother, Gertie, looming over him and Sloan on the top step. With her gray, tussled hair, pointy nose, and no more than ninety pounds covering her small, bony frame, the old woman resembled a vulture perched on the limb of a tree. Gertie scowled as she looked across the street at the girl. Harry was about to warn Charlie about the presence of his mother, but he realized it was a chance for him to have some fun at the old man's expense.

"Talk to me, Harry," Sloan said.

"She's smokin' hot, Sloan. Smokin'."

Charlie stroked his cane. "I'd like to take a bite out of her, develop lockjaw, and get dragged to death."

Gertie bounded down the steps, grabbed Charlie's cane, and brought it down on his head. "I'll give you lockjaw, you old fool!"

Harry winced as he tried to stifle a laugh. Gertie threw the cane to the ground and stomped up the steps and into the house. As Charlie rubbed his forehead, Harry erupted with laughter. "That's gotta hurt, Sloan."

"Get my cane, you ass," Charlie said.

Harry, still chuckling, picked up the old man's cane and handed it to him. Charlie whacked Harry's leg with it.

"What the hell, Sloan?"

"You knew Gertie was standing there, didn't you? You could have warned me."

"Yeah, I could have." Harry stood up and stretched. "You know, my daddy once told me something I'll never forget."

Harry crept up the steps, eased open the front door, slipped past it, and closed it quietly. "What'd he tell you, Harry?" Charlie waited for a response that wasn't coming. "Harry?"

***

Harry ate dinner alone, again. Gertie was next door with Charlie, and Joey, his grandson, was out somewhere, as he usually was these days. Harry didn't want to be alone, so when his phone rang in the middle of dinner and he saw it was Ronnie calling, he couldn't answer the call quickly enough. Harry and Ronnie went back a long way. They had played football together in high school, and they'd both fought in Vietnam. Ronnie only served one tour, but he'd seen enough action, and tragedy, to last a lifetime, as he recounted only when he went on a bender.

Like many other war vets, Ronnie could only really open up about his wartime experiences when alcohol was flowing through him.

When Ronnie returned home from Vietnam, he married his high school sweetheart, Annie, and they raised two kids. Three years ago, he quit his job as a diesel mechanic to care for Annie when she was diagnosed with middle stage A.L.S. Ronnie spent every waking moment tending to her and hoping for a miracle so they could share their golden years together, but only one year after her diagnosis, Annie had passed.

When Harry heard the news, he was at his friend's doorstep within an hour. Ronnie opened his front door, stared blankly at Harry and said, "she's…she's gone," just before his legs gave out and he fell into Harry's awaiting arms.

After several months of grieving for his lost wife, Ronnie had tried to pick up the pieces. He'd wanted – and needed - to get back to work. But despite his sterling work record and skills, his former employer had no desire to bring him back. Ronnie had been replaced by someone forty years his junior, and for half the pay. Countless hours trying to find a mechanic's job at age seventy-five proved to be an exercise in futility. Feeling stripped of his manhood, and still reeling from the passing of his wife, Ronnie turned to the bottle to dull the pain.

***

A half an hour later, Harry looked around Sam's Saloon as he waited for his friend to show. The clientele at Sam's was blue collar, local, and loyal. Harry had always felt at home here. He spun on his barstool and smiled when Ronnie "Redfeather" Wanahnton walked through the front door and grabbed a seat next to him. Ronnie shook Harry's hand and said, "Hello, White Devil."

"White Devil? What's with the name calling, Red Man?"

"Just trying to keep up with the times. Hear about the Little Hawk statue at the ballpark?"

"No. What?"

"Some assholes tore it down a few days ago. Said it was racist and disrespectful. And they're gonna rename the stadium."

"You're kidding, right?"

"Wouldn't kid you about that."

"Son of a bitch," Harry said as he sat back in his seat. "Do those assholes know that statue was tribute to the man and his tribe?"

"Don't think they give a shit, buddy. Heard it was a group from the city that did the deed."

"That statue didn't bother you, did it?"

Ronnie slugged down half of his beer. "I was good with it," he said. "I think the town meant to honor the man when they put it up. Of course, we'd prefer to get our land back and ship Whitey off to wherever the hell he came from."

"I get that," Harry said.

Ronnie chuckled.

"What's so funny?" Harry said.

"Some of you white people crack me up."

"How so?"

"They pretend to speak for my people when they do shit like this. Like they're the ones that suffered the way my people did, and suddenly they know what's best for us and what we should like and not like. Tearing down a statue makes 'em feel better about themselves, like it's helping my people somehow. Bunch of self-flagellating douchebags."

Harry's anger simmered just below the surface. "I can't believe they tore down Little Hawk. Bastards." Ronnie shrugged as he raised his beer to his mouth. A drunk man about Harry's size stumbled into Ronnie, causing him to spill his beer on Ronnies's shirt. The man snickered as he kept moving towards the front door. "What the hell?" Harry jumped off his stool. "Hey, buddy!"

The man stopped and turned to face Harry, and Ronnie grabbed him by the arm. "Let it go, Harry."

"You're one smart Injun," the man said. As Harry stiffened and clenched his fists, the man dug into his pocket, pulled a five-dollar bill out, crumbled it up, and threw in in Ronnie's direction. "Get yourself some firewater on me, Tonto," he said.

Harry broke free of Ronnie's grip. "What'd you call my buddy, asshole?"

The man locked eyes with Harry. "We got a problem?" he said.

"We sure as shit do. Looks like someone's gotta teach you some manners."

"Harry, it ain't worth it," Ronnie said as he grabbed for Harry's arm again.

The man grinned as he stood his ground. "Let's see what you got, old man," he said, tightly clenching a beer bottle at his side. Harry didn't see the beer bottle as he advanced on the man. Three seconds later, Harry was unconscious, and face down on the barroom floor.

Ronnie blew through multiple red lights driving Harry to the hospital. He watched over Harry as he lay unconscious in bed, his head wrapped in bandages. An O.R. doctor had just checked his vitals minutes ago, and she had told Ronnie that Harry was lucky to be alive. The beer bottle missed his temple by mere millimeters.

5

"Fast Freddie" Lamont, attorney at law, sat at his desk reviewing a case file. He had earned that name after making a career of playing fast and loose with the law. Fred embraced the nickname as a badge of honor. His ability to win even the most frivolous lawsuits was legendary, and he never lacked clients. Thinking about his net worth never failed to give Fred an erection.

But what really aroused him to another level of rigidity was thinking about the money he was making dealing meth and cocaine to the "local yokels," of Albrecht. Freddie despised the town and considered its residents to be simpletons, but there was serious money to be made so he set up shop in town the year before to keep an eye on his cousin, Crash, and to establish himself as "one of them." But every Friday he drove back to the city, and his half a million-dollar condo, like he couldn't get there quickly enough. Even the thought of his condo aroused him. His smile disappeared when Crash blew in through the office door.

Fred thought Crash was an idiot, and he didn't give a damn that his younger cousin was family. What mattered to him was that the boy knew all the players in town, and he didn't have a clue that Fred paid him a mere fraction of what he could earn dealing for another supplier.

"What up, Cuz?" Crash said as he slid into a chair across from Fred.

"I'm busy. What can I do for you, Francis?"

"I hate that name," Crash said.

"I know," Fred replied.

"You still nailing that secretary of yours?" Crash said, snickering.

"Why are you here?"

"We gotta talk about some shit that happened the other night."

Exasperated, Fred leaned back in his chair. *If I had a gun right now,* he mused. "What shit did you get into now?"

"Why you gotta be like that, Cuz?" Crash said, leafing through paperwork on Fred's desk. "You got any porn around here?"

Fred slapped Crash's hand. "Focus, Francis. What happened?"

Crash withdrew his hand, leaned back and plopped his feet on Fred's desk. "It's the old guy across the street."

Fred swatted Crash's feet off the desk. "Are you screwing with him again? Why don't you just leave him the hell alone?"

"He threw a rock at my wheels and knocked a taillight out. I want his ass," Crash said.

"Why did he throw a rock at your car, Francis?"

"Hell if I know. The guy ain't wired right, is all."

Fred leaned in close enough to slap the boy. "We both know you've been provoking the old man for a while now, and we don't need the attention. Leave him the hell alone."

"Are you my lawyer, or not?" said Crash.

"I am."

"Then, do something. Charge him with something."

Fred leaned back as his blood pressure started to rise. "I don't charge people with crimes. That's not how it works."

"I want his ass!"

Fred knew he had to keep the boy happy, at least until he found a new dealer he could trust. He grabbed a pen and a pad of paper. "We'll have to file a complaint, and you may have to go to court and testify against this guy," he said.

"That's cool," Crash said.

"Okay, I'll look into it. In the meantime, stop provoking the old guy, Francis. I mean it."

Crash got up and headed for the door. "Nail that bastard for me, Cuz,"

"I almost forgot," Fred said. "You're going to be taking a new guy on your next trip. Calls himself Mad Dog. He's going to be your muscle. We're going to start moving more product into Pine Ridge. Show him the ropes."

"How much we movin' this time?"

"About half a key. Leave the old man alone, Francis. Got it?"

"Yeah, yeah," Crash said on his way out the door.

6

Harry rolled over in bed and squinted at the alarm clock; it was 5:15 p.m. He sat up on the edge of his bed and stiffened up as a bolt of pain shot through him. "Shit," he muttered, as he ran a hand along the bandages still wrapped around his head. He looked up and saw Joey standing in the doorway.

"The other guy start it for once?" Joey said. Harry didn't respond. Embarrassed that his grandson saw him like this, he looked away. Joey handed a piece of paper to his grandfather. "It's from my principal. He wants to meet with you."

"What about, Joey?"

"Read the note. Go or don't go. I don't care." Joey headed for the door. "You look pretty banged up," he said. "Maybe we should pull the plug on you, too." That barb stung Harry. He buried his face in his hands as he hung his head. *It wasn't my fault, Joey*.

***

Gertie lay in Charlie Sloan's bed, taking a nap when Charlie walked into the bedroom and gently woke her. "What is it?" Gertie said.

"Harry got hurt."

"My Harry? Hurt?"

As fast as her ninety-five-year-old bones could move her, Gertie shot out of the bed and made a dash out of the bedroom. She blew through the Blake front door and nearly ran over Joey as he walked through the living room. Gertie grabbed the boy's arm.

"Where's your grandfather?!"

"He's upstairs."

"Harry!" Gertie said as she rushed up the stairs. "Harry!" she screamed.

She looked up and saw Harry standing at the top of the stairs. Gertie made it up three steps before she stopped to catch her breath. Harry descended the stairs and grabbed his mother by the arm. "You're gonna have a heart attack if you don't slow down, Ma," Harry said as he led her back to the living room. He eased her into the recliner. Gertie gently traced her hand along Harry's cheek. When she saw the bandages wrapped around Harry's head, her eyes filled with tears. "I'm okay," Harry said.

"You got into a fight, didn't you, sonny boy?"

He gently pushed her hand away. "Aw, Ma…."

Ronnie tapped on the screen door and, seeing Harry, he walked in. "How you feeling, buddy?" Catching sight of Gertie in her robe, he quickly looked away.

"See something you like, stranger?" Gertie snapped.

"Mom, that's Ronnie. You know him," Harry said. "Joey, take your great-grammy upstairs."

"What the hell am I, the family dog?" Gertie barked. She got up and stomped out the front door.

Harry rubbed his temples. "Joey, go get her before she gets hit by a car." But Joey wasn't paying attention. He was in the dining room texting on his phone. "Joey," Harry said. When he again got no response from the boy, he yelled, "Joey, go before I pitch that damn phone of yours!" Joey snapped out of his trance and headed for the front door. When he stepped outside, he saw Gertie ambling down the middle of the street and nearing a busy intersection. He broke into a sprint.

Harry settled onto the sofa, and Ronnie took a seat next to him. "How's the head?" Ronnie said.

"The last thing I remember is some asshole and something

about...firewater. But I'll never forget the bastard's face."

"He hit you with a beer bottle. You were sticking up for me, buddy."

"They get him?" Harry said.

"Not yet. He hightailed it out of the bar. I saw a swastika tattoo on his forearm. I'm pretty sure he's one of those Brownshirts."

"What the hell's that?"

"It's a neo-Nazi group. Most of 'em are from the Bremerhaven area. They meet up at an abandoned rec center up there. They talk a lot of shit about starting a revolution, and they run guns and drugs, but they do more drinking than anything else."

"How do you know this shit?"

"Got a cousin lives up that way. He works with a few of them at the foundry."

"They meet at an abandoned rec center, huh?"

"Yeah. What are you thinking, Harry?"

"Nothing."

Ronnie got up off the sofa. "I should get rolling."

"Where you headed?"

"To Pine Ridge. Check on some of my people."

Ronnie extended his hand and Harry shook it. "You take care, buddy," Ronnie said. "Get some rest."

"Will do. See you soon."

After Ronnie left, Harry sat back and thought about the man who nearly took his life. He got online and found a website with information about the Brownshirts. Known in World War 2 Germany as the SA, and acronym for the Sturmabteilung, he read that the group was the original paramilitary wing of the Nazi Party that helped Hitler gain power. A large number of former Communists and Social Democrats joined the ranks of the organization. They were called 'beefsteaks' – brown outside and red within. The World War II era SA consisted of many unemployed and working-class men. They were streetfighters, quick to beat into submission any who stood against them. Harry made a mental note of that fact.

***

Fred Lamont finally found what he was looking for after leafing through several law books: the section covering ethnic intimidation laws recently enacted in the state. As he delved into an article and grasped its ramifications, he knew he had hit paydirt. "We have a winner," he said to no one there. He celebrated by doing a line of coke off his desk.

7

On less than two hours of sleep, Harry, grumpy as hell, dragged himself out of bed at ten a.m. and drove to Albrecht High School. After waiting in the lobby just down from the principal's office for half an hour, he looked at his watch again. Principal Rhode was late, and it irritated the hell out of him. His bad knee ached, and his head still throbbed from the incident at the bar. He tried stretching the knee to ease the pain, and he searched his pockets for his pain pills. Then he remembered that he left them at home. "Shit," he muttered.

The principal's assistant, a young woman named Sandy, walked into the lobby just as Harry cursed. "Excuse me?" Sandy said.

"What?" Harry said.

"You cursed."

"Yeah, under my breath, honey," Harry said.

"I heard it," Sandy replied. "And I don't appreciate being called 'honey' by strangers."

"The name's Harry. Now we're not strangers, honey. Where the hell is the principal?"

"That's the second time you've cursed in my presence, sir. I take offense to that."

"Are you religious? Is that the problem?" Harry said.

"No, I'm a humanist."

"That's great. Whatever the hell that is."

"I'm not comfortable with your cursing, sir."

"Don't mind me, darling. I'm just irritated, is all."

"Did you just call me 'darling'?"

Harry felt a headache coming on. "Oh, Jesus. Is there any way I can ask you where the hell the principal is without offending you?"

"Do you have an appointment?"

"Yeah. The name's Harry Blake. I've got an appointment with the principal, and he's late."

"Principal Rhode has cancelled all of his appointments for the day. He asked me to reschedule you."

Harry grunted as he got to his feet. "That's just great. Thanks so much for letting me know before I hauled my ass down here for nothing," he said.

"Are you Joey Blake's grandfather?"

"Yeah. Why?"

"Your grandson harassed a fellow student."

"From what I hear, all he did was ask a girl where her family was from."

"And in doing so, he was implying that the girl was a foreigner, and that may have made her feel marginalized, and maybe even oppressed. That's a microaggression."

Harry stared, stupefied, at Sandy as he tried to process that statement. "Marginalized and oppressed? You're kidding, right?"

"No, I'm not. We don't joke about such things at this school, Mr. Blake. Everyone has a right to their dignity and their safe space on this campus."

Harry rolled his eyes and chuckled.

"Did I say something that amuses you, Mr. Blake?"

"What's your name?" he said.

"It's Sandy."

"How old are you, Sandy?"

"I'm twenty. Is my age relevant to this conversation?"

"So, you're a few years out of high school, right? Maybe you've dated a few guys, you're going to college, and you probably spend hours chatting with your gal pals about this and that. All the stuff girls your age do, right?"

"I am a young woman, Mr. Blake, not a girl."

"Who do you live with?"

"My mom and dad, if that's any of your business. Just until I finish getting my bachelor's degree."

"What's your major?"

"Gender studies."

"Gender studies? Never had an anatomy class?"

"It doesn't mean that. The term "gender" has evolved. Now it refers to the social and cultural constructions of masculinity and femininity, and not to the binary state of being male or female."

"Sure thing," Harry said. "What are you gonna do with that degree?"

"I plan to fight for women's rights, and to ensure that all women are treated fairly and with respect."

"Like for this girl my grandson supposedly harassed, right?"

"Yes. So?"

Harry chuckled again.

"Is there something funny about harassment, Mr. Blake?"

"You sure that's what happened here? You sure my boy really harassed this girl?"

"That seems to be what happened."

"Were you there when Joey was talking to this girl?"

"No, but -"

"So, you're about twenty, huh? When I was your age, I was fighting for this country in a place called Vietnam. Ever hear of it?"

Sandy placed her hands on her hips. "Is there a point to this?"

"By the time I was your age, I was into my second tour. I watched men die in ways you couldn't even imagine, little girl. I didn't have the time or luxury of worrying about whether or not everything in life was fair. I prayed every day just to get home in one piece."

"We shouldn't have been there in the first place," Sandy said. "We were only there to expand this country's empire."

"Hindsight's a wonderful thing, little lady. But I was just a grunt who did what he was ordered to do, politics be damned."

"You were a puppet," Sandy said. "A puppet for a fascist government bent on world domination."

"I was a soldier!" Alarmed at Harry's fury, Sandy backed up a step. "I saw what the real world was like, firsthand. I saw more death in a day than you'll ever see in a lifetime. I was a scared kid who just wanted to get back home alive. You wanna know what happened when I got back home? I got called a baby killer. And people spit on me! And..." Trembling, Harry tried to compose himself. "I've got nothing against you, honey, but a kid your age knows shit about real life. You want sunny skies every day? Become a painter. You want fairness? Write your congressman and see where that gets you."

"You seem to be a very angry man, Mr. Blake," Sandy said. "Maybe you should just chill."

"I should chill? That your advice, doctor? How about this? How about you come back and see me in about twenty years when worrying about everything keeps you from a good night's sleep, the boss is an asshole, and your kids make it their life's mission to drive you crazy. Then maybe your husband'll die in an auto accident, and maybe one of your kids'll die of cancer and you'll have the privilege of going on without them." Tears welled up in Harry's eyes, but he fought them back. "Wait 'til life starts smacking you around, cause trust me, it's coming. And when life starts taking things from you over and over, and when it tries beating you into a fuckin' pulp, you can look me up and bitch 'til your blue in the face. And you know what I'll tell you? I'll tell you to just chill, honey."

"I am not your honey," said Sandy. "And there's the door."

Harry got up. "I've got the number for a good proctologist, honey. He can remove that two- by- four that's wedged between your ass cheeks. Let me know." Harry left the lobby without waiting for a response.

Still seething from his encounter with Sandy and the wasted trip to the school, Harry parked his truck in front of his home, slammed it into park, and stared vacantly at nothing.

After a few minutes, he snapped out of his trance, got out of the truck, and walked toward his front door. As he neared it, he remembered that he needed pipe tobacco. The party store at the end of the block looked a million miles away, and his head and his knee still ached. He thought about grabbing his cane from the house, but he hoped to see Miss Jessica on the way to the store, and he didn't want her to see him relying on his cane to get down the street.

As he neared the last house on the block, he saw his neighbor, Phil, mowing his front lawn. Harry waved hello as he walked by, and Phil noticed Harry's bandaged head. "Hey. Harry. What happened to you? You okay?"

"Boating accident, Phil. I'm okay."

"Did you hear about Ryan?"

"No. What?"

"He got forced off the town council. Thirty years he was on it, and he was forced out. Know why?" Harry waved goodbye as he walked on. "They're here, Harry. And they're gonna eat this town alive if we let 'em."

When Harry reached the last house on the block, he saw Ms. Jessica, who looked much younger than her seventy years, swaying to and fro on her porch swing. She smiled and waved as Harry very slowly passed by her house. "Hello, Harry. Beautiful day, isn't it?"

"It is, Miss Jess. Been taking care of yourself?"

"Trying to, handsome." Jessica saw the bandages. She brought the swing to a stop. "My goodness."

"Shaving mishap, Miss Jess. I'm fine."

"You sure?"

"I am."

"Hear you had a bit of a row at Sam's."

"I don't go looking for trouble. But I got a thing for bullies."

"Violence doesn't solve anything, Harry."

"You gotta stand up to bullies, Miss Jess. If not, they'll walk all over you."

"You can try to reason with them, right?"

Harry didn't like where this conversation was headed. He already had his fill of arguing for the day. "I'm headed to the store. You need anything?"

"Would you be a dear and pick me up some tea bags? And when you get back, I've got apple pie on the table. Fresh baked, of course."

Jess found Harry's weak spot: sweets. He patted his ample belly and smiled. "I oughta say no, Jess. Thong season's right around the corner."

Jess giggled. "Let's throw caution to the wind and live a little. We've earned it. We damn well have."

He didn't know why it came to mind, but just then Harry remembered Jessica's late husband's funeral. Maybe because the man died the same week as Patsy did. Harry liked Jess' husband well enough, and the two couples even got together to play cards on the occasional Saturday night, but Harry couldn't recall his name at the moment, and he felt bad about that. And he also remembered how stoically and gracefully Jess handled losing her husband of over forty years. *Dammit, what was the guy's name?*

"It's been almost five years now, Harry."

"Since what?"

"Since you lost Patsy, and I lost my Jerry. They passed within a week of each other, remember?"

Harry's head hung low as sadness gripped him. This was another conversation he didn't want to have with Miss Jess. "Yeah," he said. "Jerry was a good man."

"He was. We both lost people we loved, Harry. It's okay to talk about it. It might even help."

"What kind of tea do you like, Jess?"

"Pekoe if they have it. Let me get you some money."

Harry waved her off. "Please. I've got money. I'll be back in about half an hour."

"The store's two minutes away."

Harry winked. "Maybe it was twenty years ago." He started down the street. And suddenly, his knee didn't feel too bad at all. And when he returned from the store, Harry had some of Jess' apple pie with a scoop of ice cream. And they talked for over three hours. And they laughed. When he left her home, Harry was glad that he took Jess up on her invitation. He hadn't felt this good in a long time.

8

Sheriff Roy Patterson, a strapping man at six foot four, leaned against his patrol car as he stared at Harry's house across the street. The sheriff had served in law enforcement for nearly forty years now, all of them in Albrecht. He loved the town, and he hadn't planned to retire for years to come, but circumstances had forced his hand. The new political landscape in Albrecht had taken its toll on the man. He couldn't, and wouldn't, take their bullshit any longer. Sheriff Roy was putting in his papers at the end of the month. The lake house down South was calling his name, as were shoals of large- mouth bass. He and his wife had decided that they would keep their home in town so they would have the option to stay there when, or if, they came back to visit.

Sheriff Roy had known Harry for what seemed like forever, and he liked Harry a helluva lot more than most of the people in town. Harry was a stand-up guy who could be counted on to help with almost anything. And the two men had shared more than their fair share of beers at Sam's Saloon over the years. He hated having to give Harry bad news. He stared at the court summons in his hand, and the restraining order, then he looked to his right. Standing in his driveway smoking a cigarette, Crash, wearing an idiotic grin, gave Roy the thumbs up. The sheriff seethed. *You little prick.*

Roy walked up to Harry's front door and knocked. Harry opened the door and smiled. "Hey, Roy, what's going on?"

"Hi, Harry. How they hanging?"

"Down to my ankles. Everything okay?"

"I hate doing this bullshit, so I'll get right to it." The sheriff handed the paperwork to Harry. "You've been charged with malicious destruction of property and ethnic intimidation."

"Ethnic intimidation? What the hell is that? This a joke, Roy?"

"No joke, buddy. It's a restraining order. It states that you cannot come within fifty feet of the petitioner, Francis Lamont, at any time."

"Who the hell is Francis Lamont?"

The sheriff pointed across the street at Crash. The boy was laughing now. "That idiot's name is Francis?" Harry said.

Sensing what was coming, the sheriff planted his feet into the cement landing. "Don't do it, Harry."

"Outta my way, Roy." Harry stepped onto the landing as Roy braced himself for the impact. Harry tried to push Roy aside, and the sheriff grunted as he wrapped his arms around the big man.

"Easy, big fella," Roy said as he fought to restrain Harry. "That asshole ain't worth going to jail for, Harry. Easy…" Harry, huffing and puffing, eased up and ceased his forward momentum. "That's it," the sheriff said, fighting for breath.

Harry snorted with rage as he stared at Crash. "The little asshole almost ran me over, Roy. And I gotta steer clear of him?"

"For the time being, yeah, you do. And there's a summons there that says you gotta appear in court to face the charges next week. Do you understand, Harry?"

"Tell me this is just a bad joke."

"Wish I could do that. The boy's cousin, a guy named Fred Lamont, is a lawyer. He got a judge to issue the order. Am really sorry it had to be me doing this."

"You're just doing your job, Roy," Harry said, looking over the paperwork. "Ethnic intimidation? What the hell is that?"

"It's legalese for a hate crime."

"What the hell's a hate crime?"

"Get yourself a lawyer and he'll explain this shit, Harry. It's complicated and a lot of it is bullshit."

"And you say this Fred Lamont is the idiot's cousin?"

"Yeah, he's got an office in town. Word is he's a real scumbag." Time passed as the two men stood there wondering what to say. Finally, Roy spoke up. "I don't want to have to arrest you, buddy. You know that. Please give the idiot a wide berth for a while."

"We'll see."

"Let's grab a beer soon," the sheriff said as he headed for the sidewalk. Crash was still standing in his driveway, grinning smugly. The sheriff crossed the street and stepped onto Crash's driveway.

"Nice work, Five-O," Crash said.

"Hate to take you away from that work you're doing on your PhD, son, but I need a minute." The sheriff pointed at Harry, who was still standing on his stoop staring pure hate at Crash. "You see that landmass standing over there? In zoology, they call that a grizzly bear."

"That right?" Crash said, still grinning.

"That's right, son. He may look like a man, but don't be fooled. See, the thing about grizzly bears is they generally won't bother ya if you keep clear of 'em and mind their personal space. But if you start poking one, you're just asking for a world of shit."

"That right?" Crash said.

Sheriff Roy pulled off his sunglasses and stared intently at the boy. "Again, it is. Now there's no law in this state says you have to be an idiot. And there's no law says you have to be a miscreant. Those are your choices. But there's consequences for your actions, and if you insist on poking that bear, then sooner or later you're gonna get your ass chewed off. Do ya understand what I'm saying here, son?"

"I'm just having some fun with the old guy," Crash said. "He can take it."

The sheriff stepped into the boy's face. "For a little while, maybe he will. But if you keep pushing Mr. Blake, I'll have a body bag in the trunk of my cruiser with your name on it. You've been warned." Sheriff Roy got into his cruiser and drove off. When he was sure that the sheriff was long gone, Crash flipped Harry off.

"Fifty feet, Harry," Crash yelled. "That's what you get for fuckin' with me, fat man." Harry's stare nearly burned a hole through the kid.

***

Later that afternoon, Harry sat on the sofa, mindlessly flipping through cable channels. The front door opened, and Gertie stepped into the living room. He tried to smile as she took a seat next to him. "Hi, Mom." Gertie noticed the paperwork sitting on the table in front of her.

"What are these, sonny boy? You get some bad news?"

"Just some legal papers. No big deal."

"I saw the sheriff drive off. Did he bring 'em?" Harry nodded.

"He's supposed to be a friend of yours. I should have shot his ass for hassling my boy," she said.

"You go out and get a gun, Ma?"

Gertie looked confused. "There's a gun in the house?"

Harry knew his mother was losing her battle with dementia. He tried to smile again, hoping to put her at ease. "No guns here, Ma. Did you eat?"

Gertie gently clasped Harry's hand. "What's going on, Harry? Tell your mama."

"I got into a little scuffle with the boy idiot across the street. He sicced a lawyer on me."

"Is that the hoodlum who goes out all hours of the night in that SS 454?"

"You know what that car's called?"

"'Course I do" Gertie said. "It's a Chevelle. Dual exhaust, Holly carb. The LS5 pumped out three- hundred and sixty horses. The idiot's got a '70 out there, right? Looks a lot like the one you had."

"How do you know that stuff, Ma?"

"I used to be a gearhead, sonny boy. I worked in a factory building

33

tanks during the war while your dad was overseas kicking the shit out of Hitler. Hell, I used to tune up your dad's car to save us some money."

"Seriously? I didn't know that."

"Sometimes I took your Chevelle out while you were overseas. I used to light those tires up. Damn, that was one badass machine."

"You drove my car around town?"

"Didn't think you'd mind, sonny boy. A car like that can't just sit in a garage. It just ain't right."

"I loved that car," Harry said.

"You're the one who sold it."

"Me and Pats needed the money."

"I know you did."

"That punk don't deserve a car like that, Ma."

"Does that boy even have a job?"

"Don't think so."

"Then how the hell did he afford it?"

Harry thought about the question for a moment. "Damn fine question."

"Somebody oughta do something about that boy. He's bad news."

"Somebody oughta," Harry said as he got off the sofa.

"Where you going, sonny boy?"

"To start dinner. Sloan gonna join us?"

"Would you like him to?"

"What the hell."

"He'll like that. I'll fetch him."

***

As Harry cooked dinner, he thought of Crash tearing up the roads in the Chevelle SS. The gods were mocking him, Harry was certain, and he swore he would get the last laugh on Crash, the gods be damned. After dinner with his mother and Charlie, Harry cleared the dishes off the dining room table. When that was done, he dropped a deck of cards on the table.

"Thanks for dinner, Harry. That pot roast really hit the spot," Charlie said. He pushed himself away from the table as Gertie grabbed his arm and led the old man toward the front door. Harry followed them.

"Where you guys going? Thought we'd play some pinochle," Harry said.

"It's almost our bedtime, sonny boy. I gotta rub Charlie down before bed," Gertie said.

Charlie winked at Harry. "If I'm smiling tomorrow, you'll know why."

"C'mon, guys, it's early. We'll just play one game. What do ya say?"

Gertie kissed Harry on the cheek. "Maybe tomorrow night, sonny. Goodnight."

Gertie led Charlie out the front door. Harry plodded towards his recliner and dumped himself into it. *Another night alone.* He turned on the local news. "And finally this tonight," the anchorman said. "A local real estate agent, Ben Robinson, was fired recently after he posted on a social media site that, and I quote, 'All Lives Matter.' A supporter of a national organization for black people contacted Mr. Robinson's employer and complained, rightfully so, that the phrase "All Lives Matter" was derogatory, inherently racist, and diminished their organization's message and goal." The anchorman turned to his co-anchor. "This story disgusts me. There's no room in our inclusive and diverse community for people like this. He deserved to lose his job."

"The intolerance of some people," replied his co-anchor, in mock disgust.

"Weather and sports are next after the break." *Poor bastard*, Harry thought. After turning off the TV, he picked up his phone and called Joey. The call went to voicemail. "Joey, it's Gramps. Where are you, boy? It's a school night. Get home soon." Harry wasn't surprised that his grandson didn't answer his phone. That was par for the course these days. He knew they would have to talk soon and hopefully reach some kind of a détente.

He looked at his watch again and it occurred to him that the next morning he was to meet with Joey's principal. Although he wasn't really tired, he had nothing to do. Lately, he didn't need an excuse to go to bed early.

9

Harry Blake Jr. smiled as he bounded down the school steps, his stomach jiggling with every stride he took. Dinner that night was lasagna, the boy's favorite, and he couldn't get home quickly enough. The boy was only twelve, but he already tipped the scales at one hundred and sixty pounds. His legs resembled tree trunks, and his upper body was wide and thick.

Harry Jr. was a mild-mannered boy who never took advantage of his size to bully anyone, but most of the kids at school gave him a wide berth just the same. A group of young thugs, led by a mean, little prick named Ricky, lay in waiting for the boy behind a van as he crossed the parking lot. As Harry Jr. walked past the van, five boys appeared and encircled him, cutting off his escape route.

"Hey, fat boy, where you headed?" Ricky said.

Harry Jr., seeing that he was outnumbered, froze. "I don't want any trouble, Ricky," he said.

Ricky eyeballed the backpack Harry Jr. held firmly in his hand. He extended his hand. "Give up the backpack, fat ass."

"I – I can't. My mom got it for me."

"Aw, ain't that sweet. We got a mama's boy here," Ricky said, laughing.

One of the bigger boys, Cal, crept up behind Harry Jr. and yanked at the backpack. When it fell to the ground, Harry leaned over to pick it up, but another boy got to it first. Harry lunged at him, but the boy had already tossed the backpack to another boy in the circle.

"Gimme it back," Harry said.

Harry lunged at another boy who was holding the pack, but it went airborne again. Harry gasped for air as he spun in circles. Then dizziness overtook him. He wobbled on his feet as he fought to regain his equilibrium.

As the boys laughed and taunted Harry Jr., Ricky saw his chance. He sucker-punched Harry, his fist landing squarely on Harry's nose. The boy backpedaled a step or two, but he didn't fall. And when the young thugs saw that the boy had taken Ricky's best shot and was still standing, the laughter quickly stopped. The boy holding Harry's backpack dropped it to the ground. Harry wiped blood from his nose, gave the thugs the finger, then he picked up his backpack and started to walk away.

"Get him!" Ricky yelled.

Cal jumped on Harry's back and wrapped his arms tightly around the boy's neck. Harry planted his feet, grunted, and contorted his meaty torso like a bucking bronco, throwing Cal nearly five feet into the air. He stared down at the other boys, waiting to see if any of them wanted to try their luck riding him. There were no takers.

***

Harry Jr. wiped his bloody nose again as he made his way through his backyard. As he quietly opened the back door, he listened for his father. He crept through the door, and he tiptoed through the kitchen. If he could just make it up the stairs…

"That you, boy?" his father bellowed from the living room.

"Shit," Harry Jr. muttered as he came to a dead stop. He thought about hightailing it out the back door, but when he saw a shadow looming over him, he knew it was already too late. Without looking up, the boy felt the weight of his father's gaze fall on him.

Lieutenant Colonel Harry Blake Sr., a burly, square-jawed man, stood over his boy. Harry Jr. continued staring at the floor. The boy knew his dad, like any military officer, was assessing the situation. Harry Sr. examined the dried blood on his boy's shirt. Harry Jr. knew what his dad was thinking; that he was on the losing end of yet another skirmish. And that he didn't fight back.

"Involved in a fray, boy?"

"I - I was coming home from school, and some boys jumped me," Harry Jr. said.

"Look at me when you're talking to me, son."

Harry Jr. slowly looked up at his father.

"Why did they jump you, boy?"

"They were trying to take my backpack."

"How many were there?"

"Five or six."

"Fucking bullies. How many of them hit you?"

"Just one. But another one jumped on my back, and I -"

"Did you hit him back?"

"I was gonna, but I thought if I did, I might really hurt him."

Harry Sr. slammed his fist on the kitchen counter. "How many times do I have to tell you, boy? When you get hit, you hit back. Hard!"

Harry Jr. hung his head as rage began to well up inside him. He wanted to hear his father tell him he did well, but he knew no reassurance or compliment was forthcoming. He wanted to tell his father how he handled the situation with the thugs pretty damn well. He wanted to tell his father that he didn't start the trouble. He wanted to tell his father that he still had his backpack, and his pride. But most of all, he really, really wanted to tell his father to go screw himself for not asking if he was okay. Where's Mom? the boy wondered.

Harry Sr. sat down at the kitchen table. He gestured for Harry Jr. to sit down as well. "Son, let me tell you a little something about the bullies of the world. The Japs and the Krauts were the biggest bullies on the block at one time. They killed and raped and did whatever the hell else they wanted for years before the U.S. of A. got into the war. One country after another fell to those bastards because they either didn't have the will or the strength to fight, or both. Bullies sense weakness, son, and they feast on it. It makes them bolder."

Harry Jr. had heard this speech before. He understood the message well enough, or so he thought, but like any other twelve-year-old boy, his attention waned. His eyes wandered for one moment, and his father saw it. He snapped his fingers at the boy, and Harry Jr. snapped to attention.

"Focus, son," Harry Sr. said. "This is important. We stayed out of the war for the first couple of years because we figured it wasn't our battle to fight. But when the Japs bombed us at Pearl Harbor, they bloodied our nose, and they made a big mistake. They should have known that you don't piss off the big boy on the block. Needless to say, we made 'em pay. Them and the Krauts." Harry Sr. lit a cigar and took a long drag on it. "Son, you're a Blake, and a Blake never takes shit from anyone. Do you understand?"

I take shit from you all the time, Dad, Harry Jr. thought.

"Bullies only understand one thing, son, and that's force. You're the big boy on the block. You got your nose bloodied today. Now you have to respond. If you don't fight back, the bad guys will chip away at you until they've taken everything." Harry Sr. took a long drag on his cigar. "I fought under a man named General George Patton, son. They called him 'Old Blood and Guts'. No one under his command ever said no to the man. No one. Ever." He grabbed his son's arm and pressed it firmly as he stared intently at the boy. "Think of me as your General Patton. You are going to fight back. And you are going to come out victorious. Is that understood?"

"Yes, Sir."

Harry Sr. let go of his boy's arm as he sat back. "Good. So, here's what you're going to do. You're going to find the little prick who hit you and you're going to beat the living hell out of him. And you're going to do it in front of his little shitheel buddies, so they get the message. Do I make myself clear?"

Harry Jr. nodded.

"Good talk we had here, son. You're dismissed."

***

The next day, Harry Jr. marched through the school parking lot like a man on a mission. Nervous adrenaline pumped through him as he sought out his quarry. He did want to beat the shit out of Ricky and his minions, but he also knew that his mother would disapprove of his actions. He knew he could have gone to her the night before and told her what his father had told him to do, but he didn't want to be the cause of tension between his parents.

The boy had his marching orders. He found Ricky at the end of the parking lot leaning against a car talking to a girl named Becky. Harry Jr. tapped on the girl's shoulder, and when she spun around to face him, he said, "Leave." Becky laughed, thinking Harry Jr. was joking. But when she saw the scowl on Harry's face, she walked away. Ricky turned to run, but Harry grabbed him by the shirt and shoved him against the car. "Wanna try takin' my backpack now, Ricky?"

"I - I was just havin' some fun with ya, buddy. You know how it is. We're - we're cool."

Harry broke Ricky's jaw with one punch. As the boy crumbled to the ground, Harry calmly walked away. The same day, he was suspended from school. When he got home, he got a "atta boy" from his dad for breaking Ricky's jaw. Then his father grounded him for not following his orders to the letter; Harry Jr. didn't take down Ricky in front of his buddies.

***

Sitting at the dinner table later that night, Harry Jr. stared sullenly at his food as his parents continued eating. "Not hungry, Harry?" Mrs. Blake said.

Harry Jr. didn't respond. His father looked the boy over. "If you're not going to eat, go to your room. Don't forget you're restricted to barracks, soldier," he said.

Harry Jr. got up, shoved his chair away and stomped off for the stairway. He slammed his bedroom door shut behind him, plopped onto his bed, and cracked open a comic book.

In the dining room Gertie stopped eating and dropped her silverware. "What was that all about?"

"I gave the boy an order and he didn't obey it."

"What order?"

Harry Sr. wiped his mouth with a napkin, then dropped it on the table. "I told the boy to beat the shit out of a kid in front of his friends, and he didn't comply."

"What did my boy do?"

"He broke the kid's jaw, but the little bastard's buddies weren't there to see it."

Gertie Blake stared at her husband. "You told your boy to beat the snot out of a kid? Why the hell did you do that?"

"Because Harry Jr. let himself be bullied. End of discussion."

Gertie pushed herself away from the dinner table. She picked up a couple of plates, turned towards the kitchen, then stopped when she saw the smug grin on her husband's face. Harry Sr., satisfied that all was right in his world, pushed his dinner plate away, sat back and lit a cigar, then he began to leaf through a newspaper.

Swallowing her anger for the moment, Gertie turned and walked into the kitchen. When she reached the sink, she planted her hands on the countertop and stared at her reflection in the window above the sink. Gertie Blake was a waifish woman who sported a pixie hairstyle just like her favorite actress, Audrey Hepburn. After seeing Breakfast at Tiffany's three times in one month at Albrecht's Stars and Screens theater, Gertie practically begged her husband to let her take acting classes, but Harry Sr., after chiding her for having such a foolish dream, reminded her of her duties to him and Harry Jr. "You've got a full life already," Harry

Sr. had told her. "What the hell else do you need?" The subject never came up again.

But Gertie didn't need to be reminded about her duties as a wife and mother. She was fiercely loyal, and committed, to her husband and son, and Harry Jr. was the light of her life. Although she and Harry Sr. had been married for only ten years, sometimes it felt like a lifetime to her already. She closed her eyes and fought the urge to cry. After regaining her composure, she stared into the window again. She saw the wrinkles, the ones she had always refused to admit existed, until this very moment. She had just turned thirty-five less than a month before, so the crow's feet at the corner of her eyes belied her age. Sadness and regret began to creep in.Gertie stiffened as she pushed away from the countertop. Enough with the pity party.

Though a small woman in stature, she never backed down from a fight, especially when her son's upbringing was the matter of contention. Knowing Harry Jr. was out of earshot, she marched back into the dining room, ready for a fight. "Happy with yourself?" she said, staring at her husband.

Harry Sr. continued to read his newspaper. "The boy didn't follow orders. He's gotta learn."

Gertie picked up a couple of dinner plates, then dropped them on the table, nearly breaking them. The noise caught Harry Sr.'s attention. He lowered the paper and looked impassively at his wife. "Something on your mind, dear?"

"Don't you "dear" me. Harry Jr. broke a boy's jaw 'cause you told him to do it. And that wasn't good enough for you?"

"My orders were explicit."

"This isn't a boot camp. Our son's not a soldier."

"The boy's in my cadet program. And the chain of command will be enforced in this household."

Gertie stared cross-eyed at her husband as she placed her hands on her hips. "You can stow that chain of command bullshit."

Harry Sr. dropped the newspaper on the table as he engaged in a stare-off with his wife. "The boy needs discipline. He needs -"

"He needs to be a boy. That's all he needs right now, you ass. He's a good kid, and you're hell- bent on sucking all the happiness out of him!"

Harry Sr. turned red as his frustration grew. "Dammit, Gert."

Gertie wagged her finger as she checked her watch. "As of nineteen-hundred hours, Harry Jr.'s no longer grounded," she said. "You're dismissed." Gertie gave her husband a mock salute before stomping off towards the stairway. Harry Sr. slammed a fist onto the table as he cursed under his breath. His chest began to tighten.

Gertie took a moment to cool off before knocking on Harry Jr.'s bedroom door. When the boy didn't respond, she stepped into the room. She waited for Harry Jr. to drop the comic book he was hiding behind, but the boy ignored her, so she sat at the foot of the bed, reached for his foot and pulled at his big toe. "This little piggy…"

Harry Jr. pulled his foot away and stayed hidden behind his comic book. "I get it, Harry Jr. You're mad. Now drop the magazine, and the attitude." The boy glared at his mother as he slowly lowered the magazine. "Let's get to it. I know your father grounded you, but now you're officially a free man."

"I am?"

"You are."

"Thanks, Mom."

"Are you…okay, sonny boy? After what happened today, I mean?"

"It didn't really bother me when I did it. Is that wrong, Ma?"

"As long as that kid was bullying you, no, it's not bad to feel that way. I'm not happy your father ordered you to do it, but he's right about one thing; bullies have to be stood up to. Don't ever forget that, sonny boy."

"Okay." Harry Jr. smiled at his mother, but his resentment towards his father for grounding him smoldered just beneath the surface, and

Gertie picked up on it.

"I know your father is a little hard on you sometimes. It's just...his way."

"Okay, Ma."

"I'd better get downstairs and get to the dishes. How much do you love me?"

The boy wrapped his arms around his mother's neck and held on tight. "More than the sun and the moon and the stars, Ma."

"You'd better." Gertie got up off the bed and stopped at the door. "I'll bring you up some dinner in a bit." Harry Jr. smiled for just the second time in the last two days.

10

Harry sat in principal Rhode's office. The principal, a man about Harry's age, stepped into the office and took a seat behind his desk. Harry looked the man over as the principal shuffled through a file sitting on his desk. Mr. Rhode looked like a tired man. A very tired man. "Thank you for coming in, Mr. Blake. I apologize for the miscommunication Monday."

"This is my second trip here, Mr. Rhode. I hope we're gonna settle this today."

"We are. Actually, Mr. Blake, we have two matters to discuss. First, your grandson was overheard asking a young woman, a fellow classmate, where her family was from."

"Yeah. So?"

"As the assistant principal explained to your grandson, what he did is considered a "micro- aggression.""

"A what?"

A micro-aggression is a statement, action, or incident regarded as an instance of indirect, subtle, or unintentional discrimination against members of a marginalized group, such as a racial or ethnic minority."

"Did you memorize that?" Harry said. "You spit that out like you're holding a press conference here."

The principal offered Harry a half-hearted smile as he rolled his eyes. "This isn't the first time I've had to have this conversation with a parent, Mr. Blake. According to the snowflakes among us, your grandson marginalized the girl in question by implying that her family isn't from this country. He may have hurt her feelings."

"Oh, Jesus..." Harry said, rubbing his temples. "Tell me you're kidding."

"I wish that I could, sir."

"Did anyone bother to ask this girl if her feelings were hurt?"

"We haven't gotten that far into the investigation yet."

Harry chuckled. "Investigation? Was there a murder committed here?"

"I understand your frustration, Mr. Blake. Let me move on to the second matter now." Mr. Rhode picked up a piece of paper off of his desk and handed it to Harry. "This is a copy of a restraining order. The court will be serving you officially soon enough. It prohibits you from coming within one-hundred feet of this school as of noon today."

"What the hell?"

"There was a complaint filed against you by Ms. Moore, my assistant. According to the complaint, you made threats against her and used abusive language. She claims that you violated her personal safe space, and that you were, and I quote, 'a mean man'. She could even charge you with a hate crime, Mr. Blake."

"A hate crime for a couple of curse words? Are you kidding me?" Harry said, staring at the principal in utter disbelief.

"These days, any incident, perceived threat, or crime which is believed to be motivated because of a person's gender can be considered a hate crime, Mr. Blake."

Harry sat back, dumbfounded. He looked through the window of the adjacent office and saw Ms. Moore sitting at her desk. She grinned and waved sarcastically at him. Harry's entire body stiffened as he turned to face Mr. Rhode. "I didn't threaten her."

"You're free to argue that in court, sir. I just wanted to give you a heads-up. I'm really sorry."

"What about my grandson?"

"Although I have the authority to suspend Joey, I've decided against it. He has been warned, and I believe that will suffice. Besides, he's a good kid and he's graduating soon." Mr. Rhode closed the file and rose from his chair. "I'll see you out, sir."

Harry got up and shook the principal's hand. "Thanks, Mr. Rhode." As he started toward the door, he stopped long enough to stare at Ms. Moore. She was texting on her phone, oblivious to the world.

"The little princess must be on a break, huh?"

Mr. Rhode, sensing potential trouble brewing, gently guided Harry out of the office and down a hallway. "The little princess is on a perpetual break," he said.

When they stepped into the parking lot, Mr. Rhode grabbed Harry by the arm. "I'm sorry for what happened to you and Joey, Mr. Blake. I really am."

"Sure thing," Harry said as he looked the building over. "I graduated from this school, Mr. Rhode. I got suspended a couple of times for doing stupid teenage shit, but now I'm banned from it for using a couple of curse words?"

"Times have changed, Mr. Blake."

"Call me Harry. Please."

"Harry, I despise my assistant principal. He's just a damn bully. And Miss Moore is a mean, spiteful, little you- know-what. I'm lucky if I get two hours of real work out of her every day."

"Why not just fire her?"

The principal nervously looked around the parking lot. Satisfied no one was within listening distance, he went on. "And give her an excuse to file a sexual harassment lawsuit against me just to get even? No way in hell. I'm less than two years from retirement. I wish to leave with my reputation and my pension intact. These days, all it takes is an allegation of misconduct and your life can be upended. Do you understand?"

Harry suddenly remembered his upcoming court date. "I'm starting to get it, yeah."

Mr. Rhode stared blankly into the distance. "I used to love my job. Now I'm afraid to pass gas once I walk into that damn building for fear of offending someone."

"Have things gotten that bad?"

Mr. Rhode turned towards Harry. "Worse. What your grandson was accused of was an absolute joke. When we were young, asking a girl where her family was from wouldn't have even raised an eyebrow."

"What the hell's happening to this world?"

"We've allowed a horde of fanatics to seize power they don't deserve and haven't earned. They've learned that if they get on social media and scream loud enough, a lot of sane people would buckle under the pressure.

And they were right. If you don't toe the company line these days, it can cost you dearly. And the meaning of words changes overnight because a minority of people decide that they should." Mr. Rhode gestured toward the school. "Do you know what the difference between a school and a prison is nowadays, Harry?"

"What?"

"In prison, the rules don't change every day."

"Meaning what?"

"I received a new directive from the school district's superintendent last week. It included a list of words and expressions that the teaching staff were told to stop using for fear that we may upset the students. It's all about coddling and indoctrinating these kids now. We're not here to teach them any longer. We're not here to challenge them intellectually or encourage them to engage in critical thinking. The school system's become an asylum, and the clueless are running it now."

"Is it really that bad?" Harry said.

Mr. Rhode pointed towards the far end of the parking lot. "There's a perfect example right there."

A group of students, both high school and college age kids, marched in a circle, and many held up signs as they chanted: "Hey, hey, ho, ho, Mr. Owen's got to go." They repeated the chant as they continued to march.

"What's that all about?" Harry said.

"They're trying to have one of our teachers, Mr. Owens, removed from his position. He teaches science and he's been one of our best for over forty years now. He loves the kids, and he really care about them."

"What's the problem?"

"He dared to say no."

"Huh?"

"The teachers in this district are being forced into taking white privilege training classes. They're being told that if they're white, they're racist, and that they're upholding racist ideas, structures, and policies whether they're aware of it, or not. Every white staff member at this school has to vow to confront and examine their white privilege, and to teach other white people to admit and confront their privilege. And every employee of the school has to commit to becoming antiracist."

Harry shrugged. "Whatever the hell that bullshit means. What's that got to do with this Mr. Owens?"

"Some of his students asked Mr. Owens if he was going to take the classes, and he laughed. When they pressed him on the issue, he told the kids to drop the subject so they could get on with the day's lesson. But they wouldn't let it go. The little bastards started screaming and calling him names. They even accused him of marginalizing them and their feelings."

"Marginalizing them?"

"It's a new page in the Victimology playbook. The always-oppressed among them complain that they're treated that way by a segment of society. The White segment, of course. So, some of the kids at the community college heard about Mr. Owens comments, and they decided to stick their noses into this nonsense. They came over and encouraged our kids to protest and to scream for Mr. Owens' scalp. Talk about the ignorant leading the blind."

Harry shook his head in disbelief. "That's the whole story? That's really the reason they're doing this?"

Mr. Rhode nodded. "Scary, no?" The principal pointed at an elderly man carrying a box, making his way slowly across the parking lot. "There's Mr. Owens now. He tendered his resignation today. We're going to keep losing the good ones."

A college student stopped and pointed when he saw Mr. Owens approaching. "Oppressor!" he yelled. The rest of the students stopped marching and stared at the teacher as if he had just clubbed a baby seal to death.

"Silencer!" another screamed.

Mr. Rhode shook his head. "They're going to eat him alive," he said. "Excuse me." Mr. Rhode walked towards the students, and Harry followed.

Mr. Owens came to a stop when the kids wouldn't allow him to pass by them. "Step out of my way, children," he said.

"We're not moving, adultist!" yelled one of the college students. "We will be heard!"

"Cancel him!" another student screamed.

Mr. Rhode stepped between Mr. Owens and the kids. "Allow Mr. Owens to pass, kids," he said.

"We are not kids!" a girl shouted, pointing a finger in Mr. Rhode's face. "You will show us respect!" Harry did a slow burn as he witnessed the complete lack of respect that the kids were showing Mr. Rhode.

Mr. Owens turned to face Mr. Rhode. He smiled. "It's okay, Charles. I'll handle this." Mr. Owens wheeled around to face his accusers. "You want respect, you coddled, pretentious, sniveling brats? Earn it! You've earned nothing but my contempt!" he bellowed. "I'd like to put all of you over my knee and give you the spankings you deserve!"

The students let out a collective gasp as they ceded a little ground to the teacher. Even Harry took a step back, not expecting such fury from the elderly man. A girl in the crowd started to sob. "I want my safe space," she moaned.

"You will listen to our grievances!" a student shouted.

"No, I will not!" Mr. Owens barked. "I give two shits about your list of imaginary grievances. If you think life is tough now, just wait, you toddlers. You'll all be shitting yourselves blind in a few years when real life smacks you in the face."

"We will not be marginalized!" another student yelled.

"Do you even attend classes here, son?" Mr. Owens said.

"No. But – ' '

"Then shut your yap!"

Another gasp from the students. A few stood their ground, but the rest backpedaled further as they began to grasp that they were not going to intimidate Mr. Owens. "I will no longer take part in a system that indoctrinates its children to the point that they become feeble- minded automatons toeing the company line for their masters. Your parents should be ashamed of all of you for your conduct."

Mr. Owens let out a long, mournful sigh before going on. "The educational system has failed you kids, and for that, I feel truly sorry for all of you," he said. "Kids, please learn to think for yourselves. Grow thicker skin. Stop being puppets. Stop playing the part of the always-offended and always-oppressed just because you're told that you are by people with hidden agendas. Stop playing the victim.

Please trust me when I tell you that this misguided sense of entitlement you all feel now will cost you dearly later in life. You children have no idea what true oppression is. You live in one of the greatest, freest, most tolerant countries on this planet. Be grateful for that. Now, get the hell out of my way."

As the students stepped aside and allowed Mr. Owens to pass by unmolested, Harry grinned and slapped Mr. Rhode on the back. "Damn," he said, "that was beautiful." He applauded as Mr. Owens drove off. The young protestors, thoroughly defeated, began to disperse. Harry watched their retreat with a great deal of satisfaction, then he turned to Mr. Rhode. "Are you going to take those bullshit classes?"

"I am. As I said, I'm less than two years from a full pension." Ashamed, he stared at the ground. "I feel like a complete sell out."

"You're just trying to hold onto what you've already earned. I get it."

A student walked past Harry with a sign that read, *Math Is Racist.* "Math is racist?" Harry said.

"Sanity eludes them, Harry. Their feelings, no matter how twisted and deluded, are all that matter as far as their concerned," Mr. Rhode said. "They're a colony of lemmings in search of a cliff. And they want to take the rest of us along for the ride."

Harry nodded. He was beginning to understand.

"They're coming for all of us," Mr. Rhode said. "Political correctness, wokeness and this cancel culture bullshit is going to eat this country alive if we don't stop it."

"How do we fight these bastards?"

"Any way we can. Goodbye, Mr. Blake."

Harry watched Mr. Rhode walk away like a beaten man, then he caught sight of Sandy looking out an office window. She gave Harry another sarcastic wave goodbye. Harry flipped her off. She pouted for a moment, but her pouting ended abruptly when she came up with what she thought was a great idea. Getting on her work computer, she logged onto various social media sites to tell the online world about Harry. She called him an "asshole" and a "douchebag," and said the "old fart" had some balls talking to her the way he did. And she proudly added that she had him banned from the school. Sandy swelled with pride and satisfaction.

She was giddy with anticipation waiting for all the "likes," and the "lol's" and the support she was certain was coming her way from her "friends" on social media.

***

Two days later, Mr. Rhode grinned as he entered Sandy's office. The girl met his grin with a self- satisfied smirk of her own. "I'm leaving early today," she said.

"You've got that right, Miss Moore. Pack your things. You've been terminated."

"What?"

"You used a school computer to commit libel on Mr. Blake, Miss Moore. That's a big no-no. Welcome to the real world."

Sandy grabbed her purse and scowled. "Don't think this is over," she said before marching out the door. That same day, she contacted a lawyer. Her attorney filed a sexual harassment suit against Mr. Rhode the next day. The school system wanted the lawsuit to go away, quickly and quietly. Three days after the suit was filed, attorneys for the school settled out of court for an undisclosed sum. The same day, the school's superintendent accepted Mr. Rhode's resignation. The elderly teacher, too tired to fight a broken, rigged system, reluctantly left his profession and his life's work behind. But his pension remained intact.

11

As the midday sun beat down on him, Harry lugged two trashcans across the backyard lawn, stopping momentarily to wipe sweat from his forehead. An intense, late spring storm the night before had littered his backyard with dead branches and garbage, and Harry couldn't rely on Joey to clean up the mess. That was fine with Harry. He knew he needed something to do, something to get the blood flowing and divert his mind from recent events. *They're coming for all of us*, Mr. Rhode had said. He had heard the same message from his neighbor, Phil, and thought nothing of it, but now those words seared into Harry's brain, and even the busy work he did now couldn't stop the phrase from running in a never-ending loop in his mind: *they're coming for all of us.*

"Hello. How's your head, Harry?" Harry snapped out of his trance. He searched for the source of the voice he wasn't sure he'd just heard. "Over here, Mr. Brake."

Harry looked toward the back of his yard and saw an elderly Asian man waving to him as he leaned against the chain link fence that divided the adjoining property. "How do you know my name?"

The elderly man held up a handful of mail for Harry to see. "I believe these belong to you."

Harry reached the fence and looked the old man up and down as he reached for his mail. "Thanks. But the name is Blake, not Brake," he said.

"I know," the man said. "That was my attempt at humor."

"Huh?"

"The joke about Asians? The problem we have with l's and r's?"

"Oh. I get it now. That's funny, Mr. –?"

"You can call me Hien."

The elderly man extended a hand to Harry. After some hesitation, Harry shook Hien's hand. "Your English is pretty good," he said.

"So is yours," Hien responded. Harry stared at Hien as if he were studying a bug under a microscope. "Have you never seen an Asian man before?"

"Seen plenty of 'em," Harry said.

"In the war, yes?"

"Yeah. How'd you know?"

"Your age. Your eyes. And that..." Hien pointed at the mail in Harry's hand. An envelope had the Veterans Administration seal on it. "Did you see much action, Mr. Blake?"

"Enough to last me ten lifetimes. You ask a lot of questions."

Hien bowed slightly. "Forgive me. But if we are to be neighbors, even just temporarily, I thought that we could get to know each other."

Harry studied Hien's face, sensing that he had met the man before. Hien appeared to be about Harry's age, and he seemed friendly enough, but something about him unsettled Harry. "You Vietnamese, Hien?"

"I am."

"Been in the U.S. long now?"

"I'm a bit of a nomad. I recently came to your country for a visit."

"Who you visiting?" Harry said.

"An old friend."

Harry glanced at the house that sat across the neighboring backyard. The Jensen family had moved out of it three months earlier. "You renting the house?"

"You ask a lot of questions, Harry."

Harry smiled. "Well, if we're gonna be neighbors..." Hien bowed again.

"Well prayed, Harry," he said.

"Prayed?" Harry said.

"The l's and r's? Once again, an attempt at humor."

"Oh, got it. Well, I should get going, Hien, is it? Got places to be."

"I hope we will talk again soon," Hien said. "Meaningful conversation can be so very good for the soul."

"Sure thing. See you around the block." Harry wasn't sure that he and Hien had anything more to talk about ever again, but he gave him a warm smile and waved a friendly goodbye before walking away.

"Good luck in court today." Hien said.

Caught off guard by that remark, Harry stopped in midstride and wheeled around. But Hien was already gone.

12

Harry sat at a table in Courtroom 1B. Sweating and irritated, he tugged at his tie as he considered walking out of the courtroom. He hated wearing a suit, and he hadn't worn one since his wife's funeral, but he figured a court appearance called for him to look like he took this matter at least somewhat seriously. Across the aisle at another table sat Crash and his attorney, Fred Lamont. Harry stared at Crash as he fantasized about the myriad ways he could kill the boy without leaving a mark. And Crash, after making sure that no one was looking, flipped Harry off.

The bailiff came to attention as Judge Bertha Davenport, a stocky woman who looked like she could wrestle a grizzly bear into submission bare- handed, took a seat behind the bench. "All rise," the bailiff said. "Department One of the Municipal Court is now in session. Judge Bertha Davenport presiding."

"Let's get this ball rolling. What have we got?" she said to the bailiff.

"The State of South Dakota versus Harry Blake, your honor. The charges are malicious destruction of property and ethnic intimidation."

The judge looked Harry over, then she stared at Fast Freddie. "And you are…?"

Fred rose from his seat. "Fred Lamont. Attorney for the plaintiff."

"Are you 'Fast Freddie' Lamont?" When Fred stared at the floor, the judge knew she had the right man. "I've heard about you, you sneaky little shit," the judge said, wagging an accusatory finger at him. "Try any shenanigans in my courtroom and I'll hang you by your nut sack. Capiche?"

"Your honor, I -"

"Shut the hell up and grab some wood, Freddie."

Fred sat back down. The judge locked her gaze onto Harry. "And who the hell are you?"

"Name's Harry. Harry Blake."

"I'm waiting."

"For what?"

"Are you slow? You're in the shark's cage now, mister. Address me correctly."

"Your…honor?"

The judge shook her head in exasperation. "Let me know when you're sure. So, where's your mouthpiece, Mr. Blake?"

"My, what?"

"Your lawyer."

"I don't have one. Figured I didn't need one."

The judge sat back. "And why is that?"

Harry pointed at Crash. "Because that little prick almost ran me over. I was just defending myself."

"Like you are here, right?"

"I suppose so, yeah."

"You ever cheat on your wife?"

"What?"

"You heard me," the judge said. "Have you ever cheated on your wife?"

Incredulous, Harry sat back in his chair. "What the hell's that got to do with anything?"

"Just trying to gauge what kind of man you are. I figure if you're the kind of guy who'd cheat on his wife, you're probably a liar as well. Answer the question or I'll find you in contempt."

"My wife's dead. And, no, I never cheated on her."

"How did she pass?"

"She stopped breathing."

Judge Davenport smiled. "You're a clever boy, aren't you?" She opened a file and quickly scanned the details of the case, then looked Harry over again. "Says here you threw a rock at the defendant's car and broke a taillight. Is that true?"

Harry visualized his hands wrapped tightly around Crash's neck as he loosened his tie. "Yeah, after he tried to run me over."

"Is that so?" the judge said.

Fred arose from his chair. "Your Honor, if I may. On the night in question, my client was carefully, and safely, navigating his vehicle down his driveway when he suffered a spasm which caused him to slam his foot hard onto the gas pedal. This caused his automobile to speed down the driveway. But thanks to my client's quick thinking and reflexes, he was able to avoid hitting the defendant. Mr. Blake then proceeded to pick up a rock and throw it at my client's vehicle, causing serious damage to said vehicle, not to mention the emotional pain and suffering my client has experienced since this incident." Never breaking eye contact with the judge, Fred leaned over and whispered in the boy's ear, "Look sad, dumbass." Crash stared at the judge like a child who was lost at a shopping mall. "My client saved a life that night. My client is a hero, Your Honor."

The judge rolled her eyes as Fred took a seat. "You're one long-winded son of a bitch, aren't you, Freddie?" She examined a picture of Crash's Chevelle taken after Harry hit it with the rock. "You call this serious damage?"

"That's a classic sports car, Your Honor. That model year is worth about one-hundred and fifty-thousand dollars at auction."

"Damn. That's a chunk of change," the judge said. She perused a file in front of her. "Says here you're a lifelong resident of Albrecht, Mr. Blake. And a Vietnam Vet. That correct?"

"Yep."

The judge eyeballed Crash. "I've seen your rap sheet, son. You're what they call a miscreant. My gut tells me that you instigated this little confrontation."

Fred stood up again. "Your honor, it's true that my client has one or two blemishes on his record, but he's turned the page. He's considering a career in social work, and he plans to devote some of his free time to reading to the blind." Fred hung his head in mock sadness. "That is, if he ever recovers from the trauma of this incident."

Judge Davenport snickered. "Trauma? Freddie, you're so full of shit, my eyes are turning brown. You oughta get an Oscar for that performance." Freddie took a seat as the judge closed the file. "Let's wrap this up," the judge said. "Mr. Blake, the court orders you to pay restitution in the amount of fifty dollars to the plaintiff. And young Mr. Lamont, I advise you to steer well clear of my courtroom in the future."

Freddie saw that Crash wasn't happy. As much as he disdained the boy, he knew that his young cousin was helping to make him rich in the drug business and needed to be placated. Freddie had one last card he could play: the race card. As the judge was about to pound her gavel, he chimed in, "What about the charge of ethnic intimidation, Your Honor?"

"What the hell is that all about?" the judge said.

"My client is Native American. He is one-eighth Sioux," Freddie said.

"What the hell's that got to do with anything?" Harry said.

"We contend that this is the reason he was targeted and attacked by the defendant," Fred said.

"Aw, bullshit," Harry said.

Fred slammed his hand on the table. "We demand justice, Your Honor!"

"Your client is part Native American?" Judge Davenport said.

"He is, Your Honor," Fred replied.

The judge looked at Harry. "Mr. Blake, how do you feel about the defendant?"

"How do I feel about him? Are you serious?"

"Sure as hell am. Answer the question."

Harry glared at Crash. The boy turned toward Harry and gave him a smug smile that no one else saw. "I hate the little bastard. One of these days I'm gonna put an end to his bullshit."

The judge sat back and stared wide-eyed at Harry. "Damn. Might've wanted to use your inside voice there. Mr. Blake, the court finds you guilty of ethnic intimidation, and it hereby sentences you to six months of sensitivity training. And you will pay restitution in the amount of one-thousand dollars for the damage done to the plaintiff's car, plus court costs."

Harry bolted out of his chair. "One-thousand dollars?! For a taillight? Are you fuckin' kidding me?!"

The judge grabbed her gavel and pointed it at Harry. "Tread lightly, Mr. Blake. One more word and I'll hold you in contempt."

Harry tugged on his crotch. "Hold this, Judge." He kicked his chair, sending it halfway across the room, then stomped off toward the exit.

"Detain that man!" the judge bellowed.

Two sheriff deputies grabbed Harry just before he reached the exit, but Harry easily shoved them aside. Two marshals quickly joined the fray. After a brief struggle with the four men, Harry finally raised his arms and gave up. The two badly-winded deputies nervously escorted Harry out of the building.

***

The metal cot and flimsy, tattered mattress that Harry laid on wasn't getting the job done. It was just after two a.m., and the big man had tossed and turned for over two hours, yet sleep wasn't coming. He grunted as he sat up. The corridor's lighting shone dimly into his cell, but just brightly enough for Harry to see someone was sitting at the foot of his bed.

"It's about damn time you kicked up a little shit, soldier."

Harry's eyes widened when he saw a man dressed in what appeared to be a military uniform getting to his feet. Pearl-handled revolvers sat snugly in holsters on the man's hips, and a riding crop dangled from his hand.

"What in the hell...?" Harry whispered.

General George S. Patton cracked Harry's foot with his riding crop. "Watch your mouth, you son- of-a-bitch!" the general barked. Howling in pain, Harry reached for his foot, but his belly stopped his forward progress. He yanked a blanket over his eyes and began to shiver. The general pulled the blanket off Harry and tossed it to the floor. "Get up, you sack of shit," Patton bellowed.

"Who - who the hell are you? How do you know my name?"

"You don't know who I am?"

Harry closed his eyes as he continued to shake. "This isn't happening, this isn't happening..."

General Patton raised his riding crop again and cracked the foot of the bed with it. "You're damned tootin' this is happening. Up, up, up!" Harry rolled out of bed and staggered to his feet, and his bad knee nearly buckled under him. "Stand up straight like you got a pair, soldier!" Harry fought the pain throbbing in his knee as he stood at attention. General Patton eyed him up and down. "I've seen better beef on a meat hook," he said, grabbing a handful of Harry's ample belly.

The general leaned in close and reached behind Harry, grabbing a butt cheek in each hand and squeezing hard. Harry tried backpedaling, but the general's steely gaze made him freeze. Patton slapped one of Harry's butt cheeks, then stepped back and shook his head in disgust. "Your ass flaps like Old Glory on a windy day, Blake. You're soft and you're a disgrace to the uniform."

"What - what uniform?" Harry said. "Who the hell are you?"

The general puffed out his chest and smiled. "I'm four- star General George Smith Patton, you worthless son of a bitch."

"Why-why are you here?"

"I'm here to help you get in the fight!"

Too scared to do anything else, Harry nodded like he understood exactly what the general was talking about.

"Get some sleep, soldier," the general said. "I'll see you again real soon. We've got work to do." The general disappeared.

***

The next morning, Harry rolled off his cot, and pain immediately shot through his body. He rubbed his bad knee and cursed when he realized that he had none of his pain medications with him. Harry looked up and saw Sheriff Roy staring at him as the cell's door opened. "Hey, Roy."

"Hey, Harry. I got you released. Let's get you out of here."

After Harry retrieved his personal effects, he and Sheriff Roy walked to the parking lot. Harry got into his truck. "Thanks for getting me out, Roy."

"Sure thing. Wanna grab a coffee?"

"Yeah. I'll call ya."

"How 'bout right now, buddy?"

Harry was tired and cranky, but he felt like he owed his friend.

"Okay. Deb's?"

"See you in ten."

***

Harry and Roy grabbed a booth at Deb's Diner and ordered lunch. Roy sipped his coffee while Harry stared out the window at nothing in particular. "Hear I missed one helluva scene yesterday," Roy said. "My boys say tangling with you was like trying to rope a rhinoceros."

Harry slugged his coffee down in three huge gulps, then ran his fingers through his hair."They screwed me, Roy. That little shit nearly runs me over, and I gotta pay restitution to him? And court costs? And I gotta go to some sensitivity bullshit classes?" When Harry slammed his fist onto the table, it wobbled. "It ain't right, Roy!" The diner's customers stopped to check out the commotion.

Roy raised his hands to try and calm Harry down. "I know, Harry. My deputies have to attend those damn things, too."

"What the hell for?"

"Couple of months ago, we're all in the break room, and one of my deputies, a black guy named Leon, was making fun of the way white people dance, and everyone's laughing their asses off, but a clerk walks by and sees Leon dancing, and when he's done pissing himself cause he's so mentally scarred for life now, he calls the state and tells the powers-that-be he was offended by what he saw.

He tells the state Leon must have been coerced into dancing for a bunch of white guys, like it was a minstrel show, so now all of my deputies have to go to sensitivity classes at that place."

"Just 'cause everyone was having a few laughs?"

"Everyone except the fuckin' idiot, social justice warrior who decided to be butt hurt over nothing. This country's changing, Harry. And it's not for the better."

"You have to go to the classes?"

"They've been trying to make me go for a while now." Roy chuckled. "I told 'em to kiss my nearly- retired ass."

"You're retiring?"

"Sure am. Putting in my papers soon. The town council slashed the department's budget by almost half. That was the last straw."

"Why'd they do that?"

"It's this defund the police bullshit that's going around the country. We had to let go of three deputies. Three good men who grew up in this town and wanted to protect it from the bad guys. And you know who's gonna suffer the most? The people on the south side of town, that's who.That area's getting flooded with drugs, mostly meth and coke, and we can't do a damn thing about it."

"Why not?"

"'Cause I don't have the manpower now to even patrol the south side since they cut my department in half. And petty crimes are way up in the past year. Vandalism, shoplifting, disorderly conduct, trespassing, you name it. The bad guys are getting' bolder cause they know even when we make arrests, the courts are tossing the cases out or the new county prosecutor's not charging 'em in the first place. They've castrated us, the bastards."

"Who's they, Roy?"

"The town council, Harry. It's gone woke."

"What the hell is 'woke'?"

"It's a disease. The council's jumped on the social justice warrior bandwagon and they're doing a self-congratulatory circle jerk with each other like they just found a cure for cancer when all they did was make life tougher for the good people in this town."

Sheriff Roy shook his head. "Our response times have almost tripled since last year, and my guys are tense and stressed out cause they're afraid to do their jobs anymore. My deputies spend more time in court defending their arrests than they do on the streets now. Hell, a lot of parents on that side of town won't even let their kids play outside anymore 'cause crime's gotten so bad. You know how fuckin' sad that is, Harry?"

"It ain't right, Roy"

"And we know the idiot across the street from you is dealing drugs on the south side and at Pine Ridge, and we can't do a damn thing about it."

Harry sat up straight when he heard that. "That idiot, Crash? No shit?"

"No shit."

"That's what he's doing when he heads out at three or four in the morning, I guess." Harry said.

"He ain't volunteering at a soup kitchen, buddy. We had the little asshole dead to rights last year on distribution, but his cousin got the case thrown out on a technicality. That still burns my ass.”

“So, no one’s gonna nail the bastard?”

Sheriff Roy downed the rest of his coffee in one gulp. “I had to turn the investigation over to the state boys. Don’t hold your breath.”

Getting angry, Harry’s hands shook as he dropped cash on the table to pay for the meals. A waitress that Harry didn’t recognize picked up the cash then walked away. “Where’s Cindy? She sick today?”

“She quit,” Roy said. “Twenty plus years here and she just up and walked out last week.”

“Why?”

“Deb’s is going corporate. Heard it got bought out by some big company and the first thing they’re gonna do is make their employees attend white privilege bullshit training. From what I’ve read ‘bout the subject, the company’s gonna try to force the employees to admit they oppress people of color, whether they know it or not.”

“People of color? Aren’t we all people of color?”

“Good point, Harry. But these days, if you’re white, you’re the bad guy. We’re all supposed to admit it, deal with it, and change our evil ways.”

“And this new company’s behind this?”

“Yup. Guess they think forcing this bullshit on its employees is gonna score ‘em big public relations points.”

Harry sat back as Roy’s words sank in. “What the hell do we do about all this shit, Roy? How do we fight ‘em?”

“I don’t know. I just don’t know.”

The two men walked out to the parking lot, and Roy shut Harry’s door after he climbed into his truck. “When’s your first indoctrination class?” Roy said.

“Tuesday night. Wonder what would happen if I didn’t go.”

“Suppose they could throw you back in jail. I’d hate to see that happen. Please go, buddy. Play along with the assholes for now.”

“‘Til when, Roy?”

"'Til you finish the damn classes, I guess. Or 'til someone blows that place to hell. I wouldn't lose any sleep over that."

Harry mulled over that statement as he drove off.

13

Later that evening, Harry sat in his recliner, staring at the ceiling. Gertie was next door with Charlie, and he had no idea where Joey was. It was just as well that the boy wasn't home at the moment, Harry figured. With the mood he was in, Harry knew any exchange between the two would probably lead to an argument right now. But he didn't want to be alone, nor alone with his thoughts. Needing to see some friendly faces, he grabbed his keys and headed out the door.

He pulled into the parking lot of the VFW Hall, Post 144. Halfway to the front door, he looked at the VFW sign perched atop the two- story building. The sign evoked a sense of pride, and sadness, in him. When Patsy was alive, Harry would stroll into the hall and brag to the guys about how he'd just liberated himself from the old "ball and chain." The gang would raise their glasses to Harry and give him a collective slap on the back in mock admiration for his heroic feat, and the boys would drink the night away.

Thinking of his departed wife brought Harry to a stop. He considered turning around and going back home, but he steeled himself and walked into the hall. Looking around, he saw perhaps fifteen men sitting at tables, drinking and playing cards, and a few more sitting at the bar. *There's less of us every time*. He thought again about leaving, but he heard a familiar voice call his name.

"Over here, Harry," Ronnie said from a table in a corner of the room. Ronnie was sitting with Jimmy Hunter, a beefy, corn-fed veteran who served two tours in Vietnam. Harry shook hands with the men before grabbing a seat. Ronnie poured Harry a beer from a pitcher. "Drink up, Harry. You're gonna need it," Ronnie said.

"Why's that?"

"We were just talking about Bobby Williams," Jimmy said.

"That's a name I haven't heard in a while. He okay?"

"He's gone, Harry," Jimmy said.

"How?"

"Suicide," Jimmy said. "I got a call from his ex-wife today. She's been trying to get him help, but…"

Jimmy turned away, but not before Harry saw tears welling up in his eyes. Harry gently clutched his arm. "He was on a waiting list for over two years at the V.A. trying to get help," Jimmy said. "Two fucking years."

"Our tax dollars at work, huh?" Harry said.

The three men sat in silence for what seemed like hours. Finally, Ronnie spoke up. "Ricky Fisher's gone, too."

"Ricky, too? How?" Harry said.

"Hodgkin's disease," Jimmy said. "He's been fighting that shit for years. It finally got him."

"Probably that fuckin' Agent Orange[1]," Ronnie said.

An uneasy silence once again hung over the men. Harry thought stopping by the hall tonight would lift his spirits, if only temporarily, and help him to forget about his day and his empty home, but the news of his fallen friends hit him hard. He hung his head in sorrow and anger and frustration clawed at his gut. Jimmy raised his glass, and Ronnie followed suit. "Here's to Bobby and Ricky. They were good soldiers. And good men," Jimmy said.

The men waited for Harry to raise his glass. "Gonna join us, Harry?" Ronnie said. Harry slammed his beer mug onto the table, sending beer and shards of glass into the air. His hand shook, but it remained tightly wrapped around the mug's handle.

---

[1] A powerful herbicide used by U.S. military forces during the Vietnam War to eliminate forest cover and crops for North Vietnamese and Viet Cong troops. It was later proven to cause serious health issues—including cancer and birth defects.

Harry stared at the floor, oblivious to everything, including his bleeding hand. Jimmy grabbed a bar towel and wrapped it around Harry's still- shaking hand. He applied pressure to the cut to slow the bleeding, and Ronnie slowly pried Harry's fingers from the mug's handle. "Harry, snap out of it," Ronnie said.

Harry clutched the towel wrapped around his hand, then stared blankly at his friends. He thought about saying something, but instead got up and walked out of the hall.

***

When Harry got home, he slammed the front door shut behind him and went to the bathroom. He rifled through the medicine cabinet until he found band- aids, a gauze pad and an antibiotic ointment. As he dressed his wound, he remembered he had an interview the next morning. "Shit," he muttered.

He thought about cancelling the interview, but he knew if he did so, the position could get filled by another applicant. For his plan to work, he needed the job. After wrapping the hand in gauze, he took a look in the mirror. The beard he had started to grow the week before was coming in nicely. He swallowed two sleeping pills and a pain pill, then climbed into bed.

14

The next morning, Harry checked his tie in the rearview mirror, then got out of his truck. His knee throbbing, he reached for his cane, but realized it wouldn't look good to walk into an interview with his cane in tow. A receptionist with Staffing Unlimited showed him into an office. Just as he got comfortable in a chair, a woman in her forties walked in. She smiled as she extended a hand towards Harry. "Hello, Mr. Blake. I'm Joanie. It's nice to meet you."

"You, too. Please, call me Harry. Can I call you by your first name?"

"Of course, you can." Joanie took a seat. Looking Harry over, she noticed his bandaged hand. "What happened to your hand?"

Harry smiled. "Shaving accident. It's almost healed."

Confused, Joanie smiled as she browsed Harry's resume. "I see you're here to apply for the custodial position at the courthouse."

"You mean the janitor's job," Harry said.

"Business jargon, Harry. And if my boss heard me call you by your first name, it would be my butt."

"You're sassy, Joanie. I like that."

"Life's too short to be uptight."

"Will you marry me? I haven't got much, but what's mine is yours when you leave me."

Joanie giggled. "That's a nice offer, but your wife might have something to say about that."

"She's passed on."

Joanie frowned as she sat back in her chair. "I'm so sorry. I didn't know."

"How could you know, honey?" *Honey? Oh, shit, I'm done here.*

But the term "honey" didn't faze Joanie a bit. "You're right, I couldn't know, but I'm very sorry just the same."

"Thank you, Joanie." *Okay. Dodged that bullet. Watch your mouth, Harry.*

"Your resume says you were a security guard for nearly forty years. Is that right?"

"Yeah, at the auto plant just north of town," Harry said.

"And you're retired now?"

"That's right. And now I sit around the house just getting fatter. I need some exercise, and this job would help."

Joanie looked at Harry's resume again. "I also see that you served in Vietnam."

"I did."

"My dad served there, too. He was really proud of that. But he didn't like to talk about it."

"I get that," Harry said. "I hope you're proud of him."

Joanie's eyes welled up with tears. "I – I am."

Harry leaned in toward the girl. "What's wrong, honey?"

"I'm sorry."

"What is it?"

"When I think of Dad…"

"Is he… gone?"

Joanie nodded as she fought back tears. Harry grabbed a tissue from her desk and handed it to her. She wiped her eyes and tried to compose herself.

"Tell me what happened," Harry said.

"He took … he took his own life. He couldn't deal with the nightmares anymore. He could never get a good night's sleep, and little things set him off all the time."

"He had PTSD."

"He did, yeah," Joanie said. "Mom said that he wasn't the same man when he came home from the war."

"War does things to you," Harry said.

Joanie nodded like she understood.

"You can't really understand, honey, but that's okay. Go on."

"Dad tried therapy and medications, but nothing really helped. He just got worse and worse. Then one day…"

There was silence as Harry struggled to find the words to express his heartfelt sympathy to the girl, but nothing came to mind.

Joanie tossed the tissue in a wastebasket. "We should discuss the job." Harry felt relief that she spoke first. "I assume that you understand what the job entails in terms of your duties, Harry."

"I can swing a mop and push a broom with the best of 'em."

"You look capable to me," Joanie said. "And they're willing to train the right person. It's only part time, about twenty hours a week. And I believe the courtroom is closing for good by the end of the year."

Or sooner, Harry mused.

"The pay isn't great, but you'll have weekends off. How does that sound?"

"Sounds good to me, Joanie. When would I start?"

"Well, I'll need to gather more personal information, like your social security number for the background check."

Harry stiffened when he suddenly remembered his recent entanglement with the court system. "Background check?"

"You sound surprised, Mr. Blake. It's standard procedure these days. Is there a problem?"

"No, of - of course not. It's just been so long since I've had to pass one of those."

"Good. We'll get the results in just a few days. Then we'll get you started."

"Sounds good." Harry said, "Is there anything else?"

"That should do it for now."

Harry got out of his chair and shook Joanie's hand. Then he started for the door. When he reached it, he turned. "Thanks for…" He saw Joanie's mouth trembling. She was about to break down and cry. Harry was again at a loss for the right words, so he did the first thing that came to mind; he opened his arms to the girl. Joanie looked confused at first, but then she walked toward him. He gently wrapped his arms around the girl. And she did the same. Holding her tightly, he whispered. "It's all right, honey. Your dad's in a much better place now. He's at peace."

Thinking that he had held on long enough, Harry let go of the girl. But when she continued to sob, and held him even harder, he embraced her again.

***

Gertie and Charlie sat on the patio in Charlie's backyard, basking in the sun. Gertie sipped her lemonade, frowned, and set the glass on the table. "The Russkies stop making vodka, honey?"

"Gertie, it's barely past noon."

"You got somewhere you need to be, lover?"

Charlie knew this was not a battle he was going to win. Grabbing his cane, he started to get up.

"I'll get it. You sit and relax," Gertie said. She returned with a bottle of vodka and poured a couple of shots into her glass. "Honey?" she said, offering Charlie a drink.

"I'm good, dear."

"You're no fun," she said as she gulped down her drink. "What's eating at you?"

"It's Harry."

"What about him?"

"I heard him talking in the backyard a few days ago."

"So?"

"He was talking to someone, but I never heard another voice."

"Maybe you were dreaming, hon."

75

"I was wide awake," Charlie said. "He was having a conversation with someone. I'm sure of it."

Gertie waved him off as she finished her drink, then poured herself another. "Damn. It's going down smooth today."

"Gertie, did you hear me?"

"I heard you. What do you want me to say?"

"Has Harry been taking his medications?"

"I think he threw some of 'em out."

"You think he did?"

"I don't know whose meds they were. They might still be in the garbage."

Charlie sat up and faced Gertie. "I'm really worried about Harry. First, he retired, then he lost Patsy, and now he's got too much time on his hands. He needs a purpose."

"My boy's hit some bumps, but he'll be fine. He's tough as nails, just like his father was." Gertie finished off her drink and poured herself a third. "He'll find his way." When Charlie scowled, Gertie said, "I'll talk to him."

"Good," Charlie said.

Gertie's head started to spin from the effects of the alcohol. "Now, how's about you and me getting in some sack time?"

"Finish your drink first, hon." *Please pass out already, Gert.*

Gertie downed the rest of her drink in two gulps. Moments later, she was out cold. "Joey, you over there? I need you," Charlie yelled across the yard.

Joey walked out the back door of the Blake house and into Charlie's backyard. Seeing that Gertie was passed out, he gently scooped the tiny woman into his arms. "Sometimes, I think you do this on purpose, Mr. Sloan."

"When you're older, you'll understand, son."

"If you say so," Joey said, walking away with Gertie cupped in his arms.

15

The town of Bremerhaven was located just off US Highway 16, twenty miles north of Albrecht. By the late 1800's, the town became home to many Scandinavian and German immigrants, and the population was just over eight thousand as of the last census. People only came to the town because they lived there, or they needed gas to continue their trip to anywhere but Bremerhaven. Smokestacks and smog dominated the skyline, and heavy industry formed a ring around the town, like a snake constricting its prey, slowly choking the life out of it.

The town owned the one-story, dilapidated building at 328 Grant Avenue. Once the town's recreation hall, it had been abandoned for over ten years, and no one in Bremerhaven seemed to notice, nor care. But Kurt Schmidt cared. The monthly rent payment on the building, zero, was the right price, and a few years back several members of the chapter, a plumber, a carpenter, and an electrician, hooked the building up with all the necessities: power, water, electricity, and a ten-seat bar.

Kurt pushed open the building's rusty, weather-beaten front door, stepped onto the walkway and lit a cigarette. His greasy, shoulder length, jet black hair belied his ancestry. Kurt was third- generation German American, and the founder of the local chapter of The Brownshirts of America. He was working class stock, believed Hitler was a true patriot, the savior and defender of the Aryan race, and like the original Brownshirts, Kurt wore a brown, collared shirt and brown tie, along with a swastika pendant on a long rope chain, and military boots.

A millwright by trade, he hadn't had steady work in nearly two years, which gave him free time to do things, mainly drink beer, and sell guns and drugs. Kurt tossed his cigarette to the ground as two of the chapter's probationary members, both in their early twenties, made their way toward him. "You boys are late," he said.

Stefan, a lanky kid sporting a death rock T- shirt and a deathhawk haircut, came to a sudden stop and gave Kurt a Sig Heil salute. "Sorry, mein Stabchef," he said. "Traffic was a bitch." The young men slid past Kurt on their way into the building.

"Traffic, my dick," Kurt said.

After slamming the front door shut behind him, Kurt followed the two young men into the building. The walls of the hall were covered with Nazi memorabilia: pictures and portraits of German leaders of the armed forces circa WW2, several swastika flags, German weaponry of the era, and portraits of Adolph Hitler and Ernst Rohm, the co-founder and chief of staff of the Sturmabteilung in the early 1930's.

Membership in the Bremerhaven chapter of the B. of A. totaled about twenty men, but today only ten showed up for the meeting. Bellied up to the bar and drinking beers, the men swung around to inspect the two, new recruits who didn't look like they could collectively fight their way out of a wet paper bag, nor outwit one. Not impressed with what he saw, Frank, one of the oldest members of the group, said, "Hope they're sterilized." He and his comrades turned to face the bar again.

"All rise!" Kurt barked. The men at the bar half-heartedly rose to their feet. The Horst-Wessel-Lied, the anthem of the Nazi Party, blared over loudspeakers mounted on the walls in every corner of the hall. Kurt and the men at the bar stood at attention while the slacker recruits, sitting at a table, checked out porn and death metal on their smartphones.

Kurt noticed. He gestured for a man behind the bar to cut the music, then he made his way to the boys. He smiled as he stood over Stefan. "What you looking at?"

"German porn. The nastiest shit on the Internet," Stefan said.

"That's great," Kurt said, before his smile disappeared. "Stow those phones or I'll shove 'em up your asses!" The boys, after nearly evacuating their bowels, quickly pocketed their phones.

"Achtung!" Kurt bellowed. The recruits jumped out of their chairs and snapped to attention.

"Yes, mein Stabchef!" they shouted. After looking them up and down, he shook his head in disgust. "Sit your asses down and pay attention. The meeting's starting." The men took seats at the table, and Kurt sat at the head of the table. "We got any new business?"

Hans, the oldest member present, chugged down half a stein of beer, then wiped his mouth. "There's a few new groups in the area kicking up shit."

"What kind of shit?"

"They're tearing down statues, trashing buildings, protesting. That kind of shit."

"What are they protesting about?"

"Word is, us, mostly." Hans said.

"Us? You mean the Brownshirts?"

"No. The whole white race. Word around town is, they think we're all evil. They apparently wanna take us down."

Kurt sat back and considered that.

"We gotta do something," said Hans. "We gotta respond."

"We got any other new business?" Kurt said.

"No."

"Meeting's over, then." Kurt got up and headed for the bar, and the rest of the men followed, except for Hans. He sat alone at the table, bitterly disappointed and angry that Kurt dismissed him without a second thought. By eight that night, all the Brownshirts were drunk except for Hans, who had walked out of the center hours before without bothering to say goodbye to anyone.

16

Every Tuesday night since Patsy's passing, Harry donned his sombrero and blasted mariachi music on the stereo as he cooked Mexican for the family. After dinner he would tell dad jokes that got groans from Joey and Charlie, then the boys would belly up to the television and watch a ballgame. Harry would do play-by-play for Charlie ad nauseum, knowing that drove the old man crazy, then Charlie would repeatedly tell him to shut the hell up, and Joey would laugh as he watched the two men go at each other. It was male bonding at its finest as far as Harry was concerned, and Taco Tuesday would go on forever if were up to him. Having the family together, especially after losing his wife, always warmed his heart. But Taco Tuesday would be canceled this night, and every other Tuesday night for the near future, unless something changed.

Things were different around the Blake house lately, and the changes irked Harry. Gertie was spending much more time at Charlie's, and Joey and he weren't talking, and that frustrated the big man to no end. Harry hoped that eventually things would get back to normal. He wanted to believe that, and he needed to believe that, but for the next six months, he was forced to attend sensitivity training classes at the C.A.T. on Tuesday and Thursday nights, and that really burned his ass.

He got out of his truck and stared at the sign facing him from just a few feet away: The Center for Alternative Thinking. For over thirty years, the building was home to the Albrecht Elementary School, but as the population of the town steadily grew older, the town council consolidated the school with another one on the west side of town just over five years ago, and it had sat empty ever since.

Harry's grandson, Joey, had attended the school, and Harry smiled as he reminisced about the hours he had spent watching his grandson and his friends play at recess. He missed those days.

The town council decided the year before, with persuasion and financial contributions to certain town council members from some loosely connected groups and organizations, that it was time to re-educate the people of Albrecht: the unwashed, ignorant masses who dared to think they were decent people. The former school was renamed the C.A.T. for short, and compulsory attendance for those deemed insensitive, oppressive or racist by the woke groups in town would ensure a steady pipeline of "students" for a long time to come.

Harry walked down the hallway on his way to classroom 7A. He saw banners covering what seemed to him to be every inch of the walls on both sides of the corridor. A banner to his right caught his eye. **Think Right. Feel Right.** He walked on as he tried to decipher the meaning of that message. He then passed another: **Legislate Hate Out of Existence.** And just as he reached his classroom, one more: **We Regress When We Oppress.** Harry felt a headache coming as he stepped into the classroom. He looked around and saw a sea of strange faces, about twenty in number, most of them staring at the floor or out the windows. No one looked happy to be there. He found an open desk in the first row near the back of the room and plopped into it.

"What are you in for?" The man sitting next to him asked.

Harry was in no mood for small talk, especially with a stranger. But he didn't want to be rude, either. "Hate crime," Harry said. "I threw a rock at some idiot's car, and it turns out the punk is part Indian, so here I am."

"You mean, like call-center Indian?" the man said.

"No. American Indian."

"Okay," the man said, extending his hand to Harry. "The name is Mike. Mike Reardon."

His right hand still- bandaged, Harry shook Mike's hand with his left. "Name's Harry. Harry Blake."

Mike pointed at Harry's right hand. "What happened there?"

"Shaving accident."

"Been shaving with your mouth, Harry?"

It took Harry a minute to get the joke, but when he did, he grinned. He liked Mike already. "What are you in for?" he said.

Just as Mike was about to respond, a slender and weak-chinned man entered the room and dropped a briefcase on the desk. He looked over the class with a smug smile. "Hello, my name is Mr. Wilkins. First name, Steve. I'm the class facilitator, slash moderator. If you're here, you've been very naughty." Mr. Wilkins waved a finger at the class and waited for laughter that never came, so he went on. "I'm here to help, heal, and enlighten. Let's get started." He passed a stack of syllabuses to the person sitting in the front seat of each row. "Please pass these back," he said.

"Let the indoctrination begin," Mike said.

Harry buried his head in his hands. "I need a drink," he said.

The syllabuses made their way to the back of the room. Harry and Mike each grabbed a copy and dropped them on their desks. "This is an unconscious bias training program which has been proven to be very effective in helping people like yourselves realize you've learned stereotypes that are automatic and deeply ingrained, and these stereotypes influence your negative behavior and actions toward other people, particularly people of color," Mr. Wilkins said. "As you can see, the syllabus is broken down into different training methods that we'll employ during the course of this course." Mr. Wilkins waited for laughter in response to his play on words. What he got was a sea of blank stares.

Harry looked over the syllabus. The first page consisted of a list of training methods. Each method was followed by a brief explanation of the goals to be achieved.

"Conform. Be like us," Mike said in a robotic monotone as he flipped through his syllabus.

"Our mission is to help all of you become more thoughtful, caring and better people," Mr. Wilkins said. "At the end of this semester, you will all be required to sign an anti-racism statement which will conclude our journey together."

"Anti-racism statement? What the hell does that mean?" Harry said.

"It means we're racist, but we just don't know it yet," Mike replied.

Racist. Harry remembered that's what the judge had practically called him, without knowing a thing about him. Crash, his cousin the lawyer, and the judge had beaten him. Harry visualized them laughing their asses off at his expense. He shifted in his seat as resentment and anger clawed at his gut.

***

After class, Harry and Mike walked to their cars. Harry looked up at a light pole and something near the top of the pole caught his eye. "Hey, Mike, check it out. Is that a security camera up there?"

"Sure is," Mike said. "There's a few of them. This place has gotten some bomb threats since it opened up."

"Just threats, huh?"

"So far. Maybe someday somebody'll get serious and follow through. We can dream, right?"

Harry chuckled. "We sure can. Want to grab a beer?"

Mike looked at his watch. "I should be getting home. Been a long day."

"C'mon. Just one. I'm buying."

"Okay. Where we going?"

Harry pointed across the street. "Ever been to Sam's?"

"Not in a long time. Meet you there."

***

The two men pulled up to the bar and grabbed a couple of seats.

Harry waved hello to a couple of the regulars, then he gestured for the bartender. While waiting for their beers, Harry turned and stared through the tavern window at The Center for Alternative Thinking. Darkness had just fallen, and the roadside sign gleamed like a lighthouse beacon that seemed to light up the entire town. Harry continued to stare at the sign.

"It's not going anywhere, Harry."

Harry turned to face Mike. "We'll see. Hey, you never told me how you got roped in."

Mike sat back. "I got charged with sexual harassment. I told a secretary at work that she looked good in a dress she was wearing. And here I am."

"Tell me you're kidding," Harry said.

"I wish I was."

"You oughta get a lawyer."

"I am a lawyer," Mike said.

"Let me get this straight. You told a woman at work she looked good in a dress?" Mike nodded yes as the bartender placed a couple of beers in front of the men. "Nothing else but that? No grab ass, no come-ons?"

"Nothing but that comment," Mike said. "And for that, you gotta go to the classes?"

Mike had a couple of gulps of his beer. "I'm a happily married guy with two kids. I'm not on the prowl. This lady at work is a big gal. Well over two-hundred pounds, and ugly as a half-shaved pug. Poor lady probably hasn't had a date since the Bush administration. I felt bad for her so I paid her a compliment, you know, hoping to cheer her up a bit. So, she gives me a look like I just stole her lunch money before she walks away. The next thing I know, I get a visit from the Gestapo two floors down. Seems this woman made a beeline to H.R. and told them that I was staring at her in a 'lustful manner' when I made the comment. I was accused of creating a hostile work environment. What a crock of shit. Now I'm forced to attend this bullshit, sensitivity classes just to hold onto my career."

"You could always work for another law firm, right?" Harry said.

"Have you been living in a cave for the past twenty years, Harry? This kind of bullshit can follow you wherever you go." Mike slammed back the rest of his beer. "I'm damn good at what I do. I do pro bono work for poor people that the other lawyers at my firm wouldn't get caught dead doing, and just like that..." Mike snapped his fingers. "Just like that my career's in jeopardy. Over a fucking compliment."

Harry gulped down his beer. "Back in my day, we didn't have to think twice about paying a woman a compliment; we just did it. Apparently now you gotta talk to a lawyer before you even look at some people."

Mike gestured to the bartender for another round. "Times have changed, Harry. Your turn. Give me the details."

"Not much to tell," Harry said. "I got a young jackass living across the street. He raises hell all the time, and late at night he hits my house with his high beams when he pulls out of the driveway."

"Late at night? How late?"

"Three, four in the a.m., some nights."

"Is he going to work, maybe?"

"The little asshole doesn't have a job, far as I know. I heard he got some family money in a trust, or something," Harry said.

"Sounds like he's up to no good."

"Probably. So, one night he wakes me up with the high beams and I head outside and tell him to turn 'em off. He tears ass down the driveway and nearly hits me. So, I picked up a rock and busted his taillight."

"That's it?" Mike said.

"Yeah. Then he hires a lawyer, and the next thing you know, I'm charged with a hate crime, and I get a restraining order slapped on me." Harry ran his hand through his hair. "I didn't know the punk was part Indian, and it don't matter, anyway. I'd have thrown a rock at a fuckin' Martian if they pulled that shit on me."

"Who represented you?"

"No one, Mike. Didn't think I needed a lawyer."

"You went to court without an attorney? That's not real smart."

"Found that out right after the judge butt-slammed my ass. I got convicted of ethnic intimidation, malicious destruction of property, the restraining order's still in effect, and I gotta pay the little asshole a thousand bucks for the damage, plus court costs. Then she ordered me to go to this sensitivity bullshit for six months."

"Remember the judge's name?"

"Davenport, I think. Big gal. And mean as a snake."

"You got Big Bertha? Tough break. We call her Judge Dread."

"Judge Dredd? Like the movie?"

"No. D-r-e-a-d. As in, male attorneys dread arguing a case before her. She's a real organ grinder. Her husband left her for a man."

"You mean, another man?"

Mike chuckled. "Good one. Anyway, she hates the entire male gender now. You say you didn't know this kid was part Native American?"

"No. But it shouldn't matter. I hit the kid's car cause he's an asshole. End of story."

"Unfortunately, these days it does matter," Mike said. "If you knew beforehand that the kid was Native American, they can charge you with a hate crime. And if the judge is convinced you did what you did because of the kid's ethnic background, you're screwed."

Harry slugged down a few gulps of his beer. "Is she gonna get in my mind? Does she know if I hate the kid, or not? Even if I do, so fucking what!" Harry said as he slammed his beer mug down on the bar. Startled by Harry's rage, Mike slowly shifted away from the big man. "What you do to a person is the only thing that should matter legally," Harry said. "Not what you think of them, or what nationality they are."

"Couldn't agree more, Harry. Sounds like you got railroaded." Harry shrugged. "You could appeal," Mike said. "I could file the paperwork for you."

Harry waved him off. "Thanks for the offer, Mike, but what's done is done. I'll deal with this shit another way."

"Meaning what?"

"We'll see. How old are you, Mike?"

"Thirty-eight. You?"

"Seventy-five," Harry said. "I'm playing on the back nine. My body's shot to hell and my mind's headed for the nearest exit. I didn't lose a chunk of my knee and lots of friends in 'Nam so I could be told what to think and what to say by a bunch of do-fucking-gooders. What the hell's happening around here, Mike? How the hell do they get away with this shit?"

"They think they can scare the rest of us into submission. They scream "racism" and "oppression" at the drop of a hat, and a lot of sane people run for cover. And guess what? It's working for them. They're winning." Mike looked at his watch. "It's late. I've got to get home." But Harry wasn't listening. He was staring at the C.A.T. again. "Harry?"

Harry turned to face Mike and extended his hand. "Was good meeting you, Mike." Harry turned to stare at the Center again.

"What are you thinking, big fella?"

Harry's gaze stayed locked onto the C.A.T. building. "You don't want to know. You really don't want to know."

17

Joey walked into the house and saw that his grandpa was in his recliner, half-asleep. Joey hadn't spoken to Harry in over a week, and he had no interest in doing so now. He crept towards the staircase, and as he neared the bottom step, a loose floorboard creaked and gave him away. Harry snapped out of his shallow slumber. He caught sight of the boy when he peered across the room. "Still giving me the cold shoulder, Joey?"

The boy stopped. "Figured you didn't want to talk to a sissy."

Harry sighed. "Joey…come talk to your grandpa." But Joey didn't budge. "Please."

Joey took a few steps into the living room, then stopped. "I'm sorry about what I said, Joey. I was angry. I didn't mean any of it." Joey refused to look at his grandfather. "Look at me, Joey. Please." Grudgingly, the boy faced Harry. "When I get mad, sometimes I lash out, but I didn't mean to hurt you. You know how that day affects me. I'm just a broken-down old man who wants his boy back. What do you say? Can we get past this?"

"We can try, I guess," Joey said.

Harry sat back and smiled. "Good deal. What do you say we get some ice cream after the news?"

"Sure thing, Gramps."

Harry gestured for the boy to sit with him on the sofa, and Joey did. The two turned their attention towards the television. "This story is just breaking," the news anchor said. "Congressman Dan Templeton, from the 15th Congressional District, is fighting for his political life today.

The congressman recently appeared on a public affairs program where the topic was the criminal justice system, and he laughed when another panel member, a spokesman for the Pinetree County Department of Corrections, announced that felons released back into society would now be called "returning residents," or 'former justice-involved persons.' When asked by the program's moderator if he would like to explain his defenseless and insensitive outburst, Templeton replied, 'You're kidding, right?'"

The news anchor went on. "The backlash was swift, as many good citizens took to social media to condemn the congressman and demand that he relinquish his office immediately. Templeton's press secretary told the media there will be a press conference later this afternoon, and the congressman - congressperson - is expected to tender his resignation." The anchor shook his head in disgust as he stared into the camera. "And not one moment too soon. We cannot allow this kind of intolerance to go unpunished in a free society."

*Poor bastard,*Harry thought.

"Good," Joey said.

"Good? What the hell does that mean, boy?"

"That guy got what he deserved, Gramps. People have to pay a price for being insensitive."

"They're going after the man's job, Joey. Felons are criminals no matter what some people decide to call them. And calling them 'returning residents' doesn't change that."

"Those people have feelings, too."

"So, we're offending them if we call them felons?"

"Yeah."

Harry turned to face Joey. "With all the real problems in this country we gotta deal with, this is something that really bothers you? Who's filling your head with this shit, Joey?"

"It's not shit. We're learning how unjust and oppressive this country is in school. That congressman is trying to shame and negate those people. He deserves to lose his job.”

“Unjust and oppressive? This country?”

“You’re out of touch, Gramps. You need to evolve. You need to be more sensitive of other people and respect and celebrate their life choices.”

Harry rolled his eyes. “Yeah, let’s celebrate criminals getting renamed by people who wouldn’t be caught dead living in the same neighborhoods as these ‘returning residents.’ I’ll break out the party hats.”

“I won’t be coming to Taco Tuesdays anymore,” Joey said.” I’m tired of you co-opting the Mexican people and their customs.”

“Co-opting? What the hell does that mean?”

“It means you’re marginalizing people of color by assimilating their customs into this white- dominated, racist society.”

Harry shook his head in disbelief. “What in the hell is wrong with you, boy? You need to stop whining about this nonsensical bullshit. I didn’t know I was raising a granddaughter.”

On the verge of tears, Joey said, “I need my safe space.” He went to his room and didn’t come out for the rest of the night. Harry shook his head wondering what had just happened.

18

Still groggy and irritated from a lack of sleep the night before, Harry fidgeted as he looked around the room. He hated being at the doctor's office. He hated the waiting, he hated the questions, and his knee began to stiffen. As he slowly extended his leg to ease the pain, Dr. Jack Palmer, a man in his early fifties, stepped into the office and smiled warmly at Harry as he took a seat behind his desk. "It's good to see you, Mr. Blake."

"You know it's just Harry, Doc."

"Of course. So, how's your mother?"

Harry tapped the side of his head. "She's in and out, depending on the hour."

"I'm sorry about that. How have you been feeling lately?"

Harry shrugged. "Older."

"At least you haven't lost that sparkling wit of yours," the doctor said as he flipped through Harry's file. He looked over the prescription drugs that he was prescribing to Harry at the moment: zolpidem to help him sleep, rizatriptan for chronic migraine headaches, citalopram for depression, tramadol for the chronic pain in his bad knee and back, and thiazolidinedione for his type 2 diabetes. "How are the headaches, Harry?"

"They still come and go."

"In terms of frequency and duration?"

"About the same as last time I was here."

"How are you sleeping?"

"Same as for the last fifty years or so."

"Have there been any delusional episodes? Any hallucinations?"

"I got a couple new buddies. One's an old, Asian guy, and the other's General Patton."

"Do you mean World War Two General Patton?"

"Sure do."

Doctor Palmer leaned in. "Are you actually seeing these people? Or are they auditory episodes?"

"Both. I see 'em and hear 'em. They show up out of nowhere, we talk for a while, then they disappear." Harry chuckled. "Can't have too many friends, right, Doc?"

"I suppose not," Doctor Jack said as he tried to smile through the sadness he felt for Harry. The doctor had been treating him for years now, with little positive results. Too much damage had already been done. Doctor Jack sat back and flipped open a second file folder. "I've got the results from your latest MRI and CAT scan here," he said.

"Hit me."

"As you already know, the head trauma you experienced in the war from the multiple explosions has done damage to parts of your brain. I'm afraid your condition is deteriorating. I'd like to order a new round of testing."

Harry wasn't fazed at all by the news. It's what he expected to hear. He hoisted himself to his feet and started for the door. "Maybe down the road, Doc. Thanks for your time."

"You're not going anywhere yet, Harry. I need to explain a few things about your condition. Sit. Please." Harry heaved a sigh as he took a seat. "We already know that you have PTSD. And you're also exhibiting signs of TBI."

"What the hell is that?"

"Traumatic Brain Injury. It's difficult to diagnose, and not well understood. The combination of your repetitive neurotrauma in the war, and your advancing age, have caused gray matter atrophy in your brain, and that can cause cognitive dysfunction."

"Laymen's terms, Doc. Please."

"In layman's terms, TBI causes brain fog. It means the potential loss of intellectual functions such as thinking and remembering things. In more severe cases, it can interfere with daily functioning." Doctor Palmer closed Harry's file. "Harry, I'm sorry to be the bearer of bad news. We can't cure you at this point, but there may be things we can do to slow the condition down. But you have to be open to more tests and possibly more medications. Do you understand?"

"My medicine cabinet looks like a mini pharmacy already, Doctor Jack. I already take enough pills every day to choke a fuckin' elephant. Hell, I have to take pills to offset the side effects of other pills. What's the point?"

"I understand that, but I want you to try another medication, Harry. The tramadol you've been taking could be causing the hallucinations, so I want to prescribe something called lurasidone. It's an anti-psychotic that may help you regulate your moods. I'm hoping it will help you when you feel anxious, like when one of your triggers kicks in. And it may help with the hallucinations. Will you try it?"

Harry shrugged his shoulders. "It's not gonna matter, but I'll humor you, Doc."

"Good. I'm going to write you a script. Like any medication, there are potential side effects. Information regarding those will be included with your prescription. If you have any questions or concerns, please call me."

Harry slowly arose. "Sure thing."

"If you need anything, please don't be afraid to call me, Harry."

"Thanks, Doc." As Harry walked out the door, Doctor Palmer made a note in Harry's file.

Patient is experiencing auditory and visual hallucinations. Possible onset of psychosis/schizophrenia.

***

After the doctor's visit, Harry was in a mood. Doctor Palmer didn't need to tell him he was slipping and was never going to get better; he knew that already. But hearing the doctor's prognosis didn't help his demeanor. He thought about stopping by the VFW hall, but decided he just didn't want to risk getting more bad news there, so he opted to grab a cup of coffee instead.

As he drove down the town's main strip, he saw a sign for a new coffee shop called The Progressive Café, so he decided to give it a try. Feeling pressure on his bladder, he knew it was time to urinate again. Entering the café, he made a beeline for the men's room. When he reached the door, he saw a young man exiting the women's restroom."Take a wrong turn, buddy?" Harry said.

"Mind your own business, cisgender" the man said as he pushed his way past Harry.

After finishing his business in the restroom, Harry stepped up to the counter. An overly cheerful young girl greeted him with a fake smile. "Welcome to the Progressive Café. How may I help you today?" she said.

"Let me get a black coffee to go, please."

"We don't use that term here, sir."

"What term?"

"Black. We believe it's insensitive, oppressive and racist to call coffee black."

"Huh?"

"Coffee beans are living beings, too, sir. Speciesism is the same sort of bigotry as racism or sexism. Giving human beings greater rights than non-human entities is as arbitrary and as morally wrong as giving White people greater rights than non-White people. Here at the Progressive Café, we don't label our products by color. It's too oppressive."

"Do they make you say that?"

"No, yeah. We had sensitivity training here."

"What if I wanted a sandwich with white bread? How would I order that these days?"

"You would ask for white bread, sir."

"Isn't white a color?"

"I guess. But it's not an oppressed color, so, like, it's okay, I guess," the girl said, giggling.

Harry was growing more annoyed with every word that came out of the girl's mouth. "Tell me you're kidding," he said.

"I'm not kidding, sir."

"What do you call black coffee now?"

"We call it inky coffee," the girl said, giggling again.

Harry rolled his eyes. "That is so cute. Can I get a black coffee to go?"

The girl pouted as she poured Harry a coffee. She handed it to him, and he paid for it. He was about to leave the cafe when he saw the man who had walked out of the women's restroom just a couple of minutes earlier. He was sitting at a table in a corner of the cafe. When a manager walked by, Harry stopped him. "Excuse me, you the manager?"

"I am. My name is Patrick," said the young man. "How can I help you?"

"You see that guy over there?"

Patrick looked across the room and saw the man that Harry was pointing at. "I do," he said.

"I just saw him walk out of the women's bathroom," Harry said.

"And what is the problem, sir?"

"What's the problem? I just told you. He was in the women's restroom."

"Sir, that man, I mean, person, probably identifies as a woman, which means either restroom is available to him or her."

"She looks like a man to me. Maybe he or she should drop his or her pants for us and we'll know for sure either way, huh?"

"That would be an act of oppression, sir," Patrick said.

"An act of oppression, huh?" Harry said as he inched closer to Patrick. "So let me get this straight, Patrick. I could walk in here, say to myself, 'I feel like a woman today,' and stroll into the women's bathroom, whip out my crank and take a piss, and it wouldn't matter to this cafe?"

"There aren't any urinals in the women's restroom, sir."

"That's not the point!" Harry shouted. Startled patrons stared at him. Harry hadn't meant to raise his voice, so when he realized he was the center of attention, he tried to calm down. "Patrick, you got any daughters?"

"Not yet, sir. I hope to, someday."

"And you'd be okay with your little girl maybe seeing a guy's schlong in the lady's bathroom?"

"Kids have to learn about sex, too, sir."

Harry's face flushed red with anger. "Yeah, when they're not kids anymore!"

Scared and intimidated, Patrick took two steps back. "I - I think you should leave the café, sir."

"Be glad to. Do the world a favor and get yourself fixed, you fuckin' idiot," Harry said. He dropped his coffee on the floor and walked out the door.

***

Still agitated when he got home, Harry tossed his keys toward the living room table, then watched them slide off and onto the floor. Ordinarily he would have picked them up, his bad knee be damned, but today his keys could take root in the floor for all he cared. He already knew, without looking around, that the house was empty, and he was good with that, considering the way the day had gone so far. He plopped into his recliner and hoped that his fatigue would morph into slumber, and soon. He looked toward the stairwell. His bed was upstairs and just thirty seconds away – on a good day - but the effort and energy required to climb the stairs was just too much for him at the moment. After about fifteen minutes, he nodded off.

Two hours later, Joey walked into the house and slammed the door shut behind him. The noise shook Harry from his sleep. He was irritated, again. "Did ya have to slam the damn door shut, boy?"

Ignoring his grandfather, Joey walked up the stairs, and when he got to his bedroom, he stuffed shirts and pants into a duffel bag, then he emptied a couple of drawers worth of socks and underwear into the bag, slung it over his shoulders, and was about to step out the front door when he heard his grandpa's voice.

"Your graduation party is a week from Saturday."

Joey walked out the front door without responding or looking back. Harry's heart sank, and he sagged into his recliner and let out a long, mournful sigh as he closed his eyes. *My own grandson hates me.*

"Life can be a real bitch, huh, Harry?"

Harry knew that voice. He shuddered but refused to open his eyes. *Go away. You're not real. Please go away.*

"I'm not going anywhere just yet," said General Patton, who was sitting on the sofa.

You're not real. You're just in my head.

"Your grandson hates you, alright. He blames you for what happened, Harry."

"That wasn't my fault."

"You keep telling yourself that. I'm sure if the wife was still around, she'd forgive you. Maybe."

This isn't happening.

"This sure as shit is happening," the general said, leaning in towards Harry. "Let's check the scoreboard, Harry. You got convicted for a hate crime by a judge who doesn't even know you, but she found you guilty just the same. Is that fair?”

“It’s not fair. Not one fuckin’ bit.”

Just then, Charlie stepped into the kitchen through the back door. He tapped his cane along the floor as he neared the living room. “Harry, you there?” he said.

But Harry didn’t hear the old man. The general had the big man’s undivided attention at the moment. He leaned in even closer to Harry as he said, “You’re damn right it ain’t fair. And it’s no wonder you didn’t go to the VFW hall today. Seems like every time you do, you get bad news about your war buddies. They’re dropping like flies, huh?”

They are.

“I know about losing good men, Blake. I watched a lot of ‘em die fighting that cocksucker, Hitler. There’s no better death, no better glory, than dying in battle. That’s the way you should have gone.”

As Charlie was about to step into the living room, he froze when he heard Harry.

“That’s the way I should have gone?!” Harry pointed a finger at the general. “I got a knee that’s as sturdy as fuckin’ oatmeal, so I’m down to one good leg. My hearing’s about shot to hell, my brain’s scrambled, and I can’t sleep most nights for more than a couple hours at a time without having nightmares. I paid my fuckin’ dues, General!”

“General?” Charlie whispered. He listened intently for another voice.

“And what have you got now?” the general said. “Half the good ole U.S. of A. hates the military and its fighting men now. They could give a shit that you risked your life for them. Their heroes now are athletes and celebrities, not soldiers.”

Harry couldn’t argue that point with the general. He knew that the country was changing, and not for the better, as far as he was concerned. Patriotism, enforcement of the laws and love for country were becoming antiquated, even disdained, concepts to a large segment of society, and knowing that angered Harry to his core. But those things didn’t matter at the moment. Right now, the general was questioning his purpose in life.

"I've got things," Harry said, not even sure if he believed it.

General Patton chuckled as he sat back. "Yeah, you've got things. You got older and more useless. Now your father, there was a good soldier, and a man's man."

"I was a good soldier, too, dammit!" Harry shouted.

"Maybe you were. But your father didn't take any shit from anybody. He'd be ashamed of you." That hit Harry hard. He sank back into his chair.

"Harry, who are you talking to?" Charlie said in a half-whisper.

But Harry still didn't hear Charlie. He was tuned into General Patton alone, who pressed on with his assault. "What about the little jerkoff across the street?" the general said. "The little prick almost ran you over, then he got a restraining order against you. You can't even cross the street without checking to see if he's around, huh? A real man doesn't take bullshit like that. Especially from a punk named Francis."

Harry's head started to throb. Pure anger had dug its claws into him now.

"That little moron's dealing drugs and we both know it. All your neighbors hate that little shit, and he's making a fool out of you. And why's he getting away with it? Cause you've got no pride, that's why. Tell me I'm wrong, Blake. I dare you."

Shame that had been buried deep began to work its way to the surface. Harry slammed a fist into the recliner's armrest. "Son of a bitch!"

"That's it, Harry. Get mad! What are you gonna do about it?"

"I'm gonna do something, General. You can count on that."

General Patton took a celebratory drag on his cigar and smiled. "That's it, soldier. Let's go to war!"

Shaking, Charlie turned and quietly edged his way through the kitchen and out the back door.

Harry spent the next two hours thinking about Joey, his truant mother, his deceased wife and daughter, and the general belittling him. Harry had heard the rumors around the neighborhood about Crash's nefarious, nocturnal activities, but the general saying it somehow gave the rumors more credence. His mind juggled all of those thoughts simultaneously to the point where he felt overwhelmed, and he knew he had to shut down and rest his mind.

He closed the curtains, turned off his phone, and lay down on the sofa. An hour later, Gertie walked through the front door. She saw her boy lying on the couch. She looked closely and noticed the beard he had been growing for several weeks now. Gertie couldn't recall the last time she had seen her son with any facial hair whatsoever. It shook her when she realized that it had been days, maybe even a week - she couldn't be sure – since she had last seen her son. She watched as Harry tossed and turned on the sofa, as if he was wrestling with a bad dream, and losing the battle. She gently touched his shoulder.

She immediately felt Harry's body convulse like a current of electricity was shooting through him. Panicked, Gertie shook Harry with all of her strength. He slowly came to. It took a moment, but when his eyes adjusted, he saw his mother hovering over him. He saw fear in her eyes.

"Mom? What is it? What's wrong?"

"You okay, sonny boy? You looked like you were having a bad dream."

Harry sat up and shook out the cobwebs. "I'm – I'm okay. Just laid down for a bit. Why are you here, Ma?"

"Why am I here? Where the hell am I supposed to be?"

"Next door, I figured."

"Next door? Why the hell would I be next door?" Gertie looked around the room as if she was seeing it for the very first time. She began to tremble slightly. "Where…where am I?"

Harry realized that his mother's condition was flaring up. And he knew better than to argue with her or agitate her in any way. He got up and gently grabbed her arm. "You're home, Ma." He sat her down on the sofa.

"Who are you?"

"I'm your son."

"You are?"

"I am." Harry looked at his watch. "It's one in the morning, Ma. You should be in bed."

Just then, Charlie walked through the front door. "Gertie? Are you here?" he said.

"She's right here, Sloan."

Charlie made his way towards the sofa. But before he could reach it, Harry crossed the room in two purposeful steps and grabbed the old man by the arm – firmly. Seething, Harry was about to shout at Charlie, but he remembered his mother was just a few feet away. He whispered, "How'd this happen?"

"I don't know, Harry. I got up to pee, and when I got back to the bedroom, she was…gone."

Harry's grip on the old man's arm tightened. "Ma could've wandered out into the street and gotten run over. You know that little asshole across the street drives like a maniac. When Mom's with you, you put a damn cowbell around her neck if you have to, you hear me?"

"I'm sorry, Harry. It won't happen again."

Harry released Charlie's arm and went to the front door. As he was about to close it, he peered across the street. A car pulled up to the curb in front of Crash's house, and Harry saw a young guy get out of the car. His curiosity was piqued.

After walking Gertie and Charlie back to the old man's home, Harry stopped when he saw a young guy, known around the neighborhood as Mad Dog Mitch, standing on the sidewalk in front of Crash's house.

Mitch lit a cigarette as he stared at Harry. Harry met the boy's stare as Crash came out his front door and pulled up next to Mitch. Harry shifted his gaze to Crash.

"What's up with the old man?" Mitch said. "He's starin' at ya like you banged his daughter."

"I would've, but the bitch is dead. Ain't that right, Harry?" Crash shouted.

The boys chuckled. Harry clenched his fists and took one step towards the street. "You little asshole…" The boys backpedaled when they saw the big man take another step in their direction. Just then, remembering the restraining order, he stopped. *Soon enough*, he mused. He took a long, deep breath. "I hope you got one helluva dental plan, Francis."

"Francis?" Mitch said.

"Yeah, so? You tell anyone and I'll kick your ass," Crash said, giving Mad Dog a shove.

Harry walked up the steps and stopped at his front door. "You boys stay out of trouble, ya hear?" he said.

"Sure thing, Uncle Harry." Crash said. "You get your old, broken-down ass to bed."

Hearing that, Harry stopped again for a moment and reconsidered crossing the street and snapping the boy's neck right on the spot. Instead, he stepped into his home. He went to the window and waited. Mad Dog Mitch followed Crash into his house. Five minutes later, with his camcorder in hand, and adrenaline pumping through him, Harry stepped out of the house.

He crept across the street and slowly ascended Crash's front steps. The wooden boards creaked and groaned under Harry's weight, but the noise didn't alert Crash. When he reached the top step, Harry crawled on all fours across the porch to avoid being seen through the front window. When he reached the far end of the porch, he stifled a grunt as he got to his feet. Creeping to the edge of the window, Harry peeked inside.

He saw Crash and Mad Dog sitting on the sofa in the living room. On a coffee table in front of them sat two plastic bags filled with cocaine. Harry pointed the video camera into the house and hit the record button. He leaned in to listen in on the conversation.

"Your real name is Francis? Seriously, dude?" Mitch said as he picked up a bag off the table and examined it.

"Let it go, man," Crash said, swiping the bag from Mitch's hand.

"How much you got there?"

"A big eight[2],[2]" Crash said. "This shit's headed for the reservation, cause my Injun brothers gotta get high, too. You and me gonna do a road trip tomorrow night. We gonna get paid!"

"What time?" Mitch said.

"Be here at two a.m."

Harry heard enough. He stopped the camcorder, crawled across the porch again, crept down the steps, and limped back across the street. His heart was still thumping as he closed his front door. He gulped down two pain pills and went directly to bed. Before he dozed off, Harry replayed the night's activities in his mind. He hoped his father and the general would be proud of him; he was finally fighting back. Harry felt good. He fell asleep with a smile on his face.

---

[2] 1/8 kilo of an illegal drug, usually of Cocaine, approx. 4 1/2 Ounces.

19

Late in the afternoon the next day, Harry parked his truck in the parking lot of the Bremerhaven Recreational Center. General Patton, who was riding shotgun, followed Harry towards the street. "You're going to meet a bunch of Krauts, Harry? Are you kidding me?" the general said.

Harry waved the general off as he neared the walkway. He stopped when he saw Kurt Schmidt standing near the building's front door, smoking a cigarette. General Patton, now standing at his side, whispered in Harry's ear, "That's the son of a bitch who coldcocked you at the saloon," he said. "Kill the bastard where he stands, soldier!"

It is him. Harry thought. He clenched his fists, counted to five, then unclenched them. As badly as he wanted to pummel Kurt into submission then and there, he knew any altercation between the two would have to wait. As Harry was about to walk through the front door, Kurt grabbed his arm. "You lost, buddy?"

Harry glared at Kurt. "The name's not buddy. It's Harry. And if you wanna keep that hand…"

Kurt withdrew his hand. "Got a last name?" he said.

"Meyer."

"That's a German surname."

"Sure as hell is."

"Where your people from?" Kurt said.

"Small village in southeastern Bavaria. You writing my biography?"

A stare down ensued between the two men. "Just like to know who I'm dealing with," Kurt said. "You got business here?"

"Heard you fellas got an organization I might be interested in joining."

"How'd you hear about us?"

"Around town. I liked what I heard."

"That so?" Kurt looked Harry over again. Then he opened the door and gestured for Harry to follow him in.

General Patton scowled at Harry. "Pussy," he said before disappearing. When Harry stepped into the hall, he looked around. He trembled slightly as he fought to conceal the resentment and anger welling up inside him when he saw the war memorabilia mounted on the walls, a portrait of Hitler, and a swastika banner hanging next to the portrait. Sensing that the other men in the room were watching him, Harry barked, "Sieg Heil!" as he saluted the portrait. He then turned to check out the rest of the room. Five men who were throwing darts and drinking beer nodded their approval, as did another group sitting at the bar.

Kurt led Harry towards the bar. "Guys, this is Harry Meyer. Harry, the guys." Hans, a man in his early seventies, looked Harry over, trying to place his face.

After shaking hands with every man, Harry leaned over the bar. "What country's a guy gotta invade to get a beer around here?" The men laughed as Klaus, tonight's barkeep, drew Harry a beer from a tap. Harry shook hands with the man before he grabbed his beer.

"The name's Klaus. Welcome."

"You keep those beers coming and I'm gonna call you Santa Klaus," Harry said.

The men all broke out in laughter. "Here's to our new brother, Harry," Klaus said, raising his mug high. The men raised their mugs. Harry spent the next three hours drinking beer and swapping stories and ethnic jokes with his new friends.

An hour later, the men began to leave the hall, and as Harry headed for the door right behind them, Hans grabbed him by the arm, "Why don't you stick around for one more beer," he said. The two men took seats at the bar.

Hans drew a beer from a tap and set in in front of Harry, but Harry pushed the beer away. "I'm good, Hans. Gotta drive home."

"To Albrecht if I'm not mistaken, right?"

"How'd you know that?"

"Took me most of the night, but I finally figured it out. Your last name ain't Meyer. It's Blake."

Harry stiffened up. "You've got me mixed up with someone else. I've got ID if you wanna see it." Harry reached for his wallet.

Hans waved him off. "Don't bother. I'm betting you were smart enough to get a fake ID before you walked in here tonight. Just in case we wanted to check you out."

Harry sat back. "So, how do you know me?"

"We met at a barbeque a few years ago."

"We did?"

"Yep. Was at my son's house in Albrecht. We were celebrating my granddaughter's high school graduation. Your mom's name is Gertie, right?"

"Yeah."

"My mom invited your mom to the party. They were friends from back in the day," Hans said. "You told me your mom dragged you to the party 'cause her boyfriend was sick that day."

"We talked?"

"For a bit, yeah. Mostly about the war."

"Sorry, I don't remember. Did you serve?"

Hans grabbed a handful of nuts and gnawed on them. "Army. Did two tours in 'Nam."

"Me, too. Marines."

"I remember you telling me that. So, what are you doing here, Harry?"

"Just trying to widen my social circle."

"Sure, you are." Hans said, smiling. "We're about the same age. Means you're way too old to be the law."

"Why would the law be interested in your group, Hans? You guys into some illegal shit?"

"Some of the guys are."

"I've heard that," Harry said.

"Sure am," Hans said. 'So, I'll ask you again; what are you doing here, Harry Blake?"

"Supposing I tell you why. Then, what?"

"I guess we'll see what."

"One soldier to another?"

"One soldier to another."

"I got coldcocked with a beer bottle at a bar in Albrecht a while back. Nearly died. Friend of mine recognized the guy who did it. Had to come here and see him face to face to know for sure. It's your fearless leader, Kurt."

"Doesn't surprise me a damn bit. Kurt's an asshole."

"If he's an asshole, what are you doing here, Hans? You a real Nazi? Or maybe you're supplementing your income selling drugs and guns?"

Hans stared at the wall. "It's nothing like that, Harry."

"What is it, then?"

Hans turned away from Harry. The big man grabbed Hans' arm and spun him around. "Why are you with these guys, Hans?"

"It doesn't matter."

"Of course, it matters. What is it?"

"I want to… belong to something."

"What do you mean?"

"Exactly that."

"You've got family, don't you? What about your mom?"

"She passed two years ago."

"Your wife?"

"The wife passed last year."

"What about your son?"

"We had a falling out. Didn't care for the way he was raising my granddaughter. He let her get her way about everything, and I told him that. Now my son doesn't let me see my granddaughter anymore."

"I'm sorry, Hans."

Hans shrugged. "That's life, huh? What about you?"

"Wife's been gone for some time now. The daughter's gone, too. And me and the grandkid aren't talking."

"Sorry. We oughta start a club of our own," Hans said.

There was silence as Hans sipped his beer. Then, Harry spoke up. "Why don't you come by and have dinner with me, Mom and Charlie sometime?"

"You mean it?"

"Sure do."

"Who's Charlie?"

"Mom's boyfriend. He's good people."

"Maybe I'll take you up on that. But I gotta ask again, Harry. Why are you here?"

"This stays between us?" Hans nodded yes. "I'm gonna take Kurt down. You got a problem with that, Hans?"

"Nah. But what happens afterwards?"

"I'm gonna take over."

Hans smiled. "Viva la revolution. Does your mom still cook?"

Harry tapped his head. "Mom's not completely with us. I'm the cook. And I'm pretty damn good. How's Friday night?"

"Sounds good, Harry."

"See you then." Harry patted Hans on the shoulder, then walked out of the hall.

20

Harry spent a good part of the next day running errands and making phone calls, including two calls to Joey, which went unanswered. At seven p.m., he cursed under his breath as he walked toward the front door of the C.A.T. building. When he reached the classroom, he grabbed a seat in the back. He looked over his classmates and saw twenty or so of the most pissed off people he could imagine. He understood their anger and resentment only too well. The animosity and pride he had to swallow by attending these classes was taking its toll on his disposition. But his mood lightened just a bit when he saw Mike, his "cell mate," walk into the room. When Mike saw Harry, he took the desk next to him. "How they hanging, Mike?"

"I left 'em at home, Harry. They're no use to me here."

Harry chuckled. "Ready for some more brainwashing?" As Mike was about to respond, Mr.Wilkins entered the room. "It's Dr. Feelgood," Harry said.

"Good evening, fellow travelers," Mr. Wilkins said. "Let's get started on the road to happier thoughts, and to being nicer, more sensitive people, shall we?"

Harry let out a sarcastic chuckle. Mr. Wilkins, hearing it, zeroed in on him. "Did I say something funny, sir?"

"No 'sir' here. Name's Harry. Harry Blake."

"Mr. Blake, care to share with the rest of the class what you find so amusing?"

"Another time."

"Since we're talking, let me ask you a question; what do you see when you look around the room?"

"I see dead people," Harry said.

There was a smattering of chuckles, but Mr. Wilkins wasn't laughing. "Is that sarcasm, Mr. Blake?"

"I sure hope so. Was supposed to be."

"Would you like to expound on that remark?"

"Expound? You sure like your fancy words, huh?"

Mr. Wilkins smiled. "I can define the word for you if it's necessary, Mr. Blake."

"I know what the word means."

"Then, please, enlighten us."

"Be glad to, Teach. I see a lot of people who'd rather be butt naked, lathered in syrup and strapped down on an ant hill than be here. I see people who are forced to be here for probably a lot of bullshit reasons. I see a whole lot of resentment and anger in this room. How'd I do?"

"You're going to make trouble for me, aren't you?" Mr. Wilkins said.

"A man's gotta have goals -"

"It's Mr. Wilkins."

"How about I call you Mr. Witch Finder instead?"

Mr. Wilkins crossed his arms. "I don't understand that reference, Mr. Blake."

Harry crossed his arms, too. "Well, Teach, a long time ago in Europe, some men were paid lots of money to find witches and bring 'em to justice. They were con men who used tricks to convince people they'd found real witches so they could get the reward money. Sound familiar?"

Harry sensed that the entire class understood what he was saying, and that they agreed with him, even if they were afraid to verbalize it. Mr. Wilkins knew he was being called a fraud by Harry, but he had no clever response to fire back at him. So, he glared at the big man instead.

"I'd like to talk to you after class, Mr. Blake."

"You mean after the indoctrination, don't you?" Harry said.

"Let's not get hung up on words here," Mr. Wilkins said. Then he smiled and extended his hands outward like a minister about to preach the Good Word to a congregation. "I'm here to help and guide all of you. We are the world. We will learn to respect and celebrate the feelings and choices of our fellow world inhabitants."

Harry scowled. "What a crock of shit. "We" is people like you," he said, pointing at Wilkins. "We is the courts and the companies who forced us to be here because they buckled under bullshit pressure from people like you. You want to make us think and act the way you do. This bullshit's all about power and coercion, Teach."

There were murmurs of assent from Harry's classmates. Mr. Wilkins' smug grin disappeared as he realized he was losing his grip on the class. Growing nervous, he cleared his throat. "We're getting off topic here. Let's begin tonight's lesson. Mr. Blake, I'll see you after class."

Harry grunted his disapproval. Mike leaned over and whispered, "You nailed him good, but this asshole's got us by the short and curlies. We have to play ball with him, Harry."

"I don't give a shit, Mike. I got a thing for bullies."

***

After class, Mr. Wilkins sat behind his desk as he and Harry engaged in a stare-off. Harry, sitting at a desk no more than five feet from Mr. Wilkins, had decided before he sat down that he wasn't going to blink first, not even if he had to sit there all night. He continued to stare at Mr.Wilkins. Finally, Wilkins spoke up. "The state has pretty much given me free reign with you. What do you think of that, Mr. Blake?"

"I think you got beat up a lot when you were a kid. So now you're getting even with the world by being a bully yourself. Is that about right, Teach?"

"You seem to be a very angry man, Mr. Blake."

"You're damn right I am."

"I read in your file that you're a war vet."

Harry leaned in towards Wilkins. "Yeah, I'm a vet. I've seen things that would have made you shit your pants and run for your mama. I fought so assholes like you could have the freedom to be assholes. But nobody's gonna tell me how to feel or what to think or say, about anything. Nobody."

Mr. Wilkins smiled as if he were playing a high stakes game of poker, and he was holding a winning hand. "I've dealt with your kind before. Real hard cases. People who weren't willing to play ball, so to speak."

"God bless 'em all," Harry said. "I hope they fought you tooth and fuckin' nail."

"Some did, for a time," said Mr. Wilkins. "But in the end, I always win. You see, I fill out reports every week and send them to the state. They're kind of like report cards for every person attending the class."

"So?"

"So, I could make your life very difficult for you. I can tell the state you refuse to cooperate, which would mean you violated the terms of your probation. That could mean jail time for you. I have that power. You need to be a good, little soldier and get with the program. Do you understand?"

"I'm done taking orders from assholes, Teach. Have been for a long time. You don't wanna push me."

Mr. Wilkins sat back. "Is that a threat?"

"I'll bet your mama wanted a boy, huh? Damn, she must've been disappointed."

Mr. Wilkins grimaced slightly, then he smiled. "Nobody beats me, Mr. Blake."

"I'll bet you and your kind are milking the government and corporations for lots of money pretending to help people, huh?"

Mr. Wilkins smiled. "I do quite well financially, yes."

Harry leaned in even farther. "You keep pushing me and I'll end your ass, you smug prick," he said.

"You're fighting a battle you can't win, Mr. Blake. You see, all we have to do is accuse people of transgressions, or of being racist, or transphobic, or whatever. We accuse them, then they have to expend energy and time defending themselves against the accusations. If you keep people on the defensive, how can they fight back?"

"Sane and decent people, when they've had enough bullshit, they'll find a way to beat assholes like you."

"We're at war, Mr. Blake, and my side is winning. We've taken most of the big cities and now we're sweeping through the burgs."

"You're like viruses, huh?"

Mr. Wilkins checked his watch. "I've really enjoyed our repartee, but it's late. Think about what I said. I can turn your life upside down if you defy me. Next week, I hope we're going to see a new you."

Harry got up and walked towards the door. He flipped Mr. Wilkins off as he left the classroom.

21

Later that night, Harry sat slouched behind the wheel of his truck, waiting for Crash to appear from his home. Just after two a.m., Crash and Mad Dog walked out of the house. Harry sank even lower in his seat, watching as the two boys got into the Chevelle. The car roared to life, and Crash snickered as he flipped on his high beams, hoping that the lights would wake Harry from a sound sleep.

But Crash didn't know that he would have Harry and his camcorder as company as he turned onto Highway 18 and headed south. Forty minutes later, Crash eased up on the gas as he neared the town of Oelrichs, a small town just west of his destination. Harry, cruising a quarter of a mile behind Crash, slowed down as well. Crash pulled the Chevelle onto the shoulder of the road about half a mile from the Pine Ridge Reservation. His eyes glued to the Chevelle's taillights, Harry killed his headlights as he eased off the road and parked on the shoulder just a few hundred feet behind the Chevelle.

His respiration quickened as he grabbed his camcorder and got out of his truck and gently closed the door. He craned his neck skyward. Harry could barely discern the New Moon that hung just above the horizon, and the light poles that lined both sides of the highway emitted a low wattage glow that rendered Harry nearly invisible.

Adrenaline pumped through him as he sidled along the shoulder of the highway. He ducked behind a rock outcropping when he saw the glare of headlights approaching. As a car was about to pass by Crash's Chevelle going west, the driver flipped his headlights on and off three times. Crash followed suit. The car did a U-turn, pulled up behind the

Chevelle, and the driver turned off his headlights as he came to a stop. Harry was less than twenty feet from the Chevelle as he remained crouched behind the rock formation. He powered up his camcorder before hitting the record button.

Two young Sioux men got out of the car, stopped, and cautiously surveyed their surroundings as they neared the Chevelle. "My brothers," Crash said as he shook hands with the two men.

Crash then opened the Chevelle's trunk and pulled out two bags of cocaine. He handed a bag to Calian, the older of the two men, and he waited as Calian dipped his finger into the bag and tasted the product.

"Shit's good. Pay him," Calian said to his friend. The second Sioux man handed Crash a huge wad of bills, and Crash started counting.

"A minute ago, we were brothers. Don't trust us?" Calian said.

"When it comes to cash money, I don't trust shit," Crash responded.

Harry saw enough. He hit the stop button on the camcorder, then, as he crept away from the rock formation, he heard a dead branch snap under his weight. He froze.

***

Suddenly, without moving even an inch, Harry was back in Vietnam. Private Blake was attached to a patrol with Company E, 2nd Batallion,12th Infantry Regiment. The unit was on a recon mission, and the private followed closely on the heels of Gunnery Sergeant Max Reegan as the platoon weaved its way through a jungle thicket. Mid-summer humidity drenched the Marines' fatigues right to the bone. The jungle was alive with the howls and trills of predatory animals seeking tonight's prey, and the terrain was rife with insects that the men tried to fend off, with little luck.

Lieutenant Andy Dillon, the son of a highly decorated colonel, trembled as he led two forward squads to the banks of a shallow tributary. The lieutenant's father pulled some strings so that his son was admitted to Officer Candidate School in Fort Benning, Georgia, despite his average grades, his nervous temperament, and his inflated ego. The men in this unit hated Dillon, but until things changed, he was in charge.

Fearing that the Viet Cong were lying in wait in the thick brush just across the tributary, Lieutenant Dillon started to sweat as he came to a stop just shy of the water's bank, and his men followed suit. Navigating his way back through a thicket of trees, he reached the platoon's rear squads.

He pointed at Sergeant Reegan. "Sergeant, I want you to take a squad on ahead. I'm gonna take three squads and head west for those hooches. I don't want to get outflanked by Charlie tonight."

The platoon sergeant unfolded his map and showed their present location to the lieutenant. "Sir, those hooches were cleared out already. There's nothing but open terrain for miles in that sector. Nothing but open fields."

"That a fact?"

"It is, sir. If Charlie's out here tonight, he'll be behind that brush. I'd need more men."

Lieutenant Dillon knew that being questioned by a soldier of lesser rank in front of his men couldn't be tolerated. He stared the sergeant down. "You got a problem with following orders, Gunny?"

"No, sir, but I was at the mission briefing, too," Reegan said. "Major Taylor ordered the platoon to stick together, sir."

The lieutenant jumped in the sergeant's face. "Major Taylor ain't here, Reegan. I'm the Word of God out here. You give us fifteen minutes before you move out or I'll have your ass court- martialed."

"Yes, sir," the sergeant said.

The lieutenant pointed to two squads. "Let's move out." Then he pointed at Private Blake. "Take the FNG with you."

Dillon and three squads headed west. Gunny Reegan shook his head in disgust as he watched the lieutenant slink away. "Asshole." he said.

Private Blake, trembling but trying to hold it together, pulled up *alongside the sergeant. "What's a FNG, Sarge?"*

"Fuckin' New Guy, Blake. That'd be you. And it ain't a compliment." The squad circled around the sergeant. "Watch your spacing" he said in a hushed voice. "If Charlie's up ahead, we're gonna be in the shit."

As the sergeant motioned for the men to move forward, he grabbed Private Blake and stopped him in mid-step. "Stay on my six, private." The men crept along until they reached the edge of the thicket. They quietly maneuvered their way around trees as they neared the bank of the tributary. Private Blake, shaking, followed five feet behind Gunny Reegan. That's when he heard it.

There was a click as the sergeant's boot caught a tripwire. A grenade, packed inside of a tin can at ground level, exploded, knocking the private into the air. After landing on his ass, Private Blake sat up and tried to grasp, through a very jumbled brain, what had just happened.

"Cover!" a corporal yelled. Then all hell broke loose. The squad hit the ground as three platoons of Viet Cong infantry, perched just across the tributary, lit up the darkness with a barrage of rocket propelled grenades, mortar shells, and AK-47 rounds. Private Blake fought double vision as he got to his feet. Chunks of dirt went airborne as a mortar shell exploded to his right, and he was tackled to the ground by a fellow infantryman.

"Stay down, private!"

The roar of gunfire and artillery was deafening as the Viet Cong continued their barrage. By the time the squad returned fire, three men were already dead.

"Where's Gunny?" a soldier yelled.

"Fuck if I know!" the corporal snapped back.

Still in a daze, Private Blake watched as a flare rocketed into the night sky, climbing higher and higher until it finally reached its zenith as it crossed the water in the squad's direction. Now the enemy had the squad's position locked in. Privat Blake, temporarily mesmerized by the eerie glow of the flare as it snaked its way earthward, snapped out of his trance when the descending flare lit up Viet Cong infantrymen slogging their way across the shallow waterway. His hands shaking badly, he grabbed his M-16, took aim, and opened up on the oncoming enemy troops. Round after round badly missed their targets. To the private's left, three men from his squad emptied their rifles' cartridges on the approaching Viet Cong.

His vision clearing, Private Blake caught sight of his fallen sergeant, propped up against a tree up ahead and to his right. Fighting abject fear, he crawled in that direction as bullets and artillery shells whizzed by from what seemed to be every direction.

Finally reaching Sergeant Reegan, Private Blake recoiled in horror. The sergeant writhed in pain, and his right leg was gone from the knee down. His femur bone, snapped in half by the force of the explosion, protruded through the skin, and his mangled leg spurted blood like a spigot that had been turned on full blast.

"Oh, Jesus," the private muttered as he unbuckled his belt. He yanked it off and wrapped it around the sergeant's leg where his knee had been just minutes ago. The flow of blood slowed as he tightened the belt, but when the private gazed at the Reegan's ashen face, he knew the sergeant was fading fast.

"Corpsman!" the private screamed. But no one heard him over the thunderous gunfire and explosions raining down all around the unit. "Corpsman!" he screamed again. But the unit's medic was nowhere nearby. He was with Lieutenant Dillon's men nearly half a mile away.

"Fall back!" the corporal roared. The last three surviving men from the squad shoved new magazines into their M-16's and again opened up on the advancing Viet Cong as they retreated into the thicket. Watching the sergeant slowly bleed to death and seeing his unit being torn apart, Private Blake's senses went into overload.

Sergeant Reegan grabbed his arm. "Private..." he said. When he didn't get a response from a very shaky Private Blake, the sergeant clutched his arm harder and yanked on it. "Private!"

"Yes – yes, sir?"

Sergeant Reegan chuckled. "That's what I get for taking orders from an asshole, huh?" Private Blake started to sob as he clutched the sergeant's hand.

"Yes – yes, sir."

The two men locked eyes. "I'm done, private. Fall...fall back with the other men. That's an order."

The sergeant's eyes went lifeless. Adrenaline and rage surged through the private as he got to his feet, drew his weapon and unloaded his clip, killing two V C soldiers. He threw his dead sergeant's body over his shoulder and disappeared into the thicket.

***

Harry snapped out of his daze and realized he was no longer in Vietnam. Trembling, he made his way back to his truck, got back onto the highway and headed home.

Harry was still shaking as he stepped through his front door and sat on the sofa. When he regained his composure and his breathing steadied, he dragged himself to the bathroom, gulped down two sleeping pills and his new medication for hallucinations, then washed them down with a healthy shot of bourbon, hoping that the combination would render him unconscious. Fifteen minutes later, he passed out cold.

22

Just after nine a.m. the next morning, Harry awoke. As he struggled to sit up, every muscle in his body screamed. As he was about to lie back down to try sleeping the pain off, his phone rang. It lay just two feet from him on the living room table, but he let it ring until it went to voicemail. He groaned as he stretched out to grab the phone. His head throbbing and foggy, he still managed to decipher the message. Albrecht's antiquated computer system apparently hadn't yet recorded Harry's conviction, so he had passed the background check and was now officially a janitor.

Sleep would have to wait. Harry had things to do. After showering, he downed two pain pills and a couple cups of coffee. Now that he could function, he went to the basement, opened the padlock on the storage room door, grabbed a chair and plopped his meaty frame into it. Just a few days earlier, the basement room was full of boxes and assorted junk that had accumulated over the years. Now the room resembled a scientist's laboratory. Boxes lined one wall, and beakers, weight scales and other mixing and measuring devices sat on a table that ran the length of the opposite wall.

Harry looked over his list, and the items on the table, one more time to ensure he had everything he needed: a gas mask, goggles, industrial work gloves, mixing equipment, scales, and nearly enough chemicals to cover the periodic table. Harry was ready to make Semtex. Enough Semtex to raise some serious hell. After securing the padlock on the door, he went to the garage. He dug out a vintage metal beer cooler that sat under a wooden work bench in a corner of the garage. The cooler brought back a lot of great memories, making him smile, but the smile was short lived. The pain came on now, like a dead-of-winter gust of wind, and it cut through Harry. His legs began to wobble, so he took a seat at his work bench.

He rested his bad knee for a couple of minutes, but he knew he had to get through the pain since there was much to do. He got to his feet again, grabbed a circular saw and went to work on a ¼ inch thick sheet of metal. He cut two small notches into the sides of the steel, one on each side, so he could lift the metal with his fingers once it was in place. His vintage cooler would now have a new feature: a false bottom.

Harry took a break. He sat on his front steps, a cup of coffee in his hand, and basked in the quiet, but he couldn't pry his eyes away from the Chevelle in Crash's driveway. Charlie stepped out of his front door and stretched. "You out here, Harry?" Annoyed that his solitude had been violated, Harry kept silent. "I know you're there, Harry. I'm coming over."

"How'd you know?" Harry said.

"I can smell your coffee from here."

Charlie found his way to Harry's front steps. He took a seat next to the big man, who grudgingly slid over to make room for the old man. "Stop staring at it," Charlie said.

"How the hell do you know what I'm looking at?"

"Just a guess. I was right, huh?"

"I had one just like it. It was a beast."

"Your mother told me that," Charlie said.

"Where is she?"

"Still sleeping. We sweated up the sheets something fierce last night."

Harry grimaced. He knew that Charlie was baiting him as he liked to do, but the thought of his own mother... "How long before she gave up trying to find it, Sloan?"

"Touché, Harry. What's the plan for today?"

"Maybe some yard work if it doesn't rain. And if the knee holds out."

"You should look into getting the damn thing replaced."

Harry shrugged. He had thought of having the procedure done years earlier, but after he lost Patsy, he just didn't care if the knee rotted off, stayed attached, or flew itself to the moon.

"Maybe down the road sometime," he said.

"Horseshit," Charlie said. "You'll never do it."

"Says you."

Across the street, Crash bounced down his front steps, flipped Harry off, and laughed. "How they hanging, fat man?" Crash said as he lit a cigarette and gave the Chevelle's exterior its daily inspection.

"Why don't you c'mon over and grab a handful, idiot," Harry shouted.

"Don't wanna see your saggy-ass, old man junk," said Crash.

"Shape up or ship out, son!" Charlie barked out.

Harry rolled his eyes. "You really told him, Sloan."

"Kiss my wrinkled ass, Harry." Satisfied that the Chevelle was spotless, Crash jumped into the car and started it. The Chevelle rocked from side to side on its chassis as he revved the engine. Crash threw it into drive and tore down the driveway like a jungle cat chasing down its next meal.

"I'm gonna get that little prick somehow," Harry said.

"Hit him where it hurts, you dolt."

"Meaning, what?"

"You can't be that thick," Charlie said as he rose to his feet. He tapped his cane on the walkway and started to walk.

"Where you going, Sloan?"

"To make lunch."

Harry frowned. As much as Charlie annoyed him sometimes, he didn't want to be alone for the rest of the day. He would never admit it to Charlie, but Harry really liked the old man. Charlie stopped halfway down the walk. "Heard from Joey lately?" Charlie said.

He hadn't seen the boy for days, and that irritated the hell out of him. "He hates me. I ain't got a damn clue where he is."

"Joey doesn't hate you. He really doesn't, Harry. You know teenagers don't want to be around us old farts."

"Sure would be nice if he at least called to tell me he's okay. That asking too damn much?"

"He called Gertie last night. He's fine."

Harry snorted as he got to his feet, and Charlie didn't need the ability to see to know that the big man was not happy. "Why didn't you tell me that already?! Where is he?!"

Charlie took two steps backwards. "Easy, big man. Apparently, Joey's staying with your brother right now. He's fine."

Harry was relieved to hear that. He sat back down, gulped in air, and the anger began to fade.

"I'm really sorry, Harry. I should have told you first thing. The boy just needs some time away is all. He'll come around."

"Yeah, sure," Harry said.

"I'd better get back to Gertie. We'll come by later and play some cards. What do you say to that?" But Harry didn't say anything. He got up and went back into the house. When Charlie heard the front door close, he hung his head and walked away.

***

Harry sat in his recliner and stared at the ceiling. The doorbell rang. Harry got to his feet and opened the front door. Standing there was a woman in her early thirties holding a clipboard. She wasn't smiling as she looked Harry over. And neither was he. "Help you?" Harry said.

"I'm an advocate for human rights, and I have a petition you should sign."

"What's your name?" Harry said. "And what's the petition for?"

"I call myself Ze."

123

"Zee? What's that short for?"

"Nothing," the woman replied. "It's a gender neutral, neo-pronoun that I refer to myself as."

"A gender neutral neo... what? What the hell is that? Didn't your parents give you a name?"

"I don't identify myself by the old male-female gender classifications. Ze is a non-binary, genderfluid person."

"Are you talking about yourself in the third person?"

"What if I am?" Ze said.

"People that do that are usually pretty pretentious."

"Are you trying to invalidate me?"

"Just making an observation, honey."

"I told you to call me Ze."

"Actually, no, you didn't. You said that's what you call yourself. And don't tell me what to call you. It's more polite if you ask."

Ze crossed her arms as she stiffened up. "You will not disrespect or dismiss me," she said.

Ze had picked the wrong day to knock on Harry's door. His mood worsened with every second he stood there. He crossed his arms. "You got thirty seconds," he said.

"Did you know that right now there are transgenders in prison who are being denied the right to gender reassignment surgery? Don't you find that appalling?"

"Trans, what?"

The young woman rolled her eyes as if she had just been asked a really stupid question. "Transgender? You've never heard the term? Seriously?"

"You can check the attitude, honey."

"Transgender means a person who doesn't identify with the gender they were born with. They can suffer from gender dysphoria. It can lead to anxiety, stress, depression, and even suicidal thoughts."

"So can life," Harry said.

"It's a very serious condition."

"So is life," Harry said. "Lemme see if I got this right. A guy who was born a guy wants to be a woman instead? That what you're getting at here?"

"Or vice-versa. And even if these transgender people are in prison, they have a right to the surgery," Ze said.

"They have a right to the surgery? Never saw that in the Bill of Rights."

"You sound just like the fascists and the homophobes in our government."

"What?"

"That's what they are if they won't help transgenders. They have to be."

Harry shifted his weight to his good knee as his agitation grew. "Look, if some dude wants to lop off his crank 'cause he thinks he's a woman, I could give a shit."

"Then you'll sign the petition?"

"Not a chance in hell," Harry said, clutching a handful of his belly. "See this belly? Can't miss it, right? If I want to get this shit sucked out, I wouldn't expect anyone else to pay for it. It's cosmetic surgery. People who want non-emergency surgery like that should pay for it themselves."

"But they can't pay for it," Ze said. "They're in prison."

"So, people who committed crimes and got thrown in prison have the right to make taxpayers pay for this surgery? Seriously? Maybe they shouldn't have become criminals in the first place, huh? We're already paying for their food and shelter, not to mention a lot of them have better medical coverage than a lot of people who work for a living. That seem fair to you?"

Ze slammed a foot into the cement landing. "That's not the point!"

"Whoa, little sister. Have a drink and mellow out."

"I don't drink anymore. I'm a recovering alcoholic," Ze said.

"Okay, but just 'cause we don't agree here doesn't mean you have to get pissy."

"We will not be denied!" Ze shouted.

"Who the hell is 'we'?"

"B.I.D. That's who."

"What the hell is bid?"

"It's an organization called Burn It Down."

"What do you want to burn down, exactly?"

"The system. The government. This whole damn country."

"This damn country? The U.S. of A.? What the hell's wrong with this country?"

"It's extremely homophobic and racist, for starters," Ze said.

"Extremely? America? Are you kidding me? We have a shitload of different ethnic groups in this country, and for the most part, everybody gets along and goes along."

"We need to burn it down."

"Just because you say we do? Try talking like this in some other countries that don't have the freedoms we have. You'd end up rotting is some prison cell. This is a great country we live in. Why the hell do you think people from all over the planet want to live here?"

"Because they don't know what it's really like to live here. They don't see the systemic racism and homophobia that runs rampant everywhere."

Harry chuckled.

"Do you find that funny?" Ze said.

"Rampant? The only thing running rampant here is your imagination."

"That's your white privilege talking."

"White, what?"

"White privilege. Because you're white, you have advantages in this country that people of color don't."

"This keeps getting better and better," Harry said. "Like what?"

"How about this nice home you have here?"

"You mean the one I worked most of my entire adult life to pay for?"

"A lot of people don't have nice homes like yours. Is that fair?"

"In a perfect world, everyone would be rich, young and beautiful, and own a mansion, darlin'. Lemme tell you something; everyone in this country has the chance to own their own home. It's got nothing to do with the color of your skin. There are a lot of people out there that have nicer, bigger homes than mine. A lot nicer and a lot bigger. And some of those people aren't white. You know why that is?"

"Suppose you tell me," Ze said.

"'Cause the only color that matters is green. If you have enough money, you can do pretty much anything you want and live anywhere you want, no matter what color your skin is. And that goes for every country on the planet. It's called the real world."

Ze stomped her foot again. "Inclusion!" she screamed.

"What?"

"Diversity!" she yelled. "Equity!"

"You got a brain tumor, darlin'?"

Ze pointed a finger at Harry. "You should be ashamed to be Caucasian."

"What color are you? You look white to me."

"I identify as a non-binary, trans-neo, pansexual, multi-ethnic resident."

"Well, I identify you as an idiot," Harry said as he checked his watch. "Wanna do something useful for society? Get a job. Or help find a cure for cancer. Do something fuckin' useful. And go peddle your white guilt shit somewhere else."

"You cisgenders are all alike."

"What the hell's a cisgender?"

"Pick up a dictionary sometime, you dinosaur."

"You smug little…."

Ze pulled out her smartphone and took a picture of Harry.

"What the hell are you doing?" Harry said.

"I'm going to post your picture and address on our site. We're going shame you, you fascist. And if I find out where you work, I'm going do my damnedest to get you fired. I'm going to cancel your ass!"

Harry took one menacing step toward the woman, stopped, and waved a finger in her face. "Be really, really careful here. I don't respond well to being threatened, you twat."

"What did you call me?"

"Pick up a dictionary sometime," Harry said before barreling through the front door and slamming it shut behind him. Ze snapped a picture of Harrys address.

"I'm coming back real soon, you bastard!" she yelled before stomping down the walkway.

***

After shoving down his meds, Harry paced the room trying to calm down. Ze had accomplished two things; she riled the big man up, and she piqued his curiosity. When his anger subsided, he got on his laptop, found the B.I.D. website and began to read.

We are B.I.D. We vow to BURN DOWN the Western--prescribed pillars that this country was founded and built on. The pillars of patriarchy, capitalism, plutocracy, majoritarianism, the Western style nuclear family structure, the class-based system, and the oppression of the masses.

We will BURN DOWN their outdated and oppressive justice system, as well as their police forces. We will BURN DOWN their prison system that enslaves the masses. We will BURN DOWN their Western-style educational system and replace it with an educational system that rewards none above the rest.

We will BURN DOWN their tax system, at every level, that steals from, enslaves and oppresses the masses. We will institute a system that redistributes this country's vast wealth so that all receive an equal share, no matter their occupation.

We will BURN DOWN their simplistic belief in a Christian "sky god." When the People assume control, his/her/its name will be stricken from every aspect of society and history.

Henceforth, we will proclaim and serve the true Trinity: Inclusion, Equity, and Social Justice.

We will BURN DOWN their concept of Loyal Opposition, for there will exist only one party: The Party of the People.

We will take power. We will take this country. By any means necessary.

Harry shook his head in disbelief. They want to destroy this country. Not on my watch, you bastards.

23

The next morning, Harry rolled out of bed, showered and downed two cups of coffee. Then, with some effort, he got into his janitor coveralls, grabbed his cooler and walked out the door. Cruising down the highway, he barely paid attention to his driving. In his mind, he was going over and over the details of his plan. He knew if his plan went sideways on him, he could go to jail for a long time. But that possibility didn't deter him. Despite the tension wracking his body, and the uncertainty of the outcome, he was hell-bent on completing his mission.

He pulled into the courthouse parking lot, turned off the engine, and exhaled deeply. He began to sweat, and he could feel his heart thumping like it was about to explode from his chest. *Breathe, Harry. It's just a dry run.*

He slipped on a pair of horn-rimmed glasses, scratched his beard, grabbed his cooler, and rifled through its contents one last time. Food and various juices packed the cooler almost right to the top. He didn't need to look under the false bottom again; he had two pieces of apple pie wrapped in plastic there.

Just ten feet from the front entrance, he stopped and surveyed the area. The courthouse, built in the early 1950's, was the lone building standing on over fifty acres of otherwise undeveloped land. Just six months earlier, a developer had finally struck a deal with the town to purchase the land, leaving him free to raze the courthouse. It was slated to be torn down in a few months, and the town's taxpayers were on the hook for the demolition.

But Harry planned on saving the townsfolk some money. Looking at the desolate stretch of land surrounding the building, he knew no one would, or should, be in the area when he did the deed.

If he managed to get that far, that is. He made his way through the front door and was greeted by a security officer, a slightly- built man named Bill, who was sporting enough hair gel to lube an automobile. Bill hit Harry with a big smile. "You must be the new custodian."

"Sure am. The name's Harry."

Bill pumped Harry's hand like a used car salesman greeting his next potential sale. "Welcome aboard, Harry. Name's Bill. Step this way." Bill led Harry to the metal detector. Harry grimaced slightly as he eyed the contraption. He knew this was coming, but now that the moment of truth was here, he considered turning tail and walking away. Instead, he sucked in air and swallowed his fear.

Harry set his cooler on the floor, emptied his pockets into a bin, and watched as Bill eyeballed the contents. Satisfied that he saw nothing that raised any security flags, Bill turned his gaze to Harry's cooler. He rapped it with his knuckles. "Damn, this thing's old school. Looks like it could withstand a bomb," he said with a laugh.

Harry let out a labored chuckle. *Or hold one, Billy Boy.*

"I gotta take a look inside." Bill said. Harry held his breath as Bill set the cooler on a table and rifled through its contents. "There's enough food here for three grown men," Bill added.

Rubbing his belly, Harry chuckled. "I'm a growing boy," he said. Bill laughed as well, and Harry finally exhaled when Bill began to close the cooler's lid. Then Harry let out a muffled gasp as Bill raised the lid again. He dug his hands deep into the cooler, and his fingers caught the notches in the sides of the container's false bottom. He yanked it out and saw the pieces of pie sitting at the bottom of the cooler.

"What's the story here?" Bill said.

Remember the story. Keep cool. "You know how it is, Bill. The wife checks my cooler before I leave the house. She gives me a world of shit if she finds any sugar. So, I got an idea…"

Bill considered this statement for a moment. He was a married man. He knew about hiding things from the wife. Men had been playing that game since the invention of fire, he figured. And he sensed Harry was a regular guy, just like himself. "That's pretty damn clever, Harry." He flashed Harry his wedding ring. "I know how it is. Twenty- two years of marriage, and I'm still waiting for a call from the governor." Bill patted Harry's belly. "Gotta keep the furnace stoked, huh, big fella?"

Harry's fake smile nearly cracked under the tension. "Yeah. Sure do, buddy."

Bill grabbed Harry's arm. "C'mon, I'll give ya the ten- cent tour of the place."

Already having the layout to the building etched into his brain, Harry followed Bill down a hallway and pretended to look around like it was his first time there. After the tour, Harry met with the head custodian, who explained the job's responsibilities. A half hour later, Harry grabbed a mop and went to work.

24

Harry spent the rest of the week establishing a good rapport with the courthouse employees. He joked with people, was quick with a smile, and he helped out around the building whenever or wherever he was needed. After work, he spent the rest of the week landscaping the backyard so it would look good for the weekend's festivities, and he made sure to check off every item on his to-do list for the party.

***

Saturday arrived, and it was a perfect day for an outdoor graduation party: sunny skies, no humidity, and a gentle summer breeze that would continue all day. A banner draped across the backyard fence read, "Congrats, Joey." Over fifty friends and family were in attendance. Gertie was working on her second vodka and lemonade of the day, and it was barely past noon. People milled around the backyard, drinking, laughing and enjoying themselves. Everyone was there - but the guest of honor.

"Harry?" Charlie said as he tapped a path across the backyard lawn.

"Over here," Harry called from the driveway, where he was keeping a look out for Joey.

"No sign of the boy yet?" Charlie asked.

"Nope. And he's not answering his phone."

"It's early. He'll be here."

"I wouldn't bet on it. How's Mom doing?"

"She's getting tight as we speak. I'd better get back to her before she starts with the dirty jokes." Charlie walked a few steps, stopped and turned. "He'll be here, Harry."

Two hours passed and Joey was still a no-show at his own party. Harry's brother, James, found Harry sulking in the kitchen. "He'll be here, Harry."

"You could've told me he was staying with you, Jimmy."

"The kid just showed up at my doorstep. What the hell was I supposed to do? Besides, I figured mom told you."

"Mom's lucky if she can remember her name some days. Has Joey asked about me?"

James hesitated. He didn't want to lie to his brother, but he didn't want to tell him the truth, either. "I'll take that as a no," Harry said. "Is he okay?"

James grabbed a beer, opened it, then stared out the kitchen window. "He's a sensitive kid. You need to ease up on him."

"What the hell's that supposed to mean?"

James turned to face Harry. "Remember how dad used to ride our asses when we were young? How he said he was going to mold us into real men? Remember that?"

"I remember. So?"

"We both resented the hell out of it, didn't we? I know I did."

"Guess I did, too."

"You're doing the same thing to Joey now. He's told me some of the things you've said to him lately."

"The kid irritates me sometimes, Jimmy. I get it, it's what kids do. So, I give him a little shit every once in a while. That a big deal?"

"Times have changed, Harry. You've got to be more sensitive when it comes to raising kids these days."

"I'm getting parenting advice from a guy who couldn't be bothered having kids? That's priceless."

"All I'm saying is you need to stop being such a hard ass. You don't have to confront him or snap at him every time you two have a disagreement. You hurt his feelings.”

Growing agitated, Harry slammed his beer on the counter. “So, I’m supposed to coddle the boy? I’m supposed to pat him on the head and tell him he’s right about everything? That’s how kids turn out spoiled. Sometimes they gotta be told they’re wrong. Sometimes…”

“What?”

“I’m raising the kid alone, Jimmy, and it ain’t fuckin’ easy.”

“What about Mom? Doesn’t she help out?”

“You’re kidding, right? Hell, I’m lucky if I see her two or three times a week these days. She spends most of her time with Sloan next door. And Patsy’s gone. And we both know you’re no help. And now the kid won’t even talk to me.” There was silence for a moment. Then Harry slammed his fist onto the countertop. “It ain’t right!”

“Nancy and I told him he should come back home.”

“Why’s that, Jimmy? The boy interfering with your jet-set lifestyle already? I’m really sorry about that.” Drained of the will to argue any longer, Harry went to the living room and looked out the bay window. He saw a truck with a trailer pull in front of his house. A man emerged from the truck, opened the trailer, and led a pony up the driveway.

James stepped into the room. “What’s going on?” James said.

“I rented a pony. I wanted to get some pictures of Joey sitting on it like he did it for his tenth birthday.” Harry grabbed a kid’s cowboy hat off the table and showed it to James. “Even saved the same hat he wore that day. Thought he’d get a kick out it.”

James pulled out his cell phone. “I’m going to call him.” James punched in Joey’s phone number and got his voicemail. “Joey, this is your uncle. The family’s all here and everyone’s wondering where you are. Please come and see everybody.”

“He’s not gonna show,” Harry said. “Tell everyone I’m sorry, Jimmy. I-I just can’t go out there and face them right now.” His head hung low, Harry grabbed his cane and hobbled out the front door like a man who had just been gravely wounded. James watched as Harry walked down the driveway, pulled cash out of his pocket and handed it to the man who had brought the pony. The man led the pony back into the trailer and drove away.

***

James didn't say anything to the party's guests, holding out hope that Joey would still show up, but by five in the afternoon, most of the family and neighbors had left, figuring that the guest of honor wasn't coming. And by seven, the backyard and the house were empty of people.

Except for Harry, who was stretched out in his recliner, his eyes partially closed and moist with tears. He dozed off just before Gertie walked into the room a half hour later.

She stood over her son, and her heart sank when she saw the sadness in her boy's countenance. She kissed Harry on the forehead, and whispered, "I'm so sorry, sonny boy." Harry awoke, and seeing his mother through blurry eyes, he turned away, not wanting her to see him in this condition.

Gertie put a light blanket over Harry and she looked in on him several times for the next couple of hours before finally retiring for the night. On the edge of sleep, Harry daydreamed: He was on a beautiful, tropical paradise in the Philippines called Palawan Island. He and a couple of buddies from his platoon were on leave, and Johnny Coleman, the radioman whose life Harry had saved, was the guy who made the trip happen. Johnny's father was an oil man with big money, and when the senior Coleman learned of Harry's daring feat, he sent his son Johnny serious money and told him to lavish Harry with anything he wanted or needed.

What Harry wanted was to forget the war, for even a few days. And he wanted to do it somewhere with beaches, friendly women, and room service. A week later, Harry, John, and a couple of buddies from the platoon were on their way to Palawan Island.

The boys raised hell. They drank from noon 'til dawn for almost the entire trip. They chased women, sometimes even catching up with them, and they managed to find the time and energy to get into a couple of barroom brawls. But none of them spent even one minute in jail. Johnny had a pocketful of cash, and after he paid off the local authorities a third time for looking the other way, the boys were escorted to the airport and asked not to return to the island anytime soon. They were on the next plane back to Vietnam. Harry smiled as he drifted into sleep.

***

Harry awoke just after ten p.m. He turned on the television, not really caring what channel was on. He just wanted background noise, any distraction at all, to block out the bad thoughts rolling around in his head. Joey walked through the front door. When he stepped into the living room, he saw his granddad. Joey started for the staircase. "Nice of you to show up to your own party, Joey."

Joey stopped. "I never told you I was gonna be here," he said.

"Your entire family showed up. Your Aunt Sadie and Uncle Sam drove two-hundred miles to see you."

"I didn't ask them to come. You did."

"You embarrassed both of us today."

"I'll get over it," Joey said. "Maybe you need to stop being so sensitive."

Joey's sarcasm hit Harry hard. He wanted to leap out of the recliner and slap the boy into next week, but he just sat there.

"I hear you got a girlfriend down the block," Joey said. "Wonder how grandma would feel about it. Oh, that's right; we'll never know 'cause she's dead."

"It wasn't my fault!" Harry bellowed. But Joey wasn't listening. He was already halfway up the stairs.

It wasn't my fault. It wasn't my fault. But doubt crept into Harry's mind now. He tried to push himself out of the recliner, but he was paralyzed by the thought that he was somehow responsible for his wife's untimely and gruesome death. A few minutes later, he watched as Joey walked out the door with a packed duffel bag. And he did nothing.

***

The next morning, Harry sat on his front steps as he sipped a cup of coffee. He tried to block out the events of the day before – the graduation party minus the graduate, and another fight with Joey, but the pain simmered just beneath. Next door, Charlie stepped out onto the front steps.

"Harry, are you there?" he said.

"No," Harry said.

Charlie walked across the lawn and took a seat next to Harry, who stared at the old man for a moment, then turned away. "It's a nice day, huh?"

"What's on your mind, Sloan?"

"I'm really sorry about yesterday. I know you're hurting."

"I'll survive."

"Is the kid around?"

"He showed up late last night to pick up more of his stuff."

"Did you talk to him?"

Harry downed the rest of his coffee. "Yep. Didn't go well. There anything else?"

"Matter of fact, there is. Last week, I walked into the house, and I overheard you talking with someone in the living room."

"Maybe you should have knocked first," Harry said.

"You're right. I should have. I'm sorry. But that's not the point. Point is, you were having a conversation with someone, but you were doing all of the talking."

"I had a mime over to the house," Harry said. "He wasn't much of a talker."

"You called him 'general'. I distinctly remember that. And you said something about how you paid your dues. What's going on?"

"Nothing's going on. Let it go."

"Talk to me Harry, Please."

"Some weather we're having, huh?" With that, Harry got up and went in the house.

25

Later that afternoon, Harry approached the rec center's front door and saw five of the BOA club's members standing in the walkway. The men slapped him on the back and shook his hand as they followed him into the building. Harry knew at that moment it was time to press his advantage. He led the men toward the portrait of Hitler and stared at it, in feigned awe, as if he were looking at the face of God. He saluted it and bellowed, "Sieg Heil!" while the other men stood there in silence.

"Well?" Harry said, scowling.

In unison, the men saluted the portrait and barked, "Sieg Heil!"

"That's more like it. Let's have a beer," Harry said. The men, twelve of them in all, filled pitchers with beer, then took seats at a long table. As Harry took a seat at the head of the table, Kurt eyeballed him. "There a problem, Kurt?"

Kurt took two steps towards Harry. "I sit there," he said.

Harry got up, puffed out his chest and smiled. "That so?"

"Sure is," Kurt said. "You need to know your place."

"Things change, Kurt. Adapt or –"

"Or, what?"

"Or we can settle this right here and now." Their eyes locked on each other. Harry's icy stare and clenched fists cut right through Kurt. The rest of the men sat back, waiting. Kurt felt their eyes on him. He took one step towards Harry, then stopped. "What ya waiting for?" Harry said. "Not so tough without a beer bottle in your hand, huh?"

That confused Kurt. He still couldn't place Harry.

"Don't remember me, asshole? You cold-cocked me with a beer

bottle at Sam's Saloon a while ago. You almost killed me, you fuckin' coward," Harry said.

The men murmured amongst themselves before Hans spoke up. "He called you a coward, Kurt. You gonna take that shit?"

"Yeah, you gonna take that shit, Kurt?" Harry said.

Kurt knew if he didn't act, he would lose the respect of the men. He charged at Harry, and Harry grabbed him by the shirt and threw him to the floor. Kurt got to his feet and lunged at Harry again. Harry caught him with a punch to the midsection that cracked two ribs, and Kurt wheezed as he doubled over in excruciating pain. Harry grabbed Kurt by the hair, pulled his head back and took aim, then he hit him with a straight right to the jaw. Kurt dropped to the floor with a thud. The men were in awe. They knew, without anyone saying it, that Harry was the new alpha male in the group. And its new leader. Harry sat back down at the head of the table.

"Anyone else got a problem with the seating arrangements?" Harry said. No one spoke up. "Okay, then. So, what's on the agenda?"

"What do you mean?" one of the younger men said.

"I mean, what are you guys doing to restore the Fatherland to its former glory?"

"The Fatherland?" Stefan said.

Harry pointed at Kurt, who still lay on the floor, out cold. "Didn't that asshole teach you guys anything about our history?" Harry got up and walked around the table. "You know the statue in the town square? Our town's named after that man. His name is Friedrich Albrecht." The men gave Harry blank stares. "He came here from the Fatherland a long time ago to spread the Fuhrer's message and the Aryan way. We're gonna spread the Aryan nation. The Aryan pride. The Aryan way of life."

"Why are we called Brownshirts?" Stefan said.

Harry stopped and pointed at the boy. "Good question, son. The original Brownshirts helped our Fuhrer rise to power. They guarded him at rallies, and they beat the hell out of anyone who stood against our leader. They were proud, blue-collar guys, they were street fighters, and they kicked ass. And they didn't take any shit from anyone. Wish I could say the same about you boys."

The men grumbled amongst themselves. "What's that supposed to mean?" one of the men said.

"Means exactly that," Harry said. "Don't know if you're aware, but there's some new groups in town, and they're tearing shit down and burning shit up. They're assholes, but they're some real go- getters."

"Why are they assholes?" Stefan said.

"'Cause they're fuckin' with the Red Man." Harry replied. "They tore down the statue of Little Hawk at the ballpark and they took away the team's name, the War Chiefs."

"Why should we give a shit what they do to the Injuns?" Stefan said.

Harry gestured that he wanted another beer. One of the younger members eagerly refilled his stein. Harry took two hearty gulps from it before going on. "Why? Lemme tell you something about the Red Man. You know the swastika on our flag? That was an Indian symbol for good luck and well-being a long time before we borrowed it from the Red Man and made it our own. And Hitler himself made a deal with some of the Indian tribes. He told 'em if they fought for the German people against the Americans, he'd give 'em some of this country after the war, if Germany had won, that is. You see, the Indians were our ally, and they can be again, but we gotta show 'em we got their backs. Plus, these new assholes in town hate white people, and a lot of 'em are white themselves."

"That's what I told Kurt. And he didn't do shit about it," Hans said.

"You were right, Hans. They blame the White Man for being racists and oppressors."

"We ain't racists," Stefan said. "We just hate anyone who ain't white."

Harry cringed at that remark, but he went on. "These new groups in town blame us for just about every fuckin' problem in the world. They wanna tear this country apart."

"Ain't that what we wanna do?" Stefan said.

Harry rested a hand on Stefan's shoulder. "We ain't tearing shit down, son. We just wanna rebuild this country in our own image."

Another member spoke up. "Are you saying we're really gonna give Injuns part of this country?"

"We'll sign a nonaggression pact with 'em, like our Fuhrer did with Stalin. And after we take this country, we'll either deport 'em all or just give 'em a few more casinos." When Harry winked at the men, they laughed. And after he raised his hand, they immediately fell silent. Harry leaned in and eyed every man at the table. "The Red Man ain't our enemy. These white people are. They hate their own kind. And they hate the Red Man. And they hate us. Remember that." As the men talked amongst themselves, Harry added, "But they're getting shit done. You're a bunch of pussies compared to them."

"No, we ain't!" Stefan said. The rest of the men grunted and nodded in agreement with Stefan.

"We'll see about that," Harry said. "Strap on your nut sacks, men. We're gonna raise some hell."

The older men at the table applauded while the younger members, filled with testosterone and a newly found purpose in life, banged the table with their fists. Harry raised his hand, and the men came to order. "Anyone here know anything about explosives?" he said. When no one responded to the question, Harry said, "Well, you're gonna learn." Harry led the men to the bar and the beer flowed.

An hour later, no one noticed when Kurt regained consciousness. Getting slowly to his feet, he rubbed his broken jaw. Then, he saw the men gathered around Harry at the bar, laughing and drinking. He knew his reign had come to an end. After slinking quietly out of the hall, he went to the local hospital's emergency room and had his jaw wired shut. The men of the B of A would never see Kurt again.

When Harry got home, he called Joey twice, got his voicemail both times, and hung up without leaving a message. Irritated and tired, he slumped into his recliner and turned on the television.

As he was about to nod off, Harry heard a clamor coming from outside. He went to the bay window and looked outside. He saw a group of people standing on his front lawn, while others marched up and down his sidewalk. Some were holding signs, and others were chanting.

Harry saw several signs that read, BID. He remembered Ze's threat to return. If she was out there, Harry was going to make her wish she were anywhere else. He threw open his front door. The protestors came to a sudden stop, like a herd of antelope that had suddenly picked up the scent of a nearby predator. They stared at Harry for a moment, then the screaming began.

"Cisgender!" one woman screamed. "Homophobe!"

"Oppressor!" a young man yelled. Harry stomped down the front steps. Reaching the sidewalk, he saw that some of his neighbors were watching from across the street.

"What's going on, Harry?" a neighbor yelled.

"Be damned if I know, Russ." The mob encircled Harry, shaking their signs in his face. "Who the hell are you people?! Get the hell off my lawn!"

A young woman got in Harry's face. It was Ze. "Remember me, you fossil? I told you I wasn't through with you."

Harry pointed a finger at the crowd. "I'll give you people -"

"'You people?'" Ze said. "What the hell's that supposed to mean?"

"It means you people here, dumbass. You got five minutes to get off my property or I'm calling the cops!"

Harry bounded up the front steps and slammed the front door behind him. He waited exactly five minutes before looking out the window. When he saw that the mob was still there, he grabbed his phone and called the sheriff's office. "Yeah, it's Harry Blake on Colonial Drive North. I gotta bunch of assholes raising hell on my front lawn, and they won't leave. Please send someone. Thanks."

Harry waited. After a half an hour passed, the cops still hadn't shown up, and he could still hear the chanting going on outside. He decided he'd had enough. Feeling a jolt of pain shoot through his bad knee, he grabbed his cane, flung open the front door and hobbled down the steps. Again, the crowd stopped and fixed their collective gaze on Harry. "What the hell's wrong with you people? Don't you have jobs?"

The crowd pressed in on Harry. "Our job is right here," said Ze. "Our job is to right the wrongs of an imperialistic, patriarchal, homophobic society that keeps us oppressed! Evolve or die, you dinosaur!" A protestor picked up a rock and threw it through the living room bay window. The crowd cheered.

Harry closed his eyes and the memories of bullies pushing him around and taunting him gushed to the surface. The utter hostility and resentment he felt when he opened his eyes and saw the mob made him turn flush with anger. He waved his cane in a wide, sweeping motion, nearly clipping one of the protesters. "Who threw that?!"

"He's got an oppression stick!" a protester yelled. A young man snagged the cane out of Harry's hand.

"Give it back!" Harry bellowed.

The crowd laughed as the young guy taunted Harry, waving the cane in the air just out of his reach. Harry charged him and grabbed him by the shirt, flung him to the ground, then grabbed his cane from the man's hand. Just then, a police cruiser rolled up to the curb. Some of the protesters helped the young man to his feet as two deputies pushed their way through the crowd.

"Oppressor!" someone yelled as they pointed at Harry.

"Hate criminal!" another person screamed.

Through the maze of people, Harry saw that Ze was talking to one of the officers. She pointed at Harry. "He pushed Eddie to the ground," she said. "He assaulted him and pushed him to the ground!" Other protestors nodded in assent of Ze's accusation.

"Officers, I want these assholes off my property. Now!" Harry roared.

Hearing the din from inside the house, Gertie and Charlie stepped out of Charlie's home and onto the sidewalk. They stopped at the end of Charlie's walkway, unable to figure out what was going on amid the chaos. Crash stood in his driveway, leaning against the Chevelle, smoking a cigarette and grinning.

"Step back!" a deputy said to the crowd that had surrounded him.

Shoving people aside like they were toys, Harry reached the deputy and pointed at the mob. "Officer, I want these assholes off my property, now!"

"Please turn around, sir," the deputy said.

"What?" Harry said.

"Turn around, sir. I'm not going to ask again."

Harry spun around. The deputy slapped handcuffs on him and walked Harry towards his cruiser. "You're under arrest for assault. You have the right to an attorney…."

"What the hell?" Harry said.

"What's going on, Gert?" Charlie said.

"They're talking my Harry away," Gertie said. She tried in vain to push her way through the crowd blocking the path to her son. "Get the hell out of my way!" she screamed.

Across the street, Crash pointed at Harry and laughed. "I'll bring some bail money, Harry!" he yelled. Harry dug his feet into the pavement and came to a full stop when he saw the kid laughing at him. The arresting deputy tried to push Harry forward, with no luck. Harry's fists were clenched, and his thick, powerful arms strained mightily against the handcuffs. The second deputy positioned himself behind Harry and the two officers, pushing as hard as they could, finally stuffed the big man into their cruiser.

Gertie pushed her way onward through the crowd. "Get the hell out of my way!" she yelled again. The mob cheered as the cruiser pulled away from the curb just as Gertie reached the street. "Bring my boy back, you bastards!" she screamed. Several neighbors crossed the street and helped Gertie, who was now crying, find her way back to Charlie.

Russ, a middle-aged, well-built man, watched in disgust as the crowd continued cheering Harry's arrest. He pushed his way to the center of the protestors and pointed at everyone all at once. "I hope you assholes are happy. You just got a decent man, a man who fought for this country, arrested. And for what? Defending his property? What the hell did Harry do to any of you, huh? Are you proud of yourselves? Get the hell out of here. Now!" he roared.

Three more of Harry's male neighbors stood alongside Russ in a show of support. Their scowls showed the crowd they meant business. They were ready, and more than willing, to physically remove the protesters from Harry's property, if needed.

The mob began to disperse. Quickly.

***

Harry posted bail and was back home later that evening. When he stepped into the house, he saw Charlie and Gertie sitting on the sofa. Gertie got up and nearly ran to her son. She wrapped her arms around him. "Are you okay, sonny boy?"

"Yeah, Ma."

"What was that all about today, Harry?" Charlie said.

Harry gently pushed his mother away, dropped his keys on the table, and walked to the staircase. "Just some idiots with too much time on their hands, Sloan. Good night, guys." Harry slowly ascended the stairs. He climbed into bed and stared at the ceiling, reliving the events of the day. Anger and exasperation gripped him. He decided at that moment that Ze had to pay a price for pushing him too far, and the bill was about due. He drifted off into a gray area between consciousness and a dream state.

***

Harry Jr.'s belly jiggled as he picked up the pace, nearing home. He was excited to see what his parents got him for his fourteenth birthday. When he stepped through the door, his father was in the kitchen, leaning against the countertop, gnawing on a cigar. Harry Jr. saw a gift-wrapped box on the kitchen table. He grinned as he made a beeline toward it.

"Hi, Dad," Harry Jr. said, standing over the gift like it was the Holy Grail. But he stopped just as he was about to tear into the box. He remembered that there was a protocol to be followed. "May I, sir?"

"Permission granted," Harry Sr. said.

Harry Jr. ripped the wrapping paper to shreds, clawed through the unmarked box, and pulled out an athletic supporter and a pair of boxing gloves. The boy's smile disappeared. "This a joke?"

"No joke, boy. You're going to learn to box."

"I don't want to box. I wanna try out for the soccer team."

"No son of mine is going to play soccer. That game is for sissies. Now, boxing, there's a real sport. It'll make a man out of you, boy. You're going to learn how to defend yourself."

"I won't be any good at it," Harry Jr. said.

"Bullshit. You've got the size already. They'll teach you technique. Plus, you'll lose that baby fat." Ashamed, Harry Jr. bowed his head.

"Where's your pride, son? You want people calling you 'fat boy' your entire life?"

"No," he murmured. What Harry Jr. wanted was to tell his father to go to hell, but he knew even looking at the man cross-eyed could cost him a weeks' worth of what his dad called "house arrest."

"Good man. Carry on." Harry Sr. said.

***

Harry Jr. took up boxing at a gym just outside of Albrecht. He lacked the conditioning to go more than two rounds of sparring for the first month, but the boy's coordination, hand speed and upper body strength impressed the boxing coach. After working with Harry Jr. for almost a year, the coach, with the consent of Harry Sr., entered the boy into a Golden Gloves tournament. Harry Jr. knocked out his first opponent with a left cross that broke the boy's jaw.

Harry Jr. fought Golden Gloves for nearly three years. His record was thirty-one wins, with twenty-nine knockouts, no losses and two draws. Harry Jr. was now more confident and more chiseled, and the fat that he carried since he was a young boy was long gone.

The coach's daughter, a pretty high school sophomore named Patsy Brown, worked part time at a thrift store next to the gym. She took notice of Harry Jr. when she stopped in one day to visit her father after her shift. In the middle of a sparring session, Harry Jr. dropped his gloves when he caught sight of Patsy watching him. Harry Jr. got tagged on the jaw by his sparring mate, but the boy withstood the punch, shook it off, then smiled and waved at Patsy. "Focus, boy!" Coach Brown yelled.

Soon after, the two teenagers became nearly inseparable. After dating Patsy for just over a year, Harry Jr. was beyond smitten; he was in love. Friends told him that he didn't have a clue what love really was, and they razzed him incessantly about being "whipped," but the boy knew his heart couldn't lead him astray. Patsy was the girl for him. Before leaving for his first tour in Vietnam, Harry Jr. married Patsy Brown, the love of his life.

***

As Harry slept upstairs, Gertie sat on the sofa in the Blake living room watching TV. Hours earlier, she had sent Charlie home alone, telling him before he left that she wanted to keep an eye on her son for the rest of the night. Just after midnight, Joey walked through the front door and poked his head into the living room and saw Gertie sitting on the sofa. Gertie caught sight of the boy. "Shit," he muttered. "Hi, Grams. Can't talk," he said as he started up the stairs.

"Don't you 'can't talk' me, boy. Get your ass over here."

Joey stepped into the room and Gertie gestured for him to sit. Knowing he was about to get lectured to, he let out a sigh as he sat.

"That was a real shitty stunt you pulled, Joey. Your grandfather put a lot of time and effort into that party, and you couldn't even bother to show up for it. Do you know how that made him feel?"

"I didn't ask for a party, Grams."

"He may not show it, but your grandpa lives and breathes for you. You broke his heart, boy."

"He'll live." Joey got up and Gertie grabbed him by the arm.

"Sit… down," she said.

Joey plopped onto the sofa again. "Your great-grandfather died before you were born, so you didn't know him. But I want to tell you something about him. My Harry, Harry senior, was tough on your granddad. My Harry was an army officer, and he was used to giving orders, so he tried to run our home like it was an army base. Me and your great grandfather used to butt heads over your granddad when he was a boy. I took your granddad's side when he, you know, screwed up like boys sometimes do, when your great grandad would really want to lay down the law. And since your grandma Patsy passed, your granddad's been raising you alone. He's had to try to be a mother and father to you."

"That's his fault," Joey said.

"Meaning what?"

"Grandma should still be here," the boy said, hanging his head.

"Your grandpa had nothing to do with your grandma dying like she did. Not a damn thing, you understand? They were at the wrong place at the wrong time, that's all."

"I heard grandpa was drinking that night," Joey said.

"Maybe he had a couple of beers. So what? The cops didn't arrest him or even ticket him." Joey conceded that fact with his silence.

"You need to let go of that, or it'll eat you alive," Gertie said. "Your grandpa's not gonna be around forever. He loves you. Tell him you love him, too. He wants to hear that from you more than you'll ever know. Stop hurting him and stop hurting yourself. Promise me you'll do that."

Tears welled up in Joey's eyes. "Grandpa's always picking on me. He's ashamed of me."

"He's not ashamed of you, Joey. He just…your grandpa's from another time. He doesn't know how to deal with…people who are a little more sensitive. Your grandpa was a lot like you when he was your age."

"He was?"

"He sure was. And your great grandpa didn't like it one damn bit, so he tried to whip your grandpa into shape, was the way he put it. That used to piss me off. And it made your grandpa a very sullen boy."

"What did you do about it?"

"When I couldn't stand it anymore, I was gonna leave your great grandfather."

"Why didn't you?"

"My Harry passed away before I filed for a divorce." Gertie made the sign of the cross.

"I'm sorry, Grams."

Gertie clutched Joey's hand and smiled through her sadness. "I know you are."

Joey didn't want to upset Gertie by telling her he was leaving for good once he had all of his belongings. He kissed her on the cheek and got up off the sofa. "I have to go, Grams."

26

Harry had been working at the courthouse for just over two weeks, and the staff had taken a liking to him. He told jokes on his breaks, did extra tasks without being asked to, and he always made sure to bring an extra piece of dessert for his new friend, security officer Bill. Bill reminded Harry of a faithful dog who eagerly waited at the door for the return of his master, and that was okay with Harry, because once he gave Bill his treat, he scurried off, leaving Harry alone for the rest of the workday.

Today was different. Today, Harry's cooler contained two pounds of Semtex hidden beneath the cooler's false bottom. Clad in his work coveralls, and wearing his horn-rimmed glasses like always, he entered through the courthouse front door, and sure enough, Bill stood there wearing a big grin. He shook Harry's hand. "How you doing, pal?"

"Doing, Billy. How's tricks?"

"Same old."

Harry pointed to his cooler. "Need to run it through?"

"Nah. You're good."

That's what Harry wanted to hear. There would be no inspection today. He dropped the cooler on a nearby bench. Bill followed closely behind like Harry was about to serve him his last meal. "Whatcha got today, Harry?"

"Let's take a look." Harry dug into the chest and pulled the false bottom up at an angle so that Bill's prying eyes couldn't see what lay beneath the two cellophane -wrapped pieces of cake. Harry pulled out a piece of chocolate cake, handed it to Bill, then he quickly pushed down on the false bottom.

"You ain't hiding a bomb in there, are ya?"

"If I was, I'd give you a ten second head start, Billy. That's what friends do."

Bill laughed, slapped Harry on the back, then scurried across the lobby like a rat with a newfound piece of cheese.

Harry grabbed his cooler and made his way down a hallway and turned left. The door leading to the basement was on his right. When he was sure that he was alone in the hallway, he quickly opened that door, and quietly closed it behind him. At the top of the stairwell, he flipped a light switch on. Battered, weather-beaten, wooden steps led the way to the basement. Harry eased down one step after another, coming to a stop when he heard the groaning of wood that bent under his weight. He composed himself, pulled his foot off the step, and skipped over it as he made his way to the bottom.

The basement resembled a dungeon. Cobwebs draped from the ceiling and every corner of the room. Harry nearly wretched as he inhaled decades of neglect in the form of dust and mold. Cold air and dampness had taken its toll on everything made of metal in the room. To his right was a window about halfway up the wall that was situated at ground level. He would run the detonating wire through that window. He looked around and saw a metal bench that he set his cooler upon, then, in the middle of the room, he saw two load-bearing metal poles, complete with decades of rust, anchored in the floor, and attached to a steel I-beam above.

When those poles give, the building's gonna come down, he thought. Harry dug two one - pound bricks of Semtex from the cooler. He unwrapped them and tore the bricks in half, then in half again. He attached four pieces of the explosive to the corners where the ceiling met the walls. Then he placed the four remaining pieces of Semtex on each side of the two metal support poles where they were bolted into the I-beam.

He grabbed his cooler and slowly and quietly ascended the steps. When he reached the top, he opened the door just a crack to check for foot traffic. The hallway was empty. Stepping out, Harry quietly closed the door behind himself and moved along.

***

When he got home from work, Harry looked around the house for Gertie and Joey, but neither was home. He called Joey's cell phone and got the boy's voicemail, again, which didn't surprise him at all. He didn't bother to leave a message. He stepped outside and walked onto Charlie's lawn, then peered into his house. He smiled when he saw his mother and Charlie holding hands as they watched TV. Returning home, he microwaved some leftover meatloaf, then took a couple of sleeping pills before easing into his recliner. He slept until after midnight.

***

It was just after one a.m. when Harry drove down Elm Street in a black, Chevy panel van that he had purchased several days earlier. When his mother asked him why he bought a van, Harry told her he needed it to haul supplies to his new job. Before Gertie even had the chance to ask her son about the job, her mind slipped out of gear and the subject didn't come up again.

General Patton rode shotgun tonight. He grinned as he chomped on a cigar. "Great night for raising some hell, huh, Harry?"

Harry checked the van's speedometer to make sure he was under the speed limit. Then he checked his mirrors, looking for any sign of law enforcement patrolling the area as he neared the edge of town. With the cargo he was transporting tonight, he didn't want to give the cops any excuse to pull him over.

He caught sight of the courthouse just half a block up the road on his right. Beads of sweat trickled down his forehead as he pulled the van into the pitch-black parking lot adjacent to the building. The city had already torn down the parking lot's light poles in anticipation of the building's imminent closure, so on this moonless night, Harry was nearly invisible.

He took a deep breath as he scanned the area for any activity. He knew the security cameras were gone as well, so he wasn't worried about getting picked up on video. He got out of the van and tested his bad knee by leaning on that leg with all of his weight. Patton got out of the van and slid up next to Harry. "How's the knee, soldier?"

With all of the adrenaline pumping through him at the moment, Harry felt no pain at all, in any part of his body. "It's okay," he said.

"That's good, my boy," Patton said.

Harry took one last look around the area. All was quiet. But suddenly, he thought about scrapping the mission. Patton jumped into his face. "To hell with that bullshit!" Patton barked as he pointed at the building. "They stole your manhood. This mission's a go, soldier!"

Harry grunted in agreement. The doubt was gone. He opened the van's rear doors and took a quick visual inventory; on the floor of the van lie blasting caps, a detonation box, a spool of detonating cord, and four bricks of Semtex. He put on a pair of work gloves, then he pulled a metal cart from the van.

After loading the explosives onto the cart, he wheeled it up an access ramp and around to a corner of the building. As he stopped to rest for a moment, he looked around the area one more time and saw no activity. When his breathing reached a normal cadence, he got back to work.

He planted the Semtex bricks at all four corners of the building, just above ground level. After attaching blasting caps to the Semtex, he took the detonating cord, which he had cut earlier into four strands, and connected each strand into each of the blasting caps. Then he walked the remaining length of cord back to the van, where he hooked the cord to the detonation box.

The general stood behind Harry, breathing down his neck. Once again, Harry thought about aborting the mission. "Don't go soft on me, soldier. Remember what these assholes did to you."

"You're right, General. I'll show those bastards a hate crime."

Harry pushed down on the detonation box's T-handle. A current of electricity raced through the detonating cord and snaked its way toward the courthouse. Moments later...contact. The explosion shattered the silence. Brick, metal and glass rocketed through the air in every direction. The general grinned and slapped Harry on the back. "That's my boy!"

Harry was flush with exhilaration. He wanted nothing more than to just stand there and bask in the moment, but he knew he couldn't. He tossed the detonation box into the van, got behind the wheel and drove off into the night. Arriving back home twenty minutes later, Harry pulled the van into his garage, killed the engine, and sat back. He exhaled for the first time all night, but adrenaline was still pumping through him. He grinned. *I did it. I really did it.*

He got out of the van and emptied its contents, then hauled the explosives down to the basement storage room. He parked himself in his recliner without checking to see if Joey or Gertie were home tonight. At the moment, it didn't matter to him either way. He cracked open a beer to celebrate the mission's success, but it was a victory he would have to celebrate alone. He couldn't tell a soul about the night's venture, at least not yet. Two hours later, and with six beers in him, he fell into a deep slumber.

***

Harry's cell phone rang just before eight a.m., jolting him from sleep. After fumbling for his phone, he answered it. "Yeah?"

"Harry, it's Bill from work. Did you hear the news?"

"No. What's going on, Bill?"

"They blew up the courthouse last night. It's all over the news."

"They blew it up? No shit?"

"No shit, buddy. I'm there now. Just wanted you to know there's no work today. I gotta go, Harry. Talk to you later." Harry smiled as he hung up his phone. He stretched his arms to shake the stiffness from them, then he turned on the local news.

"Good morning, Albrecht," the anchorman said. "Our top story. Last night there was an explosion at the old county courthouse. We go now to Tom Jensen who's at the scene." Reporter Tom Jensen, with his mic at the ready, stood in the courthouse parking lot as his cameraman slowly panned the lot, finally zooming in on the damaged courthouse.

Harry leaned in toward the TV and saw that the courthouse was still standing. "What the hell?" he muttered. Then it hit him; he had forgotten to connect the detonating wire to the Semtex in the courthouse basement. He threw the remote on the floor. "Son of a bitch."

The cameraman gave Tom got his cue. "I'm standing here in the courthouse parking lot looking at scattered debris in the aftermath of what could be an act of terrorism. Here's what we know; in the early morning hours, an explosion rocked the old courthouse, partially destroying all four exterior walls of the building. Authorities are on the scene digging through the rubble searching for clues. No one was hurt or killed in the explosion, but the courthouse will be closed for business until further notice. That's all we have for now. Live from the old county courthouse, this is Tom Jensen, Action News."

Harry sat back as tension welled up in his neck and shoulders. Gertie walked into the living room. "Hi, sonny boy. You okay?"

Harry was in no mood to make small talk with his mother at the moment. He didn't even bother to look at her. "I'm doing, Ma."

"I didn't hear you come in last night. Were you out late?"

"Was at the hall."

"You should have called and let me know. I worry about you."

"Don't. Talk to Joey lately?"

"He stopped by the house the other night."

Harry turned towards his mother. "He was here?!"

"That's what I just said."

"Why didn't you wake me?"

"'Cause I figured if you saw him, it'd just upset you more than you already were."

"You should've let me decide that."

"Guess maybe I should of. But you're the reason he left in the first place. Joey says you've been riding him kinda hard lately. I told him -"

"He'll survive a little tough love. I did."

"What the hell does that mean?"

Harry got up and stared cross-eyed at his mother. "Lemme know when you figure it out, Ma." He went to the basement and opened the padlocked storage room. He was suddenly in the mood to make more Semtex.

27

John Coleman stood on the balcony of his Tucson condo and stared out into the stillness of the Sonoran Desert. A smalltown boy at heart, the view he took in did nothing for him. And he hated the heat that a Tucson day brought with it. *Dry heat, my ass*, he thought. But his wife's family lived in the area, so Tucson was home. He missed the quaintness and intimacy that a small town offered. He missed greeting neighbors and fellow townsfolk by their first name and asking about their families. But most of all, John missed his work.

Stepping into the living room, he slid the door wall closed, slipped into his recliner, and opened his laptop. He browsed for news. An article about a damaged courthouse in South Dakota caught his attention. John, a semi-retired Intelligence Analyst for the FBI, began to read the article when his cell phone rang. The call was from his boss, Henry Wilcox, the head of the Domestic Terrorism Operations Section of the FBI. "John Coleman."

"It's Henry, John. You catch the news on the courthouse bombing in South Dakota?"

"I just tripped over it. Were there any casualties?"

"No deaths," Henry said. "And no one was hurt, apparently. Seems our bomber has some manners."

"What have you got so far, Hank?" John knew his former boss hated being called "Hank," which is why he made sure to call him that. John could nearly see the grimace on his boss's face on the other end of the line. He smiled.

"You know I don't like being called that," Henry said. "Early indications say its plastic explosives. We've got agents in route, but we could use a seasoned vet on this one. It could turn into a pissing contest between us and the local boys. We need a guy that can handle the situation before it becomes one. What do you say?"

John's pulse raced at the thought of getting back in the game, but he wouldn't give his boss the satisfaction of knowing that. "Don't know, Hank. I'm keeping pretty busy these days."

"You know I don't like that name, John."

Yeah, I know.

"Let's stop dancing here. I need an answer," Henry said.

"I can move some things around, I suppose," John said. "South Dakota, huh?"

"Yeah. A one-horse town called Albrecht." Henry chuckled. "I'm betting inbreeding's their sport of choice."

That's hilarious, you smug prick, John thought.

"There's a red eye tonight, and a ticket waiting for you at the airport," Henry said. "We can have a driver at your home in an hour."

"Send him."

"Knew the agency could count on you, John. Make us proud."

John frowned as he hung up his phone. *Wouldn't have killed you to thank me, asshole.* Then he smiled knowing that he was going back to work, even if only for a little while. He packed two bags and left a note for his wife, who was asleep. *Honey, I have to go out of town. Duty calls. Will call you tomorrow from the road.*

28

It was just after five p.m. when Harry pulled his truck into the parking lot of Jay's Diner. A tall, mustached man, about thirty years younger than himself, knocked on his window. "Harry Blake?" the man asked.

"That's me."

Harry got out of his truck and the men shook hands. "Ken Burton. My uncle, Ed, knows you from the V.F.W. hall. He says you're a standup guy. He told me you need some help."

"Your uncle's a good man. And, yeah, I need some help."

"Let's step into my office," Ken said.

Inside the restaurant, they grabbed a booth. "This is your office?" Harry said.

"It is. It saves me a lot in overhead."

Harry caught a glimpse of a 'Semper Fi' tattoo on Ken's forearm. "You a Marine?"

"Yeah. I did two tours in Iraq," Ken said.

"Come home…okay?

"More or less. You a vet, too?"

"Yeah. Did two tours in 'Nam."

"I've heard the stories. My best friend's dad was a tunnel rat. He lost a hand, and most of his mind. Took his own life a few years after he came home."

"I'm really sorry."

"How about you, Mr. Blake? You get home okay?"

Harry shrugged. "I'm still in one piece."

"And your buddies?"

"One way or another, most of 'em are gone." Ken didn't need an explanation. He knew exactly what Harry meant. A solemn silence followed. The two men looked each other over, and there was a mutual, unspoken respect between them. Harry already knew that Ken was his man. He pushed a piece of paper across the table. "Here's the information you wanted. All you really need is the guy's name?"

"That's it. My associate can do just about anything with just a name. What do you need done?"

"Can your friend put some kiddie porn on this guy's computer?" Harry said.

Ken sat back and his eyes widened. "You want kiddie porn uploaded to this guy's computer? That's some serious shit you're asking me to do, Mr. Blake. Did this guy sleep with your wife, or something?"

"Nah. The guy's a thorn in my side. He's works at the C.A.T., and he's a real piece of shit."

"Did you say the C.A.T.? The place where they're indoctrinating people?"

"You heard of it, Ken?"

"Got a friend who's going there. He told a raunchy joke to a buddy at work, someone overheard it and bitched to the H.R department about being offended, and the company told my buddy he could lose his job if he didn't play ball and sit through their bullshit classes. He is pissed."

"I have to go to classes there, too, Ken. This guy's an arrogant asshole. And he's trying to fuck with me. I want him to pay for it. Can you help me out here?"

"If he works for that organization, he is an asshole." Ken smiled. "Be glad to help."

"Good deal."

"We should discuss my fee, Mr. Blake."

"Call me Harry."

Harry left the restaurant satisfied with the price. He even gave Ken an extra five-hundred dollars, just because he could. After ordering a meal, Ken looked at the name on the piece of paper: Steve Wilkins, Harry's instructor at the Center for Alternative Thinking.

<h1 align="center">29</h1>

Just after seven p.m. that evening, Hans showed up at Harry's door. Harry introduced Hans to Charlie and Gertie, and the four sat down and had dinner. As they ate, Hans told Gertie and Charlie his story and about all of the family he had lost. Charlie mentioned that he had a sister, Mary, a widow, who was about Han's age and lived in a neighboring town. Hans took Mary's number, called her and had his first date with her that Sunday.

***

Monday morning found Harry lying in bed staring at the ceiling. It was eight a.m., and he hadn't slept well the night before, but he had no reason to get out of bed. He recalled the night of the bombing. Harry felt damn good to have an outlet for his ever-growing anger. And nobody got hurt. That thought comforted him. He'd seen enough death in Vietnam to last five lifetimes, and he had even taken lives himself. But it was the collateral damage, the civilians who died in a war they didn't want, nor understand, that could haunt a soldier for the rest of a war, if not the rest of his life. Those were the deaths that could burrow into a soldier's mind and soul and eat away at him slowly, like a vulture feeding on carrion until only dust and bone remained. He turned on his side and stretched out, hoping that sleep would come, but his mind was in overdrive, and doubt began to gnaw at him.

Could I do something like that again? He didn't know. But he had his "enemies" list ready just in case. He closed his eyes and tried again to

164

sleep, but the list continued to impose itself on Harry's consciousness, like a never-ending video loop. He went over the names: Steve Wilkins, the moderator at the CAT, was about to be dealt with. There was Crash's lawyer, Crash, the manager at the café, Ze…

Harry went down his list of names as if they were imaginary sheep that he could count in an attempt to quiet his mind and fall into a peaceful slumber. But his mind had a follow-up question for him to wrestle with. *Would Dad be proud of me for what I did?* There was someone in the room to help Harry with the answer.

"Hell, yeah, your dad would have been proud, soldier," said General Patton, who was sitting at the foot of Harry's bed. When Harry saw the general, fright gripped him. He reached for a bottle of pills sitting on his nightstand: lurasidone, the medication his doctor had prescribed to help suppress hallucinations. He jammed two in his mouth and swallowed hard. The general chuckled. "Those pills are useless against me, Harry."

"Please, go away."

"Relax, soldier. You asked a question- and a damn fine question it was - and I gave you the answer you wanted. I once said, 'accept the challenges, so that you may feel the exhilaration of victory."

"What the hell does that mean?" Harry said.

"The challenge was to put those bastards in their place, to send a message. And you nailed it, Harry. You fucking nailed it. You gave the enemy a black eye, and you feel damn good about it now, like you should. But one battle doesn't win a war."

"Maybe I should quit while I'm ahead," Harry said.

Patton pointed his riding crop at Harry. "That's horseshit. You don't bloody the enemy's nose then retreat. You never pay for the same real estate twice. Never! You take the fight to them!" the general shouted, slamming his fist on the bed. Then Patton sighed. "And you were just starting to reclaim your manhood. What a damn shame," he said.

Harry closed his eyes as he considered the general's words. His head started to throb. "We'll talk about the next operation real soon, if you're man enough to fight on, Blake." Harry nodded yes, hoping that would end this conversation. He opened his eyes again, and General Patton was gone. He rolled over and again tried to sleep.

30

John Coleman's plane touched down at the Sioux Falls Regional Airport just after eight a.m., and an FBI agent was there to meet him and drive him to the courthouse in Albrecht. When they arrived there, John was tired, but being on the job again invigorated him. Looking around, he saw that the parking lot was teeming with law enforcement personnel from seemingly every agency in the state. As he walked towards the courthouse, he was stopped by deputy Greg Jackson.

"You have business here, sir?" the deputy asked.

"I do." John showed the lawman a letter signed by the director of the F.B.I. The deputy glanced at it quickly, then handed it back.

"Welcome to Albrecht, Mr. Coleman." The deputy led John toward the building's rear entrance. "Some of your boys are already here."

"They'll keep for now. And call me John, please." John eyed the deputy's badge. "What do you have so far, Deputy Jackson?"

"We got a call last night from a woman who happened to be driving past the courthouse at the time of the explosion. We've already taken her statement."

"I'll need a copy of that. How about video?"

"The parking lot security cameras were removed a few weeks ago. The courthouse was scheduled for demolition soon, so....."

"Great," John said. He and the sheriff sidestepped shattered glass and bricks that littered the ground right up to entrance of the building. "I'd like to take a look inside."

The deputy yawned and stretched. "Been a long night, John. I've been on site since the call came in, and it's my day off."

"It won't take long," John said. "And if we find anything, I'll make sure you get the credit, Greg."

"Sure thing," deputy Jackson said. He led John through the courthouse's rear entrance. After a quick walkthrough of the ground floor, the two men made their way to an unmarked door.

"What's this lead to, Greg?"

"Basement."

"Let's take a look."

The deputy opened the door and peered down the dark stairwell. He flipped the light switch on, but there was no power. He pulled out his flashlight, aimed it at the stairwell, and took a couple of cautious steps down. "These stairs are shaky, John. Watch your step." When they reached the bottom, the deputy scanned the room. "Not much damage down here," he said. "What's your theory?"

"My wife's cooking," John said, hoping to get a laugh. But the joke blew right past the deputy. John examined the still-intact ceiling.

"I'm betting it was Muslim terrorists. And I'm betting they used C-4," the deputy said.

"The usual suspects, huh?" John said. "Why would they bomb a courthouse in the middle of nowhere, and in the middle of the night?"

"Beats the hell out of me, John. Fuckers just like blowing shit up, don't they?"

Here we go, John thought. He knew he had to jettison the deputy soon before he snapped at the man. Then he caught a glimpse of something near the ceiling. "Deputy, shine your light up there." The beam of light trailed along one of the ceiling's I-beams. "Hold it right there," said John. He reached up to the area where a support pole met with the I-beam. He grabbed a small chunk of a clay- like substance and examined it. "You were wrong about the C-4."

"How's that?" the deputy said.

"It's Semtex. Let's keep looking."

The two men found the remaining Semtex bricks that Harry had planted in the basement. John smiled as he examined the evidence.

"Something funny?" the deputy said.

"Our bomber knows his shit. He had the Semtex strategically placed down here, but something went wrong."

"Like what?"

"He forgot to attach detonation wire to this stuff. If he had done this right, he would have brought the whole building down." John smiled again.

"Something else funny, John?"

"This takes me back about fifty years. Reminds me of an old friend."

***

Satisfied that he had seen enough for the time being, John asked Deputy Jackson where he could find a decent breakfast, and twenty minutes later he was sitting at the counter at Deb's Diner. As he waited for his meal, he drank coffee and thought about Harry. The Bureau was already working on profiling the bomber, or bombers, and the agency was looking at a politically motivated angle, but John wasn't leaning in that direction. The bombing seemed like revenge to him; like a disgruntled man or group who wanted a little payback, maybe for an unfavorable court verdict. The fact that the explosion occurred in the early morning hours told him that the bomber didn't want, or need, casualties to achieve his goals, whatever they might be. John knew that most terrorist groups, either domestic or foreign, would want a big body count, and that would have meant a daytime bombing.

After finishing his breakfast, he pulled out his wallet and left ten dollars on the counter. As he was about to tuck it back into his coat pocket, he opened it again and leafed through it. He found what he was looking for after a little digging: a faded picture of himself and Harry, both clad in their combat fatigues, arms slung over each other's shoulders while standing on the tarmac of a military airport. Both young men were smiling. The two soldiers had done their duty and were going home on the day the photograph was taken. John smiled as he picked up his phone and made a call. Harry picked up on his end.

"Hello?"

"Harry?"

"Yeah. Who's this?"

"It's John. John Coleman."

There was silence on Harry's end for a moment as he tried to place the name. "Johnny? That really you? Damn, it's been forever. How you doing?"

"Not too bad. I'm in town. I'd like to drop by."

"What the hell you doing in Albrecht?"

"I'll explain when I see you."

"Where should we meet?"

"I could come by the house. Are you still at the same address?"

"Sure am. What time?"

"I should be there in less than half an hour."

"I'll see you then, Johnny."

***

Twenty minutes later, Harry opened his front door and there stood his friend. Harry was surprised to see John still had a full head of hair, even if it was now completely gray. He studied John's wrinkled face for a moment, and his smile became a frown when he realized that John, like himself, was now an old man. *Where the hell did the time go?*

"You okay, Harry?"

"Yeah." Harry gave John a hearty hug. "It's good to see you, Johnny. C'mon in."

They walked into the living room and John looked around. He pointed at a picture on the fireplace mantle: Harry and Patsy on their

170

wedding day. "I'm really sorry for your loss, Harry. Patsy was a damn fine lady."

"Yeah, she was. Thanks for sending the flowers. Can I get you something to drink?"

"I'm good. Thanks." Harry sat in his recliner, and John sat on the sofa. "They caught the guy, right?"

"Yeah, they got him," Harry said. "The bastard got ten years. I got a dead wife." Harry instantly realized what he'd just said. "Sorry, John. That sounded -"

"Forget it, Harry. You've got every right to feel that way."

Both men looked each other over again. "You look good, Johnny. Time's been your friend."

"Looks like you haven't missed any meals."

Harry grinned. "Mom can still whip up a pretty good meal. When I let her near the stove, that is."

"Meaning?"

"Alzheimer's," Harry said. "Some days are better than others. But it's getting worse lately."

"What do the doctors say?"

"She's gonna keep slipping."

"I'm sorry, Harry." John knew he had to change the subject quicky. He didn't want his friend dwelling on his deceased wife, or his mother, for too long. "How's your grandson? Joey, right? He's got to be seventeen or eighteen now."

"Yeah. He just graduated high school."

"Is he going to college?"

"You'd have to ask him. We're not exactly on speaking terms right now."

"I don't want to pry," John said.

"He blames me for his grandmother's death. And there's other shit."

"Why the hell is that? The kid knows a drunk driver was responsible for that, right?"

"Yeah. But I had a few beers that night at the restaurant, so the boy figures I'm to blame, too, I guess."

John didn't see this coming when he made the phone call: his friend was in pain, no matter how hard Harry tried to hide it. John was beginning to wish he hadn't called.

"How's Jenny and the kids?" said Harry.

"Jenny's doing well. So are the kids."

"Good to hear."

"What's with the beard, Harry? I don't recall you ever sporting one."

"Too busy to shave. So, what are you doing in town?"

"I'm consulting for the Bureau. You heard about the bombing at the courthouse, I'm sure."

Harry stiffened. He hadn't even considered the possibility that his friend was in town to investigate the bombing. "Yeah, I heard about it," he said. "Thought you were retired from the Bureau."

"Officially, I am, but I still assist in the occasional investigation. I'm what you might call a consultant."

"If you still enjoy the work, what the hell, huh?"

"It keeps the blood flowing."

"Any leads yet?" Harry said.

John smiled. "I just got to town a few hours ago. Besides, I can't talk about an ongoing investigation."

Harry leaned in towards John. "It's just me and you here, Johnny. We go back, what, about fifty years? C'mon."

"Just between you and I and the walls, we know it was Semtex. The bomber laid enough of the stuff to take down the building, but he screwed up. He didn't set off all the explosives."

Still nervous, Harry chuckled. "Not a criminal mastermind you're looking for, huh?"

"You would have never made a mistake like that, Harry. I remember watching you work with Semtex. You were an artist with the stuff."

"So, who you looking at?"

"I think we're looking at a lone gunman, so to speak. Some guy with an axe to grind with the legal system. It's just a hunch."

Hearing that, Harry began to perspire slightly as he shifted in his recliner. He knew it was time to steer the conversation in another direction before sweat started to gush out of him like Old Faithful. "You ever think about the old days, Johnny?"

"The good times we had with the guys, sure. But the rest…"

"Yeah, I know. Hey, remember the trip to the island? We sure raised some hell, didn't we?"

"I'll never forget it, buddy. And you're the reason we were there. You saved my life."

"Oh, yeah. Lieutenant Radner."

"That crazy bastard was going to shoot me that day. I saw it in his eyes. He would have killed me if you hadn't knocked him out."

"I just needed an excuse to hit the asshole. To tell you the truth, I wasn't even thinking about you at the time," Harry said.

Harry winked and both men shared a hearty laugh. "You took a bullet for me that day. How's the knee?" John said.

"It's still attached."

"I'll never be able to pay you back for saving my life, Harry. Not in a million years."

Harry waved his friend off. "That's what friends do for each other."

"Palawan was a blast," John said. "What a beautiful island."

"I took Patsy there for our tenth anniversary. We stayed in Narra."

"You did? That's right on the coast, isn't it?"

"Yeah."

"Did she like it?"

"She loved it. After we both retired, we were gonna see the rest of this country from coast to coast. And after that she wanted us to spend the rest of our lives on the island."

"What did you want, Harry?"

"I was gonna propose we spend half the year there and the other half here. I even bought a villa in Narra. It was gonna be a surprise retirement gift for her."

John hung his head in sorrow. "I'm really sorry."

Harry shrugged and smiled as he fought off the urge to cry. "That's life, huh?"

John suddenly wanted to leave. Very badly. He looked at his watch.

"How long are you in town for?" Harry said.

"That's hard to say. Hey, I overheard something about the War Chiefs. Isn't that the local baseball team?"

"Yeah. They were a double-A club called the Lakota War Chiefs. They played at Sioux Stadium."

"Played?"

"They're not the War Chiefs anymore, John. Some people bitched the name was racist and oppressive, so the town council changed the team's name, the stadium's name, and some assholes tore down a statue of Little Hawk that was in front of the stadium, too."

"I don't recognize that name."

"He was an uncle of Crazy Horse. He died fighting for his people. The town erected a statue of him at the stadium to honor him and the Sioux tribes."

"I heard a couple of the locals talking about it at the diner. Damn shame if you ask me."

"The War Chiefs name ain't racist. And neither was the statue. It was a tribute to the man and his people," Harry said.

"I'm betting the people who tore it down don't know that or don't even give a damn if it's true. Some people are looking for racism around every corner these days. They probably tore it down because they figured if white people erected the statue, it had to be a racist act. And because they could get away with it," John said.

Harry stiffened as he sat up. "Little Hawk fought for his people. He was a warrior," he said. "That statue's been in front of the stadium for over twenty years. And the high school's nickname was the Chieftains, and they took that away, too." Harry slammed a fist into the recliner's armrest. "They had no fuckin' right!"

John eyes widened. He was taken aback by Harry's rage. "I read a report about the incident," John said. "It was a group called TID. It's an acronym for Tear it Down. Apparently, they've set up shop here in town."

"TID, huh? I had a run-in with someone from a group called BID last week. Some crazy bitch showed up at my door trying to get me to sign a petition. She told me BID stands for Burn It Down, as in the entire country. Then she said something about cancelling me, whatever the hell that means."

"It means they're going to try to make your life a living hell because you don't agree with them. Or because you pissed them off. Or you said something that they didn't like. They're pretty easily offended. Or they pretend to be."

"They sound like a bunch of whiny-ass brats," Harry said.

"And fairly-well organized, whiny-ass brats. Apparently, TID brought in people from the city to tear the statue down."

"Any of 'em get arrested yet?"

"There was video footage of the statue being torn down on some social media sites. It would be easy enough to round them up and charge them. But with the current political climate? No, I seriously doubt that they'll make any arrests," John said.

"The current political climate? What the hell does that mean?"

"I'll give you an example. A while back, a mob tore down a statue of Ulysses S. Grant at the Golden Gate Park in San Francisco. These 'social justice warriors' didn't care that Grant led the Union Army to victory over the Confederacy in the Civil War, assisted in the Reconstruction, fought the Ku Klux Klan, and advocated for the Fifteenth Amendment. To these assholes, the general was a symbol of oppression because he married into a slave-owning family, so none of the good things he did matters to them, apparently.”

“Damn,” Harry said.

“It gets better. When the ‘Frisco Police arrived on the scene, they didn’t intervene. The mob pelted the police with everything that wasn’t nailed down, but there were no arrests made.”

“Why the hell didn’t the cops do anything, John?”

“I’m assuming they were told to stand down by the higher-ups and the politicians. It happened in California, so that should tell you something.”

“Is this what we fought for? So, people can pull this shit and get away with it?”

“Some people just hate America, my friend. They believe it’s evil. They want to erase our history, deny it, or rewrite it to conform to their political beliefs. They’re trying a myriad of ways to undermine this country. And if sane and good people don’t fight back, this country is screwed. It’s a brave new world. Wear a helmet.”

An uneasy silence followed as Harry sat there and sulked. John looked at his watch again. “I should be on my way,” he said as he got up off of the sofa. Harry followed him to the front door. When they stepped onto the sidewalk, Harry stopped and stared at the ground, and John turned to face him. “How about we get dinner while I’m in town?” But Harry wasn’t listening. Rage and disgust gripped him as he thought about the town council’s decision to rename the town’s baseball team. And thinking about Little Hawk’s statue being so unceremoniously torn down ate at him as well. “Harry?”

“Huh? Yeah. That’d be great, John.”

Harry walked with John, then he stopped at the curb. John kept walking towards his car as Harry opened his mailbox. A novelty, coiled snake sprung out of the box and launched itself at the big man. “Shit!” Harry bellowed as he tripped over his feet and landed on his rear end. John turned around in time to see Harry get back to his feet. “Dammit, Sloan!” Harry roared.

He grabbed the mailbox with both hands and yanked on it, snapping the wooden support post in half in the process.

John was awe struck at the physical feat he had just witnessed. Even from more than ten feet away, he could almost feel Harry's rage. "You okay, Harry?"

Harry gave John a sarcastic smile. "Fuckin' great, John!" Harry effortlessly carried the mailbox, and the attached broken post, to the far edge of his lawn. Stopping there, he launched it ten feet into the air, and it landed on Charlie's front lawn. Satisfied with his effort, he turned to face John, who stood there, dumbfounded. Harry pointed to Charlie's house. "The old man next door likes to pull a prank on me now and then. He's a real fuckin' card. Was good seeing you, John." Harry snorted as he stomped up his front steps. John trembled slightly as he got into his car.

31

Harry stepped into the house, sat down and drew in eight or ten deep breaths, but the anger- reducing technique didn't work this time. He was still seething and looking for a fight. He got on his laptop and checked out the TID website. The group planned to meet at Higgins Park at six p.m. to protest against the basketball courts, swing sets, jungle gyms and park benches that had been built years ago by a company owned by a white contractor. The group was thirsty for more social justice, diversity, equity and inclusion, even if it meant that the townsfolk would be excluded from enjoying the park's amenities. He made a few phone calls to his Brownshirt minions and told them to pass the word. The social justice warriors from TID were going to have unexpected company.

***

At six p.m., Harry stood in the Higgins Park parking lot, looking skyward. The skies were overcast, and the local weatherman had called for rain by mid-afternoon, but none had fallen. Harry was hoping for rain. He wanted the park to be empty so he could turn his men loose on the TID group without kids witnessing the fight. His plan was to call the police when the two groups faced off and fought, have them get arrested, then hope that the resulting media coverage would awaken the town by exposing the two groups and their odious goals. But when he looked around the park and saw families barbequing and children playing on the swings and the jungle gym, he knew he had to change the game plan.

Fifteen members of the B.O.A. stood behind Harry and waited. They ranged in age from eighteen to seventy. Harry turned around and looked the men over as if he were reviewing troops. "Nobody brought any weapons, right?" Stefan looked away from Harry, sheepishly. "Hiding something, boy?"

Harry spun Stefan around, pulled up his shirt and found a pair of nun-chucks stuffed into the boy's waistband. He grabbed them and tossed them at Stefan. "Get rid of these," Harry said. "Now!" Stefan pouted as he walked to his car. Harry looked the men over again. "Anyone else packing?"

The men said "no" in unison. "Better not be," Harry barked. "There's kids around." Harry looked at Hans, whose fists were clenched and ready for battle. "You consult with your doctor before the rumble, Hans?"

"I can still kick some ass," Hans said.

Harry smiled and patted Hans' shoulder. "I'll bet you can. But you've got a woman now. You don't want her knowing you're getting into trouble. There'd be hell to pay, right?"

Hans mulled it over. He conceded Harry's point by taking a few steps back behind the group. "Good man," Harry said. He turned and caught sight of a group of about thirty people from the TID organization, chanting slogans and carrying TID banners, marching towards the middle of the park. One sign read: **Whitey Built these Swing Sets.** Another read: **What the White Man Built, We Will Tear Down.** A few men in the group were carrying large duffel bags.

As Stefan returned to the group, he pointed at the TID mob. "Let's bust some heads!" he said.

The other members of the group shook their fists and grunted in agreement. General Patton appeared at Harry's side, nearly giving the big man a heart attack. "Hell, yeah. Finally, a soldier with some balls!" As Harry was about to respond to the general, he realized that his men would think he was crazy if they saw him conversing with someone he wasn't even sure existed. "They sure as hell would, soldier," Patton said. "The kid's right. Let's bust some heads!"

Trying hard to ignore the general, Harry turned to face Stefan. He grabbed the boy by the shirt and pulled him close. "We don't bust heads with kids around. Got it?" Stefan gulped and nodded, then Harry let him go. "Wanna know why we're here?" Harry said, addressing all the men. "'Cause these assholes are gonna try tearing down the playground equipment."

"Why they doing that?" Karl said.

"'Cause the stuff was built by a white man. I told you guys they hate white people. Us included."

"So, what the hell we gonna do, then?" Stefan said.

Harry turned and watched as the TID protesters reached the swing sets. Several of the male protesters dropped large duffel bags onto the ground, unzipped them and pulled out sledgehammers and pry bars. A man approached the group. "What's going on here?" he said.

"We're setting things right," a TID protester said, handing the man a TID flier.

"Setting what right?" the man said.

"These swing sets were built by the White Man for the White Man. They're oppressive and not inclusive. Read the flier." The TID members chanted as they marched around the area, "Tear it down!"

Harry turned to his men. "It's time. Men, let's show those bastards who owns this town!"

"How the hell do we do that if we can't kick their asses?" Karl said.

"Just start walking like you got a purpose."

"Seriously?" Stefan said.

"Yeah, seriously. When they see you badasses coming, they'll run like the cowards they are." Harry thrust his fist in the air. "Who are we?!" The men stood mute, as if they were just asked a trick question that stumped them. "We are BOA!" Harry bellowed. "We are BOA!"

Harry began to march. The men chanted, "We are BOA!" as they followed behind the big man. As they neared the swing sets, one of the male TID members saw them coming. "Oh, shit," the man said. The other TID protesters stopped chanting and lowered their banners when they caught sight of the Brownshirts closing in on them. Park-goers gathered from a safe distance and watched.

"We are BOA!" Harry's men roared as they formed a semi-circle around the TID members holding the tools near the swing sets. The Brownshirts clenched their fists, glared, and snorted. The TID members looked at each other, all of them wondering what to do. A young male shouted, "We are TID!"

"Whatcha are is dead meat if you don't walk away right now," Harry said. Tools were dropped and banners lowered before every member of the TID group vacated the park, quickly. The crowd of onlookers cheered their departure.

***

Back at the rec hall, Harry stood in the walkway and shook hands with every one of his fellow B of A members before they entered the building. When the last member walked past him, Harry closed the front door and followed the young man inside. He was met with a cheer as he strode into the hall. The men saluted Harry. "Sieg Harry!" they roared.

Harry raised his arm, and the men came to attention. "Did you see those pussies run? Did you?!" The men cheered. "And did you hear the people cheer? Did you?!" There was hooting and more cheers from the men. Again, Harry raised his arm, and once again there was silence. "You take a country with an army! You keep a country when you win the hearts and minds of the people!"

The men howled their approval. Harry knew at that moment that the group would do anything for him. "Last one to the bar is a rotten Bolshevik!" he said. The men laughed as they followed their leader to the bar. Just as the men started to chug beer and sing a song of victory, Harry quieted them. "Anyone here know anything about Semtex?" he said. The men fell silent. It was the response Harry hoped for. "Well, you're gonna learn," Harry said.

***

On his way home from the rec hall, Harry got a call from Ken Burton. "Hi, Ken."

"Can we meet, Harry?"

"Sure. Where?"

"My office okay?"

"I can be there in fifteen minutes."

"I'll see you there."

***

At Jay's Diner, Harry got out of his truck and saw Ken walking his way. The men shook hands. "What's the story, Ken?"

"My associate loaded enough kiddie porn on the asshole's computer to sink a ship. Just let me know when you want me to make the call to the cops."

"Will do." Harry gave an envelope stuffed with cash to Ken. "Thanks for your help."

"Thanks, Harry. Don't forget about me if you or a friend ever need my help," Ken said.

"Matter of fact, I do need you again. You say your associate's really good with computer shit, right?"

"My guy can hack a lady's panties off with a couple of keystrokes. What do you need?" Harry showed Ken a picture of Ze on his phone. "This a missing persons situation?" Ken said.

"In a way, yeah. I want her to disappear."

"I'm not a hit man, Harry."

"Didn't mean it that way. Her name's Ze. She's been making my

182

life miserable. I want her to pay for it."

"Any idea how you want it done?"

"I read about a guy who lost his job just 'cause people online found out he wore blackface at a Halloween party. Figured we could maybe do the same to her."

Ken looked over Ze's picture closely. "She looks mean. If she's causing you problems, I'm betting she's from out of town, right?"

"Pretty damn sure she is, Ken."

"I'm getting tired of these assholes. Yeah, my guy could photoshop this picture, put her in blackface and upload it to the Internet in his sleep."

"It's kinda scary what people can do with a computer these days, ain't it?"

"Technology cuts both ways, Harry. It's all about how people use it. I'll give you a discount on this one. How's two-hundred sound?"

Harry pointed at the envelope in Ken's hand. "It's already in there. Plus, a little extra."

Ken smiled as he shook Harry's hand. "Thanks," he said. He started to walk away, then stopped and turned. "Remind me to never piss you off, Harry." Harry smiled as he waved goodbye.

*** *** ***

When he got home, Harry went online and created a handful of new email accounts, then he went to the TID website. Scrolling down to the bottom of the page, he left a series of comments, each under different screennames, for the organization to ponder. One read: *Was at the park today and saw your "men" about to tear down defenseless playground equipment. And when they were confronted by some real men, men that could fight back, they ran away. Bunch of pussies you got working for you. The leader of this group oughta be ashamed. If this is all you got, get the hell out of our town. We've got enough women already.*

Harry had accomplished a lot today. He slept well that night.

***

The next morning, Tim Baxter, the president of the local TID chapter, sat behind his desk on the second floor of the town's old library, reading some of the comments Harry had left on the TID website. Ralph Simmons, a beefy young man and the organization's top thug, stepped into the office. Tim gestured for him to take a seat, then he scowled at Ralph. "So, you're telling me the playground equipment at the park is still intact?"

Ralph squirmed in his chair. "We got ambushed by some of the locals, Tim."

"Word around town is you and the rest turned tail and ran."

"I was ready to fight, but the others went chicken shit on me. What the hell was I supposed to do?"

"You're supposed to be a leader. You should have stood your ground. You made the organization look bad, Ralph. You made us look weak." Ralph lowered his head in shame. "We're supposed to tear down the statue of that Kraut in the town square next week. We can't look weak to the local rubes again. Do you understand?"

"We need more men, Tim."

"Then hire some goons."

"Goons?"

"Yeah, goons. Go to the Supply Depot and round up some illegals."

"You mean undocumented peoples?"

"What's with the p.c. shit, Ralph? We doing a press conference here?" Tim didn't wait for an answer to his rhetorical query. "I don't give a shit what you call them. Offer them twenty bucks a man. And if that's not enough, tell them we'll grant them citizenship, too."

"Citizenship? Seriously?"

Tim sneered at Ralph. "No, not seriously. But tell them that, anyway. Now get the hell out of my sight.”

32

Later that afternoon, Harry went to the basement, opened the padlock on the storage room door, and closed it behind him. He pulled two burner cell phones out of a bag and opened up one of the phones to expose its internal circuit board. He soldered two wires to the circuit board and closed the phone's casing, making sure not to pinch the wires. Then he hooked the other ends of the wires to a blasting cap, plugged the cap into a quarter pound of Semtex, and pulled an old, nondescript cigar box off the shelf and placed the homemade bomb into it.

He shut the storage room door, closed the lock, then yanked on it to ensure it was locked. He grabbed his car keys off the table, and twenty minutes later he was sitting across the street from Fred Lamont's office: a single-story building sitting on the corner of Main and Oak. He grabbed a pair of binoculars and scanned the office's interior. Fast Freddie, slouched in his chair, was talking on the phone. *Bastard*, Harry thought as he swept the binoculars from one side of the office to the other.

He eyed a bookcase that ran the length of the far wall. It was filled with books and pictures, and it looked like the perfect place to store the cigar box. No one would even notice it until it was too late. Harry got out of his van, walked up the street, turned at the corner, and continued down the adjacent alleyway. Seeing no foot traffic coming or going, he casually strolled down the alley and slowed when he saw the rear entrance to the building.

Reaching the back entrance, he looked it over. He saw a sturdy, steel security door, but figured the lock would be easy enough to pick. Harry assumed that the building had an alarm system, but that didn't matter. He planned on being in and out of the office long before the authorities arrived. He returned to his van and drove to Sam's Saloon. After drinking a few beers with some of the regulars, he drove home. Once there, he turned off his phone and climbed into bed, hoping to sleep. He knew he had to be wide-eyed and alert later that night.

***

Just after three a.m., Harry awoke. He gulped down two cups of black coffee, then grabbed a duffel bag off of the table on his way out the front door. As he started up his van, he was barely startled when he saw that General Patton was riding shotgun.

"Hot damn, Harry, it's good to see you back in action," the general said. "What's our target tonight?"

"The scumbag lawyer," he said.

"We gonna kill him?"

Harry didn't respond as he drove on. Ten minutes later, he pulled his van into a parking lot three blocks away from Fast Freddie's office. Patton opened the duffel bag and pulled out a cigar box.

"What the hell is this?"

Harry grabbed the box from the general. "That's a bomb."

"No shit? How do you detonate the damn thing?"

"You'll see." Harry grabbed a ski mask and a tool bag before getting out of his truck.

"You're going to kill this bastard, right?"

"Nope. I'm just getting a little revenge."

"Pussy," Patton said. With the general at his side, Harry made his way towards the office's alleyway. As he walked, he wondered if anyone could see the general besides himself.

"That's a negative," Patton said. Turning into the alleyway, Harry slipped on a pair of gloves, then pulled the ski mask over his head. When he reached the back entrance of Fast Freddie's office, he went to a knee and dug through his tool bag. He unzipped his lock pick set and pulled out a rake pick and a torque wrench, then he went to work on the lock. "You know how to pick locks?"

"I learned how on the Internet," Harry said.

"What the hell's the Internet?"

"Quiet," Harry said as he tried to listen for the sound of the lock's pins dropping.

"Tread lightly, soldier. You're talking to a four-star general here."

Harry fumbled with his tools as he jammed and poked at the lock. The general squatted down next to him, getting into Harry's personal space. "Stop crowding me."

"Or what?" General Patton said. "You sure you want to lock horns with this bull?"

Harry sneered at the general as he kept fumbling with the lock. "I'm trying to do something here."

The lock's pins finally dropped. Harry packed up his tools, got to his feet, opened the door, and turned on a flashlight. A silent alarm was triggered. He was on the clock now. He strode through a small reception room, pushed open a door, and found the office in only a matter of seconds. He swung the flashlight to his right and caught sight of the bookcase. Harry placed the cigar box behind a row of books on the top shelf so he could come back and retrieve it in case something went wrong and the bomb failed to detonate. Less than one minute later, he was back in the alley. The general was waiting for him.

"Well?" Patton said.

"Well, what?" Harry said, as he started to walk.

"Where the hell's the explosion?"

"It's coming. Hold your urine."

The general followed closely behind Harry. When they reached the side street, Harry pulled off the ski mask and tucked it into his tool bag. He pulled out a burner phone and continued down the side street towards his van. Fifty feet away from the mouth of the alleyway, he stopped and punched a number into the phone. In the cigar box perched on the shelf in Fast Freddie's office, the cell phone's display screen lit up, announcing an incoming call. Electricity surged through the wires connected to the phone's circuit board and ran to a blasting cap, which set off a quarter pound of Semtex. The explosion shattered the stillness of the night. Hearing it, General Patton looked back and saw brick and glass littering the street.

"Wasted damn munitions," the general said, looking Harry's way.

But Harry was already halfway down the block. Just like the courthouse bombing, he knew he couldn't stick around to admire his work. Nearing the van, he was surprised when he saw that the general was already sitting in it. "How the hell...?" Harry mumbled.

"Never mind that."

Harry hauled himself into the van. As he pulled away from the curb, he smiled. But the general scowled. "You proud of yourself?" Patton said.

"Why wouldn't I be?"

"You blew up another building. Wow."

"I took action. What's the problem?"

"What's the problem? There's no body count."

"Nobody needs to die."

"You killed in Vietnam, soldier. You can do it again."

"That was different. That was -"

"Was, what?"

"It was kill or be killed over there."

Patton eyeballed Harry "It was against the Nazis, too. But you're swapping spit with a group of 'em now. I lost a lot of men fighting those bastards. Your father fought those sons of bitches. He'd be real proud of you, you traitor."

Harry looked at the general but saw his dad instead. Unnerved, he jerked on the steering wheel, sending the van into the path of a big oak tree. He regained control just in time to avoid a collision. When he looked at the general again, Harry saw that he was gone. Still trembling, he slowly made his way home.

***

John Coleman climbed out of bed just after eight a.m., stretched his arms and legs, and yawned. His day had just begun, and he was already irritated. John's sleep was interrupted by a phone call from one of his field agents around five a.m. He was informed that a local attorney's office had been destroyed, and traces of Semtex were found at the site. Now there was another bombing for him to deal with. He thought about climbing back into bed for a little more sleep, but when his phone rang, he knew he had to answer it. It was the boss. "Hi, Hank."

"That's 'sir' to you, John. You sound tired. Getting too old for the job?"

Kiss my wrinkled ass, Hank. "I got a call in the middle of the night. I had a hard time falling back to sleep."

"Another bombing. A lawyer's office, right?"

"You've already heard about it?"

"Someone's got to be on top of things. What do we know?"

We both know you're an asshole, Hank. "Our bomber, if it's the same guy or group, likes Semtex."

"Is it untraceable again?"

"I won't know until I get the report. But I'm betting there were no tags or chips again, just like the courthouse."

"Need any more resources?"

"I think we're good for now. But that's your call."

"I'm thinking about bringing in another team to assist. I'm already catching heat from the higher-ups. They think you may not be up for this one John."

The hell they do. "Do what you have to do, Hank."

"We'll see. Keep your nose to the grindstone, old timer. Make us

190

proud."

The line went dead. John closed his eyes as he did a slow simmer. Henry was the worst boss John had ever dealt with, a ladder climber who had used any opportunity - or person – to claw his way to the position he held now. *Screw you, Hank, you prick.*

John sat back, closed his eyes, and thought about his old friend. *Are you the bomber, Harry?* Even though he had no evidence yet, Harry fit the profile. He had a temper, he was an expert with explosives, and John sensed that there was something off - or different - about the friend he thought he knew pretty well. *Life can change people,* he mused. Then he remembered the letter sitting on the coffee table in Harry's living room when he dropped by to see him. He didn't know the details of the letter, but John was sure he had seen a court seal on the envelope.

Having trouble with the law, Harry? John hoped not. He considered Harry to be a good friend despite the fact that the two had lost touch over the years. Harry was a good man, and he had saved his life, but as head of the Bureau's Behavioral Analysis Unit for the last fifteen years before his retirement, John possessed the experience needed to come to this conclusion: there was a high probability that Harry was the bomber.

That thought disheartened him. While showering, he made a mental list of his itinerary for the day. And he knew he would have to pay Harry another visit at his home to snoop around. *I hope I'm wrong about you, my friend. Please let me be wrong.*

33

Harry Blake Jr., now a full-fledged combat engineer, was on his second tour of duty in Vietnam. He was attached to the 1st Battalion, 3rd Marine Regiment at the Khe Sanh Combat Base, an outpost south of the DMZ in South Vietnam. General William Westmoreland, the commander of U.S forces in Vietnam, saw the base as a bulwark against the advancing NVA[3] and the Viet Cong, and an airstrip was built at the base that U.S. forces used to fly recon missions over the Ho Chi Minh Trail, the main artery that the Viet Cong used to transport men and weapons into South Vietnam.

The U.S. Marines stationed at Khe Sanh had been under attack for weeks by the Viet Cong, who shelled the base with artillery, mortar and rocket attacks on a near-continuous basis. The order finally came from on high: the base was to be abandoned, and everything that wasn't nailed down was to be taken or destroyed so that the V.C. couldn't reap anything of value.

1st Lieutenant George Easton swept the outer perimeter of the base with his binoculars as Marines loaded armaments, communication and hospital equipment onto an ever-moving convoy of cargo trucks. Lance Corporal Harry Blake Jr. pushed his way through a throng of infantrymen who were tired, shell shocked, and thrilled that they were going to be anywhere but here come the end of the week, or, God willing, sooner. The corporal stopped when he saw Lieutenant Easton turn to face him.

"You my sapper, Marine?" Easton said.

---

[3]NVA In the context of the Vietnam War (1955–1975), the army was referred to as the North Vietnamese Army

"I am, sir. Lance Corporal Blake, sir."

"We're pulling up stakes, Corporal. My orders are to blow this place to hell so Charlie gets squat when we leave. Your mission is to make me happy and blow it to hell. Can you do that, Corporal?"

"Sir, yes, sir."

"Then get to it. Start with the command-and-control bunker."

Corporal Blake gave the bunker a cursory glance. It was pockmarked with enemy shells, and in its present state, it seemed to the corporal that a gentle breeze could topple the structure. "Looks like the Cong started the job for me, Lieutenant."

"You a wiseass, Corporal?"

"No, sir," the corporal said as he stiffened up.

"Then stow that shit and get it done, ASAP. We'll try to cover you."

"Cover me, sir?"

"The VC's got the entire area surrounded with beaucoup artillery, and they're raining hell on us. Carry on."

Within half an hour, Lance Corporal Blake had planted enough Semtex in the bunker to bring it down. He rolled a spool of detonating wire from the interior of the bunker and set it on the ground fifty feet from the structure's entrance. Lieutenant Easton, sweeping his binoculars to the south, caught sight of a squad of Viet Cong infantry manning a battery of Soviet-made 122 mm howitzers. Corporal Blake didn't hear Easton mumble, "Oh, shit." The lieutenant dropped his binoculars. "Incoming!" he shouted. "Cover!"

Every soldier within a hundred-foot radius heard the lieutenant's order, and as a barrage of artillery shells rocketed toward the base, they scurried for shelter. But Corporal Blake had re- entered the bunker to double check the connections on the Semtex. A high-pitched shriek filled the air just before an artillery shell slammed into the roof of the command-and-control bunker, and the corporal was knocked unconscious by a falling chunk of the cement ceiling.

***

When Corporal Blake awoke, he found himself lying in a bed at a military hospital. His head ached and his vision was blurry, but he could make out rows of beds lining both walls, and every bed seemed to be occupied, as far as he could tell. As the corporal shook loose the cobwebs, Doctor Weiland, favoring one leg, walked past the corporal's bed and saw that he was awake. The doctor checked the chart for the soldier's name, then he smiled. "Welcome, Corporal Blake," the doctor said.

"Where am I?"

"The Forward Aid Station outside of Khe Sanh."

"How long have I been here?"

"Two days now. You're being treated for a concussion. You're lucky to be alive, young man." The doctor checked the gauze wrapped around the corporal's head. "You've got thirty stitches up here, so no head-butting any officers for a while, understand?"

"Sure thing, Doc."

The doctor caught sight of a man making his way down the aisle. "Speaking of officers..."

Lt. Colonel Will Duncan, a stocky, scar-ravaged man, strode up to the corporal's bed and looked the patient over. Corporal Blake tried to sit up as he saluted the colonel. "At ease, Corporal. How's the head?"

"Fine, sir. Just got my bell rung, is all."

"He's not fine, Lieutenant," the doctor said. "He's got a grade three concussion. We're -"

"That's Lieutenant Colonel, Doc."

Doctor Weiland didn't give a damn about rank at this point. Not after watching five soldiers die overnight, and not after being on the ass-end of a fourteen-hour shift. "We're going to transfer the corporal to Saigon for observation and more testing," he said.

The colonel shoved paperwork into the doctor's hand. "These orders say otherwise, Doc. Corporal Blake, as of zero- nine- hundred hours, is back on active duty."

As the doctor looked over the paperwork, the colonel turned to the Corporal Blake and stared at the boy like he would give him an unlubricated, full-fisted prostate exam if he didn't get the answer he wanted and expected. "We still need to take out the airstrip at Khe Sanh. Are you a team player, son? Do you want to make your country proud?"

"Yes, sir."

"That's what I wanted to hear," the colonel said, swiping the paperwork from the doctor's hands.

Doctor Weiland stood nose to nose with the colonel. "He is not fit for duty," he said.

The colonel scowled. "If you don't take two steps back, you won't be either, Doc." The doctor stood his ground, and the colonel smiled. "Suppose you tend to the other fighting men here. The ones that really need you. Run along now."

The doctor knew he was fighting a losing battle. The release papers confirmed that. He set a hand on Corporal Blake's shoulder. "Keep your head down, Corporal."

Corporal Blake saluted him. "Will do," he said.

"On your feet, Marine. We're rolling," the colonel said.

When the corporal got to his feet, dizziness overtook him, and he fell to the floor. The doctor was about to help the boy up when the colonel pushed him aside. Then, he looked at Corporal Blake and sneered. "You're not going yellow on me, are you, son?" the colonel said.

The corporal slowly got to his feet, "No, sir."

Doctor Weiland watched Corporal Blake follow the colonel out of the infirmary. The boy wobbled the entire way to the door. "Bastard," the doctor muttered.

***

Less than two hours later, the corporal found himself back at the Khe Sanh base. Barracks and bunkers were in shambles and still smoldering from artillery fire, and the outpost was a flurry of controlled chaos as Marines, still taking shelling from the Viet Cong, continued to empty the base of everything that could be stowed onto M-35 cargo trucks. Corporal Blake got out of a jeep and saluted Lieutenant Easton. "Reporting for duty, sir," he said.

The lieutenant pointed to the north end of the airstrip. "Your munitions are stacked up at the end of the strip. I'm giving you two PFC's[4] to help you, Corporal. They're cherries, and I don't want to hear shit about it."

The hairs on the corporal's nape stood on end as he surveyed the carnage all around him. "What about the Cong, sir?"

"What about 'em?"

"Why are we trying to blow the airstrip, Lieutenant? If the Cong take this base, they'll just rebuild it, right?"

"Because the brass says we blow it. You got a problem with that?"

"Sir, no, sir," the corporal said, as he saluted.

"Di di mau[5], Corporal!"

Corporal Blake humped it down a dirt embankment. He cringed at the sound of an artillery shell exploding just fifty feet from him. He reached the airstrip, and as he crouched down to pull a mine from its metal crate...

"Incoming!" Lieutenant Easton yelled. Within seconds, a barrage of shells rained down on the base. Corporal Blake scrambled for cover in a nearby trench, but before he could reach it, a shell exploded just to his left, and the shockwave knocked him unconscious as he hit the ground.

---

[4]Private First Class, an enlisted rank in the U.S. Military.

[5]Di di mau: "Hurry up" in Vietnamese.

***

When he came to, Corporal Blake once again found himself lying in a bed at the Forward Aid Station, and once again he saw Doctor Weiland standing over him. The doctor wasn't smiling this time around. "I thought I told you to keep your head down, Corporal."

"It was down. Down in the dirt," said the corporal, hoping to elicit a chuckle. But the doctor wasn't in the mood for levity.

"Corporal Blake, do you know what day it is?"

"Thursday?"

"It's Tuesday, Marine." The doctor sighed as he pulled a penlight out of his lab coat pocket and shone it in the corporal's eyes.

"That hurts," the corporal said, turning his head away.

Doctor Weiland tucked the penlight away and made a notation in the corporal's chart. "You've got another concussion, Corporal. I'm putting you on the bench."

"But, Doc -"

"Have you got a death wish, son? Are you really in a big hurry to return to combat duty?"

"You heard the colonel. They need me."

"Fuck the colonel."

"But the airstrip…"

"Fuck the airstrip, too, son. Even if we blow it up, the Viet Cong will rebuild it when they take the base."

"That's what I told the lieutenant."

"And what did he say?"

"He told me to follow my orders."

"You shouldn't have been out there, son. And your superiors knew that, but they don't give a shit." The doctor sat down at the foot of the bed. "Corporal, you've got your whole life ahead of you if you survive this hellhole. Then, what?"

"What do you mean?"

"Are you going to blindly obey everyone and anyone who tells you what to do for the rest of your life?"

"Guess it depends on who's giving the orders."

"You volunteered, right?"

"Yeah," said Harry.

"Why?"

"I wanted to fight the bad guys."

"Is that the real reason?"

"What do you mean?"

"Your father was in the military, right?"

"How'd you know?"

"Was he a domineering man?"

"Guess you could say that. Hey, what do you mean, was he?"

"I've seen your file, Corporal. I know your father's deceased. I'm betting you enlisted because your dad would have wanted you to join the service, right?"

"Maybe."

"Maybe? Bullshit, son. You're on your second tour, right?" Harry nodded. "Have you got a girl back home?"

Harry smiled. "Yeah. Her name's Patsy. We got married before my first tour."

"Go home to her, son. You've done your part."

"You want me to turn tail and run? You want me to abandon my buddies?"

"I want you to get home in one piece, soldier. You've taken two blows to the head within a couple of days. Two serious blows. God only knows the damage that's been done long term. You want to press your luck?"

"I can't leave my buddies behind."

"Your loyalty to your friends is noble, son, but do you want to go home to your wife in a body bag?"

"Course not. But it's my duty to stay. What do you know about fighting a war, Doc?"

"Have you ever heard of a conflict called the Korean War?"

"You fought?" the corporal said.

"Until I couldn't fight anymore." The doctor pulled up his pant leg and tapped on his prosthetic leg.

Corporal Blake's resentment towards the doctor immediately turned to sympathy. "Shit. I didn't know. How'd it happen?"

"Following fucked-up orders and charging up a hill with no strategic value is how." The doctor clutched Corporal Blake's arm as he looked him in the eye. "Be wary of people who throw orders around; some of them are incompetent, some have hidden agendas, and some of them haven't earned the power they have, son." The doctor limped away.

34

Harry rolled over and squinted at the alarm clock; it was just past noon. Demolishing Fast Freddie's office the night before kept him from getting to bed until almost five a.m., and his nocturnal activities were beginning to take a toll on his body clock, but his "things-to-blow- up" list was shortening, one building at a time. He shifted his weight towards the edge of the bed and managed to set his feet on the floor in one motion. He yawned and scratched his beard before getting to his feet. The adrenaline that surged through him the night before was long gone. He felt achy now, but he smiled just the same as he lumbered down the stairs and into the kitchen.

After downing two cups of black coffee, he stepped into the backyard. A mild, sunny day greeted him, and he was feeling pretty damn good about himself today. Things were getting accomplished.

"It's good to get things done," said a voice coming from the adjacent backyard. "Depending on what those things are, of course."

Harry shaded his eyes from the sun's glare as he tried to locate the person behind the voice. "Over here," Hien said as he waved hello.

Harry limped slightly as he made his way across the yard. He was almost panting by the time he reached the fence.

"You're not in the shape you once were in, Harry."

"Don't have to tell me twice…"

"Hien."

"Hien, right. Sorry. The memory ain't what it used to be, either."

"The price we pay for getting old, yes?"

Harry nodded. He hated that he couldn't do the things he used to do effortlessly when he was young. And he hated admitting it to anyone, too.

"That's just your misplaced pride, my friend. It brings no shame to you to admit such things. It is merely the cycle of life."

"How the hell do you know what I was thinking, Hien?"

"Some men of your age feel anger and bitterness for losing their youthful vigor."

"You look about my age. Don't it bother you?"

"When one truly understands the cycles of life, one can find it easier to accept the changes that occur as we age. And there is something so much better than this life awaiting all of us."

"Know that for a fact, do ya?" Harry said. His mood began to sour. He didn't know if there was an afterlife. He just knew that he'd spend the rest of this life without his beloved wife and daughter. Suddenly, he was no longer interested in prolonging this conversation. "Well, got things to do, Hien."

"I'm sorry if I've touched a nerve, Harry. That was not my intention. Please forgive me."

"There's nothing to apologize for." Harry waved goodbye as he walked towards his house.

"Patsy misses you very much."

Harry stopped and turned. "What did you say?"

"I said that your wife misses you a great deal. She says that you gave her many years of happiness, and that she's worried about you."

"Is that a joke? 'Cause I'm not laughing."

"I would not joke about such matters, Harry."

"What do you know about my wife?"

"I know her, and I know how she passed away. I'm very sorry about that."

Harry took a step back. *Get out of my head.* "Who the hell are you?"

"You already know who I am, my friend. Be at peace with yourself and all around you, please. We will hopefully speak again soon."

Hien bowed, then disappeared right before Harry's eyes.

"Who the hell are you?!" Harry shouted as he clutched the fence and yanked on it. "Come back! Come back, dammit!"

Harry waited but Hein didn't reappear. Instead, he heard Charlie shouting from his patio. "Harry, is that you? Who are you yelling at?" Harry waved the old man off as he marched back into the house.

***

Harry was sleeping in his recliner when the doorbell rang. He wasn't in the mood for company, unless it was his grandson coming by to see him, but Joey had a key to the house, and Harry wasn't about to change the locks on the boy, no matter their estranged relationship at the moment. He waited, hoping whoever was at the door would just leave. Then his phone rang. John Coleman's name appeared on his caller ID, so Harry picked up. "Hi, John."

"Are you home, Harry? Your truck's out front," John said.

"Yeah. I'm here."

"I'm at your front door."

"I'll be right there," Harry said. "Shit," he muttered under his breath. As fast as he could move, he descended the basement stairs and checked the storage room door to make sure the padlock was secure. Satisfied it was, he climbed the steps, and his bad knee nearly buckled as he reached the top step. He leaned against the wall to catch his breath. After about a minute, the pain subsided and when he got to the front door, he inhaled again and opened the door with a smile.

"Sorry 'bout the wait, John. C'mon in."

"If I'm interrupting something…"

"Not at all," Harry said, gesturing for John to sit. "Just let me get my coffee. Can I get you some?"

"I'm good. Thanks."

When Harry stepped into the kitchen, John stood up and looked the room over. He wasn't sure what it was he was looking for, but when Harry returned just moments later, he sat in his recliner and sipped his coffee. "I heard about another explosion in town. Maybe a ruptured gas line?" Harry said.

"Not likely, Harry."

"Okay. Important thing is nobody got hurt, right?"

"That's right. Hear about the Masters?" John said.

"The golf tournament?"

"Yeah, the golf tournament. They just renamed it."

"Why the hell they do that?"

"Apparently, the powers-that-be decided the term "masters" had too negative a connotation attached to it. The slavery thing. You know how it works these days. A few people get offended, or claim they are, then they scream and cry on social media. Then, P.R. departments panic, the sponsors panic, then the bigwigs cave in, and next thing you know, the Masters is no longer the Masters. Now they're going to call it 'The Tournament'."

"Is there something in the water? What the hell's the matter with these people?"

"It's political correctness, the cancel culture and wokeness, Harry. They're all cancers. And they're spreading."

"I read about a guy who went to a Halloween party dressed as a black rapper a while back. A picture of him showed up on that social media shit, and some people got on that social media thing and pissed and moaned that this guy was a racist, so he lost his job. A fuckin' costume cost the guy his job. How can that be possible, John?"

"It's a scary, new world we're living in. Gotta watch your step, and your mouth, these days."

"I read about safe spaces John. They're big on campuses these days, apparently. Bunch of kids cringing in fear when they hear something they don't like or agree with. And triggers -"

"Triggers are a legitimate psychological condition, but some people have appropriated its meaning so anyone can use the term these days for even the most trivial nonsense."

Harry sat back in his recliner. "I know about triggers, John. What's the other shit you mentioned? Wokeness and cancel, something?"

"The cancel culture. It's the latest version of the Salem Witch trials. And wokeness is… you should do some reading on the topics."

Harry wasn't interested in reading at this very moment. He wanted to know if his friend was any closer to making an arrest for the bombings. "Maybe I should, at that. So, what's going on with the investigation? Any new leads?"

"We're looking into the lawyer and the kind of cases he's handled. He seems to be a shady character. He's represented some real scum bags," John said.

"A courthouse and a lawyer's office? They could be related, huh?"

"I'm betting they are."

Harry sat up as he considered John's words. *Is he onto me?* A part of Harry really wanted to tell his friend that he was the man that the authorities were looking for. But another part of him was truly enjoying his nocturnal escapades, and telling John would put an end to that. And there was still more to do. "Why do I feel like you want to ask me where I was last night, John?"

John hit Harry with a disarming smile. "I'm assuming you were fast asleep. At our age, what the hell else would we be doing?"

Harry chuckled. He sensed that John knew more than he was letting on, and that troubled him, but he would have to settle for a stalemate at the moment. "So, with a second bombing, you gonna stick around town longer?"

"Seems so."

"We never grabbed that dinner."

"My fault there. We'll do that soon. Hey, how about giving me a tour of your castle? It's been about thirty years."

"Hasn't changed," Harry said, pointing in different directions.

"Living room, basement downstairs, bedrooms upstairs, yard in the back."

"Show me the place, Harry. C'mon." John got up and grabbed Harry by the arm and tried to hoist him up. "We could both use the exercise." Grudgingly, Harry dug himself out of the recliner and showed John around the first floor and then the upstairs. John took mental images of every room, hunting for anything out of the ordinary. After a quick look at the backyard, Harry led John down to the basement. John did another quick scan. To him, it looked like any other suburban, middle-class basement: sports memorabilia hung on the walls, there was a sofa, chairs and a wall-mounted, big screen TV.

And there was a padlock on the door to a room. "It's kinda messy down here, John. Didn't know I was doing tours today."

"The life of a bachelor. I remember those days." When Harry winced, John realized what he had just said. *Life of a bachelor.* "Shit, Harry. I didn't mean –"

"I know, John."

John pointed at the storage room. "What's with the lock? You hoarding old Playboys in there? Hiding them from Joey, maybe?"

"Nah, I got enough explosives in there to take out a small city, is all."

John chuckled. "Of course, you do, Harry." Harry led his friend back up the stairs. "I was hoping to see your mother before I left."

"She's probably next door at the boyfriend's."

"Seriously?"

"Yeah. He's a war vet named Charlie."

"Good for mom. Never too old, huh?"

As they stepped into the living room, Gertie walked through the front door. She scowled when she saw that John was wearing a suit. "This another shit-heel lawyer come to hassle you, sonny boy?"

"No, Mom. This is an old war buddy. Say hello to John."

John gently shook Gertie's hand. "You fought with my boy?" Gertie said.

"I did. It's a pleasure to see you again, Mrs. Blake."

Gertie smiled. "Any man that fought those commie bastards with my boy is welcome in my house. Did you feed your friend, Harry?"

Harry wanted this conversation to end. Now. "No, Ma. John needs to get to work."

"Horseshit. He's not leaving until he's had some of my meatloaf. Lemme just fire up the oven."

"Mom, it's nine a.m."

"It is? Where the hell did the day go?"

"I could use a cup of coffee," John said.

Harry wasn't happy to hear John wanted to stay, but he smiled just the same. "I'll grab you some," he said, heading for the kitchen.

Gertie took a seat next to John on the sofa. "So, you and my boy are friends, huh? How come I've never met you before?"

"We have met, Mrs. Blake. I spent a weekend here after Harry and I got back home. But that was a long time ago."

"You get home...ok?" she said.

"I did, thanks to your son. He saved my life over there."

"My Harry saved your life? No shit?"

Harry stepped back into the room with John's coffee. "Language, Ma."

"Oh, blow it out your ass, sonny boy. I'm too damn old to be putting on airs."

"Bravo, Mrs. Blake," John said.

"You can call me Gertie, young man. So, what do you do?"

"I'm semi-retired. I worked for the F.B.I. Now I consult for them."

"A G-Man, huh? Bet you've got some good stories. You one of the guys that got Dillinger?"

"That was a little before my time, Miss Gertie."

Gertie suddenly grew agitated. She grabbed a Kleenex and started to shred it into small pieces. Her smile disappeared as she stared at John.

"Gertie? Getting a little familiar here, aren't you? Harry, who the hell is this man, calling me by my given name? Why is he here?"

Harry hung his head, and John knew it was time to leave. He rose from the sofa. "I should get back to the office."

"I'll see you out," Harry said.

Harry grabbed his cane as he led John to the front door, then down the steps. They stopped when they reached the walkway. "The dementia, Harry?"

Harry nodded. "It's taking her a little at a time. One minute she's good, the next she's gone."

"I'm sorry."

"What the hell you gonna do, huh?"

John noticed the new mailbox near the curb in front of Harry's house. "See you replaced the old mailbox," he said.

"Yeah. I dumped the old one in the trash right after you left that day. I didn't want the old man to know I pitched the damn thing on his lawn." Harry pointed. "Speaking of the old man…"

Charlie stepped out his front door. "That you, Harry?" he said.

"Is that the boyfriend?" John said.

"That's him," Harry said. "Sloan, say hi to John, my old buddy."

Charlie waved hello as his cane guided him down his front steps. "Is he…?" John said.

"As a bat." Harry replied. Charlie approached the two men. "Mom's left the building again, Sloan. You wanna tag team her?"

"Of course," Charlie said. He extended a hand in John's general direction. "I'm Charlie."

"Pleasure, Charlie. I'm John. Harry tells me you're a vet."

"Am that, John." Charlie pointed to his eyes. "That's how I lost these."

"You never told me that, Sloan," said Harry.

"You never asked, you big lummox. You really call Harry a friend, John?"

John chuckled. "I do. He's good people. I'm betting you've got some great stories about the war. I'd love to hear some of them while I'm in town."

Charlie looked away. "No offense, but I don't care much for talking about the war. Not with civilians, anyway. I don't expect you to understand."

"I do understand. I fought in Vietnam with Harry. The big guy saved my life."

"Bullshit," Charlie said.

"It's true," John said. "He took a bullet in the knee protecting me. I'll tell you the story someday if you're interested."

"I may take you up on that. Been a pleasure, John. I'd better get my girl."

"Sure thing," John said, stepping aside and watching as Charlie stepped into the Blake house. "How long since your mom was diagnosed, Harry?"

"A few years now. Her doctor calls it amnestic MCI. I've got locks on half the stuff in the house so she can't get into things."

"Like the room in the basement?"

Harry nodded and smiled. "Can't have Mom playing with explosives, right?"

"I don't mean to scare you, but you know they think dementia's genetic, right?"

"Yeah, but I'm not worried about it," Harry said, tapping his head. "Got my own shit going on up there."

"One too many explosions, I'm betting. Are you getting any help from the V.A.?"

Harry shrugged. "I've had tests, meds, that kinda nonsense. Doesn't matter."

"How the hell can you say it doesn't matter? You earned all the help they can give you. All the guys do."

"It's too late for me, John. Too much damage's been done."

There was a long silence as John struggled to find the right thing to say to his friend, but he came up with nothing. Harry turned towards the front door. "I should get back in there. Mom can be a handful when she's like this."

"I understand. We'll talk soon. Good luck, Harry."

John got into his car and saw Harry wave goodbye before he grabbed the railing and pulled himself slowly up the steps. John hung his head for a moment, then he pulled away from the curb thinking how sad he felt for Harry and just how unfair life could be. But John knew that Harry was still his prime suspect in the bombings that had rocked the town, even though he had found nothing in the house but the padlocked basement room to bolster his suspicions. Then he remembered that Harry's mother had thought he was "another lawyer." *What the hell did that mean? You have legal problems, Harry? Maybe criminal ones?* John decided that it was time to do some digging into Harry's past, as much as it bothered him to do it.

***

Two hours after John left, Gertie was calm and back to being herself, so Charlie took her to his home and laid her down for a nap. Harry wanted his mother to stay with him for the rest of the day, but Charlie convinced him that she would be fine staying with him. And Harry, as always, had a hard time saying no to the old man. So, he pulled the lawnmower out of the shed, hoping that some busy work would soothe his foul mood.

As he cut the grass, he thought again about the town council's decision to rename his beloved baseball team, and the stadium that the team called home. *Did they put it up for a vote? Bettin' they didn't. Bastards.* For the hour it took him to mow the lawn, Harry's mind went over a list of all the things that were pissing him off these days. And the list was long. When he finished cutting the grass, he shoved the lawnmower aside like it had sprouted a mouth and insulted him.

Having nothing else to do, Harry decided to take John's advice and do some reading. After showering and having lunch, he sank into his recliner, opened up his laptop and got online. He wanted to learn more about some of the changes that were going on in his town and around the country.

His first stop was the Albrecht town website. After a bit of poking around, he managed to find the minutes from the town council's past few meetings. He read that the council had banned the song *Jingle Bells* from the grade school's Christmas pageant because it was possible that the song was first performed in a minstrel show in 1857. The school's principal agreed with the decision, saying the song would be replaced because it had "the potential to be controversial or offensive." And the Albrecht Central School District Superintendent agreed as well, saying, "we couldn't be more proud of our staff" in their ongoing effort "to be more culturally responsive, thoughtful and inclusive," adding that "this is not a political situation" and "was not an attempt to push an agenda." Harry shook his head in bemusement. *Jingle Bells is racist? Are they really serious?*

He went on to read that the town council, at the behest of the superintendent and the school district, also voted in favor of teaching Critical Race Theory to grades three through twelve, effective immediately. Having never heard the term before, Harry looked it up and learned that CRT was an academic and social movement based on tenets of Marxism. He dug deeper into the topic and found one of its updated definitions. This definition of Critical Race Theory maintained that many institutions in the U.S. were built on, and still enforced, systemic racism and oppression of people of color, and that this racism and oppression have a long history in the U.S., and that they are ongoing and driven by white supremacy. *White supremacy? Is the country run by the Ku Klux Klan?* Harry mused.

Harry read for nearly three more hours before taking a break to stretch, check his phone for any messages, and make supper. Ordinarily he would have thought about inviting his mother and Charlie over for dinner, but he was in no mood for company today. After eating, he poured himself a cup of coffee, sat back down and got back online. He read various articles about triggers, the cancel culture, the woke movement, micro-aggressions, and political correctness.

He read about a well-respected writer and Hollywood director, who had been in the movie business for decades, declare that he might never do another movie with the studio system ever again because of the p.c. climate and how it cast a pall over the entire movie making process. The director was quoted as saying: "You can't make a film without a sensitivity counselor these days. It's ridiculous."

He went on to read about writers, editors, commentators and people from various other professions who had been either censored, censured, or lost their jobs and reputations because they dared to go against the "prevailing wisdom" of the day. They dared to challenge the p.c. movement, and they paid for it dearly. Harry's blood pressure began to rise.

He poured over articles about the cancel culture and how it cost many decent people all across the country, and the world, their livelihoods and their reputations because so many companies and corporations - always posturing for image and marketing purposes - an article called it virtue signaling - were unwilling to stand up to the allegedly aggrieved and offended social justice warriors who wanted blood, and anyone's blood would do the trick.

He read about an ice cream maker that had dropped its decades-old logo of a smiling Eskimo child because the ice cream's parent company decided it was racist, and because the term Eskimo was considered derogatory by some people because the term meant "eater of raw meat." *Don't they actually eat raw meat? Does eating raw meat somehow make them bad? Do Eskimo people stay up at night worrying about this shit?*

He read one more article. It concerned a large cosmetics company that decided to remove the word "whitening," a word it had used for decades to describe the products' effect, from its skin lightening products because the word, seemingly almost overnight, offended some people. It occurred to Harry that some social justice warriors were people who thought that they knew what was best for everyone else. They apparently saw racism, injustice and unfairness around every corner and in every crevice.

And the "neo-woke," whom the day before seemed to be unoppressed, were suddenly offended and oppressed the moment they rolled out of bed one day, got online and read that they were indeed oppressed, but just didn't know it until social justice warriors on the Internet told them that they were.

Harry realized he couldn't swing a dead cat on the Internet without finding story after story about people who were suddenly oppressed, offended over trivial matters, or both. He also realized that all of these movements were ultimately about one thing: power. Tired and disgusted, he closed his laptop, washed his meds down with a healthy shot of bourbon, then crawled into bed.

35

The following morning, just after nine a.m., Harry was asleep when he felt something poking his ribs. Opening his eyes, he saw his mother standing over him. "Up and at 'em, sonny boy." She prodded him again with a bony finger.

His brain fog dissipating, Harry remembered he'd promised his mother a trip today. "Gimme another hour of sleep, Mom."

"I'm not falling for that." She poked him again. "Get up."

Harry groaned as he rolled out of bed. After packing for a picnic, he and his mother got on the road. Gertie listened to an oldies station and held Harry's hand as he cruised down the highway. They had picked a perfect early -summer day for the trip. "It's a beautiful day, sonny boy."

"Sure is, Ma."

Gertie loved the park, and seeing her smile always put a smile on Harry's face as well. As he neared his exit, his phone rang. Harry saw that it was his boss from the courthouse calling. He let it go to voicemail, knowing already what the call was about. Harry's boss was calling to tell him that he could return to work when the new courthouse opened, but Harry had no intention of going back. His nocturnal activities were keeping him busy enough, and he certainly didn't need the money.

Harry was a saver and had been since his first job. His pension was a generous one. He was collecting Social Security, there was the money from the civil suit – well over a million dollars – that he had won against the driver who killed his wife, and the lawsuit he won against the manufacturer of the defective airbag that contributed to his wife's death. His house had been paid off for over twenty years, and the windfall from wise investments he had made over the years dabbling in the stock market amounted to just under half a million dollars.

Harry was worth just over three and a half - million dollars, and he had more than enough money set aside to send Joey to the college of his choice, if the boy decided that's what he wanted.

He and Patsy had planned to buy a luxury RV and take to the open road when she finally retired, and Joey was in college. Her career as a physician's assistant still gave her a great deal of satisfaction, and she ended every discussion on the subject by telling Harry that there would be plenty of time for their plans when she was really ready to "hang up her stethoscope." The couple planned to visit family and friends all over the country, stop and see the sights along the way, and they were going to take their time getting wherever they were going, just because they could. Then the villa on Palawan Island beckoned. Life was going to slow down. Life was going to be good.

***

On the day Patsy finally retired, she and Harry went to dinner to celebrate. He sat in the booth next to her so he could hold her hand, and he laughed heartily whenever Patsy said anything even remotely clever or funny. Everything in Harry's life was good at that moment. Joey was a happy kid, and he was getting good grades in school. Gertie had Charlie, a good man who would always do right by his mother, and he and Patsy had their health. They had played by the rules, and they were ready to reap the rewards of a lifetime of hard work. Harry had never been so happy in his life. On the way home that night, he sat at a traffic signal and held his wife's hand as the light turned green. He rolled into the intersection.

Harry never saw it coming. Up the avenue a few hundred feet, a drunk driver, with two county sheriffs trailing in hot pursuit, rocketed through the intersection. Before Harry could react, the SUV lost control, veered and slammed head-on into Harry's sedan at over eighty miles an hour.

Metal collided violently with metal. The force of the collision activated the driver's side airbag, and it slammed into Harry's head, knocking him unconscious. But the passenger side airbag malfunctioned. When Harry came to a few minutes later, his vision was blurry and the effects of head trauma were already kicking in, but he immediately reached for his wife. He called her name repeatedly but got no response. Patsy's body was contorted, and blood crept down her face.

Harry gently turned her head towards himself. Patsy's skull was fractured from the impact with the dashboard. He gently cupped her head in his hands and sobbed. "Don't go, Pats." He continued to sob as the paramedics took her away twenty minutes later.

***

At the hospital, Harry sat slumped in a chair in the emergency department's waiting room. When a nurse passed by, he grabbed her arm. "Can I see my wife?"

"What's her name, sir?"

"Patsy. Patsy Blake."

"I'm afraid she's still in surgery," the nurse said.

Six hours later, just after Harry had finally nodded off, he was awakened by a surgeon, who took a seat next to him. "How is she, Doc?"

"Not well, Mr. Blake, I'm sorry to say. Your wife has suffered a traumatic brain injury. We had to induce coma to relieve the swelling in her brain. She also has internal bleeding and a Grade A spinal cord injury." The doctor paused as he allowed Harry to digest the news. "Even if she emerges from the coma, her motor and cognitive skills will never be what they were before the accident." The doctor paused again and sighed. "If your wife lives, I'm afraid she will never walk again. I'm

215

very sorry."

Harry hung his head as he fought back tears.

"We have counselors here at the hospital, Mr. Blake, if you'd like to talk to someone."

"When can I see her?"

"She's in post-op. Maybe later today. Go home and get some sleep, please. You've been through a lot." The doctor gently patted Harry's arm as he rose from his seat and walked away. But Harry didn't go home. He paced in the waiting room until his bad knee forced him to sit.

Then he shifted in his chair every ten minutes until the staff found him a sofa to lie down on. But Harry didn't sleep, and night became morning. At a little past nine a.m., he snapped out of his sleep-deprived stupor, looked at his watch and realized that he hadn't called anyone to tell them the news.

He picked up his phone and made several of the most difficult calls he would ever make.

***

For the next two years, Harry spent almost every waking moment at Patsy's bedside. Some days he read to her, and others, he just talked to her. And some days he just sat there, staring at his wife and hoping for a miracle. But no miracle came. Patsy was still comatose, and the doctors told Harry that there was little hope that she was ever going to regain consciousness.

Many years before, Patsy had granted Harry power of attorney concerning her medical treatment in case something like the accident occurred. She had told Harry that she would not want to continue living if it meant being kept alive by artificial means, or if the quality of her life was going to be severely compromised by a significant injury or illness. So, after two years of watching his beloved wife waste away, Harry made the decision to end Patsy's life.

***

Harry and Joey stood at Patsy's hospital bed. Harry had an arm slung around Joey's shoulder, and he clutched Patsy's hand and held on firmly. "Say goodbye to your grandmother, Joey."

"I – I don't want to," Joey said, staring at his grandmother. The boy and his grandfather had spent countless hours arguing over Patsy's fate. Just a week before this day, Joey tried to convince his grandfather that his grandmother would someday soon make a miraculous recovery, and everything would get back to normal.

"You know how many doctors I've talked to, Joey. And you know what they've all said. Your grandmother is never going to be well again. We have to let her go. We have to...let her go."

Joey yelled at his grandfather for over an hour before he finally broke down and cried. Harry tried to hug the boy, but Joey pushed him away, ran upstairs and didn't leave his room for two days.

***

"Say goodbye to your grandmother," Harry said again. Joey took one last look at his grandmother, then he walked out of the hospital room. Harry didn't have the energy or desire to chase after the boy. His hand remained clutched in Patsy's, and tears streamed down his face. "Go to a better place, my love." A few minutes later, Harry's beloved wife of over fifty years was gone.

***

Reliving the day of his wife's death distracted Harry. He was still driving down the highway but wasn't paying attention to the road. "You okay, sonny boy?" Gertie said. "That's our turn you just missed."

"Aw, shit," Harry said. He got off at the next exit, then turned back onto the highway headed east. After pulling into the park entrance, he got out of the truck and helped Gertie out. She held onto Harry's arm as they took a footpath that led them to a picnic table in a secluded spot near a pond. Gertie started to unpack the cooler while Harry placed a seat cushion on the bench. "Sit, Ma. I can do that."

"I can help," Gertie said as she continued to unpack food from the cooler.

"I got it."

Gertie pouted, but she finally sat down. "Did you remember my stuff, sonny boy?"

Harry pulled a fifth of vodka and a container of lemonade from the cooler and set them on the table. "Hot damn," Gertie said.

He filled her glass, then he sat next to her and cracked open a beer. "I remember bringing you here when you were knee high to a grasshopper," Gertie said. "We'd come almost every weekend and you used to chase the geese and the ducks around 'til I thought you were gonna drop dead right on the spot. One time you fell into the pond chasing one of those damn birds. It jumped into the water, and you couldn't stop in time, so you went headfirst into the water, too. You flopped around like a small mouth bass trying to spit a hook. I thought you were drowning. I ain't moved so fast in my whole life trying to drag you out of the water. Do you remember that, son?"

Harry smiled as he sipped his beer. "Yeah, I remember. I was scared shitless. Dad was supposed to teach me to swim the summer before."

"Your father had his career, sonny boy. The army had him traveling all over hell back then."

Harry sighed. "I remember."

Gertie put her drink down and looked at her boy. "Your father had his faults, but he was a good man just the same. But when duty called…"

"He dropped everything, including us," Harry said as he slugged down the rest of his beer.

"We turned out fine, son. Where's this coming from?"

"Let's drop it, Mom. Just forget I said anything."

"I'm not gonna just forget it. What's eating you?"

"Mom…"

"I'm too damn old for this shit. Spit it out, boy."

"I was just thinking 'bout my buddies from the war."

"And?"

"A lot of 'em are dying lately. If they were just going from old age, that's one thing, but they're not. Most of 'em are dying from shit caused by the war."

"I'm sorry about that, but what's that got to do with your father?"

"If I hadn't gone off to fight…"

"You wouldn't be dealing with your buddies' dying like they are. That it, son?"

Harry nodded as he cracked another beer open.

"And you're blaming your father for wanting you to enlist, huh?"

"Dad didn't just want me to enlist. He told me I wasn't his son if I didn't."

Gertie looked aghast. "Your father never said that."

"He sure as hell did. The day I graduated from high school."

"I – I didn't know that, son. Why didn't you tell me?" Agitated, Harry got up and started to pace. "Why not, Harry?"

Harry stopped pacing and pointed a finger at his mother. "'Cause you didn't want to know, Ma."

Gertie gasped. "What the hell's that mean?"

"Means exactly that. You didn't want to know. When dad used to ride my ass, you – you didn't stick up for me."

"That's horseshit, boy. Me and your pa got into it all the time over you. I read him the riot act more times than I can remember."

"I don't remember it that way."

"That's 'cause I tried to keep that nonsense with your dad between me and him. I didn't want you to see me and your dad fighting if I could help it."

Harry stopped pacing long enough to consider that.

"You were five when you fell off the bike we got you for Christmas. Remember that?"

"Not really, Ma."

"Well, I do. You were tearing ass up and down the sidewalk when you hit a bump and went flying right over the handlebars. You hit the pavement head first and got one helluva gash. You started howling like a banshee with its ass on fire."

"I did?"

"You sure did. So, I came running out of the house and did some of that mothering stuff. I hugged you and kissed your boo boos and told you you were gonna be alright. Then your father walked out and saw you on the ground with tears in your eyes, and you know what he said to you? He said, 'get up, boy, and get your ass back on that bike, pronto.' Well, I about lost my shit. I cursed at him like I just caught him tapping my kid sister."

"Tapping?"

"Yeah, you know, like he was having sex with her."

"Where'd you hear that word?"

"I learned it on one of those Hip-Hop channels I used to watch before you had it blocked. Where was I? Oh, yeah. So, your dad starts marching down the walkway like he owns the damn cement, and I told him to turn his ass around."

"What'd he do?"

Gertie smiled. "What do ya think he did? He turned his ass right around and went back in the house. And that was the first and last time I ever let you see me and your dad fight over you."

Harry, less agitated now, took a seat next to his mother. "I didn't know that, Ma. I never wanted to start any trouble between you and him. I'm sorry."

Gertie grabbed Harry's hand and held on tightly, but he turned away. "Look at me, son." Gertie tugged at him, and Harry finally faced her. "You weren't the problem. Your father was. He saw everything as a battle, including the way we raised you. It's just the way he looked at life. And, yeah, he could be a hard ass sometimes, but he's gone now, so try to remember the good times and remember he loved us. Get past your anger and maybe you'll stop blowing shit up."

"What?"

"I may be old, but I ain't no fool, boy. I know it's you that's been bombing buildings around town. You could always find trouble when you had too much time on your hands." Harry was dumbfounded. He stared at his mother as he tried to process the U-turn the conversation had taken. "Go deaf and dumb, son?"

"I'm - I'm not blowing shit up."

"Don't you dare lie to your mother. I've seen your van pull out of the driveway at all hours of the night. Then, the next day, I hear about a bombing, and I remember what you did in the war. And I saw that letter you got from the state after Sheriff Roy showed up at our door a while back. You had to go to court for some shit, then a little bit later, the courthouse got blown up. And then a lawyer's office gets blown up…"

"You must be drunk, Ma."

Gertie slapped her boy. "Sass me like that again, and I'll knock you into next week, boy."

Harry recoiled. He started to say something, but quickly decided that the better move was to keep his mouth shut. He started to clear the picnic table as he did a slow burn. "We're leaving," he said.

"The hell we are. Sit down, Harry."

Ignoring his mother, Harry jammed food and bottles into the cooler. Gertie hoisted herself up from the table and, after a few labored steps, faced her son. She gently touched his arm, and when he brushed it away, she pinched him with all her strength. "Dammit, Ma!"

"Sit down, son. Please." Harry sat, and Gertie took a seat next to him. "We both know what you've been doing, so stop denying it. I just want to know why."

"Cause I'm mad as hell."

"Did the court screw you over? Or some lawyer?"

"Both."

"Then get a lawyer and fight 'em."

"I'm too damn old for that, Ma. Besides, I'm not spending one damn minute fighting with these assholes in court."

"They must've really pissed you off."

"They did. I'm fighting 'em the only way I know how. I hate bullies."

Gertie clutched her son's arm. "I know you do. And there's only one way to deal with 'em. But it'd break your momma's heart if you got caught or you hurt someone. Promise me no one will get hurt."

"I don't want to hurt anyone. I thought I was done destroying shit when I came home from the war. But they kept pushing me." Harry's chest heaved as he grew agitated. "Now I'm blowing up parts of our hometown because of them, and I hate it. But I - I had to do something."

"I understand, sonny boy," Gertie said. "But what about your F.B.I. friend? You think it's a coincidence he looks you up after all these years?

"He's in town investigating the bombings. He's got no reason to suspect me."

"You mean, yet."

"I'm being careful."

"Should we have him killed?" Gertie said, winking.

Harry wanted to laugh, but he just couldn't. "I've lost enough friends already."

"When's it gonna end, son?"

"Soon. I promise. You gonna keep this between us, Ma?"

Gertie winked. "Of course. It'll be our secret."

Knowing that his mother's mental condition could betray her at any given time worried Harry, but he smiled just the same. "Then let's drink to that."

Gertie held up her glass and Harry filled it with more vodka and lemonade. "A toast," Gertie said, raising her glass. "Here's to my boy kicking the shit out of the bullies."

Mother and son spent the rest of the day drinking, reminiscing, laughing and soaking up the sun. It was a day that Harry knew he and his mother needed. And it was a day that he would always cherish.

***

When they returned home from the picnic, Harry walked his mother into Charlie's home, then looked around for the old man. "Sloan?"

"I'm in the kitchen," Charlie responded.

Harry stepped into the kitchen and saw Charlie was seated at the table drinking coffee.

"How'd it go, Harry?"

"Pretty good. Sorry we couldn't bring you along."

"It's okay. I know you needed some time with your mother."

"She's half in the bag. I give her an hour, tops, before she taps out."

Charlie chuckled. "Thanks. I owe you."

Charlie followed Harry into the living room. Harry gave his mother a hug and a kiss. "I love you, Ma," he said before walking out the door. After stepping into his home, he collapsed into his recliner, wiped out from the day. Harry needed to recharge. He had plans for later that evening.

36

Despite the humidity that gripped Albrecht at three a.m., Harry sported a black ski mask and a light jacket. Its pockets were stuffed with phones and various tool of the trade. Reaching his destination, he wiped sweat from his forehead as he went to one knee. A waxing moon lit up the night, and Harry used the natural illumination to his advantage as he went to work on the door's lock. After hours of meticulous practice picking locks in his basement, he beat this one in mere seconds, even with gloves on. He bagged his tools then slid through the back door and into the Progressive Café. And General Patton followed right behind him.

"A coffee shop, soldier? Did they piss in your java?"

Harry ignored the general as he stopped in the middle of the cafe and waited for his eyes to adjust to the dimly lit room. A streetlamp bled in just enough light for him to locate the sales counter. His heartbeat quickened as he placed a shoe box, packed with one-quarter of a pound of Semtex, on a shelf beneath the counter. Harry figured that was enough to do the job. He didn't want to bring the building down; he just wanted to make a statement.

The general shook his head in mock admiration. "Let the carnage begin," he said. Harry retraced his steps towards the café's back door. Nearing the rear entrance, he turned and saw the general still standing in the middle of the café. "Why don't we go after the Japs? Those little, Asian bastards are tough as nails. Now there'd be a fight worth fighting."

"They're our allies now," Harry said.

"Bullshit."

"No bullshit. They have been for a long time. C'mon, we'll get some pancakes."

The general grumbled as he walked in Harry's direction. When they stepped outside, Harry looked up and down the alley and saw no signs of foot traffic. He strode to the mouth of the alley. Reaching it, he pulled off his ski mask. He turned down a side street and walked on. A block from the coffee shop, with the general at his side, Harry stopped and pulled out a cell phone.

"This isn't war," the general said.

"It's war. Just a new kind with a new enemy." The general shrugged his shoulders like he wasn't convinced. "Improvise, adapt and overcome, George."

"What's with the 'George' shit? Getting awfully familiar, aren't you?"

Harry punched a number into the cell phone. Two seconds later, the coffee shop's windows exploded, ejecting glass and shattered wood into the street. The store's chairs and tables were turned into kindling. There would be no coffee available at the Progressive Café for some time to come.

Harry and the general walked toward his van. "You call me by my first name, right?" Harry said.

"You're growing a pair, soldier. I like that."

Harry got into his van and pulled into the street. He wanted to take a look - even a quick peek would do - at the fruits of his labor. As he turned into the intersection, the van's rear doors swung open, and a wooden crate tumbled out and landed on the street. "Aw, shit," Harry barked as he slammed on the brakes, put the van in park, and jumped out. Moving with a purpose, he lifted the crate, walked it to the van and shoved it back into the vehicle. He slammed the rear door shut then yanked on the handle to make sure it was closed. Knowing he had no time now to revel in his work, he cursed under his breath as he yanked the van into drive and sped away.

37

It was just after eight p.m. the next night when John Coleman got on his laptop and entered Harry's full name into the F.B.I.'s criminal database. Within seconds, he saw results he didn't want to see. He read that Harry was convicted of a hate crime in county court. The same courthouse that had been bombed just a few weeks ago. "Dammit," he muttered, before reading on. Harry was given one year's probation and was ordered to attend sensitivity training at a place called the Center for Alternative Thinking. *Alternative Thinking? What the hell does that mean?*

John's phone rang. He saw it was his boss calling. "Hi, Hank."

"You know I don't like being called that."

John grinned. "I keep forgetting."

"The clock's ticking. I need something, John."

"I may have hit pay dirt."

"What have you got?"

John sat back in his chair. "A local militia group that's involved in some heavy stuff. Drugs, gun trafficking, etcetera."

"They have a name?"

"I'm looking into it. They may be loosely affiliated with several other groups around the country."

"Got a guy on the inside that I don't know about, John?"

"Nothing like that. Just a hunch."

"Why the hell would a militia blow up a coffee shop?"

"Maybe they didn't like the coffee," John said, rolling his eyes. *Lame, lame, lame,* he thought. He waited for a response from his boss, but he got nothing but dead air. John's boss had less than no sense of humor. "The bombings may not be related, Hank. We could have a copycat."

"I really wish you'd stop calling me that," Henry said. "But your hunches usually pan out. Send me what you've got."

"Got to follow up on a few things. You'll hear from me soon."

"John, I need -"

John hung up his phone. *I could give one half of one good shit what you need, Hank.* It wasn't like John to be caught flat-footed like he just was. He could have just let the call go to voice mail, but he knew Henry would keep calling every five minutes until he picked up. Seeing Harry's name in the Bureau's criminal database had rattled him, and now he had to throw his boss a bone, and soon.

He didn't even need a real militia at the moment. *I can always create a group and give them a name,* he thought. *Hell, I can even give them a secret handshake, a fight song, a web site, and a damned mascot if I want to. I'm the frigging F.B.I.*

John was not about to hand a friend over to his boss. A friend that had saved his life. He knew that he had just bought himself some time, but just how much he didn't know. If he could pull it off, John was going to have his boss chasing his own tail until he dropped from dizziness and exhaustion. He got back onto the Bureau's criminal database. And he ordered out for dinner. There was some serious digging to be done. It was going to be a long night.

***

By the time John crawled into bed at three that morning, he knew the name of every doctor Harry had seen for the past forty years, and he had a list of every medication his friend had been taking for the same amount of time.

After running a DMV check, John also knew that Harry had recently

227

purchased a 2006, black, paneled van, and he had the plate number.

With all of the tools at his disposal as a G-Man, and an Internet connection, John could have dug much deeper into Harry's life, but he knew enough. At least for now.

38

Harry sat on the living room sofa browsing the Internet on his laptop. He searched for stories about people from all over the world who had lost their jobs and reputations because of the cancel culture movement. He read an article about a school board proposal in a northern California city. It had voted to rename forty-four of the area's public schools, including those named after former presidents George Washington and Abraham Lincoln, whom, according to the board, "engaged in the subjugation and enslavement of human beings, oppressed women, led to genocide, or diminished the opportunities of those amongst us to the right to life, liberty, and the pursuit of happiness."

Opponents called the school board's action liberal overreach, woke insanity, and cancel culture run amok. Besides conservative condemnation to the progressive proposal, the board also faced backlash from the left. The city's mayor, a Democrat, joined the chorus of criticism, calling the plan "offensive" and a distraction from more pressing issues.

After reading a few more articles about the damage done to the lives, careers and reputations of decent, sane people caught in the sticky web of the cancel culture, he began to grasp the true scope, and danger, of the movement.

He then read up on all the new gender pronouns that had somehow made their way into the modern- day lexicon, and he learned there were many more genders than he'd had previously known about. He'd been taught in school, as he assumed almost every other human being on the planet had been for centuries, that there were only two genders, male and female. But some websites, including a very popular social networking website, claimed there were now over fifty genders. Questions raced through Harry's mind. *Where in the hell have these fifty genders been hiding? Who in the hell are these people making these claims? What the hell is their agenda? The world has gone fuckin' nuts.* Harry was officially awake.

About to close his eyes for a much-needed break from his reading, he heard a knock at the front door. He grunted as he hoisted himself off of the sofa. Without checking the peephole first, Harry swung open the front door. He smiled when he saw Ze standing on the porch with her arms crossed and a scowl on her face. "How you doing, sweetie?"

"I got fired from my job," Ze said. "Know anything about that?"

Harry was still smiling. "As a matter of fact, I do, hon. I'm the one that got your ass fired."

Not expecting to hear that, Ze took a step back. "What? You - you really did it?"

"Just said I did. I warned you not to screw with me. Now we're even."

Ze pointed a finger in Harry's face. "We're not even. Not by a long shot."

"You should just walk away, honey. Turn around, forget about me, and walk away."

"I'm gonna get you!" Ze screamed.

"I've had it with your bullshit. Get the hell off my property! Now!" Harry roared.

Ze stomped off down the walkway. Harry slammed the front door shut behind him. Attempting to calm himself, he drew in a couple of deep breaths before sitting in his recliner. He closed his eyes and tried to focus on the problem at hand. He realized that Ze could cause more trouble for him, and he would have to deal with her once and for all. Suddenly, something came to him. *I'm an alcoholic,* he remembered Ze saying during their first entanglement. A plan began to take form in his mind.

He grabbed a legal pad and started to scribble down some dialogue. Harry would take no pleasure in the ploy, but Ze had been warned more than once to just walk away. For the next three hours, he went over his lines. When he was sure he had his act down cold, he treated himself to ice cream.

***

The next afternoon, Harry stood in front of the B.I.D. building, a two-story edifice built in the mid-forties that, until a year ago, was the home of the town library. The Internet had gradually rendered the library obsolete, and the town's council had decided that it couldn't justify the funds needed to keep it open any longer. Another piece of the town's heritage was gone, relegated to the ash heap of history, and what took its place, like an unsightly patch of weeds among a bed of flowers, was the B.I.D. organization. The building was now a haven for a new, more enlightened form of education, and the four tenets of B.I.D.'s manifesto were Inclusion, Diversity, Ubiquitous Oppression, and Victimhood for All. Real learning and independent thinking had no home, nor relevance, within these walls now.

Harry stepped into the building and was met by a young man named Jeff, who wore a smile as wide as it was fake. "Hello," Jeff said. "How may I help you?"

"I'm here to see Mr. Barrett."

"Do you mean Ne?"

"I guess so."

"Do you have an appointment?"

"Yeah."

"What's your name?"

"Harry Blake."

"Follow me, please," Jeff said.

231

Walking behind Jeff, Harry surveyed the first floor, noting the absence of tables and chairs that once accommodated students and other library patrons. In their place now were rows of cubicles and the social justice warriors who toiled in them. When they reached an office near the rear of the building, Jeff knocked on the door. "Your one o'clock is here to see you, Ne."

When Harry stepped into the office, he looked over the man sitting behind the desk: a mousey young guy who arose and offered his hand to Harry. "Welcome..."

"The given name is Harry." Harry gave Barrett a firm handshake. "But I call myself Xem now."

"You've discovered the gender pronouns? Excellent. My pronoun is Ne."

Harry smiled as he fought back the urge to gag. "Hey, that's great," he said. The two men sat. "This used to be the town library," Harry said.

"So, I hear. I'll bet its shelves were filled with oppressive stories and outright lies on just about every subject imaginable. *Their* version of history. We'll rectify that soon enough."

"Good for you. What's on the second floor now?"

"A sister organization rents that space. They're called TID."

"Tid?" Harry said.

"T-I-D. It's an acronym for Tear It Down. They have some of the same goals as we do."

"They're tearing and you're burning, huh? You guys must have lots of energy."

Ne grinned smugly as he sat back in his chair. "We're reshaping the entire country one hick town at a time. That takes energy, all right."

Harry cringed but kept his cool. "What do they want to tear down, exactly?"

"The American political, economic and justice system. It's so oppressive and outdated."

"How about their god?"

Ne rolled his eyes. "A White, bearded cisgender man in the sky who created everything? How quaint."

"What about the family unit?"

"You mean *their* belief that every child should have a female mother and a male father? Such nonsense. We fight for inclusion, diversity, equity and social justice."

Harry, seething below the surface, remained calm as he leaned in towards Ne. "You say you're for inclusion, but it seems like your organizations want to exclude a lot of people for their beliefs and way of life. Or maybe even purge them."

Ne frowned. He didn't like being challenged with logic. "That's a conversation we just don't have time for today. So, how can I help you?"

"I came here for two reasons. Someone named Ze came to my home a while back with a petition. She, he, it said ze, zir, hir works for your organization. She, he, it was a delight and I'd like to get in touch with ve, ver, vis."

"Oh, I see," Ne said, even though he didn't have a clue what Harry meant, except for the part about Ze. He fumbled with a pen. "Unfortunately, Ze no longer works for our organization."

"That's a shame," Harry said. "What happened?"

"We found something from her past that forced us to let her go. We discovered that she's a very intolerant person, and the one thing we don't tolerate here at B.I.D. is intolerance."

It took some effort, but Harry managed to subdue the glee that tried to surface through his stern countenance. "That's really sad. But don't we all have something in our past? Something that could bite us on the ass later, no matter how innocent it was?"

Ne's mouth flattened in disapproval. He knew that to respond yes would be the honest answer, but doing so would open up a can of worms that he didn't want to deal with. "Ze now works for TID on the second floor."

"Is that so? She, he, it told me a little bit about your organization, and at first I didn't take it too seriously, but after going to classes at the C.A.T. for a while..."

"You attend classes at the center?" Ne said. "Was it mandatory?"

Harry hung his head in mock shame. "Yeah, it was. The judge, bless her heart, found me guilty of a hate crime, ethnic intimidation. I was oppressing a young man from the neighborhood, and I didn't even know it until I started taking the sensitivity classes."

"Bravo for seeing the light, Harry, I mean, Xem. They're doing wonderful work at the center remolding the minds of these...people."

Hearing the words, *these people*, irritated the hell out of Harry, but he knew he had to keep his cool. His body tensed as he shifted in his chair. "You're not from around here, are you?"

Ne chuckled. "Even if I were, I'd never admit it to anyone. I was transferred here to help with the 'Awakening', so to speak. I cannot wait to get back to civilization. So, what else can I help you with today?"

"I want to help you, actually. I want to join the fight. I thought I could pass out fliers, make some phone calls, that sort of thing. Anything to help the cause."

"That's wonderful. We can always use an extra hand." Ne looked Harry over. "You call yourself Xem now, right? Your gender expression seems to lean towards male. Are you questioning?"

"I sure am," Harry replied. "I thought I was a cisgender, but I'm just not sure now. For a while, I thought I was a demiboy, but now I think I may be a non-binary, but sometimes I think I'm demigender, and just yesterday I felt like I was genderfluid. Last week I thought I was transfem, but then I realized I might be agender." Harry let out a mournful sigh. "I just want people to accept me for who I am. I want validation. I want respect."

Ne, completely lost trying to follow Harry's verbal gymnastics, smiled and nodded just the same. "I understand. Our kind will get the respect we demand and deserve."

"Great. About the job...?"

"You're welcome aboard, Xem. Unfortunately, we can't offer you a paying position at the moment."

"That's not a problem. I don't need the money."

"When can you start?"

Harry winked. "Just as soon as I figure out who I am." Harry roared with laughter, and Ne followed suit. Ne then handed Harry a binder with the acronym B.I.D. on the cover. "Please read this. It includes our mission statement, and the steps we're taking to achieve our goals. I'll answer any questions you might have. And..." Ne's eyes widened when he gazed over Harry's shoulder. "Excuse me for a minute," he said as he shot out of his chair and scurried out of the office.

Harry got up and poked his head out the door in time to see Ne grab Ze's arm and spin her around. "You're not allowed on this floor, Ze." Ne's voice carried across the room. Heads turned from the rows of cubicles.

"Get your hands off of me!" Ze screamed as she slapped at Ne's hand. "I'll come down here anytime I want!" Seeing that she was the target of employees' stares, she shouted, "what the hell are you assholes looking at?! Fuck all of you and fuck B.I.D.! I'll burn this place down!"

As Ze stomped off with Ne in pursuit, an idea came to Harry. He started to walk. He surreptitiously opened several doors until he found a janitor's closet. Peeking inside, he found the room was full of cleaning supplies, including trash bags, mops, brooms and dustpans.

Closing the door, he returned to Ne's office, scooped up the binder Ne had given him, and left the building by the back door. Once it closed behind him, Harry stopped and eyed the door over. He saw that it was a standard, double-paned security door, and he knew that it wouldn't present a problem. On his way to his truck, he scanned the parking lot, searching for security cameras mounted above on poles, or at ground level. Seeing none, he got into his truck and drove off.

***

When Harry returned home, he looked around the house and saw that, once again, he was alone. Ordinarily, that would have bothered him. He thought about calling Joey for the fourth time this week and begging the boy to pick up his phone, or at least return his call, but realizing that his effort would just bring him more frustration, he dismissed the thought. Instead, he punched in another number.

"Ken Burton here."

"Hey, Ken, Harry Blake. I need your services again."

"How's seven o'clock at my office sound?"

"I'll be there."

***

The two men sat in a booth at Jay's, and after ordering, passed their menus back to the waitress. "You notice anything different about the town, Ken?"

"Well, there's the bombings. That's got everybody's attention."

"Anything else?"

"Some of the locals seem more tense these days. You know, like they're watching what they say and who they say it to. Like there's someone looking over their shoulders and all the time."

"Like we're kinda living in a police state, huh?"

"You could say that, yeah. I was at the bakery the other day, and old Mrs. Thompson was in a pisser of a mood."

"Mrs. Thompson? I've never seen anything but a smile on that woman's face in my life."

"Same here, Harry. So, I asked her what was wrong, and she told me she got accused of being racist by a group of people last week."

"What people?"

"Some group that apparently set up shop in town a while back. You know that young, black kid that lives over on Elm Street? I think his name is Wesley."

"Yeah, I've seen him around town. Heard he's a good kid."

"I've heard the same. Anyway, Wesley apparently goes into the old lady's shop a couple of times a week to buy bread and such for the family. And the way the old gal tells it, the two of them needle each other just for fun. So, Wesley's in there messing around near the back of the shop and Mrs. Thompson says to him, 'knock it off, boy.' Well, some young woman was in the store at the time and overheard that, and she nearly pissed herself right on the spot. Guess the woman screamed at Mrs. Thompson and nearly gave her a heart attack. Then she said something about outing the old gal as a racist. Mrs. Thompson told me the next day there was a protest in front of the shop, and these idiots were yelling at her from the sidewalk, calling her a racist, and trying to block customers from going into the shop. Then some asshole picked up a trashcan and threw it through the bakery's window. They ran before the cops showed up."

"Did anyone get arrested?"

"Not as far as I know. That the kind of shit you're talking about, Harry?"

"Yeah, it is. There're people in town that are starting a lot of shit here. Bunch of douchebag outsiders who think it's their place to tell us how to talk and how to act. And I'll bet my last dollar that psycho Ze was the ringleader at the bakery."

"Who?"

"Remember that woman I had your friend put in blackface? Nasty piece of work named Ze?" A waitress set a couple of plates of food in front of the men, and the men dug into their meals.

"Yeah, I remember," Ken said, "My guy uploaded that picture to some social media sites for you. Did it work?"

"It sure as hell did. She got her ass fired from B.I.D."

"What's that?"

"An organization that's set up shop in the old library. B.I.D.'s short for Burn It Down. They're a bunch of assholes who want to destroy this country from the inside. They started shit on my front lawn a while back and I was the one that got arrested."

"No shit?"

"No shit. Anyway, I've got a ham radio at home. You think your friend could connect it to the Internet for me so people can listen in?"

"I don't think it's difficult to do with the right equipment. You going to do a podcast?"

"Don't know what the hell that is, Ken. But I'm gonna try and wake this town up. I'm gonna tell everybody about this BID organization and the bullshit they're starting."

"Are they fanatics?"

"That's one word to describe them. And they're not the only ones in town doing what they're doing."

"Do you think they're responsible for the bombings?"

"Nah. They're assholes, but they're not the bombers."

"You say that like you know something the rest of us don't Harry." Harry grinned as he sat back as he continued eating. "You do, don't you?" Ken said. "C'mon, talk to me."

Why the hell not? Harry figured. He knew that word was starting to spread around town already, or would soon enough, that he was the bomber, so over dinner he told Ken everything, including his intention to burn down the B.I.D building. "They wanna see things burn. I'm gonna help 'em with that," Harry said.

Ken wiped his mouth with a napkin and stared at Harry like he had just been told the secret to eternal life. "Damn, Harry. Damn." When they finished their meals, Harry paid the bill, and the two walked out to the parking lot. "I'll have my associate over to your home tomorrow afternoon. If there's anything else I can do…"

"You've done plenty already, Ken. Thanks."

The two men shook hands. "Harry, are you really going to do it?"

"Sure am."

"Remind me to never piss you off."

Harry smiled as he walked away.

***

The next afternoon, Ken's associate, a young man named Mark, showed up at Harry's door with a canvas tote full of electronic and computer components slung over his shoulder. He knocked on the door. Harry opened it and looked the boy over. "Help you?"

"Hi. Ken sent me."

Harry let the boy into the house, then he led Mark down the basement stairs. "This them?" Mark asked, gesturing at the computer and a ham radio sitting on a desk in the corner of the room. He didn't even wait for Harry's response before unpacking his bag and taking a seat at the desk.

"You need me for anything?" Harry asked.

"Nope. I'm good," Mark said as his fingers started to fly on the laptop's keyboard. Less than an hour later, Mark was finished hooking up Harry's ham radio to the Internet. He left Harry step-by- step directions on how to transmit online, and he gave him his cell number in case he had any problems or questions. Harry was impressed with the boy's expertise, and he was grateful. He gave the boy one-thousand dollars in cash for services rendered, and the kid smiled like he had just hit the lottery as he left the house.

Harry spent the rest of the afternoon knocking on his neighbors' doors to let them know he would be broadcasting very soon. When several neighbors asked what he planned to talk about, Harry told them to tune in to find out. He did the same with the gang from Sam's Saloon when he stopped in for a beer later that day.

That night, Harry returned to his basement and took a seat at the desk. He went to the town's website and smiled when he saw that the B.I.D.'s manifesto was uploaded to the site. At the bottom of the page, he saw only several comments regarding the manifesto and the organization itself. The town was still asleep, and that angered and disappointed Harry.

***

The next morning, Harry wore a Panama hat, sunglasses and had a messenger bag slung over his shoulder as he left his house. The bag contained a pair of gloves, a bottle of whiskey and a newspaper. He drove to the B.I.D. building, parked his truck and slipped the gloves on before exiting the truck. After entering the building, he took the stairway to the second floor and stopped to look around. A banner hanging on the wall to his right exclaimed, *Tear It Down!* He shook his head in disgust as he looked around the room. The worker bees were busy in their cubicles, and no one bothered to greet Harry or even look at him.

He made his way down an aisle that separated cubicles on each side. As he walked on, he saw what he was looking for on his right: a nameplate on a desk that read, Ze. Seeing that the cubicle was empty, Harry slid into it, grabbed the whiskey bottle from his bag and placed it on Ze's desk before heading back to the stairwell. A note attached to the bottle read: *I never got you a parting gift. Enjoy. Ne.*

Harry took a seat on a bench near the stairwell, placed his gloves into his bag, then pulled out a newspaper. He flipped casually through it, pretending to read it as he waited. He was willing to sit there the entire day if that's what it took. But only five minutes later, he caught sight of Ze walking towards her cubicle.

He got up off the bench, tucked the sunglasses and newspaper into the bag, then descended the stairs to the first floor. Turning to his left, he walked towards Ne's office. He peeked in and saw Ne seated at his desk. He tapped lightly on the door. "Hey, remember me? Am I interrupting?"

"Of course not. Please have a seat."

Harry took a seat and chuckled. "That was some scene the other day,

240

huh?"

"Oh, you mean with Ze? Yeah, that was a bit ugly. She knows she's not supposed to step foot on this floor."

"I figured it was best if I just left." *C'mon, Ze. Take the bait.*

"I'm sorry you had to see that. We have therapists available to talk to if you feel traumatized or triggered."

"I survived two tours in Vietnam. I think I can deal with a little spat without pissing myself."

"Very well. Now, where were we before... the incident?"

As Harry was about to say something, he saw Ne's eyes lock onto something, or someone, behind him. Ze stood at the door, holding a liquor bottle and snorting fire.

"You can't be here, Ze. You know that," Ne said.

"You think you're funny, Ne?"

"What are you talking about?"

"You rotten son of a bitch! You know I'm a recovering alcoholic!"

Harry grinned as he slouched in his chair and lowered his head. He knew what was coming. Ze wound up and fired the bottle at Ne. He ducked to his left, and the bottle exploded against the wall behind him. Employees working near to Ne's office heard the noise. They fixed their astonished gazes on Ze.

"I'll burn this fucking place down, and you with it!" Ze screamed before she marched away. Ne bolted out of his chair and scampered out of the office. Still grinning, Harry got up and peeked into the hallway. He saw Ne ascending the stairwell, in pursuit of Ze. Harry figured he had only a few minutes. He stepped into the hallway, turned a corner, and slipped into the janitor's room. He grabbed a broom and a dustpan, then he made his way back to Ne's office.

He closed the office door and went to work sweeping up every shard of glass on the floor that he could find. He dumped the dustpan full of glass into his messenger bag, slung it over his shoulder and, with his head hung low, he brushed past several employees as he left the building through the back exit. He now had Ze's fingerprints.

***

When Harry returned home, he went straight to the garage. He emptied the shards of glass onto a table. Then he grabbed a paint brush and dipped it into a jar of gasoline. He coated the shards with a light layer of gasoline, then with motor oil. While the glass dried, he had lunch. An hour later, he donned his gloves again and shoveled the broken glass back into the messenger bag. Feeling satisfied with what he had accomplished with his day so far, Harry took a very long nap.

***

Harry was wearing black slacks, a black sweater and steel-toed boots when he walked into his garage just after 3 a.m. He grabbed several empty liquor bottles from a recycle bin. General Patton stood right behind him. "We going to have a body count tonight, soldier?" Hardly surprised to see the general, Harry brushed by him and grabbed a few rags off the work bench. "Ever hear of personal space?" the general said.

Harry waved the general off as if he were a fly buzzing around his head. He filled the bottles with four parts gasoline and one part motor oil. After jamming the rags down the neck of the bottles, he placed them into a small cooler, then stuffed the cooler into a large duffel bag. He hauled the bag to the van and stowed it in the rear of the van, then quietly shut the door. The general stood next to the van. "I want to see some carnage tonight."

"Piss off," Harry said. The general glared at Harry as Harry got into the van, turned the ignition, and put it in drive. Patton jumped in the van just before Harry pulled onto the street. Minutes later, he turned onto Division Street and slid the van up to the curb.

He pulled a black ski mask over his head, slipped on a pair of gloves, grabbed the duffel bag and began the short hike across the street, the general walking alongside him. When he reached the west side of the parking lot, pain shot through his bad knee, so he stopped to rest.

Leaning against a lamp pole, he scoured the area for any sign of activity. Albrecht was fast asleep. A gentle summer breeze tussled his hair as Harry's pulse cranked up and the soreness he felt just moments ago abated as adrenaline shot through him. When he reached the back steps of the old library, he stopped to surveil the area one last time.

"Is this a library?" the general said. "Is literacy the enemy now?"

"If it was still a library, we wouldn't be here," Harry said as he stepped onto the concrete landing. He set the duffel bag on it, unzipped the bag and pulled two Molotov cocktails from the cooler. After carefully placing them on the landing, he retrieved the bag full of glass shards and scattered them over the landing. He then faced the door. He closed his eyes as he reared back his right foot, then fired it into the bottom glass pane. The glass shattered completely. Backing up a step, he grabbed a lighter from his pocket, lit the rag on one of the bottles, and tossed it through the gaping hole in the bottom of the door. Crouching down to peer into the building, he felt a jolt of exhilaration when he saw the bottle explode and send a trail of flames down the hallway. He lit the second bottle and tossed it in. It exploded, and fire quickly spread to the cubicles on both sides of the aisleway.

Satisfied with the results, Harry repacked his gear. Descending the steps, he stopped when he heard the general, who still stood on the landing, grunt. "What's wrong, George?"

"There's no carnage or death. This ain't war."

"Sure, it is. Just not like you remember it." When Harry looked at the general, he saw his father instead.

"You disappoint the hell out of me, son," Patton said, before disappearing. Harry stood there questioning his sanity, wondering if he had truly just seen his father. Shaking off that unsettling thought, Harry's attention turned toward the building. His eyes filled with tears as he reminisced about his childhood and the carefree hours he had spent in the old library. They were happy times for the boy. But at this very moment, a part of the town's history was being obliterated before his eyes, and the old man knew that he was the architect of the destruction.

Guilt hung over him. He now wished that he hadn't done the deed. He despised *them* for intruding on his town. And he hated *them* for forcing his hand. His entire body trembling, he tottered towards his truck. And the building continued to burn.

***

Three hours later, Harry lay in his bed, tangled in his sheets, staring wide-eyed at the ceiling. He dragged himself out of bed and went to the kitchen. Figuring a full belly might help him sleep, he downed two chicken sandwiches and a tall glass of milk, then went back upstairs. He looked into his mother's room. Her bed was empty. Then he peeked into Joey's bedroom. Harry found another empty bed. He stepped into the room and checked the closet. It was empty, as was the dresser. *He's never coming home.*

Harry was glad that Mom had someone, but the two empty bedrooms and the king-size bed that he now slept in alone forced him to finally acknowledge, if only to himself, the profound loneliness he felt. *Life's funny the way it works out. It's a regular fuckin' hoot.* He trudged back into his bedroom, swallowed an anti-psychotic med, a pain pill, and a sleeping pill. He climbed back into bed, but he tossed and turned for hours.

***

When he awoke late the next morning, Harry was ornery from lack of sleep, his knee was stiff and sore, but worse, he felt the wet chill of the bed sheets beneath him. He yanked back the blankets and gazed,

244

sickened and humiliated, at the urine-stained bed sheets. Harry had never bothered to read about one potential side effects of his new anti-psychotic medication: bed wetting. "Son of a bitch..." He glared at the smorgasbord of prescription medications sitting on his nightstand. *I'm done with these bastards.* With a swipe of his arm, the bottles scattered in every direction.

General Patton sat in a chair in a corner of the room, sporting a smile. "About damn time, Blake. Pills are for weak people." Harry glared at the general. "I see you pissed your bed." Patton chuckled as he took a deep draw on the cigar dangling in his mouth. "Time for some adult diapers?"

"Go fuck yourself, George." Harry stomped out of the room.

"C'mon back, Harry. I was just pulling your chain." The general waited, but Harry didn't return. Fifteen minutes passed and Patton was still alone in the room. Sneering, he whispered, "I'm not done with you, Blake, not by a long shot." Then, he disappeared.

Harry knew he needed to do something, anything, to try to shake the memory of wetting his bed, so he stepped into the backyard and grabbed a rake. "Good morning, Harry," Hien said from the adjoining backyard. Harry winced when he heard Hien's voice. Although he felt, in a way he couldn't describe in words, that he and the elderly, Asian man were becoming more than neighbors, he was in no mood for a chat. He kept raking the grass as if he hadn't heard Hien's voice. "The accident you had in bed could have happened to anyone, Harry."

Harry kept raking. "Don't know what you're talking about," he said.

Hien regarded Harry with sympathetic eyes. "Please listen to me, my friend. It is nothing to be ashamed of."

"Let's drop the subject, okay?"

"Very well," Hien said. "Did you hear the one about the Asian guy, the priest and the rabbi?"

"You can't tell those kinda jokes anymore, Hien. They'll crucify you for it."

"I understand that. Why do so many people in this great country seem so easily offended and uptight these days?"

Suddenly, Harry wanted to talk. He walked to the fence. "It's this p.c. and cancel bullshit. If you don't toe their company line, they scream, they piss themselves, and then they try to destroy people's lives."

"That is so sad. Diverse viewpoints help to make a country stronger and freer. Silencing people for dissenting views is the trademark of a totalitarian regime."

"Sure as hell is." Harry looked around at nothing in particular. "I used to love this country."

"You still do."

"I don't recognize it anymore, Hien. It's going…bad."

"How so, Harry?"

"I got gas pumps screaming ads at me when I'm just trying to get gas. Newspeople and politicians screaming at each other and saying how evil the other side is. Half the stuff on the Internet is bullshit and lies. People accuse others of shit just because it's easy to do. Everything's gotten so…loud." Harry shook his head. "Albrecht's changed. Sometimes I just wanna…"

"What, Harry? Blow the town to kingdom come and let the chips fall where they may?"

"Sometimes you have to destroy a village to save it," Harry replied.

"To keep it from falling into enemy hands, yes? Wasn't that your country's policy in Vietnam?"

"Yeah. We called it Scorched Earth. When we pulled out of a village or city, we didn't want to leave anything behind the 'Cong could use. So, we burned everything on our way out."

"I know the term. And I recall another strategy that was used as well."

"You mean pacification?"

"Yes, Harry. Pacification. The attempt to win the hearts and minds of the people. Your government wanted to hold and protect the anyone who didn't toe the company line, even if it meant turning on family or friends. And they were taught to never question the authority of the Nazi Party, and they got away with this bullshit for years.

We've got new groups invading our town and acting like Nazis, telling us and our children how to talk and what to think. The Nazis sent dissidents to concentration camps. The bastards invading our town are sending people to sensitivity training classes. Ever hear of the Enabling Act of 1933? It gave the Nazis the power to repress their opponents and limit free speech. See any similarities here? These assholes are trying to exert power over the rest of us, power they didn't earn and power they don't deserve. They want to destroy our way of life and our beliefs. Are we gonna let them get away with it here? Is that what you want for our town? Is that what you want for your country?!"

Harry paused for a moment as he struggled to maintain his composure. "And did you know they tore down the statue of Little Hawk at the ballpark? Apparently, a new organization that set up shop in our town brought in some people from the city to help tear the statue down. You good with that, Albrecht? Are you okay with a bunch of assholes coming to our town and tearing down our monuments? That was our statue! That statue was our way of honoring Little Hawk and his tribe. And they tore it down! And they got away with it!"

Harry rubbed his temples again as his head began to throb. "And they're planning on doing it again. One of these groups, it's called TID, is gonna try tearing down the statue of our town's founding father real soon. These assholes are so fuckin' bold now they're posting this shit on their website. You know what that sound is you're hearing? That's them laughing at us, Albrecht. Laughing!"

Harry gripped the radio's mic and squeezed hard. "C'mon out and show 'em we're not gonna take their bullshit anymore, but keep the kids at home, 'cause it ain't gonna be pretty. That's all I got for now, Albrecht. Show up and show 'em whose town it is." Harry was spent, both physically and emotionally. He turned off his laptop and ham radio, then he called Hans and told him to ready the troops for the upcoming showdown. Sleep came easily to him that night.

***

Only a handful of Albrecht's residents had tuned into Harry's maiden broadcast, but the next afternoon he was visited by a group of neighbors. They asked Harry if what he had said the night before was true. When he assured his neighbors that everything he had said could be verified, they all agreed something needed to be done. They encouraged Harry to keep up the good work, and they assured him that they would pass the word about his broadcasts. One woman suggested that he should give himself a catchy handle to spice things up a bit. Harry agreed that was a good idea. When he asked the group if they were going to attend the clash the next morning, everyone gave him a resounding cheer for an answer.

After the neighbors left, Harry ran some errands, had dinner alone, then he called Joey. And like always of late, he got the boy's voicemail. The good mood he enjoyed for most of the day was suddenly gone. At eight p.m., he climbed into bed and spent most of the night tossing and turning.

***

An eight-foot limestone statue of Friedrich Albrecht stood in the middle of the town square. Most of the townsfolk who traversed the square barely took notice of the statue as they went about their business, but some stopped when they saw two groups assembled on opposite sides of the plaza. The TID faction, about one-hundred strong counting supporters of the group, cheered, waved signs and chanted on bullhorns while several men in the group rested sledgehammers at their feet.

Harry and his men were gathered across the square. Harry saw law

252

enforcement officers from three nearby towns standing at the ready along all four sides of the plaza, waiting. That made him smile. Like the confrontation at Higgins Park two weeks earlier, Harry hoped that the authorities would arrest both groups and charge them with rioting, thus thrusting both organizations into the public spotlight and putting them out of commission.

Harry looked around for any sign of familiar faces amongst the crowd and saw none. Disappointed and angry, he crossed his arms and glared across the square at the TID mob. Behind him stood twenty men from the B of A, and friends of the group, men who didn't need a reason or an excuse to bust some heads.

Ralph Simmons, the TID's top thug, stood off to the side of his group. He smiled when he saw two pickups packed full with Mexican men pull up to the plaza and come to a stop. Luis, the leader of the group, got out of a truck and looked around. Ralph rushed to meet him. "You boss man?" Luis said.

"I am," Ralph said.

"A guy at Supply Depot say you have work for us. Tells us to come here."

"Yeah, I've got work for you and your men," Ralph said.

Luis looked around the plaza and saw people everywhere. "Is a lot of people here. How we work with so many people around?"

"Walk with me," Ralph said, slinging his arm around Luis' shoulder. Ralph led Luis towards the edge of the square. When he saw Harry's men, he stopped and pointed. "You see those men there?"

"Si."

"They're evil gringos."

When Luis caught sight of Harry, he began to figure out what was going on, so he played dumb.

"Que?" he said.

"They're evil gringos. They hate your people. You help us fight them, si?"

"Que?" Luis said again.

Ralph faced Luis and raised his fists. "Your people… good fighters, right? I pay you and your friends mucho dinero and you fight."

Luis gave Ralph a blank stare. "Que?"

Ralph threw his arms up in exasperation. "You were speaking English a minute ago. What the hell?" Harry walked towards the two men. Ralph took one step back when he saw Harry approach.

"Hola, Luis," Harry said. "How's it goin'?"

Luis shook hands with Harry. "Bueno, mi amigo," he said.

"How are Angelina and the ninos?"

"They're good. Thanks for asking, Harry."

"What the hell? You guys know each other?" Ralph said.

Harry sneered at Ralph. "This is my town, asshole. I know everybody. What's going on, Luis?"

"This puto wants to pay my men to fight his battle."

"Is that so?" Harry said.

"Sure is." Luis looked over the B of A men gathered behind Harry. "Got some new friends, Harry?"

"Wouldn't call 'em that exactly. Long story, Luis."

"They look like bad men." Luis turned around and checked out the TID mob. "What about them?"

"They're outsiders, mostly."

"They the ones starting shit all over town?"

"Yep," Harry said.

"Your boys gonna kick their asses?"

"If they don't walk away right now, yep."

"You want help?"

"Don't want you getting into any trouble, Luis. You got a family."

Luis spat on Ralph's shoes. "Walk away, pendejo, while you still can."

Ralph pointed at Harry. "We're tearing that statue down. If you try to stop us, you'll be sorry."

Vietnamese population and turn them against the Viet Cong."

"That was the goal."

"And you hope to achieve that here in Albrecht?"

"You're damn right I do. I'm gonna wake this town the hell up."

"He who wishes to fight must first count the cost," Hien said.

"One mark of a great soldier is that he fights on his own terms or fights not at all," Harry said.

"The wise warrior avoids the battle," Hien said.

"But he fights when he must. And attack is the secret of defense. Sun Tzu. *The Art of War*."

Hien bowed. "I'm impressed."

"I've done some reading."

"But you're no longer a soldier."

"The hell I'm not. I'll always be a soldier, and I'm not gonna let these bastards have a safe haven. Not in my town."

"And where is your safe haven, Harry?"

Harry stared at the ground. "My safe haven? She's…she's gone."

Hien bowed his head. "And I'm truly sorry about that, my friend."

Harry gripped the fence as he tried to steady himself. "I miss her so much."

"I know you do. But what would your Patsy think about your recent activities, Harry? Do you think she would approve?"

"She's gone, dammit! What the hell does it matter?!"

Hein bowed his head again. "I have agitated you, and I sincerely apologize. We can talk another time, when you're ready. You know where to find me."

"It ain't you that's eating my ass, Hien."

"Harry!" Gertie barked from Charlie's backyard.

Harry turned. "Yeah, Mom."

"I need a ride into town, sonny boy."

"Gimme a minute. I'm…" Harry looked around for Hien, but he was gone.

***

A group of the town's residents stood behind police barricades at the B.I.D. building and watched as A.T.F. CFI's[6] scoured the parking lot of the old library in search of clues that might lead to the identity of the arsonist responsible for the fire the night before. The interior of the building was charred to a near pitch black on both floors, and if the Albrecht fire department hadn't gotten assistance from departments in three nearby towns, the building would have completely burned to the ground. John Coleman walked the first floor, making a visual and mental inventory of the damage. A forensic evidence tech approached him holding shards of burnt glass. "Molotov cocktail?" John said.

"Yes, sir."

"I saw shards on the rear landing when I walked in. Make sure to bag them as well, Agent. Have them analyzed and dusted."

"Yes, sir."

John suspired as he looked around the building. Across the room he noticed an agent talking to a man. He joined them and extended his hand to the man. "John Coleman. I'm with the Bureau. And you are?"

"Ne," the man answered.

"Ne? As in, knee?"

"As in N-e. It's my preferred pronoun."

"He's the office manager here, sir," the agent said. "He claims he knows who's responsible for the arson."

"Is that right?" John said.

"Yeah," Ne replied. "I'm pretty sure it was Ze, Mr. Coleman."

"Ze?"

"Yeah. That's her preferred pronoun. Some employees heard her threaten to burn the building down."

---

[6]ATF Certified Fire Investigators (CFIs) are special agents with highly specialized training in investigating fire and arson-related crimes.

"Let's take a walk, young man," John said.

"I don't identify as a man. I am Ne."

You're so special, John thought. After listening to Ne's account of the argument he had with Ze, and after interviewing several employees who corroborated Ne's story, John had Ze picked up and arrested. She was booked and printed, and she screamed like a banshee at everyone who came within ten feet of her throughout the entire process. The next day, prints lifted from the glass shards found on the library's landing were an eighteen-point match to Ze's. She was charged with arson and advised to seek legal representation.

39

Thursday night at eight, Harry sat at the desk in his basement. He started up his laptop and ham radio. As both started to hum, he checked his watch and saw that it was time. New to the broadcasting game, he was a bit nervous. He inhaled deeply, then exhaled, trying to settle his nerves before starting. Then he picked up the mic. "Hello, Albrecht. How are ya feeling about your town these days? Do you like what's going on? Do you even know what's going on in your town?" He paused and rubbed his temples before going on.

"How about all of you parents out there that have kids going to Albrecht Elementary? Did you know the school is teaching Critical Race Theory to your kids? If you're not sure what that is, look it up. I did. It's scary shit. They're telling your kids they're racist if they're white. And if they're another color, they're told they're oppressed by all white people. Nice thing to teach children, huh?

These cowards want to steal your kids' childhoods, Albrecht. What child needs to hear this bullshit at such a young age? Do they care what they're doing to our kids? Hell, no, they don't, the soulless pricks. But decent people should. You should. They want to indoctrinate your children, Albrecht. You okay with that?!" Harry slammed his fist onto the desk as he sat back and gulped in air, attempting to fight off hyperventilation.

"There was a guy in Germany that did the same thing with young people; his name was Hitler. Ever hear of the Hitler Youth or the League of German Girls? They were organizations set up by the Nazis to indoctrinate their children into the Nazi belief system. Kids were brainwashed and taught to conform. They were taught to snitch on anyone who didn't toe the company line, even if it meant turning on family or friends. And they were taught to never question the authority of the Nazi Party, and they got away with this bullshit for years.

We've got new groups invading our town and acting like Nazis, telling us and our children how to talk and what to think. The Nazis sent dissidents to concentration camps. The bastards invading our town are sending people to sensitivity training classes. Ever hear of the Enabling Act of 1933? It gave the Nazis the power to repress their opponents and limit free speech. See any similarities here? These assholes are trying to exert power over the rest of us, power they didn't earn and power they don't deserve. They want to destroy our way of life and our beliefs. Are we gonna let them get away with it here? Is that what you want for our town? Is that what you want for your country?!"

Harry paused for a moment as he struggled to maintain his composure. "And did you know they tore down the statue of Little Hawk at the ballpark? Apparently, a new organization that set up shop in our town brought in some people from the city to help tear the statue down. You good with that, Albrecht? Are you okay with a bunch of assholes coming to our town and tearing down our monuments? That was our statue! That statue was our way of honoring Little Hawk and his tribe. And they tore it down! And they got away with it!"

Harry rubbed his temples again as his head began to throb. "And they're planning on doing it again. One of these groups, it's called TID, is gonna try tearing down the statue of our town's founding father real soon. These assholes are so fuckin' bold now they're posting this shit on their website. You know what that sound is you're hearing? That's them laughing at us, Albrecht. Laughing!"

Harry gripped the radio's mic and squeezed hard. "C'mon out and show 'em we're not gonna take their bullshit anymore, but keep the kids at home, 'cause it ain't gonna be pretty. That's all I got for now, Albrecht. Show up and show 'em whose town it is." Harry was spent, both physically and emotionally. He turned off his laptop and ham radio, then he called Hans and told him to ready the troops for the upcoming showdown. Sleep came easily to him that night.

***

Only a handful of Albrecht's residents had tuned into Harry's maiden broadcast, but the next afternoon he was visited by a group of neighbors. They asked Harry if what he had said the night before was true. When he assured his neighbors that everything he had said could be verified, they all agreed something needed to be done. They encouraged Harry to keep up the good work, and they assured him that they would pass the word about his broadcasts. One woman suggested that he should give himself a catchy handle to spice things up a bit. Harry agreed that was a good idea. When he asked the group if they were going to attend the clash the next morning, everyone gave him a resounding cheer for an answer.

After the neighbors left, Harry ran some errands, had dinner alone, then he called Joey. And like always of late, he got the boy's voicemail. The good mood he enjoyed for most of the day was suddenly gone. At eight p.m., he climbed into bed and spent most of the night tossing and turning.

***

An eight-foot limestone statue of Friedrich Albrecht stood in the middle of the town square. Most of the townsfolk who traversed the square barely took notice of the statue as they went about their business, but some stopped when they saw two groups assembled on opposite sides of the plaza. The TID faction, about one-hundred strong counting supporters of the group, cheered, waved signs and chanted on bullhorns while several men in the group rested sledgehammers at their feet.

Harry and his men were gathered across the square. Harry saw law

252

"You've been warned, asshole," Harry said.

Ralph walked back to his men. He pointed at the statue as he addressed them. "You see that statue? His name was Albrecht, and he was an Aryan."

"Didn't he start an orphanage for homeless kids?" a member of the group said.

"He might have," Ralph said.

"And didn't he raise a lot of money for the town's first hospital?" another member said.

"How the hell should I know? I'm not from around here," Ralph said.

"Pretty sure he did," the man replied. "Seems like the man did some good shit for this town." Other men in the group nodded in assent.

"He hated gays and transgenders! And all people of color!" Ralph exclaimed. "He was an oppressor, a homophobe and a racist! And he probably owned slaves!" It didn't matter to Ralph that all of his claims were outright lies. His assertions had the effect he was hoping for. The men processed what they had just heard. They took the bait.

"Tear it down!" a TID member yelled as he picked up his sledgehammer and headed for the statue. Other men with sledgehammers followed. The rest of the men from the group marched towards the center of the plaza, led by Ralph.

Seeing this, Harry turned to face his troops. "Men, the Fatherland is watching what we do here today. This is what you were born to do. Make me proud. Take 'em!"

With Harry leading the way, the men from the B of A began to march. The two groups met in the middle of the square and the melee was on. Fists flew in every direction as onlookers recorded the fight on their phones. When Harry and Ralph caught sight of each other, they squared off. Ralph threw the first punch. It caught Harry on the chin. The big man stumbled backwards one step before he regained his balance. He grinned. "That all you got, Sally?"

Ralph threw another punch that Harry blocked, then Harry threw a left hook that splattered Ralph's nose and sent him to the ground, unconscious. Satisfied that Ralph wasn't getting up, Harry looked around the plaza and saw that his men were easily plowing through the TID men. Seeing that they were being routed, the rest of the TID group, the ones not lying on the ground battered and beaten, retreated. The TID supporters watched in stunned silence. They stopped chanting, lowered their signs and banners, and walked away.

Harry, still huffing and puffing from the battle, watched the lawmen converge on his men. As the BOA members readied for a second fight, Harry shouted, "Stand down!" The men watched as Harry extended his arms, allowing a cop to handcuff him. All his men did the same. Every BOA member was arrested and taken away. All of the TID members were allowed to walk away from the scene. The statue of Friedrich Albrecht stood unscathed.

40

Charlie sat at his kitchen table having lunch when he heard a knock on his front door. He stiffened up as he stopped eating in mid-bite, debating whether or not to answer the door. Normally, the old man would have done so without any hesitation, but things had changed in Albrecht. Crime was up, and Charlie had heard stories about a spate of home robberies occurring in the neighborhood lately, some during the day. The Defund the Police movement, like an infectious virus, had gained a foothold in Albrecht, and the town's reputation, and its residents, were paying the price.

Charlie had spent his entire life in Albrecht. He cherished the town's serenity, its friendliness, and the townsfolk's steadfast faith in their police force and judicial system. But Charlie sensed that the town's faith in its institutions was slowly fraying at the seams. Opening his front door now without knowing who was on the other side made him skittish, and that angered the old man. "Who is it?" he called out as he reached the front door.

"It's John Coleman, Mr. Sloan."

"Can you prove it?"

"I've got ID."

"Your I.D. does me no good to me unless it's in braille."

"I forgot about that. So, how do we do this?"

"Who shot Kennedy?"

"John or Robert?"

"Who was the first director of the F.B.I.?"

"J. Edgar Hoover. He served under eight presidents."

Charlie opened the front door. "No miscreants would know those things. Sorry for the delay, John.”

“I understand, Mr. Sloan. You have to be careful these days.”

“Never had to be in this town,” Charlie mumbled.

“Excuse me?”

“Nothing, John. Just an old fool reminiscing about better days.” Charlie gestured for John to come in. The two men walked into the living room and John took a quick look around before taking a seat on the sofa. “If you’re looking for Harry, he’s the house next door.”

“I know, but he's apparently not home, so I figured I’d drop by to see you since I was in the area. I hope I’m not imposing.”

“Not at all. My car’s in the shop, so I’m stuck at home,” Charlie said as he eased into his recliner.

“You drive?”

“That was a joke,” the old man replied.

“Oh. Got it now.”

Ordinarily, Charlie would have offered his company something to drink, but not today. He knew this wasn’t a social call. John looked the room over again. On the mantel above the fireplace sat a set of framed photos. “Family pictures?”

“And some from the war, John. Feel free.”

John went to the fireplace and picked up a photo of two young soldiers standing on a tarmac next to a B-17 Flying Fortress. “Is that a B-17?”

“It is. You know your planes.”

“Did you fly?”

“God, no,” Charlie said. “Heights scared the hell out of me. I was a grunt. Third Army. ‘Tertia Semper Prima’ was our motto. Third always first.”

“Did you serve under Patton?”

“I did. That photo you’re looking at was taken at Midland Army Airfield in Texas. Spent a couple of days there with a high school buddy before my deployment. He’s standing next to me in the picture. Name was Eddie Turnbull. He was at the base training to fly."

"Did he get his wings?"

"He did. On his first mission he flew co-pilot over Germany in '44. The plane took heavy flak and went down. The entire crew was lost."

"I'm sorry, Mr. Sloan."

"So am I. He was my best friend. War is hell."

John set the photo on the mantle and sat down again. Silence hung over the room as he searched for a seamless way to steer the conversation toward his purpose for the visit. "Want to tell me why you're really here, John? Have something to do with Harry?"

Damn. The old man is sharp. "I apologize for the subterfuge. I am here to talk about Harry."

"As a friend, or a law enforcement officer?"

"As a friend. For now."

"That so? How much time have you spent with Harry since you got into town?" Charlie said.

"Not as much as I would like. The bombings have kept me pretty busy. But enough to see he's changed."

Charlie stuffed a pipe with tobacco, lit it and took a long draw. "I've known Harry for over twenty years now. Been with his mother about as long. Losing Patsy and his daughter took a big toll on the man, but haven't seen this change you speak of, John."

"No?"

"Not really. Am pretty sure he's off his meds. Maybe that's affected him, but I couldn't say for sure."

"Pain meds?"

Charlie pointed at his head. "For up here, too. Gertie found a bunch of prescription bottles in the garbage recently, all of 'em half full or more. When she asked him what was going on, Harry walked away without a word."

"Damn," John said.

Charlie already suspected that Harry was responsible for the recent bombings in town, and now he realized that John felt the same. But the old man wasn't about to have a hand in sending Harry to prison. Sensing that he had already said too much, and feeling guilty about it, he hung his head.

"Are you okay, Mr. Sloan?"

Charlie straightened up in his recliner. "John, are you investigating Harry? Is he a suspect in the bombings?"

John started to fidget. "Do you think -?"

"That Harry's the bomber?" Charlie said, chuckling. "Oh, please. Harry couldn't even couldn't even take a dump without a schematic and a pit crew. We both know why you're here, so out with it, son. They say confession is good for the soul."

Caught off guard by Charlie's candor, John sat back in his chair like a chess master who had just been checkmated by what he thought was an inferior opponent. He knew he had to end the visit now. He didn't want to lie to Charlie, but he couldn't discuss details of the investigation, or the short list of suspects, with the old man. He knew now that talking to Charlie was a mistake. John didn't want Harry to find out that an old friend was digging into his private life. A friend that could possibly have Harry incarcerated for the rest of his natural life. And if Charlie were to say anything to Harry… "I should be on my way back to the office," John said, rising from the sofa.

"Humor an old man for just a minute, John, please. Seems to me the bombings aren't related. My guess is you've got more than one bomber, like a copycat, maybe. Sure, the courthouse and the lawyer's office could be related, but what about the coffeehouse and the old library? What's the connection? Just don't see it."

"You have any suspects in mind, Charlie?"

"Well, there are a few militia groups in the area, as I'm sure you're well aware by now."

"We're already looking into a few local groups."

"That's why they pay you the big money, right?"

"You know it," John said. "I really should get going now."

Charlie got to his feet, and he winked at John. "I'm glad we could put our heads together and rule Harry out as the bomber here. I'll send you a bill for my time." Charlie led John to the front door. When the two stepped onto the porch's top step, John thought about asking Charlie to keep their conversation between just the two of them.

"We'll keep our chat just between us, John. No need in Harry knowing, right?"

Damn, this old man is really sharp. "That sounds like a good plan, Charlie. Thanks."

John was halfway to his car when he spotted a black Chevy van parked in front of Harry's home. Harry had parked it there only a few minutes ago, figuring it wouldn't hurt to leave the vehicle in front of the house just this once. But he didn't know that John was talking to Charlie next door.

John stopped suddenly when he recalled a small detail from a report that came across his desk just after the bombing at the Progressive Café. A cabbie parked on a side street adjacent to the café reported seeing a black panel van stop near the intersection where the explosion had just occurred. The report stated that the cabbie saw a wooden crate lying on the street just behind the van, and a large man got out of the vehicle, picked up the crate and shoved it into the back of the van before speeding off. *Explosives get packed in crates.* John dug out his notepad and scribbled down the van's plate number, then he crossed the street and opened the trunk of his car.

He pulled out a magnetic GPS transponder, turned it on, and made his way to the rear of the van. He swept the street for any sign of foot traffic. When he saw none, he dropped to his knees and ran his hand under the van's chassis. Finding a smooth, dirt-free area on top of the rear axle, he attached the transponder to it, then pulled at it to make sure that it was securely attached. He got to his feet, got in his car, and drove away. When he returned to the office, he sent a text to a friend.

41

Harry called Mike Reardon from the police station and told him his situation. Acting as Harry's attorney, Mike went to Barry's Bonds on Elm Street, just off the town's main drag. Mike gave Barry, the proprietor, a check for fifty-thousand dollars to post bail for Harry and all the incarcerated members of the B of A, plus five-thousand dollars in fees for services rendered. Barry assured Mike that the men would be out on bond by the end of the business day. At five that afternoon, Harry walked out of the county jail, followed by his men.

"How'd we get out so soon?" Stefan said.

"I bailed us all out," Harry said. Then he thrust a fist into the air. "We are BOA!" he shouted.

His men encircled the big man, cheered, and took turns shaking his hand. When they settled down, Harry said, "Men, you're all heroes. Today we bloodied the enemy, but it was just one battle. Now we lay low for a while. Our next mission is coming soon. Sig Heil!"

The men saluted Harry. "Sig heil!" they barked in unison. When they dispersed, Harry went home.

***

Harry was relaxing in his recliner when his phone chirped, signaling an incoming text. Hoping it was Joey, he picked up his phone and squinted at it. The text read: *I know what you're doing, and I don't approve. Please stop before someone gets hurt or before you get caught, or both. Your friend, God.* Hoping that he had misread the text, he read it again, but the message was the same.

"Shit," Harry muttered, dropping the phone on the table. *Did someone see me at one of the bombings? Is it John, maybe?* Someone knew, and it didn't matter who it was at the moment. He suddenly remembered the room full of explosives in the basement. He pushed himself out of the recliner, went to the kitchen and poured a cup of coffee. As he sipped his coffee, Harry began making a mental list of the things he would now have to do as a result of the text.

At the top of his list was removing the bomb-making materials and explosives from the storage room and moving all of it to a more secret, secure location. And it would have to be done at night. Harry picked up his phone and punched in Ronnie's number.

"Hey, stranger. Where been you hiding?" Ronnie said.

"Been busy, Ronnie. I need a favor, buddy."

"Name it."

"That old barn on your property still there?"

"Sure is. Why?"

"I need to store some shit. Could I rent a little space in it?"

"Rent? C'mon, buddy, you're kidding, right? How much space you think you need?"

"One corner of the barn should be plenty."

"You need a hand moving the stuff?"

"I got that covered. You got a lock on the barn?"

"I'm in the middle of nowhere, Harry. Why would I?"

"Just curious," Harry said. "Would you mind if I slapped a lock on the doors?"

"Gonna be hiding dead bodies in there?"

"Sure am," Harry said, chuckling.

"If you need something more secure, ever consider a storage unit?"

Harry had considered that, but he figured any self-storage facilities would be armed with security cameras. "Ronnie, if it's a problem…"

"It's no problem," Ronnie answered. "Hell, if it wasn't for you, I wouldn't still have my home."

"Good deal. Was thinking about moving the stuff later tonight. That okay?"

"Sure. Remember how to get here?"

That question stung Harry. He knew it was Ronnie's way of saying that he hadn't been out to see him for quite some time. "I remember, Ronnie."

"When you're done, we'll tip a few."

"Just might do that. If it's not too late."

"It's never too late to have a couple with your best friend."

"See you later tonight, buddy," Harry said before hanging up. Ronnie's last words echoed in his mind as he set down his phone. *It's never too late to have a couple with a buddy.* These days, it was never too late for Ronnie to start drinking. Or too early, for that matter. Harry's heart ached for his best friend. He'd dragged Ronnie, nearly kicking and screaming, to an A.A. meeting a couple of years before, but Ronnie wouldn't admit to himself, nor to a room full of strangers, that he had a drinking problem. When he was asked to introduce himself by the moderator, he stood up and said, "My name's Ronnie, and I don't need this shit," before walking out of the building, leaving Harry sitting there wondering what the hell had just happened.

Harry felt guilty about drinking with Ronnie, but he figured if his friend insisted on "putting a few down," he shouldn't be drinking alone. At least he could make sure Ronnie got home safely if they were out drinking together. Harry knew the sadness and loneliness that his friend was trying to cope with. He knew Ronnie's agonizing grief and bitterness. Once Harry joked that they should start a "dead wives club," adding they could collect dues, have a secret handshake, and do the other things clubs do. He hoped to get a laugh, or at least a chuckle, out of his friend.

But Ronnie didn't find Harry's attempt at humor even remotely amusing. After calling Harry an asshole, Ronnie punched the big man and nearly knocked him on his butt. Harry rubbed his jaw and thought for one brief moment about taking a swing at his buddy. Instead, he just walked away, figuring that maybe he deserved exactly what he got. Harry felt guilty for not having visited Ronnie at his home in what seemed like months. Stowing the explosives at the farmhouse would give him an excuse to see his friend, at least. Thinking that eased his guilt a bit. He lay down and managed to sleep for a couple of hours.

***

It was just after eleven p.m. when Harry finished loading the van with most of the explosives from the basement. When he slid the last crate into the back, he shut the rear door and leaned against the vehicle, sweat pouring from what seemed to be every gland in his bear-like frame.

After wiping his brow, he went back into the house, grabbed a bottle of bleach from the kitchen and headed for the basement. He spent the next hour wiping down the floor and every wall and shelf in the storage room.

Then he grabbed a steel, security trunk off of the table and hauled it behind the shed in his backyard. He set the trunk into a hole. The box contained Semtex, blasting caps, and notes with detailed instructions on how to detonate the explosive. After refilling the hole, he patted down the dirt to smoothen it out.

Harry was about to get into his van when he saw Crash skipping down his front steps. "Headed out to get some ass, Harry?" Crash said, snickering.

"Don't start with me, boy."

"Or what, old man? I'll stand here talkin' shit all night if I wanna. And ain't dick you can do about it."

Harry took two steps toward the boy, and Crash hightailed it to his car, jumped in it and fired up the engine. Harry's body shook with rage when the roar of the Chevelle's motor shattered the nighttime's tranquility. Crash rocketed down the driveway. He cut the wheel hard and hit the brakes, and the Chevelle screeched to a stop just inches shy of the van's rear end. Crash poked his head out of the car and grinned. "Scare ya, Harry?"

Harry smiled and winked at the boy. "It's coming, boy. It's coming."

Crash laughed as he sped down the street. Harry got into the van and headed for Ronnie's farm. After merging onto the highway, he checked his speed every ten seconds or so to make sure he wasn't speeding. He didn't want to give the police any excuse to pull him over tonight. As he continued down the two-lane highway, he fantasized about the different ways he could get even with the boy idiot. *I can blow up his house. Maybe make it look like a gas leak.* Then he realized the homes on either side of the boy's house could be damaged as well, and Harry liked his neighbors. He then considered option two.

I can kill him. I could do it lots of ways. Who'd miss the little bastard, anyway? The idea sent a warm tingle throughout his body. *Hell, I'd be doing society a favor. Might even be Time's Man of the Year.* The tingling ended abruptly when Harry remembered his Catholic upbringing and the Commandment: "Thou shall not kill."

"Aw, the hell with that nonsense," said General Patton, who was now sitting shotgun in the van. Harry's body spasmed when he heard the general's voice. Quickly regaining his composure, Harry eased off the gas and brought the van to a stop on the shoulder of the road. He had a death grip on the steering wheel as he drew in a deep breath, held it, and began counting under his breath. When he reached five, he slowly exhaled. The general chuckled. "Breathing exercises again? They're not gonna help."

Harry didn't respond. He continued to draw in huge gulps of air then exhaled deeply as he stared out into the blackness of the night. "Men didn't get therapy in my day, Blake. They sucked it up and they did whatever they had to do. Men are pussies these days, you included. They're told now it's good to get in touch with their feelings. Horseshit!

Lemme tell you a little story…" Harry groaned his disapproval, but that didn't stop the general. "Back in '43, there were a couple of soldiers in a field hospital that said they were hurt. The doctors said they had shell shock. What a crock of shit. You know what I did? I slapped the shit out of both of 'em. Ike made me apologize to the sniveling bastards. Can you believe that bullshit?"

Harry closed his eyes and continued taking deep breaths. "Men didn't cry in my day," Patton said. "We bottled it all up like a real man's supposed to. We never asked for help, for anything. Men in my day-"

"Died of heart attacks in their fifties, like my dad did. Right, General?"

Patton grimaced. "Your father was a warrior, but he was cheated of his legacy. He was meant to die fighting. The best death for a soldier is to die on the battlefield trying to kill the enemy. Remember that."

"I'll keep it in mind," Harry said. His breathing finally evened out. "I'm gonna leave my own legacy, General. You can count on that." Seeing no traffic on the road in either direction, he put the van in drive and pulled back onto the highway.

Patton looked towards the back of the van. "You've got enough munitions in the back to blow us to hell and back, soldier. What's the target tonight? Tell me it's those fucking Russkies. I hate those commie bastards."

"This stuff's going into storage."

"Storage? What's the hell?"

Harry caught sight of the frontage road exit, and slowing, turned on his blinker. "I've got a war buddy who's an FBI agent. He's in town and he's been sniffing around."

"That Coleman guy? Let's kill him."

"That your answer to everything?" Harry said as he caught sight of a billboard coming up on his right. As he passed it, he thought it read, *Be Less White, Albrecht,* but he wasn't sure, so Harry pulled onto the shoulder of the highway and backed up until the van sat alongside the billboard. He was right. The sign did read, *Be Less White, Albrecht.* This time, Harry understood the message. Infuriated, he got out of the van and yanked open its rear doors. He grabbed a gallon of paint and tore off the can's lid. Then he spun in the billboard's direction and took aim. Filled with adrenaline and rage, he hurled the paint can at the sign. When it collided with the sign, the paint splattered on the billboard, blotting out a portion of the sign's message. Harry grunted with satisfaction, but his anger demanded more from him. Now, he wanted a fight. Now, he needed a fight. He climbed into the van and saw that the general was gone. He pulled back onto the highway.

A few minutes later, Harry turned onto the dirt road that led to Ronnie's property. Breathing a sigh of relief now that he was off the main thoroughfare, he flipped on his high beams and slowed just in time to avoid potholes ahead on both sides of the narrow road. "Damn slalom course," he muttered. He had told Ronnie more than once to have the road resurfaced, and he had even offered to pay for the work, but Ronnie always put it off. He had let his property deteriorate over the past few years, and that irritated Harry to no end.

Rounding a bend in the road, Harry slammed on the breaks when he saw a state police cruiser, its light bar still flashing, idling about a hundred feet up ahead of him. Beyond the cruiser, in the near distance, he spotted the farmhouse, but he couldn't get to it without passing the patrol car.

Shit. Harry turned off his headlights and put the van into park. *What the hell's a cop doing here in the middle of the night?* Craning his neck out the window, he peered through the darkness. When his eyes adjusted for the dark, he spotted Ronnie's truck in front of the cruiser. Harry figured that Ronnie had gotten pulled over for drunk driving. He went over his options: he could hightail it out of there and leave his buddy to fend for himself since the cops hadn't seen him yet. Or he could intervene and hope like hell he could somehow help his buddy to avoid spending a night, or more, in jail.

Sweat poured down his face as he sat back and mulled over the two choices. The trouble with option two was that he knew some of the state troopers that patrolled the town's highways could be hard asses. They might decide to search the van if he even stared at them the wrong way. But Harry couldn't leave his friend to fend for himself. Grabbing a towel, he dried his face, stiffened his spine, flipped on the headlights, and put the van into drive.

When Harry pulled up behind the cruiser, he saw two state troopers standing on either side of Ronnie. Trooper Maxwell, a lanky, young guy well over six feet tall, looked in Harry's direction, shielding his eyes from the glare of Harry's headlights. As Harry cut the van's engine, Maxwell pulled out his flashlight, shining it on the van as he cautiously approached it.

"You lost, sir?" the trooper said.

"Nope," Harry said. "Just came to see my buddy."

"Who's that?"

"The guy you're talking to over there. His name's Ronnie. Ronnie Wanahton."

"You're his friend?" the trooper asked.

Harry nodded. "Why'd you pull him over, officer?"

"Can I see some ID?"

Harry softly exhaled as he handed his license over. The trooper studied it for a moment. Harry kept a wary eye on the trooper in his sideview mirror as Maxwell did a slow walk around the van. When the trooper stopped at the rear of the van, Harry's pulse quickened. Maxwell finished circling the van, and he stopped when he reached the driver's side door. When the trooper looked up his gaze narrowed. "Tinted rear windows, huh? Not hiding something illegal in there, are you, sir?"

"Just a couple of dead ex-wives, officer."

Maxwell smiled. "Please remain in your vehicle, Mr. Blake. I'll be right back."

The trooper got into the cruiser and ran a "wants and warrants" on

Harry. Ronnie, with nearly a fifth of whiskey in him, slouched against the side of the cruiser as the second trooper kept a close eye on him. Ronnie snapped out of his stupor when he caught sight of Harry. "That you, Harry?"

"Yeah, Ronnie. How you doin'?"

"I went out for a pack of smokes and Barney Fife here pulled me over."

Trooper Washington, a powerfully built man about half Harry's age, wasn't amused by Ronnie's sarcasm. Harry watched as Washington grabbed his baton and used it to push Ronnie against the cruiser. "Take it easy there, buddy," Ronnie said. Washington smiled at Harry as trooper Maxwell returned to the van. He handed Harry his license.

"You're good to go, Mr. Blake."

"What about my buddy?"

"Your friend was all over the road when my partner and I spotted him," Maxwell said. "He just blew a one-point-six. He's way over the limit."

"He's a vet, like me," Harry said. "He lost his wife a few years ago. That kicked the shit out of him. And his own kids disowned him, so now he drinks. I tried to get him help a while back."

"Any luck with that, Mr. Blake?"

"He's on and off the wagon all the time. I try to keep an eye on him, but-"

"Can't be there all the time, right?"

"Exactly. Look, officer, my buddy could lose his license and do some serious jail time over this. Couldn't you look the other way just this once? I mean, what's the harm? He's already home, right? Would mean a lot to me."

"I wish I could. What brings you out this late, anyway?"

"Came to check on him. Called him a little earlier and he didn't pick up his phone, so here I am."

"My partner's got a thing for drunk drivers, Mr. Blake. I'm afraid we're going to have to take him in."

"He didn't hurt anybody, right?"

"Not this time, no."

"Please, officer," Harry said. "Talk to your partner. It would mean a lot."

"Sit tight."

"I got a bum knee. I'd like to get out and stretch it out, if that's okay."

"Sure thing," the trooper said as he walked away. Harry eased out of the van and locked the doors. Hearing Ronnie yell, "Harry, you still there?" he answered, "Sure am, buddy."

"I went out for smokes and Barney Fife here pulled me over."

"Yeah, I heard that, Ronnie."

Trooper Washington grabbed Ronnie by the shoulders and shook him. "That's real funny, loser." he said. He spun Ronnie around, then cuffed him. "Fucking no-good drunk." Trooper Washington deliberately rammed Ronnie's head into the roof of the squad car before stuffing him into the back seat. For good measure, the trooper shoved his boot into Ronnie's ass to finish the job.

"Hey!" Harry yelled. "What the hell, asshole?"

Washington glared defiantly at Harry. Trooper Maxwell, who stood between the two men, knew there was about to be trouble if he didn't intervene. With his arms up in a gesture of non- aggression, he walked back toward Harry.

"We got a problem, Max?" Washington said.

"I hope not," Maxwell answered.

Harry's fists were clenched as trooper Maxwell reached him. "Mr. Blake, I need you to get back into your vehicle and vacate the premises."

His chest heaving, Harry pointed at Washington. "Ain't nobody gonna treat a buddy of mine like that. Ever!"

Trooper Washington slammed the cruiser's back door shut, then he marched toward Harry. Snorting with rage, Harry began to advance on

Washington, but Trooper Maxwell stepped into his path. "Please get back into your vehicle and go home, Mr. Blake." Harry slammed into him, almost knocking him to the ground. Maxwell quickly regained his footing, then he grabbed Harry in a bear hug, slowing the big man's forward momentum. "Let me at the prick!" Harry bellowed.

As Trooper Washington approached, his hand rested on the Taser gun stowed in his duty belt. "We got a problem here?"

"You're damn right we do," Harry said.

"Let me handle this, partner," Maxwell said as he turned to face Harry. "Mr. Blake, this is your last warning. Get in your vehicle and go home. Now."

"Not until that asshole apologizes for what he did."

"I got shit to apologize for, old man. Move it along or you'll be sharing a cell with your buddy," Washington said.

His chest heaving, Harry easily pushed trooper Maxwell aside. "You didn't have to rough him up. I'm more your size. Wanna try strapping me on, tough guy?"

"Are you challenging me to a fight?" Washington said.

"I'd drop you without breaking a sweat," Harry responded.

"That's it. You're under arrest for disturbing the peace. Cuff him, Max."

Harry grinned. "Why don't you try cuffing me, Officer Badass."

Maxwell again positioned himself between the two men. "He's serious, Mr. Blake," he said.

"So am I."

"That's it," Washington said. Standing within swinging distance of Harry, he unholstered his Taser and aimed it at Harry's chest, but before he could pull the trigger, Harry knocked it from his hand. Washington lunged, chin first, at Harry, and Harry nailed the trooper on the jaw with a roundhouse right. Washington's knees buckled before he hit the ground. Rubbing his knuckles, Harry glanced at Maxwell. The trooper stood there stunned at what he had just witnessed. Then he grinned.

"Something funny?" Harry said.

"You're right. He is an asshole," Maxwell replied. "Nice right, Mr. Blake."

Harry extended his arms towards Maxwell. "Now you can arrest me."

"Sorry. I have to do this." Maxwell cuffed Harry, and the big man put up no resistance as the trooper put him in the back of the cruiser. Ronnie snapped out of his stupor when Harry leaned into him.

"Where've you been, Harry?"

"Busy knocking a cop out."

"Wish I'd seen it," Ronnie said before he passed out. He remained in that condition until the two men were booked and thrown into the county jail for the night.

***

The next morning, Harry called Mike Reardon. Mike rescheduled a meeting to go downtown and bail out Harry and Ronnie. Harry thanked him profusely after putting Ronnie in a cab, then he took Mike to lunch and recounted the events of the night before. "I wonder if those troopers had body cameras on them." Mike said, sipping his coffee. "I'll have to check into that. You say the one cop tried to tase you while you were just standing there?"

Harry nodded. "I challenged him to a fight. He came at me, and I knocked him out."

"I got a copy of the police report on the way here, Harry. You didn't just knock him out. You broke his jaw and knocked out three of his teeth." Mike took another bite of his Reuben sandwich, while Harry, who barely slept the night before, yawned. "There'll be an arraignment," Mike said. "But we can have it waived."

"What are they charging me with?" Harry said.

"Assaulting a peace officer and resisting arrest. That's some pretty serious shit. You're already on probation, right? And you're still facing charges for the fight in the town square. You could do some time."

"Buy me some time if you can, Mike. I'll pay you whatever you want."

"Will do what I can."

Harry knew he needed a little more time to finish what he had started, and he couldn't accomplish his goals from the inside of a jail cell. He got up and dropped some cash on the table.

"Thanks, Mike."

"See you at class tonight?" Mike said.

"Yeah, but I don't think we'll have to worry about going to those bullshit classes for much longer."

"You're being a little cryptic here, Harry."

"You'll find out soon enough. The whole town will."

"Where are you headed?" Mike said.

"My buddy's house."

"The buddy they arrested for drunk driving?"

"Yeah. If you'll represent him, too, I'll pay you."

"I don't handle drunk driving cases, but I know someone. She's good."

"Okay. And thanks again for today. I gotta go get my van." Harry started to walk to the front door.

"Assuming it's still there," Mike said as he finished his coffee. "They may have impounded it."

Harry froze. He had no idea that the authorities could impound his vehicle, and he suddenly realized that he never got the chance to unload the explosives from the van the night before. He dug out his phone and frantically punched in Ronnie's number. One ring. *C'mon, Ronnie. Pick up.* Then a second, unanswered ring. He turned towards Mike. "Mike, just curious. Can they search my van if they impounded it?"

"They can. They don't even need a search warrant. Why?"

Oh, shit. "No reason." Another ring. *Get up, Ronnie. Get your ass out of bed and tell me it's still there.*

Ronnie finally answered his phone. "Yeah?" he said in a voice still raspy from alcohol and fatigue.

"It's me, buddy. Is my van still there?"

"I don't know."

"I need you to check, Ronnie. Now."

"I'm in bed. Can't it wait?"

"Now, Ronnie!"

Startled, Mike looked up from the paperwork that he was leafing through. Harry smiled as if everything was just fine, but panic gripped him. His hand throbbed as he clenched his phone. *C'mon, Ronnie.* After what felt like an eternity… "Yeah, it's here," Ronnie said. "Coming to get it?"

"Sure am. I'll be there soon." Harry hung up his phone.

"Need a ride, Harry?" Mike said.

"Yeah, but I didn't want to bother you. Figured you needed to get back to the office."

"I moved some stuff around 'til later this afternoon. I've got time."

"You sure, Mike?"

"It's no problem."

After Mike dropped him off at home, Harry got into his truck and drove up the highway. Moments after he pulled onto the access road leading to Ronnie's farmhouse, he saw that his van was parked where he had left it the night before. As he got out of the truck, he looked the surrounding area over. Except for some wildlife scurrying around on the property, he was alone. When he reached his van, Harry yanked on the driver's side door handle; it was still locked. Breathing a sigh of relief, he looked toward the house. He figured that Ronnie would still be in bed, continuing to sleep off last night's bender.

He swung open the barn's wooden door and guided the van into a corner of the barn next to a row of horse stalls. He locked the van, then he attached a heavy-duty padlock to the barn door after closing it. He then made his way towards the house.

Harry stepped into the living room and the stench stopped him in his tracks. The room reeked of spoiled food, and it looked like it had caught the business end of a tornado. The coffee table was littered with food containers, some still half full of food. Harry guessed that much of it had gone bad some time ago. Unlaundered clothes were draped over every piece of furniture, and the entire room was covered in dust. Harry hadn't stepped foot into the house for months now, and remembering that, he hung his head in shame. *I'm sorry, Ronnie.* His best friend was living like a true recluse; a man who had given up on life. Ronnie was completely alone, except for his one- hundred-and-ten- pound chocolate lab, Rex, who, upon hearing footsteps, snarled as he stepped into the room. Harry smiled and opened his arms wide. "C'mere, boy."

Rex recognized Harry immediately. He ran to the big man, nearly knocking him to the floor when he reared up on his hind legs and jabbed his front paws into Harry's chest. Harry gave the dog a hearty hug, then led him to the kitchen. He winced when he saw the neglect: dirty dishes stacked high in the sink gave off an odor that nearly caused Harry to wretch. After shaking the stench off, he saw that Rex's bowls were empty. He set them on the counter. As he filled them with water and food, Rex yelped when he saw that he was about to be fed. Harry set the bowls on the floor, and the dog dug in.

Harry went to the first-floor bedroom. He opened the door slowly and saw that Ronnie lay in the bed, sleeping. He bent over his friend. Ronnie's breathing was shallow and labored, and he still reeked of alcohol. Harry gently shook him. "Get up, buddy." Ronnie grunted and pulled a blanket over his head. Harry shook him again, this time a little harder. "C'mon, Ronnie. Rise and shine."

"Leave me alone," Ronnie murmured as he rolled onto his side.

Harry grabbed him by a shoulder and spun him on his back. "Let's go, Ronnie. It's time."

Ronnie opened his eyes. "Let me sleep, Harry."

"Had a rough one last night, huh?" Harry said.

"No rougher than usual."

"How much do you remember, buddy?"

"Too damn much. I'll have to start upping the dosage," Ronnie said, pointing to an empty liquor bottle toppled over on the nightstand.

"You remember the cops hauling us off to jail?" Ronnie nodded. "And why we were there?" Ronnie nodded again. "Both our asses are in a sling," Harry said. "You understand that, buddy?"

Ashamed, Ronnie slung an arm over his eyes as he began to sob. "I - I got us into some shit, didn't I? I'm sorry, buddy."

"You need help, Ronnie. We're gonna get you some."

Ronnie sobbed more as Harry gently grabbed his arm and helped him get out of bed. "Grab a shower. Then pack a bag or two. You may be gone a while," Harry said.

"What about Rex?"

"He can stay with me 'til you get back home."

While Ronnie showered and packed, Harry made a few phone calls. When Ronnie was ready to go, Harry helped him into his truck, then he let Rex into the rear cab. He pulled onto the highway; his destination was a detox center just outside of Albrecht.

***

An hour after Harry left Ronnie's property, John Coleman pulled up to the barn in a nondescript, gray sedan. A tracking program on his laptop pinged loudly, telling John the GPS device that he had planted on Harry's van was working and located nearby. He got out and looked around the property. The farmland looked barren and neglected, as if an Arctic squall had just rolled through this small section of South Dakota.

He walked towards the barn's wooden double doors. When he saw that the doors were padlocked, he kicked at the dirt in frustration. John knew that Harry's van was parked in the barn, even without actually

277

seeing it. He stared skyward and sighed, debating whether or not to make a phone call and get a search warrant. A very brief tug of war between his head and his heart ensued. When the battle was over, John got back into his car and drove off.

***

After dropping Ronnie off at the rehab center and spending a little time with his friend, Harry returned home. He yawned as he slipped into his recliner. When his phone rang, he saw it was Ken Burton calling, a call he had been waiting for. "Hey, Ken."

"Hi, Harry. They should be coming for your friend at the C.A.T. tonight."

"Thank, Ken." Harry hung up his phone and closed his eyes. He grew irritated thinking about having to attend another class at the B.I.D later that night. But being fairly certain about how the class was going to end, he smiled as he nodded off.

42

Harry had a bounce in his step as he walked through the front doors of the C.A.T. building later that evening. His classmates didn't know it yet, but they were about to have an unscheduled break from their indoctrination classes. Harry's only regret was that he didn't have a yearbook that he could have everyone sign before they left. When he stepped into the classroom, he saw it was filled with the usual, resentful faces. Mike, seated in the back of the room, waved, and Harry took a desk next to him, then shook his hand. "Hey, stranger."

"Stay out of trouble today, Harry?"

"So far." Harry winked at Mike. "I should've brought popcorn for the show."

"What show?" Mike said.

"You'll see." Mr. Wilkins stepped into the classroom, sporting a shit-eating grin as he stared at Harry. Remembering their post-class standoff after their last encounter, Harry knew that Wilkins would be gunning for him tonight, but he wasn't worried. He met Wilkins' stare and raised him a sneer. "Good evening, class," Mr. Wilkins said. "Are we still on the road to being better, more tolerant people?"

"Gag," Harry said loudly enough for the entire class to hear, including Mr. Wilkins. There were snickers and guffaws.

Mike leaned in towards Harry. "Don't provoke the asshole," he whispered.

"Was that the class clown I heard?" Mr. Wilkins said.

The class fell silent. No one wanted to anger Mr. Wilkins. They knew he could make their lives even more miserable with one bad evaluation. "Mr. Blake, might it have been you, I wonder?"

"Wonder no more, Teach," Harry answered.

"Come on up here, if you don't mind."

Mike grabbed Harry's arm as he arose from his seat. "Careful, Harry."

"I'm good," Harry said before striding down the aisle. He smiled as he pulled up next to Wilkins. "Why don't you tell the class why you were ordered by the court to attend these classes, Mr. Blake."

"No sweat, Teach." Harry faced the class. "I threw a rock at some idiot's car 'cause he pushed me too far. The court called it ethnic intimidation, or a hate crime, or some shit, and they convicted me of a hate crime 'cause it turns out the boy idiot's part Indian."

"Indian? Do you mean a person from the country of India, Mr. Blake?"

"No, I mean an Indian from this country. The boy's one-eighth Sioux and seven-eighths asshole." The class snickered.

"I noticed that you used the term 'boy' when you described the young man. That's a very derogatory term, Mr. Blake."

"Everything's derogatory to a guy like you, Teach. He is a boy. A young, punk-ass boy. Got anything else?"

Mr. Wilkins grimaced as the class snickered again at Harry's response. But then he smiled, thinking he had found an opening. "I thought you said he was Native American."

"That's what his lawyer says. Hell, he looks whiter than me."

"When you hear the term, 'redskin', what do you think, Mr. Blake?"

"Bad football team. Their front office is a mess. And they overpay for free agents past their prime."

"I'm not talking about the football team. And I'm sure you know they're not called the Redskins anymore."

"You guys won that one, huh? Yeah, fuck finding a cure for cancer, right? Your kind is tackling the really serious problems in the world." Harry rolled his eyes. "You should be really proud of yourselves," he added.

Still more snickering came from the class. Mr. Wilkins crossed his arms. "Doesn't the term 'redskin' offend you?"

"Nah. Why the hell should it?"

"Exactly, Mr. Blake, Why should it? You're not Native American. You can't understand, or you just don't care, about their plight, about the way they've been treated for over three centuries by the white man. So, what's the big deal about a white man like yourself assaulting a young Native American man, right?"

"I threw a rock at the idiot's car after he nearly ran me over. I never laid a hand on him. And if the rest of the people here knew this kid, they'd of done the same damn thing. It had nothing to do with him being part Sioux. I don't give a shit about that."

Mr. Wilkins smirked. "So, what you're saying is you don't care about Native Americans. In fact, it seems to me that your actions tell us you harbor a hatred for all of them. That offends me."

"Just so happens my best friend is a Sioux Indian. His name's Ronnie, and he's from Pine Ridge. Want me to bring him to class sometime? We could do a Show and Tell kinda thing."

"Ah, so, it's the old I-can't-be-a-racist-because-I've-got-a-friend-of-color argument? Is that it, Mr. Blake? I find that offensive."

Harry yawned as if he were in the ring beating the hell out of a one-armed man and was growing bored by the mismatch. "Well, I'm offended that you're pretending to be offended, Teach. Two can dance to that song." There was more laughter from the class. Louder and more boisterous laughter. Harry reveled in it. "You ever been to the Pine Ridge Reservation, Teach?" Harry said.

"I can't say that I have," Mr. Wilkins said. "Why do you ask?"

"You're practically pissing yourself about what I did to the boy, like you really care, but you've never been to the reservation? It's just a stone's throw away."

"I'm a very busy man, Mr. Blake."

"Of course, you are, Teach. You're busy telling other people, like me and my classmates here, what bad people we are. And you're busy collecting paychecks for doing it, right?"

"I'm helping people. I would do this job for free."

"Some kids pull the wings off of flies for free, too."

The class laughed again, and Harry noticed that Mr. Wilkin's hands were shaking and his eyes twitched. "Do you have a point here, Mr. Blake?" he said.

"You say you'd do this job for free, huh? If that's so, why don't you donate some of your income to the Sioux people at Pine Ridge if you care so much about them? Did you know it's the poorest reservation in the state?"

"The economic plight of those people is tragic, and we can have a conversation about the underlying causes another time. But for now, I'd like to play a little game, Mr. Blake. What do you say we do a little role playing?"

"Why the hell not."

"Good. Let's pretend that you and I are walking down a street toward each other, and you stare at me as I pass by."

"Okay," said Harry.

"So, I see you staring at me, and I stop and say to you, 'Haven't you ever seen a Native American man before?' How would you respond to that?" said Mr. Wilkins.

"I'd say, 'Of course I've seen an Indian before.' What's your point?"

"I didn't use the word, Indian. Mr. Blake. I said, Native American."

"Tomato, tomato. Calling a man an Indian isn't a slur."

"But what if I wish to be called Native American? What if I find the word Indian offensive?"

"Who decided it's offensive? You? And exactly when did that word become offensive, like you say it is?"

"Society decided it is an offensive term, Mr. Blake."

"That so? What's your definition of 'society'? Is it just you and your kind? You think you speak for everyone in this country? Why do people like you get to decide what's offensive and what's not? Who the hell put you in charge of the language?"

"Yeah, who?" a classmate said.

"What if I demanded that you call me a Native American, Mr. Blake? Out of respect?"

"First off, calling someone an Indian isn't disrespecting them. And second, if you demand my respect, you probably already lost it. People have to earn respect. Do you respect me, Teach? And do you think I care either way?"

"My feelings towards you are not relevant to this exercise, Mr. Blake."

"Lemme tell you what is relevant. Assholes like you are trying to force the rest of us into compelled speech. You're trying to make the rest of us say things we don't want to say, or don't have to say. That's really fucked up."

Harry had the class's full attention. Growing agitated, they sat up and fixed their gazes on Harry as if he was descending a mountain carrying two stone tablets. Mr. Wilkins took notice. And he began to perspire. "We're – we're getting off topic here, Mr. Blake. You seem unwilling to admit your prejudice to me or the class. That's a problem."

"I'll tell you what the problem is," Harry said, turning to face Mr. Wilkins. "You're trying to make me look bad in front of everybody here by implying I'm racist. That's what assholes like you do when you can't beat a guy fair and square. You try to trap people by twisting their words around or by calling them racists. It's the coward's way. You're a fuckin' coward, Teach." The class fell into a silenced awe. Then, murmured assents rippled through the room.

Mr. Wilkins took a step back, knowing that he was losing the battle, and the class. "That's – that's not true, Mr. Blake. We're merely role playing here. We are trying to help you overcome your hostility towards Native Americans."

"Lemme tell you something about Native Americans. I served with a few of 'em in Vietnam. Lakotas. Some of them were from this area. They were good soldiers, good men, and their people were great warriors. They fought for this great country even after we took their land from them and forced them onto reservations. I keep hearing all this talk lately about reparations. If we're gonna do it for anyone, how 'bout we do it for the people who had their land and homes stolen from them?"

"Right on, Harry!" Mike said. Harry's classmates roared their collective approval.

Caught off guard by the growing boldness of the class, Mr. Wilkins backpedaled until he nearly bumped into the wall behind him. After a few moments, he regained his composure. "That's an interesting point, Mr. Blake. So, you feel guilt - white guilt - for what we did to the Native American peoples, right?"

"I'm not buying into your white guilt bullshit, Teach. I wasn't around when we took their land, so no guilt here. But do I feel bad for 'em? Sure as hell do. There's a difference. But we oughta make it right by them."

"How so, Mr. Blake? By assaulting them with rocks?"

"We're back to that again? You're one sorry-ass, broken record."

"That's just your white privilege talking. You're in denial, Mr. Blake. But I'll break you of that before we're through here."

Harry chuckled. "Good luck with that. You probably couldn't even break wind." The class snickered.

Mr. Wilkins smiled through Harry's barb. "That's very clever, Mr. Blake."

"Gotta question for you, Teach. You're white, too, right?"

"That is the skin pigmentation I was born with, yes."

"You feel guilty for being white?"

"Of course, I do. And this is my penance for it."

"Penance?"

"Yes, penance. I'm here to help white people confront their implicit and aversive racism, and to conquer it. I'm trying to have an open and honest dialogue with you here. But it seems you're unwilling to do that."

Harry glared at Mr. Wilkins as he took a step towards him. "You want honest dialogue, Teach? People like you really piss me off."

"People like me?"

"Yeah, people like you who are quick to accuse other people of shit at the drop of a hat. People like you who piss and moan and scream that you're offended by every stupid ass little thing, people like you who pretend to know what's in a stranger's heart or mind when they say or do something you don't agree with, without knowing one fuckin' thing about that person. People like you feel better about themselves by tearing other people down. Little people like you who try to ruin other people's lives just because they don't buy the bullshit you spread around like horse manure, and 'cause they don't kowtow to pissants like you."

A hush descended over the class. It was broken by a single person's applause. Soon, the entire class was clapping. Adrenaline rushed through Harry. He knew he was saying what every person in the class had been thinking but was afraid to articulate.

Mr. Wilkins raised a shaky hand to restore order. "That was some speech, Mr. Blake. You certainly have a lot of misguided anger in you, which is why you're here. We need to love and respect all people, and their feelings. We're here to learn to do just that."

"What about little boys, Teach? Do we need to love and respect them, too?"

"Of course. Why would you ask that?"

"You seem to love little boys - a lot. Your computer is packed with pictures of them, isn't it? Lots of young, naked boys, from what I hear."

Stunned, Wilkins' knees began to wobble. The class let out a collective gasp, and they stared at the instructor with accusing eyes. "I – I don't know what you're talking about."

Harry looked towards the door and saw two sheriff deputies enter the classroom. "They're here for you, Teach."

Wilkins pointed at Harry as he addressed the class. "This – this man is lying. There's no truth to his allegations."

Harry leaned in towards Wilkins and whispered, "I told you not to push me, you little prick." Mr. Wilkins eyes widened in panic when he saw the deputies approach him.

"Are you Steve Wilkins?" a deputy said.

"Yes. But -"

"Mr. Wilkins, you're under arrest for possession of child pornography." The deputy spun Wilkins around and cuffed him. The class watched as the two deputies walked Mr. Wilkins out of the classroom. Then they turned their awe-struck gazes towards Harry. They stared at him as if he had just invented fire before their very eyes.

"School's out," Harry said. The room erupted in applause as Harry marched triumphantly out the door.

43

The next morning, Harry awoke with a smile just after eleven a.m., showered, then splashed on some aftershave. Satisfied that he looked presentable, he left the house and headed toward the convenience store. He didn't really need anything, but he wanted an excuse to walk down the street in case Miss Jessica was up and about. As he neared her house, his heart started to pound. He felt like a boy at his first school dance. He caught sight of her just a moment later, sitting on her porch swing.

"Hello, Harry," Jessica said, smiling warmly.

Harry stopped and smiled. "Hi, Miss Jess. How are you?"

"I'm fine. On your way to the store?"

"Am. Need anything?"

"Just the usual, if you don't mind, handsome."

"Not a bit."

After picking up Jess's favorite brand of tea, Harry returned to her house and saw that Miss Jessica was still on her swing. He climbed her front steps with little difficulty today and handed her a small paper bag.

"Thank you, Harry. Didn't you shop for yourself?"

Harry had forgotten to buy anything for himself to maintain the ruse. "Yeah, but I put it on layaway." Jessica laughed as she gestured to Harry to sit next to her. The wooden swing groaned under Harry's weight as he eased himself onto it. "You must have a defective swing here, Miss Jess. It's either that or one of us has gotta lose some weight."

Jessica giggled as the swing began to slowly sway. "You are a funny man, Harry Blake."

"I have my moments. How's your day so far?"

"Just fine. I did some gardening earlier, and I was about to make

287

lunch. Interested in joining me?”

“That sounds good.”

“Oh, I almost forgot to tell you,” Jessica said. “A few days ago, I saw a man crouched under your van.”

Harry dug his feet into the porch’s floorboards and the swing came to an immediate stop. “Crouched under it? What did this man look like?”

“I’d say he’s about your age, short and full head of gray, wavy hair. I think I’ve seen him stop by your house a couple of times. He looked kind of... official.”

John, Harry thought. “And you said he was under my van?”

“He was. That’s not something you see every day, is it?”

Harry got to his feet. “I just remembered there’s something I gotta take care of, Jess. Sorry, I’ll have to take a rain check on lunch.” His pulse rate climbing, he bounded down the steps.

“Is everything okay, Harry?”

Harry didn’t stop to respond. His mind racing, he hurried down the street and blew through his front door. He threw his keys on the table, then drew in a deep breath. *First things first, Harry.* He had to find out why John was poking around underneath his van. He grabbed a boxful of rags and a bottle of bleach from the garage. After throwing the items into his truck, he drove to Ronnie’s farmhouse. Once there, he opened the padlock on the barn’s door and went in.

He crouched beneath the van’s rear end, turned on a flashlight, and scanned the underbelly of the vehicle. He located the tracking device where John had mounted it on the axle. Pulling it loose, Harry examined it. He surmised it was some sort of tracking device, then he realized that John had plenty of time to locate the van by now and would have found the explosives stowed in the rear. *Why ain’t I behind bars already, John?* But Harry did know one thing: the device complicated things.

After emptying the van of all of the explosives and stacking them on a wooden pallet in a corner of the barn, he draped a tarp over the pallet. Then he thoroughly and methodically wiped down the van’s interior with bleach, spending most of his time and effort on the rear cargo area of the vehicle, making sure to erase any trace of the explosive materials that had been stored there.

Harry pulled the van out of the barn, fastened the padlock on its door, then he drove to an electronics store just a mile down the highway from Ronnie's house. He showed the device to a salesman who explained that it was, in fact, a GPS tracker. And a very hi-tech one, the salesman added. Harry slipped the man a twenty-dollar bill and thanked him. Before leaving the parking lot, he crouched beneath the van and carefully reinstalled the tracker in its original location.

His next stop was the Chevy dealership off of Route 7. Walking into the showroom, he picked out the first available salesman he saw, a man named Chuck, who, when he saw Harry, rocketed out of his chair and eagerly shook Harry's hand. Chuck's desperate grin told Harry all he needed to know; Chuck would make a deal right now that would include his mother, if need be. Harry told Chuck what he wanted, and that he was in no mood to haggle today. Within an hour, the deal was done. Harry left Chuck the keys to the old van and drove off the property in a new one. When he got back to Ronnie's farmhouse, Harry parked the new van inside the barn, padlocked the barn doors again, then drove home in his truck.

***

When Harry stepped inside his home, Rex greeted him with a gleeful yelp, and he gave the dog a hug. "I know, boy. I missed you, too." He walked into the kitchen and rifled through a box on the counter, digging out a bag of dog snacks. Dropping the bag on the table, he went through the box again and found a rubber ball. "Want it, boy?"

Harry opened the back door and Rex eagerly followed him into the backyard. He tossed the ball, and the dog took chase. Harry smiled as he watched Rex gobble up the ball, then trotted it back to him. Rex let the ball drop to the ground, then barked as he waited for Harry to pick it up and toss it again so the game could continue. Charlie, leaning against his fence, heard the dog bark. "You get a dog, Harry?"

"It's Ronnie's dog, Rex. I'm gonna be watching him for a while."

"Is Ronnie okay?"

"I put him in detox."

"I'm sorry to hear that. He's a good man. Hopefully they'll be able to help him."

"We'll see."

"You okay, Harry? Haven't seen much of you the past couple of days."

"You a truant officer now?"

"Was worried about you, is all. Forget I even asked, you schmuck." Charlie started to walk away.

"Hold on, Sloan." Charlie stopped. "I was in jail the night before. I hit a cop. And if you tell Mom, I'll kill you."

"You're kidding, right?"

"About killing you? Nope."

"I meant about hitting a cop."

"Nope," Harry said as he tossed the ball again.

"Why'd you do it?"

"He roughed up Ronnie, so I knocked him out. Where's Mom?"

"Changing the bed sheets. We got it on last night something fierce."

Harry sat down at the patio table as Rex returned with the ball. "Yeah, right," he said, tossing the ball again.

"Can I come over?" Charlie said.

"Can I really stop you?"

"Is the dog friendly?"

"There's only one way to find out."

Charlie slid his hand along the top of the fence, using it as a guide. He followed the fence to the gate that led to Harry's backyard. When he got past the gate, Charlie used his cane to lead him across the patio and to a deck chair. As Charlie sat down, Rex trotted onto the patio deck and stopped just a foot from the old man. Rex let out a full-throated bark that caused Charlie to rear back in his chair in fright, making Harry chuckle. "Sounds like a big dog, Harry."

"He's the size of a small sedan. Go ahead, call him. Let's see what happens."

Trembling, Charlie said, "Here - here, Rex."

Rex licked Charlie's hand. After the old man's body slackened, he petted the dog.

"Damn," Harry said. "Was hoping Rex was gonna bite you on your bony ass."

"Your ass could feed him for about a decade, Harry."

"Good one. What's on your mind, old timer?"

Charlie sat back as he debated whether or not to have this talk with Harry. He always tried to respect Harry's privacy, but he figured the big man had a right to know what was going on. "It's about your friend, John. He stopped by the house the other day."

"That so?"

"It is. He asked me some questions about you. He says he's worried about you. Then the bombings came up. I tried to throw him off the trail by telling him you're dumb as a stump, and there's no way you could pull off anything that complicated without getting caught."

"Thanks for the vote of confidence, Sloan."

"John's a smart guy. I'm pretty sure he thinks you're the bomber."

"Why would he think that?"

Charlie chuckled. "C'mon, Harry. Let's not do this."

"Let's not do what?"

"I know, Harry. I know."

Harry sat back and did a slow burn. *My mother, the rat.* "Mom told you, didn't she?"

"Your mother? No, she didn't tell me. I was bluffing. Is it really you, Harry? Are you really the bomber?"

"You're hallucinating, Sloan. Take a pill and sleep it off."

"Or maybe I'll just ask your imaginary friend if it's you. You know, the general?"

Suddenly irritated, Harry got out of his chair and stood over the old man. "Think it's time for you to leave, Sloan."

"I'm not going anywhere just yet. And you don't scare me, so sit your ass down." But Harry didn't budge, and Charlie sensed that Harry was still hovering over him. "Harry, please sit down. This will stay between us. I swear it. But I need to know."

"You don't need to know shit. Stay out of my business."

Charlie reached for Harry's hand. When he found it, he squeezed it with all of his strength.

"We're family, big guy. You know I care. I'm worried about you. Really worried." Grudgingly, Harry sat back down. He wanted, maybe even needed, to tell someone about the general. It was a secret that weighed on him so heavily that he felt he couldn't carry the burden much longer. "Talk to me, Harry."

Harry sat back as if he was about to tell a long tale to the old man and needed to be comfortable. He told Charlie about the first time the general appeared, and every other time since. But he neglected to tell Sloan about Hien and their conversations. Recounting that "relationship" with anyone was off limits, at least for now. The talks Harry had with Hien were much too personal to share, especially because their conversations sometimes broached the subject of his dear, deceased wife, Patsy. After finishing the story, Harry exhaled as if a great weight had been lifted from his shoulders.

"That's about it, Sloan. Tell Mom this shit and I'll deny it, then I'll choke the life out of you."

"You know Patton's dead, right, Harry?"

"I know. But he seems pretty damn real."

"Did you tell your doctor about this?"

"Yep. He gave me more meds. They didn't help."

"Maybe a shrink could help," said Charlie.

"Patsy made me see a shrink when I got back from 'Nam. I was having night terrors that scared the hell out of her. She told me sometimes I'd toss and turn in bed, then I'd get out of bed and roll around on the floor like I was back in the war trying to duck enemy fire. One time she tried to hold me down while I was thrashing around and apparently I threw her across the room. The next morning she told me what happened. I didn't remember any of it."

"Have you tried anything else?"

"There was some biofeedback bullshit, hypnosis, sleep studies, you name it. Nothing helped."

"And…?"

"And what, Sloan?"

"What are you taking now?"

"Pitched them all except the pain meds."

"You think that was smart?"

"Don't care either way anymore."

"You know, I served under Patton for a short time. He rode his men hard."

"He still does."

"What do you guys talk about?"

"The old man next door who asks too many questions, mostly." Harry got up and walked into the house, then he eased into his recliner. When he saw Sloan walk through the door, he grunted. "I've had rashes that went away quicker," he said.

Charlie took a seat on the sofa. "Take me with you, Harry. Please."

"Where the hell am I supposed to take you?"

"If you're going to blow anything else up, I want to come with you."

"Why would I take you?"

"Then it is you? Hot damn!" Charlie exclaimed, slapping a hand on his leg.

"I didn't admit shit here."

"It all adds up. Your bomb making skills, your temper…"

Harry slammed his fist onto the table. It shook, and so did the old man. "My temper? Gee, I wonder why I have a temper. This country's gone bat shit crazy, and I don't like it one fuckin' bit. I got an idiot, juvenile delinquent across the street I can't go near 'cause he's part Indian, whatever the hell that's got to do with anything. I got strangers telling me what words I can and can't use. I got idiots trespassing on my property screaming for my scalp 'cause I don't buy their bullshit, and when I try to have them removed off my property, I get arrested. And the court says I'm some kind of hate criminal so they make me go to classes so some asshole can try to indoctrinate me and a bunch of other sane people into their fucked-up way of thinking."

"Things have changed, Harry."

"'Things have changed'? That's all you got?"

"Channel your anger, somehow."

"Those buildings didn't blow themselves up. How's that for channeling my anger?" Harry felt like a pressure cooker that needed to blow its lid before it went airborne. "Yeah, it's me! Okay?! I've had enough!"

After recoiling for a moment from Harry's rage, Charlie leaned in towards the big man. "This is serious stuff, Harry. Have you thought it through?"

Harry sucked in air as he tried to calm down. "I've been careful."

"How many places have you blown up now? Is it four so far?"

"Sounds about right."

"Why the courthouse?"

"The judge pissed me off."

"And the coffee shop?"

"The manager pissed me off."

"And the lawyer's office?"

"He represented the little prick across the street that dragged me into court. He pissed me off."

"What about the old library?"

"You sensing a theme here, Sloan?"

"Suppose I am. But your friend John's a federal agent. He's sworn to take you in if he finds out you're the bomber."

"John's gonna do what he's gonna do."

"If there's another bombing, take me with you, Harry, please." Charlie clutched Harry's hand. "Give an old man a thrill, son."

"I'll think about it," Harry said. "But if you breathe one word of this to anyone…"

"I know, I know," Charlie said. "You'll choke the life out of me."

***

After Charlie left, Harry got comfortable in his recliner. As he was about to nod off, a thought occurred to him. He still didn't know why only the B.O.A. men were arrested for the brawl at the town's square the previous week, so he got online and went to the town's website. A link led him to a statement from the county prosecutor, a Progressive, who had taken office just six months ago.

The statement read: ***Recently, there was an altercation in the Albrecht town square between two groups: a popular, benevolent organization called T.I.D., and a neo-Nazi hate group known as The Brownshirts of America. After a thorough investigation of the incident, this Office declines to prosecute members of the T.I.D. organization, but charges will be brought against The Brownshirts of America for their part in the disturbance. All members of the latter group will be charged with disturbing the peace, assault, and affray.***

It is the determination of this Office that the members of the T.I.D. organization involved in the aforementioned incident have experienced either racial or economic oppression, or both, and thus were, justifiably, seeking redress in a manner that this Office respects and sanctions. The people shall always be afforded the right to protest in

any comportment which they deem to be appropriate or necessary to express their grievances against an unjust, racist, non-inclusive, non-equitable society such as the one in which we are forced to live.

Let's have a conversation. Let's raise awareness. Let's discuss renaming our town. The man our town was named after, Friedrich Albrecht, was a cis, patriarchal white man, a capitalist, an oppressor, and a Christian. Should we honor such a man? This Office thinks not. We can do better. We can send a signal to the world that we are better.

And let's explore ways to remedy the injustices inflicted on the oppressed peoples of this town, especially those of the LGBTQ community, who have been seriously scarred, traumatized, marginalized and endangered in so many ways by the events of that day. And if conversations don't produce the results we seek, we shall reconstitute Albrecht, by any means necessary.

They Collins
Pinetree County Prosecutor

Instead of trying to process everything he had just read, Harry focused on just one fact at the moment. Only the Brownshirts were to be charged with crimes. His head throbbing, he took a migraine pill and lay down on the sofa.

His slumber ended an hour later when his phone rang. Mad at himself for not turning off his phone, he let the call go to voicemail. Miss Jessica left a message reminding Harry about their date later that evening. He grunted as he sat up. He was tempted to give Jessica an excuse for backing out of the date but decided that it would be good to see a friendly face, if only for even a few hours.

After having dinner, Harry and Jessica went to a movie of her choice, a romantic comedy that Harry somehow got through without nodding off or scoffing at the ridiculous premise of the story. Halfway through the movie, Jess clutched Harry's hand and held onto it. Harry, taken slightly aback by her gesture, continued to watch the movie like nothing had happened.

When he brought Jessica home, Harry walked her up to her front door. They stood on the porch and Harry stared at his feet like a teenage boy on his first date. "I'm up here, Harry," Jessica said. Harry blushed as he looked at her. He thought about kissing her, but remembering his deceased wife, he took a step back.

"I should get home, Jess. I want to call Joey before it gets too late," he said.

"Call him? Isn't he still home with you?"

"He moved out."

"Where's he living?"

"Rapid City," Harry answered quickly, not wishing to tell Jessica the truth, or why he and the boy weren't on speaking terms.

Jessica gave Harry a kiss on the cheek. "It's really nice to have someone to spend time with. I hope I'm going to see you again soon, Harry."

"Night, Miss Jess."

When Harry got home, Rex was eagerly waiting at the door. "Hi, boy," he said as he hugged the dog, then fed him. As Rex dug into his dinner, Harry sat in his recliner and called Joey. The call went straight to voice mail. "Joey, it's grandpa. Pick up the phone, please. I know you're getting my calls. I miss you. Please come home." He hung up the phone and ran his hand through his hair. His heart aching, Harry didn't even have the energy to peel himself out of the recliner. He turned on the TV and hoped sleep would come soon. Rex pulled up alongside the recliner and stared at Harry. As Harry petted him, he heard a voice.

"Your grandson still AWOL?" General Patton said, chuckling.

Harry glared pure hate at Patton. "Go fuck yourself, General."

"Did I hit a nerve?"

"Keep Joey out of this."

"You pulled the plug on the boy's grandmother. No fucking wonder he hates you."

"She was in a coma, for chrissake! She would have been paralyzed for the rest of her life. She didn't want to live like that!" Harry started to sob. "I put her out of her misery."

"Or maybe out of yours, huh? Fess up, Blake. You know you would have had to spend every waking minute wiping her and feeding her. What kind of life is that?"

Harry bolted out of his recliner and snorted as he hovered over the general. "I would have been glad to do that for my Patsy, you prick!"

"There's the fire!" the general said. "Let's harness it. When's our next mission?"

Emotionally drained, Harry shrugged as he sat back down. "I don't know. I'm tired."

"You can stow that 'I'm tired' shit, soldier. We need to escalate. I need blood!" Harry buried his head in his hands, and the general pointed an accusatory finger at him. "Grow some balls and make it soon." The general disappeared.

Harry got up and paced the room. He thought about calling his brother to tell him he was on his way to see Joey, but he wasn't about to take any excuse, or a no, for an answer over the phone. He pocketed his cell phone, grabbed his truck keys and got on the highway. He was going to see his grandson, and no one was going to stop him.

***

Harry's brother, James, lived in Brushwind, a small town just over an hour south of Albrecht. As Harry cruised down Highway 18, he struggled to recall the last time he had visited his brother at his home. The two hadn't been close for many years now, but it wasn't any one incident or argument that led to their estrangement. James and his wife, Nancy, were living the good life. Their home was easily the biggest in town, the couple traveled often, and they spent well beyond their means, even though both James and his wife earned hefty incomes.

298

Harry didn't mind too much when his brother called from time to time looking for money, because he was behind on the bills. Although their conversations about politics could get heated, Harry didn't mind that politically they were on different ends of the spectrum. Harry even forgave his brother, eventually, for not attending Patsy's funeral because he and his wife were vacationing in Mexico, a trip they couldn't bother to cut short to come home for the funeral.

What really irked Harry was that his brother rarely spent time with Joey since Patsy's death. There were no trips to an amusement park, a baseball game, nor anything else. James always had an excuse. Either he was just too busy, or he and his wife had plans that didn't involve a kid tagging along, like one of their many trips around the world. That was the last thought Harry had as he pulled up to James' house and got out of his truck.

As he strode towards the house, he saw a brand- new BMW X5 M parked in the driveway. Instead of ringing the doorbell, he pounded on the front door loudly enough to be heard down the block, then he did a slow burn as he waited. James finally opened the door.

"Harry, do you know what time it is?"

"Nice car, Jimmy. What'd that run you?"

"Just over a hundred grand. Like it?"

"You trade the Jag in?"

"It's in the shop getting detailed. We're taking the Beemer to Vegas tomorrow."

"That's great. I wanna see Joey."

James' eyes shifted away from Harry. "He's – he's not here."

"Where is he?"

"He's gone. He left last week."

"Where the hell did he go?"

"He moved to California."

"You let him move to California? What the hell were you thinking, Jimmy? The kid's only seventeen. I'm still his legal guardian."

"It was his decision, Harry."

"It wasn't his decision. It was mine!"

James took a step back. "You don't own the kid. Besides, he doesn't want to talk to you."

"Tell me where he is, Jimmy."

"I can't. I promised Joey I wouldn't."

James' wife Nancy stepped into the doorway. "It's kind of late for a visit, isn't it, Harry?" she said.

"Stay out of this, Nancy. Tell me where he is, Jimmy."

"I told you I can't do that. Joey doesn't want to have anything to do with you anymore," James said. "You need to just accept that, Harry."

"And don't blame us if the kid hates you," Nancy said.

James grimaced when he heard his wife's remark. It took a moment, but when Harry processed Nancy's barb, he hung his head in complete defeat. Nancy tapped her watch. "If we're done here, we need to finish packing," she said. "Have a nice drive home, Harry."

Harry glared at Nancy with pure contempt. "You miserable…"

"Don't say it, Harry," James said.

Harry stomped down the walkway and got into his truck. He jerked it into reverse and backed it into the driveway directly across from James' house. Then he slammed it into drive and hit the gas pedal, hard. The truck barreled across the street and slammed into the BMW's rear end, setting off the car's alarm. Harry slowly backed out of the driveway, put his vehicle in park, got out and inspected the damage. His grill and bumper were caved in, but the engine still purred like it had just rolled off the production line. James and Nancy looked on in horror and shock when they saw that their new car's trunk was now located in the back seat. Harry got back into his truck, smiled and waved goodbye to James and his wife. "Enjoy your trip," he said as he drove off.

***

When he got home, Harry grabbed a beer and downed it in just a couple of gulps. He went to the basement and sat on the sofa. He was tired, but still had anger-fueled adrenaline pumping through him. Silence invaded the house and having only his thoughts for company made him grow more agitated. He needed an outlet. He needed to vent. So, he flipped on the power to his ham radio. "Hello, Albrecht. This is Hoppin' Mad Harry. Anyone in town besides me feeling angry these days?

Feeling like something's off kilter in Albrecht? Did you hear about Ben Robinson? He's been a realtor in our town for over twenty years. Good guy. He got fired for saying all lives matter a while back.

He got on social media and said exactly that, and nothing else. And...he...got…fired. Did he say something racist? Nope. Did he try to incite violence in any way? Nope. He just stated his opinion. That's all. But apparently some of these douchebag social justice warriors screamed bloody murder and the realtor's parent company caved in and fired him. Ben's a decent, family man who a lot of you know. He lost his job over an opinion. You okay with that, Albrecht? You okay with a good man losing his livelihood for stating an opinion on this social media bullshit?"

Harry opened up a book sitting on his desk and flipped to a dog-eared page. "This is a quote from one of the Founding Fathers, Benjamin Franklin. 'Without freedom of thought there can be no such thing as wisdom; and no such thing as public liberty without freedom of speech.' Think about that." Harry closed the book and sighed.

"They're witch hunters, these assholes taking over our town. And to them, we're all witches. They're like locust eating everything in their path, and we're all on their menu. You okay with that, Albrecht? I'm not. I'll fuckin' die before I let these bastards get me or my hometown. That's all I got tonight, Albrecht. Sleep well while they steal our town right out from under us. Hoppin' Mad Harry, signing off."

Harry turned off the radio, then slowly climbed the basement steps.

Reaching the living room, he stopped when Rex came to him. Rex whimpered as if he could sense the big man's deep sadness. Harry went to a knee and hugged the dog, holding him tight. Returning the gesture, Rex set a paw on Harry's shoulder. "I love you, boy," Harry said. He got to his feet and eased into the recliner, and Rex lay down next to the chair. Harry petted the dog until sleep came.

44

As he ate lunch the next day, for no reason in particular, Harry thought of Hien, and he grew agitated. He wanted an answer to a question that had been plaguing him for some time now. He dropped his half-eaten sandwich, plowed through the back door, then through the gate that led to the Jansen's backyard. When he reached the back door of the house, he knocked on it. "Hien, you there?" When he got no response, he banged on the door. "Hien!" The door opened and Harry stepped into the house. He looked around the first floor and saw that it was completely empty of furniture and appliances, and the walls were bare. He started up the stairs.

"Hello, Harry." Hearing Hien's voice, Harry spun around and nearly lost his balance. He grabbed the banister, then stared at Hien, who stood in the living room waving at him. "It's good to see you again, my friend."

Harry eased his way down the stairs. "The house is empty. I thought you were staying here."

"I never said that. You just assumed it was so."

Harry continued down the stairs. "Let's stop with the games. I want some answers. Who the hell are you?"

"You already know who I am."

Hien took a seat on the bottom step of the stairwell. He gestured to Harry to join him. His gaze never leaving the elderly man, Harry cautiously sat down next to Hien. "I don't know who the hell you are," he said.

"Look at me, Harry. Really look at me."

Harry studied Hien's face closely. The elderly man's visage slowly transformed right before his eyes. Hien's wrinkles and liver spots faded away, and his pale skin gave way to smoother, much younger skin. Hien was no longer an old man; he was now a teenage boy. Harry did know him. The memory he had tried to block for nearly fifty years came rushing to the surface. He closed his eyes and fought it no longer.

***

Corporal Harry Blake Jr. stood in a trench, swatting away a horde of flies buzzing around his head as he scanned the village a few hundred feet in front of him with his binoculars. It was a typical mid- summer day for this area near the southern Laotian border: brutal heat with stifling humidity. The Viet Cong was transporting men and artillery through the village on a dirt road that linked up with the Ho Chi Minh Trail just south of the hamlet. Corporal Blake and three men from the platoon had spent most of the previous night laying land mines along the road to disrupt the flow of men and ordnance into South Vietnam. He was tired and irritable, and he just wanted a shower and some serious sleep.

Lieutenant Bob "Body Count" Radner stood alongside Corporal Blake. Radner was hated by almost every enlisted man who had ever served under him. The lieutenant was notorious for inflating the number of dead Viet Cong soldiers in his reports, and Corporal Blake had even heard that the lieutenant was the target of two fragging attempts.

As Corporal Blake continued to sweep the village for enemy activity, Radner was busy bitching out his radio man, Private Johnny Coleman, about something or other, just because he could. Corporal Blake knew that Radner would take full credit for the day's mission, if it went off as planned. And that pissed him off. The lieutenant turned his focus to him.

"Any activity, Corporal?" Radner said.

"That's a negative, Lieutenant," Blake replied.

Radner spat at the ground in disgust. "Fuckin' 'Cong. Don't they know I got places to be?"

Corporal Blake wanted to tell the lieutenant to shut the hell up, but he just grunted instead. He glanced at the lieutenant, then quickly looked away. "Got something to say, Corporal?"

"No, Lieutenant."

"Out with it."

"Just wondering what we're doing here, sir."

"We're here to stem the Commie tide, Corporal. And we're here to win the hearts and minds of these savages," Radner said.

"And if we don't, sir?"

"Then we lose. I hear you're the A-number-1-go-to-guy for demolition OPS, Blake."

"He's fuckin' Rembrandt with Semtex," said Private Coleman.

Radner shrugged like he wasn't impressed. "Those claymores better work, Corporal. I want a big body count today."

Radioman Coleman snickered, and Radner shot him a dirty look. "Something funny, Private?" he said. The private stared at the ground. Corporal Blake chimed in to deflect the lieutenant's ire away from the radioman.

"Lieutenant, the claymore's an anti-personnel mine. I got my hands on some Soviet TM-forty- sixes. They'll take out a deuce-and-a-half[7]," Blake said.

"They'd better," Radner said as he spat in the private's direction.

"We got movement," Corporal Blake said, pointing toward the north end of the village. He refocused his binoculars and saw a Vietnamese, teenage boy riding a bike down a trail that was laden with the Russian land mines. The corporal gasped. "Oh, Jesus," he said.

The lieutenant grabbed his binoculars and swept the village. "What is it, Corporal?"

"It's – it's Choo Choo."

"Who the hell's that?"

---

[7]An Army tactical cargo truck that could carry 2 ½ tons of materials on-road or off-road in all weather.

"His names Hein Chu. I call him Choo Choo. He's a kid from the village. He's been feeding us intel on the Cong for over a year now. I gotta go get him!" Blake started to scale the trench wall.

Radner grabbed the corporal by his belt and pulled him back down. "Stand down, Corporal! You think we're gonna scrap this OP for one gook kid?"

"He's with us, Lieutenant. He's a good kid. We gotta do somethin'!"

"The hell we do," Radner said.

The boy continued peddling down the trail. Corporal Blake tensed up as he watched Choo Choo approach the edge of the village. "Turn around, Choo Choo. Turn around...." Blake muttered. Seconds later, the boy pedaled directly over a mine, and the corporal watched in horror as the explosion ripped Choo Choo's body in half, propelling his severed upper torso into a nearby ditch. Through his binoculars, corporal Blake stared, transfixed, at the boy's face. Choo Choo's lifeless eyes remained open. What was left of the boy's upper body contorted and twitched, then went rigid.

"This OP's a fuckin' soup sandwich," said Radner. "Charlie'll have the skinny soon enough."

Falling to his knees, Corporal Blake began to sob. "Buck up, Corporal," Radner said. "That's one less zipperhead who's gonna breed. We'll call it, say, ten dead Cong in the report." Radner looked over at radio man Coleman just as the private grabbed the field radio's receiver. "What the hell you think you're doing, Private?"

"New directive, Lieutenant. I gotta call in any civilian casualties to HQ."

Radner unholstered his .45 and aimed it at the private's head. "I don't think so, Private."

Seeing the gun in the lieutenant's hand snapped Corporal Blake out of his anguished stupor. He jumped to his feet. "What the hell, Lieutenant?!" Blake shouted.

"Stay out of this, Corporal," Radner said.

Staring at the business end of the lieutenant's .45, Private Coleman's voice shook as badly as the hand that held the radio's receiver. "I – I have to call it in, Lieutenant."

Radner cocked the hammer of his .45. "Drop that receiver. I will not repeat that order, Private."

Corporal Blake grabbed the lieutenant's shoulder, spun him around, and caught him squarely on the jaw with a roundhouse right. The Lieutenant's eyes rolled up as he collapsed, but just before hitting the ground he squeezed off a round that tore into Corporal Blake's right knee.

"Son of a bitch!" the corporal yelled as he backpedaled and slammed into the trench wall. Private Coleman, still shaking, dropped his radio, grabbed a field dressing from his pack and ran to the corporal.

After the My Lai massacre earlier that year, the military's upper brass was ready to come down hard on any officer violating its Code of Conduct and Rules of Engagement. When radioman Coleman recounted the incident and backed Corporal Blake's story, Lieutenant Radner drew a two-year sentence at a military prison. Corporal Blake attended the funeral for Choo Choo. He sobbed uncontrollably and needed nearly as much consoling as the young boy's family.

***

Harry snapped back to the present. He opened his eyes and stared in disbelief at his dead friend, Choo Choo, sitting right next to him. "No. It can't be," he mumbled.

"Yes, it's really me, Harry. Your friend, Choo Choo."

Harry buried his face in his trembling hands. He closed his eyes, hoping that when he reopened them, the nightmare would be over. "This is not a nightmare, my friend. I am here," Hein said in a hushed, calm voice.

"I-I saw you die."

"You did, yes, but my death was not your fault. I know you tried to save me."

Harry's mind raced as his eyes remained closed. He wanted to run out of the house and never return, but he didn't have the strength to move. "This – this isn't happening. This isn't real," he whispered as his hands continued to shake.

"You came here to know the truth, and I have told you the truth," said Hien. "You must let go of the guilt, my friend. It's unnecessary, unfounded, and it's eating you alive. Look at me. Please."

Harry slowly opened his eyes and saw that Hien was still sitting next to him. "If you're real…." Harry waved a hand in Hien's direction. When it passed right through the man, he exhaled. "I knew it. You're not really here. You're not real."

Hien smiled. "I dwell on a different plane of existence now. You and I cannot connect physically since I no longer have human form. Where I now exist, time is meaningless. And there is no more sadness, no more sickness and no more death. Do you understand, my friend?"

Harry, fighting back the urge to scream, chuckled instead. "Sounds nice."

"It is well beyond nice. Your Patsy is there. And your daughter as well. They are perfectly happy and perfectly content."

Harry shook his head. "You can't know them."

"I know everyone in the next life, Harry. As I said, time no longer has its limiting effect since it doesn't really exist where I now reside."

Harry felt lightheaded, but he got to his feet. When his legs began to wobble, he grabbed the banister to steady himself, then he turned to face Hien. "Then how come I can see you but I can't see them?"

"I'm sort of an… emissary. You've been allowed to see me because there's a purpose in it. But seeing your wife and daughter now, in their new form, it is not allowed."

"What the hell does that mean?"

"It means that you're not ready to see them, my friend. It's not your time."

"You're dead, so you're not really here. Hell, I'm not even sure if I'm here." Releasing his grip on the banister, Harry staggered towards the front door.

"Is the general still pulling your strings?" Hien said.

Harry stopped and turned. "What's that supposed to mean?"

"I know the general and his kind. He attacks your manhood; he belittles you, and he eggs you on. He uses your weaknesses against you. He's leading you down a bad road."

"I decide what I do. Nobody else does."

"But he influences you just the same, Harry. He has told you that your father would be proud of you for the things you've been doing, hasn't he?"

"Maybe. So?"

"And if your father is proud of you, that would make you happy, no?"

Harry chuckled. "I'm getting shrunk by a ghost."

"There is no such thing as ghosts, Harry. Please, answer the question."

Growing agitated, Harry started to pace the living room floor. "Yeah. No. I don't know. What the hell do you want from me?!"

"I want you to be free, Harry. And you cannot be as long as the general torments you. He uses memories of your father to shame you, and to goad you on. The general intimidates you, just as your father did. Tell me that I'm wrong."

Confusion and anger welled up inside Harry as he continued to pace back and forth, trying somehow to make sense of this encounter.

"It makes sense, does it not?" Hien said.

Harry stopped pacing. "It's not really General Patton, is it?"

"No, Harry. It's not really General Patton. It has assumed the general's appearance and mannerisms because that's what its kind do.

They're crafty. They deceive, and they demean. They do whatever they can to achieve their nefarious goals."

"I'm losing it. You're not real. None of this is," Harry said, walking towards the back door. When he reached it, he stopped. "But just for the hell of it, tell Patsy I love her, and I miss her. And my daughter, too."

"They know, Baloo. They know. Be at peace."

Harry's eyes widened in disbelief. "How can you know that?!" he said to an empty room.

Patsy's nickname for Harry was Baloo, the bear from *The Jungle Book* story. She started calling him that after dragging him out on the dance floor on their second date. Harry danced like the big bear, flailing his arms in every direction like his rear end was on fire. Patsy had tried to keep a straight face while he stumbled around the floor, but she finally doubled over with laughter. Harry had pouted, then stomped off. When Patsy caught up to him, she apologized, kissed him and told him he would always be her "Big Baloo." That made Harry smile.

***

Still shaking, Harry strode through his backyard. When he stepped through his back door and into the kitchen, he heard a knock at the front door. In no mood to see anyone, he sat at the kitchen table and stared at the floor, willing to just sit there until whoever was at the door went away. Then he heard, "Harry, you home?" He recognized the voice. It was Lou, his neighbor.

When he opened his front door, Harry saw that about ten neighbors lined the sidewalk and cheered when they saw him. Lou pointed towards Harry's banged-up truck.

"What happened, Harry? You okay?"

"Had a little fender bender. I'm fine, Lou."

"Me and the wife heard your broadcast last night," said Lou. "She's more pissed than I am."

310

"Did Ben really lose his job over that bullshit, Harry?" Tom asked.

"He sure did, Tom."

"He helped us buy our house," another neighbor said. "Got us a helluva deal, too. He's a good man. What happened to him isn't right."

"No, it's not," Harry said. When he told the neighbors about the C.A.T., and what was being taught there, a woman quipped that maybe the town should kick the C.A.T., and everyone laughed.

Harry told his neighbors that his next broadcast would be at eight p.m. Friday night, and the crowd nodded their approval and promised to pass the word along to others before they left. Harry smiled as he walked back into his home.

But his happiness was short-lived when he remembered what day it was: the anniversary of his wife's death. He grabbed his keys and got into his truck. After Harry pulled away from the curb, John, who was parked down the street, pulled out into the street, too.

***

As Harry pulled into the parking lot of the Our Lady of Hope Cemetery, John parked his sedan across the street from the cemetery and grabbed his binoculars. He watched Harry make his way through rows of headstones and graves before finally stopping at a burial plot. He didn't have to guess the name on the headstone that Harry stood by, or the one next to it. He knew Harry's wife and daughter were laid to rest there.

John lowered his binoculars and bowed his head in respect. After a few moments, he trained his binoculars on Harry again, who was now sitting on a bench just feet away from his wife's grave, staring at the ground. John could almost feel the sadness and grief he saw on his friend's face. *Jesus, he's so lonely.* It broke John's heart to see his friend like this, but he wanted to put an end to their game of cat and mouse and confront Harry about the bombings.

John debated joining his friend on the bench. He could throw an arm around Harry's shoulder, they could talk about the old days, and maybe even share a few laughs before he steered the conversation towards the bombings. But he knew this wasn't the appropriate time. He knew better than to intrude on his friend at a moment like this. And he remembered that just a few weeks ago Harry, in a fit of rage, had dismantled and unearthed his mailbox with virtually no effort. John realized that if he challenged Harry about the bombings right now, he could lose a friend, and maybe his head.

He watched as Harry stared at the ground, then the sky, then at nothing in particular, until he could watch no longer. He still had no concrete proof that Harry was the bomber, but he knew deep down – he just knew – that he was. And John knew that, one way or another, this matter needed to be resolved soon.

John had to fight the inertia that was taking hold of him. He took one last mournful look at Harry before driving away. When he arrived at his office, he sat at his desk and unwrapped a roast beef sub. As John ate his lunch, he turned on his laptop and checked the tracking program that linked up with the transponder he had installed on Harry's van. John peered closely at the screen to make sure he was reading the location correctly. The van was over six – hundred miles away. In Missouri. *What the hell…?*

***

After lunch, John paid the local Chevy dealership a visit. He showed his government identification to the sales manager, who promptly supplied him with the information he sought. Harry had sold his van to the dealership as a trade-in, and the van was then sold to a man residing in Missouri. The buyer had paid a driver to have the van delivered to him. John also found out that Harry had purchased a new van the same day, and the license plate number was on a printout that John folded in half and tucked in his pocket as he left the dealership.

John sat in his car and considered his options. He knew he could get a court order to tap Harry's cell phone, but that would leave a paper trail that he just couldn't risk. He didn't want anyone at the Bureau knowing that he was investigating a friend. He rubbed his temples as he once again tried to figure out his next move. Then he grinned when he realized that Harry had gotten the best of him by swapping out the vans. As much as he wanted to resolve this case, he decided at that moment that he was done tracking Harry or following him around town. Whatever was going to happen going forward was up to Harry.

Although he didn't agree with Harry's methods, John at least understood his friend's anger. *The man's taking a stand,* he thought. *I respect the hell out of that.*

45

Harry arrived at the rehab center. Walking through the front door, he saw Ronnie sitting in the day room.

"Hey, buddy."

The two men hugged. "You came," Ronnie said.

"Told you I would. How you feeling?"

"Aw, you know. How's Rex?"

Harry pulled out his phone and showed Ronnie several pictures of the dog. "He's doing fine. But if it ain't nailed down, he eats it."

Ronnie smiled. "That's my boy. Gotta be careful not to overfeed him. He'll keep eating 'til he explodes if you let him."

"I'll keep it in mind."

"C'mon," Ronnie said. "We need to talk somewhere private."

Ronnie led Harry to his room just down the hallway. He sat on his bed and gestured for Harry to take a seat in a chair in the corner.

"What's going on?" Harry said, suddenly worried.

"I was in the barn the day before I came here. Guess what I found on the ground near your van."

"No idea, Ronnie. What?"

"A brick of Semtex. I thought your demolition days were over, Harryy."

"So did I."

"I didn't break into your van, just so you know. It was just lying there."

"I believe you, buddy. I didn't mean for you to get involved. I just needed somewhere out of the way to hide the stuff. I'm sorry. I didn't think it through. I'll move the van today."

"So, it is you, huh? You're the guy they're calling the Mad Bomber?"

"There any point lying to you?"

"What's going on with you? Why are you doing this shit?"

Harry kept Ronnie's glance. "I'm tired of getting pushed around, so I'm channeling my anger. Isn't that how they put it these days?"

"Guess so," Ronnie said.

Harry sat back and folded his arms. "So, now you know. What're you gonna do?"

"You think I'd turn you in, Harry? That what you're asking me? Jesus, you're my best friend. Keep the van in the barn. Hell, I'll make room in there for a tank if you need it."

"You mean it?"

"What are they gonna do to me even if I admitted I knew you were stashing the shit there? They gonna throw me in prison? Let 'em."

"I don't ever want it to come to that."

Ronnie smiled. "It don't scare me, buddy. Nothing does anymore."

Harry saw past Ronnie's half-hearted smile. He sensed that something was wrong. Very wrong. He took a seat on the bed next to his friend.

"What is it, Ronnie?"

"I wanna go with you the next time."

"What?"

"They ran some tests. I got what they call decompensated cirrhosis. My liver's on its last leg. Without a new one, the doc gave me six months, tops."

"We'll - we'll get you another liver, then. We'll get your name on a list and -"

Ronnie waved Harry off. "The doctor said the same thing. I told him not to bother."

"Why the hell not?"

Ronnie stared out the window as he let out a mournful sigh. "I'm tired, buddy. Real tired. I'm ready to... leave."

"Bullshit. You've got plenty to live for."

"Annie's gone. My kids won't talk to me anymore. I can't go back to my old job. I can only watch reruns of Mannix so many times. It's time."

"Don't say that," Harry said. "We'll get you fixed up and we'll figure it out."

"Wanna fix things? Can ya turn back time? Can ya do that, buddy?" Ronnie said. Having no answer, Harry simply looked away. Ronnie leaned in and whispered, "It's okay." Then he wrapped an arm around Harry. "You're the best friend a guy could have. You were always there for me."

Harry gently pushed Ronnie away, then got up off the bed. "There's gotta be something…"

"There is. Promise me you'll take me with you next time. Gimme one last thrill."

"If there is a next time." Harry knew this visit had to end now. He knew he could say nothing to cheer his friend up, and he needed time alone to process the bad news he just received. He went to the doorway, then stopped. "I'll be back soon, alright? Next time I'll bring Rex."

"Dogs aren't allowed here."

"Let 'em try and stop me."

"Okay." Ronnie walked with Harry to the center's front entrance. They hugged again, then Harry pushed through the door and took several steps before stopping to look back. Ronnie still stood there, waving goodbye. Harry forced a smile as he returned the gesture. He kept it together until he got to his truck. When he reached it, he reared back and kicked the fender with all the strength he could muster. Then he lowered his head and started to sob. After composing himself, Harry looked at his watch and realized he had somewhere to be.

46

With his arms folded, Harry stood tall as the B of A men stepped into the rec hall, saluted him, then took seats. Two of the older members walked towards the bar. "Bar's closed 'til after the meeting," Harry said. The two men stopped and turned towards the big man, and Harry stared them down. The two took seats with the other men without saying a word.

Harry stood between two tables and looked the men over. "It's good to see my brothers-in- arms again. It's been too long," Harry said. The men clapped. "The last time we met here, we celebrated a victory. Do you remember?" The men clapped again. "But that was just one small victory in what's gonna be a long war. It's time to plan for our next mission, men." Harry picked up a duffel bag off the floor and set it on the table. He unzipped the bag and pulled out a couple of bricks of Semtex, blasting caps and detonators, and set them on the table. "Anyone know what this is?"

The men had no answer for Harry. "This is Semtex. It's a plastic explosive and it packs one helluva punch. You're gonna learn how to use this stuff for our next mission."

"What's our next mission?" Stefan said.

"The baseball stadium."

"Why the stadium?" Frank said. "Don't you like baseball?"

"Remember how it used to be called Sioux Stadium? It ain't anymore. And remember the team used to be called the Lakota War Chiefs? Well, they ain't called that anymore. Don't you guys keep up on current events?"

"So what?" Stefan said.

"So what? The Red Man's our friend, dummkopf. Remember? And you know who renamed the team and the stadium? The assholes that invaded our town. The same assholes that hate us. The same assholes we kicked the shit out of in the town square."

"They're still around?" Otto said.

"Yep. So, we need to send the bastards another message. The people of Albrecht love the Red Man. And when the people of this town see we're sticking up for our Indian brothers, our movement's gonna gain more steam." The men nodded in agreement. "But we need to bomb the stadium during the day."

"Why's that?" Stefan said.

Harry picked up a brick of Semtex and showed it to the group. "'Cause this shit'll explode if the temperature's under seventy-five degrees. We gotta do it when it's hot or we'll blow ourselves to hell. Got it?" None of the men thought to check the temperature of the rec hall at that moment. The thermostat was set at sixty-five degrees.

"Why do we have to learn how to use this shit? Ain't you gonna be there?" Otto said.

Harry winked. "I'll be on the other side of town creating a diversion," he said. The men nodded and laughed. "Okay, let's get to it," Harry said as he passed the detonators and blasting caps around the table for the men to inspect.

***

An hour later, after the rest of the men had left the hall, Harry and Hans sat at the bar and had a beer. "So, you're the bomber, huh?" Hans said.

"I am."

"You've got some nut sack, Harry. Are we really going to blow up the stadium?"

"There's no 'we'. You're not getting involved in this, Hans."

"It ain't MENSA guy's you're dealing with here. If they get caught, they'll go to prison."

"Yeah, guess they will."

"Some of these guys are my friends."

Harry eyeballed Hans. "Bullshit. They're nothing to you. Do you hear me? Nothing. They're just a bunch of young punks, drug dealers and gun runners. They're a cancer on this town." Hans considered that.

"You've got a woman now, and you're happy, right?" Harry said.

Hans nodded yes. "Suppose that's true," he said. "Mary's a good woman."

Harry grabbed Hans's arm. "Then build a life with her, Hans. And be fuckin' happy, you schmuck."

Hans chuckled as he pushed himself away from the bar and patted Harry on the back. "Good night, Harry."

47

When he got home, Harry put on a clean shirt and combed his thinning hair to look presentable for Miss Jessica. Looking at his watch, he remembered that he had told his neighbors that he would be on the air in ten minutes. He called Jessica and told her that he would be a little late. He then went to the basement and fired up his ham radio and computer.

"Evening, Albrecht, it's Hoppin' Mad Harry," he said. "How are you feeling about your town these days? Did you hear it was our town council that voted to rename Sioux Stadium and the War Chiefs? It's true. The spineless bastards sold us down the river in the name of this p.c., woke bullshit that's invaded our town. And did you know a teacher at Albrecht High was forced to quit 'cause he refused to attend sensitivity training classes that tell people that they're racist and oppressors if they're white? True shit. These assholes are Nazis without the jackboots, and they're trying to silence anyone that doesn't think the same bullshit they do.

And guess what they did at the elementary school last week? Some fucked-up teacher gave the eighth graders an assignment that had to do with pizza and sex. The kids were supposed to tell what their favorite pizza toppings were, and every different topping meant something sexual, like kissing and oral sex."

"So, the kids were told if they like cheese on their pizza, that meant they like kissing. And if they chose olives, that means they like oral sex, and so on. And then the kids were supposed to share their preferences with the other kids in class." Harry paused for a moment as his blood boiled. He slammed a fist onto the desk. "These sick ass people are sexualizing our kids, Albrecht! This is fuckin' child abuse! And your town council signed off on this bullshit, too, the bastards.

Is this the Albrecht you remember growing up in? Is this the kinda town you wanna raise your children in still? How the hell are they getting away with this shit?! How in the hell can this happen in our town?! Wake the hell up, Albrecht!" Exhausted, Harry exhaled. "That's all I got tonight. Sleep well while these soulless assholes take your town."

Harry went upstairs and sat on the sofa. On the verge of hyperventilating, he breathed in and out repeatedly as he tried to compose himself. Soon his nerves steadied, as did his breathing. He pushed himself off the sofa and walked out the front door. Halfway down his steps, he heard a voice.

"Got a date, fat man?"

Harry stopped when he saw Crash in the driveway across the street. He considered ending the boy's life right then and there, but instead, he kept walking. "Going to see the old bitch down the street, Harry? You get into her adult diapers yet?"

Harry stopped and wheeled around. "Watch your mouth, boy."

"Or what?"

"Or I'll call your parents and tell 'em you need a good spanking. Oh, I forgot, your parents are dead, huh?"

That remark wiped the grin off the boy's face. Crash clenched his fists and Harry clenched his as well. "Wanna discuss your feelings on the matter, son? C'mon over and we'll talk."

Crash stayed put. "I'm gonna nail you, fat man. Count on it."

Choking down his rage, Harry walked on. Jessica was standing on her porch when he reached her house. Her arms were crossed, and she was frowning.

"I'm sorry if you heard that, Jess," Harry said, joining her on the porch.

"I did, Harry. And I'm not happy about it."

"That kid needs to be taught a lesson."

"Or maybe you do."

"Me? What'd I do?"

"That was very insensitive of you, taunting that boy about his dead parents."

Harry was flabbergasted. "You're mad at me? That kid's an asshole. You heard what he said about you, right?"

"He's obviously in pain and he's just lashing out. You could be a little more sensitive and understanding."

"I can't believe you're defending that little prick."

"He's just a lost, little boy. He needs compassion."

"He needs jail time," Harry muttered.

"What was that?"

"Nothing. Can we just forget about it?"

Jessica took a moment, and then said, "C'mon in."

As they ate homemade spaghetti, the tension between Harry and Jessica eased, and their conversation was light and easy throughout the meal, but Jessica still sensed that Harry was preoccupied.

"What's wrong, Harry?"

He set his fork down on his empty plate. "Just one of those days. I'll live."

"Want to talk about it?"

"Nah. Dinner was great. Thank you."

"You're welcome. I miss watching a man enjoy a meal. Why don't you turn on the TV and find us a good movie."

"Will do," Harry said. He stepped into the living room and grabbed the remote. He flipped through the channel lineup and remembered that *Gone With the Wind* was about to start.

"Did you find anything good, Harry?"

"Gone With the Wind is on in a few minutes."

Jessica joined Harry in the living room. "I don't think it is. I heard they pulled it off the air. And not a moment too soon, if you ask me."

"What do you mean, they pulled it?"

"They decided that the movie was too racist, and non-inclusive. It triggers too many people."

"You're kidding, right?"

"Not at all," Jessica said as she sat on the sofa next to Harry. "Some people find the film offensive, and it can traumatize them as well."

"Jess, is it a story about the KKK lynching black people? No, it's not. If it was, I'd get people being angry about that. It's a fictional movie that takes place in the South during slavery. You're telling me that watching this movie can trigger people? Seriously?"

"It can, yes."

Harry grew slightly agitated. "Lemme tell you what a real trigger is, Jess. Try walking down the street sometime and hearing a car backfire, and you nearly shit yourself 'cause you think it's an artillery shell going off. And then you check to see if you still got all your limbs attached. And when the shock wears off and you know everything's still where it was five seconds ago, then you look over and see your buddy's been cut in half by the shell, and his lower half's about ten feet from the rest of his body, and his upper half is still shaking while the guy's screaming for help just before he chokes to death on his own blood. A guy who was a good soldier. A guy who was a good friend. A guy who had his whole life in front of him if he could just get home in one piece. That's a real trigger, Jess."

"I understand, Harry."

"No offense, but you don't. I can't watch a movie or documentary about Vietnam 'cause it hits too damn close to home, but I don't try to stop other people from watching it. That's what this crap's about, don't you see? A small group of people are trying to tell the rest of us what we can and can't say. And what to think. And now, they're gonna start censoring movies? Are books next? Are they gonna tell us it's for our own good? That it's gonna make us better people?"

"You need to be more sensitive, Harry."

"What if I don't wanna be more sensitive? What are they gonna do with me, then, Jess? They gonna throw me in jail? Where's this stuff coming from, anyway?"

"I'm taking a class at the Center for Alternative Thinking. It's opened my eyes in so many ways."

"You're going there? Who's making you do it?"

"No one is making me. I read their mission statement, and I was curious. So, I started taking a class a few weeks ago."

"And...?"

"And I realized that I was enabling these kinds of movies by watching them. It's a culturally offensive movie. And it ignores the horrors of slavery."

"It's a fictional story written nearly a hundred years ago. It was a different time, Jess. Is pulling the movie off the air gonna erase slavery from our history?"

"No, but we don't have to condone it, either. And they didn't ban the movie. They're going to show it again soon with a disclaimer and a denouncement of the movie's depiction of race relations."

"A denouncement? Do people really need to be told by some corporation that slavery was bad? Wow, that is so damn brave of 'em to go out on a limb like that." Jessica, slightly shaken by Harry's growing anger, shifted away from him. Sensing Jessica's uneasiness, Harry's tone softened as he clutched her hand. "Look, Jess," he said, "be as sensitive as you want, okay? But do it because you want to, not because other people tell you you have to."

"I've got my own mind, Harry, but I've learned that there are a lot of oppressed people out there that I wasn't aware of. And I've had a part in oppressing them myself," she said.

"How so?"

"Some of the words I've been using for so long, for example. Now I know that some of them were oppressive and non-inclusive, and that they may have marginalized others. I'm guilty of anthropocentrism and ethnocentrism, too.”

“I guess you didn’t know you were such a bad person ‘til those assholes told you you were, huh?”

“Don’t try to marginalize me or my feelings, Harry.”

“That’s twice you’ve used that word in about ten seconds, Jess. It’s one of the words they throw around a lot these days when they wanna play the victim. Cry wolf enough and people are gonna start tuning you out.”

“If they’re victims it’s because we’ve made them victims.”

“That’s exactly what they want, Jess. They want you to think you’re one of the bad guys. And the more guilt you feel, the more they can push you around and manipulate you. It’s all about power. Don’t you see that?”

“Not at all,” Jess said. “I’m evolving. And apparently you need to do the same.”

“Evolve into what? A spineless jellyfish?”

Jessica pulled her hand away from Harry’s. “I don’t appreciate that.”

“Guess this is where I’m supposed to say I’m sorry for hurting your feelings, huh?”

“Harry, come with me to a class sometime. Please. It may help you.”

“I already go,” he said. “The state’s making me.”

“You are? Why?”

“I hit the boy idiot’s car with a rock. The court said I needed sensitivity classes ‘cause they say I was ethnically intimidating the little asshole.”

“Why did you do that?”

“He nearly ran me over with his car, Jess. In your lingo, he was trying to marginalize me.”

“He’s just lashing out against society. Victims of oppression sometimes do that.”

Growing more agitated, Harry got up of the sofa. “You’re calling that little shit heel a victim? And oppressed? His parents supposedly left him money. The asshole doesn't even have a job. Oh, I forgot, he's got a job; he sells drugs. And he harasses me every chance he gets. He still a victim?"

"We'd have to look at the root causes of the boy's anger."

Harry chuckled. "Yeah, you and your new friends do that. Make excuses for the little asshole."

"I don't appreciate your tone, Harry."

"Look, if you wanna feel guilty about some of the imaginary bad things you say or do, that's your call. But you and others who think like that just make it easier for some people to claim they're victims."

"That is so insensitive."

"People need to grow a backbone, Jess. And they need to stop pretending like every little thing offends 'em or hurts 'em."

"Harry, can't you see you're enabling racism by watching a movie like 'Gone With the Wind'? Do you understand that? People like you are enabling racism whether they consciously know it, or not. And whether they admit or, or not."

"Who the hell is *they*?"

"White people, of course."

Harry stared at Jessica as if she were speaking a language he didn't understand. "All white people? Are you saying if you're white, you're racist?"

Jessica's posture stiffened. "On some level, yes, Harry. All of us are. It began with slavery, and if any white person denies being racist, that means they are, but they're afraid to admit it."

"So, all Germans are Nazis, right?"

"That's ridiculous. Why would you say that?"

"If all white people in this country are racist 'cause they were born in a country that had slavery, then all Germans must be Nazis 'cause that's a part of their history. That what you're saying, Jess?"

"Harry, you're trying to confuse me, and I don't appreciate it."

"I'm just taking your logic a little further. Why's that confusing you?"

Jessica got up off the sofa. "I think we're done here," she said.

"Why? 'Cause you started something you can't finish, Jess? Don't people like you always say you want an open, honest dialogue about this kinda shit? Or does the conversation end when you start losing?"

"It's not a contest, Harry. And I'm not losing. You're just showing your white fragility."

"Do I seem defensive to you? Do I seem uncomfortable talking about race with you?"

Jessica looked surprised. "Yeah, I know what the term means, Jess. I've done a bit of reading lately about all this bullshit. If you and your new friends really want to find out who's racist, you can do the Swimming Test on all of us, I guess."

Jessica crossed her arms. "And what is that?"

"They did it in Salem way back when to decide if a person was a witch, or not. They'd strip a person naked, hog-tie their hands and feet, then they'd toss 'em into water to see if they floated or sank. We could do that now with white people. If you toss 'em in and they float, that proves they're racist, so you can then throw 'em in prison, or whatever. But if they sink, then you have to let 'em go free 'cause that means they're not racist. Of course, some people drowned back then proving their innocence, but what the hell, huh? You gotta break some eggs to make an omelet, right?"

"I seriously doubt it will come to that."

"Jess, if all white people are racist, what does society do about it, exactly?"

"We step in and educate them, of course."

"And if they refuse to be 'educated'?"

"Then we do it by any means necessary. You're either racist, or you're anti-racist, Harry. There's no middle ground. You can't be simply not racist. Treating everybody fairly is not enough. White people have to actively participate in seeking to root out racism, or they're oppressors.

That's the only way to cleanse this world of racism and homophobia."

"Now we're dragging homophobia into this? Doesn't phobia mean a fear of something? Are all straight people suddenly afraid of gay people?"

"That may have been the strict definition of the word years ago," Jessica said. "But the word has evolved. We know now that the word means more than just an irrational fear."

"Who the hell is *we*? Some people try and change the meaning of a word and the rest of us are just supposed to just accept it?"

"Anyone who doesn't like gay people or doesn't celebrate their lifestyle is homophobic, Harry."

Harry stared at Jessica, completely dumbfounded. "If I don't celebrate gay people, whatever the hell that means, that makes me homophobic? Are you losing your mind, Jess?"

Jessica crossed her arms again. "People like yourself need to adapt."

"To this bullshit? Never, Jess. Not in a million years."

"I didn't know you were such an intolerant man."

"And I didn't know you were so damn gullible. People like the assholes at the C.A.T. want to tear this country apart. Congrats, Jess, you've become a useful idiot for them. You should be really proud of yourself."

Jessica walked to the front door and opened it. "I think it's time for you to leave."

"It sure as hell is," Harry said as he walked out the door without looking back.

***

When Harry got home, Rex was at the door, waiting. Harry fed him, then he went through the day's mail. Just as his anger and frustration were beginning to abate, he opened an envelope with the court seal on it. The letter stated that his sensitivity training courses would resume the next week with a new moderator. And Harry's presence was mandatory. His bile began to rise. He hadn't expected to be summoned back to the C.A.T. so soon after taking down Mr. Wilkins. He tore the letter to shreds and threw it in the trash.

Then he called Ronnie's kids, speaking first with his daughter, Maggie, and then with his son, William. Harry explained to both that Ronnie was dying and begged them to reconcile with their father before it was too late. But both Maggie and William made it clear that they had no intention of seeing, or speaking to, their father ever again. Harry seethed as he told them that they'd regret their decision until the day they died before hanging up on both of them.

A text had come in while he was talking to Ronnie's kids. *There are cameras everywhere these days. Just saying.* "Son of a bitch!" His heart rate climbing, he went to the bathroom and downed a couple of aspirin in anticipation of an oncoming headache, then hauled himself up the stairs and fell into bed. Rex climbed into bed with him and snuggled up against the big man.

Harry petted the dog for a few moments before rolling over on his side. After tossing and turning for over an hour, he cursed as he got out of bed.

48

Just after two a.m., Harry sat on a bench at Higgins Park facing South Street. A warm gust of wind rushed through the trees. Harry remembered a time - it felt like a lifetime ago - when a soothing breeze blowing through the bedroom window would have lulled him into a peaceful slumber. He shook off that depressing thought by reminding himself that his trip to the park tonight had a purpose. He pulled a pair of night vision binoculars from a duffel bag and trained them on the lower wall of the C.A.T. building. He spotted patches of weeds that ran along the length of the entire wall. Harry already knew, without needing to look, that South Street fed into Highway 16 less than a quarter of a mile down the street from where he sat. *This will work*, he thought.

He stared at the C.A.T. building. Its very existence seemed to mock him. *Why the hell doesn't this piss off everyone in this town?* He couldn't stomach looking at the edifice for even one second longer. As he stowed the binoculars back in the duffel bag, he heard a voice.

"Hi, Harry."

Harry should have been surprised to see John, but he wasn't. He greeted his friend like they had plans to meet then and there.

"Hey, John. Got insomnia?"

"Something like that. How about you?"

"Same."

"Word around town is you like to spend time here, so I thought while I was out, I'd swing by and maybe see what the attraction is."

"I don't come here nearly as often as I used to."

"Why is that?" Harry pointed to the C.A.T. building, and John looked across the street. "That's the place, huh?"

"Yep," Harry said.

John read the sign aloud. "The Center for Alternative Thinking. Sounds almost innocuous, doesn't it?"

"Don't know what that word means, John."

"It means something that's harmless, or at least seems harmless."

"Oh. Suppose it does at that."

"Have they broken you yet? Made you see the error of your ways?"

Harry wasn't surprised that John knew about his court-ordered attendance at the C.A.T. He figured it was only a matter of time. But if John was hoping to catch Harry off guard, it didn't work.

"We both know that ain't gonna happen."

John chuckled. "I figured as much. They met their match in you."

Harry grinned. "Course, they did."

"I heard your old instructor is facing some serious criminal charges. His name is Wilkins, if memory serves."

"That's him. Guy's apparently a real pervert. The cops nailed him for kiddie porn."

"They'll replace him. Are you planning on going back when classes resume?"

"Nah," Harry said, gesturing for John to grab a seat on the bench. "I'm through with their bullshit."

John took a seat on the bench and stretched out his legs. "I figured that as well. I heard your broadcast the other night. Stirring oration, my friend. Kind of a call to arms, huh? I almost got aroused listening to it."

Surprised to hear that, Harry turned to face John. "You heard it?"

"I've been tuning in for a while now. Does that surprise you?"

"Guess it does. Have you told your Fed pals about my broadcasts?"

John sat back and drew in the warm summer air. "No, I haven't. But I had to give my boss something, so I just sent him a file on the Brownshirts. You're running with some bad guys, Harry. They're into a lot of bad stuff. Gun running, drug dealing…"

"And if they weren't drunk all the time, they might even try starting a new Nazi regime here, John. But I'm not running with 'em. I'm running 'em."

"You are?"

"They had an opening at the top," Harry said. "I applied. I got the job."

"How involved was the application process?"

Harry wiggled his fists for John to see. "Not very. Only took about thirty seconds, or so."

John smiled. "You were always good with them." John grabbed Harry's arm. "Harry, we both know the Brownshirts aren't responsible for the bombings, but they're going to be surveilled soon, which means you will be, too. I'm sorry. I covered for you as long as I could."

"I appreciate you buying me some time, John. Really do. I'll hand 'em to your boss on a silver platter soon enough."

"Do I want to know?"

"No, you don't."

"So, when's it going to end?"

"It'll all be over real soon."

"You're in deep, my friend. You know that, right?"

"I don't give a shit," Harry said as he rose from the bench. "This is my town, John. My home. I made a life here. Lots of really decent people live here, and we don't need any uppity, know-it- all assholes from the big city strolling into town and telling us how to think and what to say. They think we're rubes. Country- ass bumpkins. They look down on us and they act like they have some kind of divine calling to show us just how racist and stupid we are and how we'd see the light if we'd just obey them. Fuck 'em!"

"I'm with you, Harry. I get it." John patted the bench. "Have a seat." Harry stared aimlessly into the night sky. "Please," John said in a calm voice. Harry finally sat down. "I don't want to see you spend the rest of your life in prison."

"If you're covering for me, why'd you stick a GPS tracker under my van?"

"I'm still a law enforcement agent. I was tracking you because I wanted to know."

"All you had to do was ask, John."

John considered that statement for a moment. It hit him that it was one of the funniest things that Harry had ever said, even if Harry wasn't trying to be clever. "All I had to do was ask?" he said.

"Yeah."

John chuckled. "Seriously? All I had to do was ask?"

Harry looked at John with bemusement. "Yeah, all you had to do was ask."

John doubled over as his chuckling grew into hearty laughter. Harry, finally getting the humor in what he had just said, chortled along with his friend. John straightened up as he wiped tears from his eyes. The moment passed and they gathered their composure. Then both men stared at the C.A.T building.

"So, when's it going to happen?" John said.

"You really wanna know?"

"Yeah."

"The night of the Fourth."

"Independence Day? That's fitting."

"Guess it is at that," Harry said. He grasped John's arm. "I'm sorry I got you involved in this shit, John. I really am. I had no idea they'd call you in on this thing."

John clasped Harry's hand and smiled. "It was my decision to come. Besides, it gave us an excuse for a reunion, right?"

"Sure did."

"Make this the last one, Harry. Please."

"I promise, buddy."

"I'm holding you to that." John looked at the C.A.T. building again and scowled. "Blow it straight to hell."

"That's the plan," Harry said as he arose from the bench. "I'm going home and try to sleep, John. You should, too. You look like warmed-over shit."

"Thanks," John said as he arose as well. "You missed your calling. You should have written for Hallmark." John started to walk away.

"Maybe in the next life. By the way, I got your text - God," Harry said.

John waved without looking back, and he disappeared into the night. Harry decided he wasn't ready to go home just yet. He sat back down on the bench and and drew in the warm summer air as he took in the sounds of the park animals that stirred about. A raccoon scurried up to Harry's feet, stopped and stared at the big man. Harry dug into his duffel bag and pulled out a bag of nuts, then tossed a few to the ground He smiled as he watched his newfound friend gobble up the late - night snack.

Soon, several more raccoons gathered, and he gladly fed them as well. A gentle breeze wafted through the park as Harry sat back and took in the tranquility all around him, wishing this moment could last forever. With his mind calm and clear, and his pathway mapped out, Harry was now certain of how it was going to end. He was at peace with himself for the first time in years.

But the serenity was short lived when he thought of Joey. The boy still hadn't returned any of his phone calls. And the private detective he had hired to track him down was unable to locate the boy yet. Harry knew he was to blame for his grandson's animosity towards him. And he didn't know how to repair the damage.

Then he thought of Ronnie, who was dying. His inability to help his best friend frustrated the big man beyond words, and seeing Ronnie waste away reminded him of how helpless he had felt watching his wife languish a little bit more every day until she finally passed. Harry got up and went home. He wanted nothing more than to sleep.

49

Harry arrived home just after three a.m. Rex greeted him at the door and followed him to the kitchen. He gave Rex a snack, then parked himself on the sofa, kicked his feet up on the table, and turned on the TV, not paying attention, nor caring, what was on. Rex climbed onto the sofa and laid across his lap. Harry petted the dog gently as he closed his eyes.

It took hours for Harry to finally fall asleep, and when he awoke just after one p.m. the next day, he didn't bother to turn on his phone, check the weather outside, or even pour himself a cup of coffee. Instead, he dragged himself up the stairs and crawled into bed and tossed and turned for hours. Just after midnight he awoke, fed Rex, and parked himself on the living room sofa again. And he slept through the night.

***

It was just before dawn the next morning when, clad in work coveralls, Harry pulled his truck to the curb near the intersection of Woodmere and Parklane, on the southwest side of town. He got out, locked the truck, and started to walk. He put on a pair of gloves as he neared his destination: the parking lot of the *Weedless to Say* Lawn Service Company. Harry checked his watch; it was five- thirty- five, and sunrise was at five- fifty this morning. Being the Fourth of July weekend, Harry figured most of the company's employees, if not all, would have the day off, which meant they probably wouldn't notice one missing van.

Three rows of vans sat in the lot, and the gate at the lot's entrance was unlocked, as usual.

Harry knew, by way of a chatty company employee who had done work on his backyard the summer before, that the vans were left unlocked overnight with the keys tucked under the floor mats. He crossed the street and entered the lot. Reaching a van in the back of the lot, he opened the driver's side door, pulled back the floor mat, found the keys and started the van. He maneuvered the vehicle onto the street, parking it directly behind his truck.

Harry grabbed a five-gallon bucket out of his truck and put it in the van. He slid back behind the wheel of the van and headed for the highway. Ten minutes later, he turned onto South Street. The C.A.T. building came into view up ahead on his left. He pulled into the parking lot, parked the van, put on a ball cap, grabbed the bucket and got out. The sun was just rising over the horizon. Keeping his head down, he walked towards the northeast corner of the building. His bad knee was throbbing and swollen, but he knew he couldn't risk bringing along his cane today. Grimacing, he fought the pain as he reached the corner of the building without even the slightest hint of a limp.

He dropped the bucket onto the ground next to the wall. Planting his good knee into the ground, he pulled a tool bag out of the bucket, removed a trowel, and set it on the dirt next to him. Keeping the bag close to his body and making sure that his broad back blocked the security cameras above from seeing what he was about to do, Harry pulled out a brick of Semtex and lay it on the ground in front of him. He checked to make sure that a cell phone and a blasting cap were securely attached to the explosive.

Using the trowel, Harry unearthed a small patch of weeds just inches from the wall. He tossed the weeds aside then dug a small rectangular hole about three inches deep where he had just dredged out the weeds. He placed the brick of Semtex in the hole, then covered it with dirt and smoothed it over with the trowel. Harry got to his feet, and his bad knee nearly buckled on him. He grimaced again as he braced himself against the wall and rested for a couple of minutes. Then, making sure to keep his head down, he picked up the trowel and the tool bag and walked ten feet along the wall, stopped, and went to his knees again. He dug out another small patch of weeds just inches from the wall, then he jammed the trowel into the earth and shoveled out another hole. He placed another brick of Semtex into the hole and covered it with dirt.

He grabbed the bucket and trowel and made his way along the wall another ten feet. It was not even six a.m. yet, but humidity hung heavy in the air already. Sweat ran down Harry's neck and back as he dug another hole and buried a brick of Semtex. He repeated the process around all four walls of the building. Just after seven a.m., he buried the last brick and covered it with dirt. Harry slowly rose to his feet, fighting the pain that shot through his back and legs. He tossed the trowel and tool bag into the bucket and kept his head down as he made his way towards the van.

After tossing the bucket into the van, he eased behind the wheel and pulled out onto South Street. He was on the highway a few moments later. When he pulled onto Woodmere Street, Harry slowed the van to a near crawl as he approached the lawn care company's parking lot. He watched as a couple of employees shuffled through the front door of the building. Harry assumed that they would be headed for the vans shortly. His pulse raced. He knew it had to be now. Harry cut across two lanes of traffic, yanked hard on the wheel, and pulled the van into the parking lot. He killed the engine and tucked the key underneath the floor mat, then grabbed the bucket from the back. His head down, Harry walked toward the gate, then made his way down the street. He turned the corner and saw his truck still parked where he had left it. He hoisted himself into it and drove off.

50

Mike Reardon sat at his desk thinking about something Harry had said to him just a few days ago when they were discussing the resumption of classes at the C.A.T. *Wouldn't worry about that if I was you, Mike.* As he pondered Harry's cryptic words, a knock on the office door snapped him out of his trance.

"C'mon in," he said. A legal secretary walked into the office holding a file folder.

"This is everything I could find on Mr. Blake." The secretary handed the folder to Mike, then turned to leave. As she was about to close the door, Mike said, "No one else has seen this, right?"

"No one, Mr. Reardon."

"This is confidential client information, Liz. You're not to discuss this with anyone. Do you understand?"

"I do."

Mike leafed through the folder until he found what he was looking for: a file that contained Harry's military records. Once he had grasped the extent of Harry's experience with explosives, he knew he didn't need to read any further. And any questions he had for Harry would be answered in an hour.

***

Just after eleven a.m., Harry stepped into Mike's office. The two men shook hands, then Mike gestured for Harry to sit.

"How you doing, Mike?" Harry said.

Mike gave Harry a forced smile. "I'm doing, Harry." Until the moment before Harry walked into his office, Mike was certain that he was going to confront the big man about his suspicions, but now he wasn't so sure now that was a good idea. He did consider Harry to be a friend, even if their relationship was more business than personal, and he felt uneasy about getting into Harry's business. Still, he really wanted to know.

"Ready to do some paperwork?"

"I am," Harry said. "But you look like a man with something on his mind."

Mike squirmed in his chair. "I - I'm sorry, but I did a little digging into your past, Harry."

"And?"

"I found your military records."

"Are you about to ask me something as my lawyer or my friend, Mike?"

"Both, Harry. But right now, as your attorney."

"Then whatever I tell you has to stay between us, right? The lawyer-client thing?"

"Yeah. It's called confidentiality. What you say now stays between you and I."

"Okay. It's me, if that's what you're wondering."

Stunned, Mike sat back. "Are you saying…?"

"Yeah. I'm the mad bomber. That's what they're calling me, right?"

"Yeah, that and a domestic terrorist. You're really serious, Harry?" Harry nodded. "The courtroom, the coffee shop, Fast Freddie's office…"

"Don't forget the old library. I did them all."

"I knew you were pissed, but…damn. You said something about not having to worry about going back to the classes. What did that mean?"

"Do you really wanna know?"

"I kind of do, yes."

"I'm taking the C.A.T. down."

"You're kidding, right?"

"Nope. I'm not going back there, Mike. Neither are you."

"This is serious shit, Harry. You know I hate that place and everything it stands for, but…damn."

"I know you do. You can have a ringside seat if you want."

"I can?"

"Why the hell not? Mom and her boyfriend are going, and so are some friends and neighbors. The more the merrier."

"When's it happening?"

"Tomorrow night."

Mike grinned. "Independence Day? That's fucking poetic, Harry."

Harry shrugged. "I suppose."

Mike's smile disappeared. "As your attorney, I have to tell you what's going to happen if you get caught."

Harry waved him off. "Don't have to bother, Mike. I know how this is gonna end already. I've got a plan."

"Want to tell me the plan?"

"Not really."

"Okay, then. Let's take care of that will."

It took just over an hour for Mike to draw up Harry's will. Harry left his home and one million dollars to Joey, another million to his mother and Charlie, a half a million to Mike, and the rest of his estate, another million, to the Sioux Nation Relief Fund. Mike and Mr. Reynolds, the firm's estate planner, witnessed the signing, making it legal. Harry shook hands with Mr. Reynolds before the attorney left the office.

"Got a minute, Harry?" Mike said.

"Sure."

"Why the hurry to get your will done today?"

"Been putting it off for too long, Mike. It was time."

"Is there anything you want to tell me?"

"Not really."

"You've got to appear in court in two weeks on the assault charge against the state trooper. I held them off as long as I could. I'm sorry."

"No need be sorry, Mike. You did right by me."

"Will I see you at the arraignment?"

"We'll play it by ear."

"You don't seem too worried."

"Not a damn bit. Let 'em do their worst." Harry shook Mike's hand. "Thanks for everything. You're a good man." Harry headed for the door.

"Are you sure there's nothing else you want to talk about? Anything?"

"I'm sure, but thanks for the offer." Harry said. "Just make sure you read the will over really good before it gets filed, please."

"Can I bring anything tomorrow night?"

Harry winked. "Hot dogs and marshmallows are always good over a roaring fire."

***

After leaving Mike's office, Harry drove to Don's Auto and Body Shop. Don Hopkins, a seventy- year- old man who still worked six days a week because he loved his job, wiped his greasy hands clean as he stepped into the parking lot. Harry climbed out of his truck and the men shook hands.

"Your rental's over there, Harry," Don said, pointing towards the rear of the lot.

"Thanks, Donnie."

Don looked the truck's front- end damage over. "Damn. Hit a deer, buddy?"

"Nope. Hit my brother's car."

"Accident?" Ron said.

"Nah."

Don chuckled, but then he saw that Harry wasn't kidding. "Remind me to never piss you off, Harry. It's gonna take a couple of weeks to get the parts and put her back together."

Harry dug the truck's title out of his wallet and signed it over to Don, then he handed it to him. "Take all the time you need, Donnie. She's yours."

"You know I've had my eye on this truck for some time now. You serious?"

"Sure am, buddy."

"Lemme write you a check for it."

"Don't want your money, Donnie. Don't want it and don't need it." Harry patted the hood of his truck. "Be good to the old girl."

Don handed Harry the keys to his rental car. "Thanks, Harry. Say, that thing still on for tomorrow night?" he said.

"Sure is," Harry said. "You gonna be there?"

"Wouldn't miss it for the world, buddy." The men shook hands, then Harry walked away.

***

After returning home, Harry went next door and invited Charlie and Gertie to dinner that evening, telling them that he wouldn't take no for an answer. Then he spent the rest of the afternoon cleaning his home. A sense of calmness washed over him as he scrubbed and dusted every room. He boxed up clothing, labeled the boxes to be taken to the local Goodwill, and stacked them in the garage.

When the house was cleaned to his satisfaction, Harry went through his mail and paid all of his bills for the month. Then he called Joey, and as always, the call went right to his voicemail. "Joey, it's your grandpa. I really wish you'd pick up your phone and talk to me." He stopped for a moment as he searched for the right words. "I – I want to apologize for some of the things I said to you. I didn't mean any of 'em. I'm just an angry old man who doesn't know when to shut the hell up sometimes. I hope you can find it in your heart to forgive me someday. No matter what happens or what you hear about me, just remember I love you, kiddo."

After hanging up his phone, he put a put a pot roast in the oven, played out in the backyard with Rex for a while, then laid down for a nap.

***

Around seven, Gertie and Charlie came over for dinner. As they ate, the three laughed and enjoyed each other's company like three friends at a reunion that was long overdue. After dinner, they watched Gertie's favorite show, *Murder She Wrote*. Gertie and Charlie held hands on the sofa as the show started, but she only made it through half the episode before nodding off. Harry looked at his mother and smiled, knowing that she was happy and with a good man who truly loved her. He leaned in towards Charlie and touched his arm, whispering, "She's out." Charlie gently woke Gertie, and while she used the restroom, he and Harry waited at the front door.

"You okay, Harry?"

"Sure. Why do you ask?"

"You seemed awfully calm and carefree tonight, like you haven't got a damn care in the world. You back on your medications?"

"Nah. Just enjoyed the night, is all."

Charlie reached for Harry's arm. When he found it, he grasped it firmly. "I don't buy it, son. What's really going on inside that head of yours? You know you can talk to me."

Gertie joined them at the door. She pulled Harry towards her and kissed him on the cheek. "We had a nice night, sonny boy. You want me to stay here tonight?"

"No, Ma. I'm good." He looked at Charlie, then he winked at his mother. "You keep the old goat warm tonight."

"You sure?"

"Am. Sleep well, kids. And don't forget about tomorrow night."

343

"You're gonna stick it to some bullies, right?" Gertie said.

"I sure am." Harry kissed his mother on the cheek and watched her and Charlie cross his lawn on their way to Charlie's house. Normally, seeing people walk on his lawn would have bothered the big man, but not tonight. Harry waited at his door until he saw them walk into Sloan's house. After closing the front door, he cleared the table, gave Rex a snack, started the dishwasher, then climbed into bed.

Across the street, Crash started up his Chevelle and snickered as he hit Harry's home with his high beams. Harry's bedroom lit up with a blinding light. Ordinarily that would have set the big man off, but not tonight. He turned on his side away from the glare and grinned, knowing that this would be the last time the boy idiot would ever pull this stunt. Ever. Harry slept through the night like a man who was truly at peace with himself and the world.

51

Harry awoke with a smile early on the Fourth of July. He was more content than he had been in years. After showering and getting dressed for the big day ahead, he bounded downstairs and saw Rex eagerly awaiting him at the bottom of the stairwell. He hugged the dog, fed him, then brewed coffee. After a hearty breakfast, Harry went next door. As he was about to knock on Charlie's front door, Gertie opened it and smiled when she saw her son clad in his full-dress uniform. She beamed with pride as she kissed her son on the cheek.

"You look handsome, sonny boy. Your father would be so proud."

"Thanks, Ma." Harry helped Gertie and Charlie into his rental car, then drove downtown. He parked just off of Main Street. As he helped Gertie and Charlie get out of the car, he smiled when he saw Ronnie get out of a cab just down the street. As Ronnie began to walk in his direction, Harry noticed that his friend's stomach was badly distended, he looked frail, and his gait was labored and unsteady.

"I gotta go, Ma."

"We'll be fine," Gertie said. "Go."

Harry hurried to Ronnie. He grabbed his friend and steadied him just as Ronnie started to wobble. "You okay, buddy? You don't look too good. You sure you're up for this?"

Ronnie smiled. "Sure, buddy. Let's go."

The aroma of grilled hot dogs, hamburgers and spent fireworks permeated the air as several thousand of Albrecht's citizens, lined up on both sides of Main Street, awaited the beginning of the annual parade. Harry and Ronnie joined a group of other war veterans behind the high school band. The men shared laughs, tears, hugs and handshakes as the band tuned their instruments and gathered in formation.

The townsfolk cheered in unison when the grand marshal blew his whistle. The band struck up The Star-Spangled Banner, and the vets, lined up in rows behind the Veterans of Foreign Wars banner, saluted as the American flag passed just ahead of them. The band began to march, and the vets followed closely behind. When Harry saw that Ronnie, who was at his side just moments before, was struggling to keep up, he slung his arm around Ronnie's shoulder and helped him continue on.

Harry looked around at the sea of faces standing on both sides of Main Street as he and the other men marched on. Lucille Branston, the ninety-year-old widow of Harold Branston, a World War 2 vet who had passed just the year before, smiled warmly and waved to Harry as he passed by. Harry smiled and waved back to her, wishing he could stop and give the elderly woman a hug, but with Ronnie draped on him and using him as a rudder, he knew he had to keep moving.

The crowd applauded when the band segued into God Bless America, and it cheered loudly as the vets continued down the avenue. Harry spotted two more familiar faces among the crowd.

Paul Harrison, a thirty-five-year-old mechanical engineer who lived down the street, and his eight-year-old son. Both father and son saluted Harry and the other vets as they passed by. Their gesture nearly brought Harry to tears.

Then Harry saw a group of teenagers with their noses buried in their smart phones, oblivious to, and unmoved by, the living history marching right past them. Anger and disappointment churned in him, but his ire wasn't directed at the young people. Harry knew it was Albrecht's school system that shouldered the blame for the teenagers' obvious lack of appreciation for his and his fellow soldiers' service to their country. Harry knew that the schools' administrators and teachers weren't interested in teaching civics any longer. They were focused on trying to convince students that "White people's math" was racist. They were also intent on sexualizing grade school-aged children. And they were determined to teach the students that America wasn't worthy of their patriotism, loyalty, or pride.

As he and his fellow vets continued to march, Harry beamed with pride when he saw a multitude of American flags waving on both sides of the street. But an unsettling thought hit him: his beloved hometown was losing the battle for its soul. Harry sensed that the good people of Albrecht were slowly but surely ceding ground and authority to the interlopers who were seeking to make the town, and the entire country, conform to their distorted agenda, beliefs, and values. He knew they had to be stopped, no matter the cost. By the time the vets reached the south end of Main Street, Harry was nearly carrying Ronnie. He eased Ronnie into a patio chair at an outdoor café.

"You okay, buddy?" he said.

"Little tired," Ronnie said with a sad smile.

"I'll get the car and we'll head for the house. You can lie down when we get there."

Harry made the trek back up Main Street. He found Gertie and Charlie having drinks with some neighbors just off the main drag. Harry's neighbors assured him that they would get Gertie and Charlie back home later in the day. That was fine with Harry. He wanted a quiet house for Ronnie to rest. On the way home, Harry saw that Ronnie looked even worse than earlier in the day. "You don't look too good, Ronnie. Maybe I should take you to the hospital," he said.

"Nah. I'm good. Just need to lie down for a bit."

"You sure?"

"Yeah."

When he arrived home, Harry hauled Ronnie up the front steps, laid him down on the sofa, and went to the kitchen to make his friend a couple of sandwiches. By the time he walked into the living room, he saw that Ronnie had already passed out cold. He left the sandwiches on the table, then realized he was tired as well. Harry knew he needed to be alert and well rested for the night's activities, so he climbed into bed for a nap.

***

Just after eight that evening, Harry and Ronnie stepped out of the house. As he and Ronnie crossed the street, Harry saw Crash and Mad Dog Mitch leaning against the Chevelle smoking cigarettes. "Hey, Harry, the old bitch down the street any good in bed? Was thinking I might wanna tap that ass."

Ronnie looked the Chevelle over when he and Harry reached Crash's driveway. The car still gleamed from the wash the boy had given it that afternoon. "Damn. That's a beautiful car," Ronnie said.

"It sure is," Harry said as he planted his feet behind the car's rear end and slammed a fist onto the trunk lid. Dents formed in it as Harry slammed his fist onto it again. Crash took one step towards Harry.

"What the hell, asshole?!"

"Gimme the keys, punk," Harry said, extending his hand towards Crash.

"Eat shit, fat man."

Harry pounded on the deck lid again. "Give me the keys. Now!"

Crash's fear of the big man was the worst kept secret in the neighborhood, and ordinarily the boy would have turned tail and run, but Harry was pounding his Chevelle into submission. And when neighbors began to step out of their homes to check out the commotion, Crash knew he had to act or risk losing face. But he was still too scared to move.

"You going to kick the idiot's ass, Harry?" a neighbor said.

"Thinking so, Dave," Harry said, clenching his fists. He pounded the deck lid again.

"Get him, you pussy," Mad Dog said as he shoved Crash towards Harry.

After stumbling to within just a couple of feet of Harry, Crash came

348

to a sudden stop. Harry grinned as he waved for the boy to keep coming. Shaking badly, Crash backpedaled. "Just- just walk away right now and I won't have to fuck you up, old man," he said.

Harry slammed a fist into the deck lid one more time. "I got things to do, you little bitch. Gimme the keys!"

"He just called you a bitch, buddy," Mad Dog said. "You gonna take that?"

"You steppin' in when I whip your buddy's ass, Injun?" Crash said.

"My buddy don't need my help," Ronnie said. "I'd do what he says."

Crash lunged at Harry. The big man grabbed the boy and easily tossed him to the ground. Crash got to his feet, then pointed at Harry. "You're a dead man!" Leading with his chin, Crash charged again.

Harry hit the boy with a right cross that landed squarely on the boy's chin. Teeth flew from Crash's mouth and his jawbone cracked. He crumbled to the ground. Harry dug a set of keys out of Crash's pocket. As he handed the keys to Ronnie, he glared at Mad Dog.

"You want some, son?"

Mad Dog raised his arms in a gesture of surrender. "I'm cool, man," he said. Then he walked away.

Harry got into his van, and with Ronnie trailing closely behind him in the Chevelle, they got on the highway. After exiting onto South Street, they pulled into the Higgins Park parking lot. Harry smiled when he saw that the crowd was much larger than he had anticipated.

Most of the crowd was oblivious to the threat that the C.A.T represented to their lives and their town. The majority were there simply because it was a tradition to attend the fireworks show at the park.

Harry parked his van and grabbed a duffel bag from the front seat. Ronnie parked the Chevelle alongside Harry's van and Harry tossed the duffel bag into the Chevelle, then he and Ronnie made their way towards the crowd. Mike Reardon was flipping burgers on a grill when he saw the big man.

"There he is!" Mike shouted.

"Looks like you're the man of the hour," Ronnie said, elbowing Harry.

Harry shook Mike's hand before walking to a bench that faced South Street. Gertie sat with Charlie on it, and they were smiling and holding hands. He kissed his mother on the cheek, then gently clasped Charlie's shoulder.

"Hi, sonny boy," Gertie said.

"Hi, Harry. What type of explosive you using tonight? C-4, maybe?" Charlie said.

"Semtex."

"Is it showtime yet?" Gertie said. "I ain't getting any younger here. And I'm hungry, dammit."

"Have a burger, Ma." Harry walked towards the parking lot, passing by Mike on his way.

"You're really going to do this, Harry?"

"Sure am."

"What about the cameras?"

"I'd be disappointed if they're not on."

Harry got into the Chevelle and fired up the engine. He smiled as he revved it, remembering a time when he was young and full of testosterone, behind the wheel of his own Chevelle SS 454, and tearing ass around the neighborhood with Ronnie riding shotgun. But his smile faded when he realized those good times were long gone. *Let it go, Harry. Let it go*. He drove across the street. When he reached the C.A.T. parking lot, he pointed the car's front end towards the near wall of the building, left the car running, and tossed the duffel bag to the ground.

He checked his watch. The sun had set fifteen minutes ago, and the annual fireworks show at Takoda Park, just two miles east, was due to begin. Most of the town would be there watching the festivities, or they would be home, watching from the comfort of their front porches. And Harry didn't have to worry about any of the town's deputies interfering with his mission tonight. Sheriff Roy had assured him that all of his deputies would be patrolling on the other side of town, giving him time to make his escape.

Harry took a seat on the hood of the Chevelle. He looked to the sky, and as if on cue, it lit up in a dazzling display of light and sound. Across the street, the crowd applauded, and oohed and aahed as the show began. General Patton appeared, but Harry was not surprised at all to see him. Patton, with one hand on his hip, surveyed the empty parking lot.

"I don't see the enemy, soldier."

"This enemy fights like the 'Cong," Harry said. "They were clever. They'd shoot at us from a village, then they'd blend in with the locals so we wouldn't return fire." Harry pointed at the C.A.T. building. "This enemy's clever, too. They attack with their bullshit accusations and hide behind their made-up words. They gotta be rooted out."

"What in the hell are you talking about?" Harry didn't respond. "You just keep disappointing me, soldier," Patton said, his tone edged in disgust. "I want some carnage and death."

"Next mission you'll get it. I promise," Harry said. The general disappeared. Harry continued watching the show. A half hour later, the sky came alive with a dizzying barrage of fireworks, signaling the grand finale. When the show ended, he slid off the hood of the car.

Harry looked up at the security camera mounted high on a light pole to his right. After waving at it he squeezed into the Chevelle, buckled up, exhaled, and floored the gas pedal. The Chevelle's tires tore into the pavement, and it hurtled toward the building. Adrenaline coursed through Harry as he braced himself for impact. The Chevelle rammed into the building, buckling the car's hood. Harry's head snapped forward, but the seat belt held tight. The Chevelle was now part of the wall.

His body aching from the impact, Harry slowly unbuckled himself, then put his shoulder into the driver's side door. It gave with a groan, and he fell out of the car, got to his feet, and staggered momentarily before regaining his equilibrium. He checked out the Chevelle. The front tires were blown, the hood caved in, and the punctured radiator hissed as coolant fluid leaked from it. He looked up to the security camera, grinned and pointed at his groin, mouthing the words, "Watch this." He unzipped his fly, pulled out his organ and hosed the driver's side of the Chevelle with a steady stream of urine. When he had nothing left in the tank, he zipped up and retrieved his duffel bag. He pulled a Molotov cocktail from it, lit it, and tossed it into the car.

As he started to walk away, the car exploded, ejecting metal shrapnel and glass into the air. He then put more distance between himself and the C.A.T. building. Setting the duffel bag down, Harry again rifled through it and pulled out a burner phone. He braced himself as he punched in a number.

The Semtex bricks buried around every wall of the building exploded simultaneously, sending a thunderous roar through the night. Shards of glass and chunks of brick and mortar soared across the parking lot in every direction. The crowd watched in a hushed awe as what was left of the building's walls buckled under the weight of the roof. When the roof slammed into the ground with a near- deafening thud, a cloud of pulverized mortar and brick dust billowed into the air. The dust soon dissipated, leaving a view that resembled a post-apocalyptic landscape.

"Hot damn!" Gertie shrieked. The crowd was still shouting and cheering when Harry reached the parking lot. His friends and neighbors encircled him, applauding their hero.

"Hell, yeah, Harry!" one man said.

"Way to go, Harry!" another yelled.

"Hope everybody enjoyed the show," Harry said, grinning and glad-handing with the crowd. Harry knew that most of the crowd was stunned and confused by what they had just witnessed, but he didn't have time to explain to these people why the C.A.T. building had just met its end. He eased past the crowd and spotted and Mike. "Mike, you sure you can get Mom and Charlie home?"

"No problem," Mike said as he shook Harry's hand and gave him a hearty hug. "You're the man, Harry. This oughta shake the town awake."

"We'll see, Mike," Harry said before he and Ronnie left the park.

***

Five minutes later, two sheriff deputies' cruisers, their light bars on and sirens wailing, sped down South Street and pulled up next to the park. Getting out of their vehicles, they surveyed the damage across the street in astonishment. They spent the next two hours questioning the crowd about the explosion. No one mentioned Harry's name.

***

"That was one helluva show," Ronnie said from Harry's kitchen.

Harry eased onto the sofa. "Glad you liked it, buddy."

Ronnie returned to the living room with a beer and a glass filled with whiskey. "We need to celebrate," he said. He gave the beer to Harry, sat down on the sofa, and Rex settled in at his feet. Ronnie bent down to scratch the dog's ears. "That'll rile up the troops, huh?"

Completely exhausted, Harry still managed to smile. "We'll see."

Harry stiffened as he watched Ronnie down nearly half the glass of whiskey in one gulp, but then remembered his friend was dying. *What the hell.*

"Here's to good friends," Ronnie said, lifting his glass to Harry.

"Best of friends," Harry said.

Ronnie finished his drink with two more gulps. He glanced at Harry, then looked away. Something in Ronnie's expression, something dark and sad, scared Harry.

"What is it Ronnie?"

Ronnie smiled. "I think it's time."

"What do you mean?"

"I've been talking to Wakan Tanka[8] and he told me he and Annie are waiting for me."

Harry got up off the sofa. He stood over Ronnie, who continued to smile, even with tears in his eyes.

"I love you, buddy," Ronnie said. "You're the best friend a guy could ever have. We're going to see each other again. And it'll be great. And it'll be forever."

Harry started to hoist Ronnie off the sofa. "C'mon, let's get you to the hospital."

Ronnie gripped Harry's arm and whispered, "It's time. Let me go, buddy. Please let me… go." Reluctantly, Harry released his grip, letting Ronnie sink back into the sofa. Harry fought back tears as he knelt down and gently cupped Ronnie's hand in his. Ronnie smiled again as he gripped Harry's hand. His breathing grew labored, then shallow, then his head listed to the side.

Helpless to do anything else, Harry watched as Ronnie took his last breath. "No," Harry whispered. "Don't go, Ronnie. Don't …go."

Harry gathered his friend into his arms, the tears pouring freely now. He rocked Ronnie gently as he held on harder. Rex, sensing that his master was gone, whimpered as he snuggled against Ronnie's feet. Harry finally let go of Ronnie, easing him into a lying position on the sofa. Then he buried his face in Rex's nape and held the dog tightly.

Harry finally eased away from Rex and dried his tears. He sat back and studied Ronnie's face. He saw complete peacefulness in his friend's countenance. It struck Harry as ironic that this was the happiest he had seen Ronnie in many years. Finally able to break off his gaze, he pulled out his phone and called the sheriff's office.

"Put me through to the Sheriff Roy, please. Tell him it's Harry Blake."

After telling Roy that Ronnie had passed, Harry stepped out into the

____

[8] Wakan Tanka: In Lakota spirituality, Wakan Tanka is the term for the supreme deity, or "Great Spirit".

front yard. He looked skyward, wondering if God already had his best friend cradled in His welcoming arms. He wanted badly to believe that there truly was a higher power, an infinitely benign being, that gave eternal refuge, joy and peace to all of his departed family and friends. But he just didn't know.

He sat on his front steps and waited. A half hour later, a county vehicle pulled up to the house. Dave Windham, the town's coroner for over thirty years, shook Harry's hand as his two assistants went into the home. After exchanging pleasantries, Dave asked Harry a series of questions concerning Ronnie's death, and when Harry explained to him that Ronnie was recently given only a few months to live, Dave said, "Ronnie was a good man, Harry. I'm really sorry." Harry nodded in agreement.

Harry watched Dave step into his home. Then he bowed his head and ran his fingers through his hair. "Ronnie…" he whispered. He didn't move until Dave's assistants carried Ronnie's body out. Rex trotted out behind the men, whimpering as he tried to follow his master, but Harry gently grabbed the dog by his collar and held fast.

When Dave reached the bottom step, he stopped and patted Harry's shoulder. "I heard you put on one helluva show at the park tonight. Wish I could have seen it. If there's anything you need…" Without looking up, Harry waved goodbye to Dave. As the coroner's van pulled away from the house, Harry wrapped his arms around Rex and held on tightly. He and the dog sat there for the next two hours, sharing their grief.

52

John dragged himself out of bed at six a.m. and checked his phone. He saw three missed calls from Special Agent Brooks. He showered, dressed and chugged down a cup of coffee as he braced himself for a long day. When he reached the C.A.T. parking lot, he got out of his car and surveyed the damage. What was left of the C.A.T. building was being combed over by the local authorities as well as his own team. Special Agent Brooks approached John holding a plastic evidence bag in his gloved hand.

"I see the local boys sniffing around my crime scene. Why is that, Agent Brooks?"

"I'll run them off, sir."

"Before you do, tell me what you've got."

"The explosion occurred at exactly nine fifty-five p.m., sir."

"Exactly? How do we know that?"

"We have multiple witnesses, sir. People across the street at the park were watching last night's fireworks at the time of the explosion."

"Seems they got two shows for the price of one. Anything else?"

"We've got him, sir."

"We do?"

"He mugged for the cameras like he was taunting us. We ran him through FACE[9]. His name is Harry Blake. He's a local."

"Let's go have a look at that footage, Agent."

After reviewing the footage, John realized that he could no longer cover for Harry. And Agent Brooks informed him that their boss, Henry,

---

[9]The FBI's Facial Analysis, Comparison and Evaluation service (or FACE) allows for broad matching capability in criminal investigations.

had already issued an A.P.B. for one Harry Blake, Jr.

***

The entire town was talking about the C.A.T. bombing. Bob Haig, a retired deputy sheriff, was bellied up to the bar at Sam's Saloon having a beer with Hal Owens, the owner of the local funeral parlor.

"Why the hell would Harry bomb those places?" Hal said.

"Heard he got tired of getting pushed around," Bob said.

"He get pushed around at that coffee place?" Hal said.

Vince Thornton, the town's retired butcher who was just shy of ninety years old, was sitting next to the two men as he downed his fifth bourbon and water of the evening.

"Gents, forgive my eavesdropping, but Don told me Harry had his truck in the shop a while back, and Harry was really agitated. When Don asked him what was eating his ass, Harry told him he saw a man use the lady's room at that new coffee shop, and when he complained to the manager, the manager told him it was company policy to allow that nonsense. Apparently, the proprietors of said coffee shop aren't judgmental in such matters as the sexes co-mingling in their restrooms."

"That's awfully progressive of 'em," Bob said. "If that's the case, and if it was Harry who blew the place to hell, then he's my hero. Fuck those people, thinking they can come to our town and force- feed us their bullshit, and we're supposed to just bend over and take it. Fuck 'em."

"It was Harry," Vince said. "I was there when he took down that re-education center. It was beautiful. Harry did what we all wish we had the balls to do."

"Then here's to Harry," Bob said as the three men clinked glasses. After downing the rest of his beer, Bob looked Vince over. "Thought you passed a few months ago, Vince."

"Misinformation and propaganda, Bob. And wishful thinking on the wife's part."

The men laughed as they clinked glasses again. As the night passed, they shared more drinks and more laughs. More of the bar's regulars gathered around to share in the camaraderie and talk about the local bombings, and the reason, or reasons, for them. Everyone present hated the scumbag lawyer, Freddie Lamont, whose office was blown to bits. No one knew exactly why Harry would have blown up the courthouse, but they surmised that it may have had something to do with the tight-ass lady judge and her newfound wokeness. If that was the case, everyone agreed that they could live with that. And the gang agreed that anyone willing to work at the C.A.T should have been drawn and quartered, then drawn and quartered again, just for the hell of it.

And they all agreed that the Progressive Cafe's coffee was obscenely overpriced, the staff was phony, and that their restroom policy was nothing short of immoral.

As they toasted Harry once again, the man of the hour was getting out of his rental car in the saloon's parking lot. Harry needed to see some friendly faces tonight. He wanted to be with people who knew Ronnie and would share in his grief. He needed to have some laughs, tell stories and forget about life for one night. When the gang saw Harry walk through the front door, the tavern erupted with applause. Harry smiled as he was greeted with hugs and handshakes. The drinks were on him tonight, he declared, and the alcohol flowed until well after closing time.

***

The Wayside Motel, just north of Albrecht off Highway 18, received an average of two stars in the most travel guides for the past ten years, and any of the locals would say that was a generous score. But plush accommodations weren't high on Harry's priority list at the moment. He awoke in room 114 around noon, fighting a nasty hangover. He gulped down a couple of aspirin, showered, shaved his beard, and soon after, felt slightly better. He slipped on a pair of sunglasses and a Panama hat before stepping outside. Following closely behind Harry, Rex jumped into the front seat of the rental car as Harry got in and drove off.

After pulling into the Higgins Park parking lot, Harry led Rex to a bench facing what was left of the C.A.T. building across the street. He took a seat and Rex lay at his feet, basking in the sun. When a group of pigeons sensed the dog wasn't a threat, they drew near, waiting. Harry scattered a bag of bird seed on the ground and smiled as his winged friends gobbled up dinner.

Then Harry gazed with great satisfaction at the charred, battered remains of the C.A.T. building. He watched as federal crime scene investigators sifted through shattered glass and chunks of concrete in search of evidence, and he smiled as a tow truck hauled away what was left of Crash's Chevelle. Just then, a man crossed the street and approached the bench. It was John.

"You mind?" John said as he reached Harry.

Harry gestured for John to sit. "Not at all," he said.

"I'm looking for a friend of mine," John said, taking a seat. "He lives in Albrecht and goes by the name of Harry Blake. He's a big guy, and he's good at blowing things up. Can you help me?"

"What's your business with this Blake guy, stranger?"

"I'm an old friend who lost touch with the man for way too long. I need to apologize to him for that and hope that he'll forgive an old fool before it's too late."

Harry smiled. "I'm betting your friend feels exactly the same way. Hope you catch up with him real soon."

John smiled and clasped Harry's arm. The two men watched a dump truck haul away rubble from the explosion.

"Some men go to extreme lengths for a cause," John said.

"Maybe they feel the cause is worth it."

"They're calling you a terrorist."

"They say one man's terrorist is another man's freedom fighter. It's all perspective, huh?"

"Indeed. I heard about your friend, Ronnie. I'm really sorry."

"Thanks, John. You'd have liked him. He was a good man."

"Hopefully, he's in a much better place." John looked Rex over. "Who's this big guy?"

"That's Rex. He was Ronnie's."

John petted the dog. "I love dogs. Had a couple myself that I didn't spend enough time with."

"The job?"

"Yeah. I spent thirty plus years on the road. I missed out on a lot of things. And even when I was home…"

"Was it worth it? With the all the things you missed?"

"I don't know, Harry. I just don't know. Are you keeping the dog?"

Harry shrugged as he fed the pigeons more seeds. "We'll see."

"Looks like you've made new friends here."

"They're old friends, John. Just haven't seen as much of them as I used to."

"Why is that?"

Harry pointed at the now-defunct C.A.T. building. "I didn't like the view."

"That's not a problem anymore, is it?" John said.

"Not really. How's the investigation going?"

"There's an A.P.B. out on you. Every law enforcement officer in the state is looking for you as we speak."

"'Cept for Roy."

"Sheriff Patterson?"

"You met him, John?"

"I had dinner with him a couple of weeks ago. Seems like a good man. He's getting ready to retire soon, I believe."

"What did you guys talk about?"

"Life. Family. Our careers. You. And how he was planning on keeping his deputies clear of this area when you took down the building."

Harry sat back, stunned. "He told you about that?"

John smiled. "Only after I loosened him up with five or six beers. I sensed he wanted to tell me something the moment we met. But he needed to feel me out first. And I, him. So, we danced around for a while, and when he was convinced I could be trusted, he told me his plan."

"You're not going to charge him - ?"

John smiled. "Of course, not. He's fed up with a lot of the bullshit that's happening in town, just like any sane person should be. You can only push a man, even a law enforcement officer, so far before something gives. Pretty sure you understand that."

Harry smiled. "Sure do. I heard you got a suspect for the library bombing."

John pulled out a pipe, stuffed it with tobacco, and lit it. "We do. She calls herself Ze. I had the privilege of questioning her. When I refused to call her by her preferred pronoun, she screamed like a banshee and called me names that would make a sailor blush. I should have had a whip, a chair and some raw meat when I talked to her. Mean-ass woman."

"Got any evidence on her?"

"We do. But there's a problem. There were security cameras inside the old library. And one of them recorded a man that strongly resembles you placing a liquor bottle on her desk."

"No shit?" Harry said.

"No shit. I warned you that there's cameras everywhere these days. We found shards from that bottle outside the building, with her prints on them. The office manager told me that she threw a liquor bottle at him, which would explain the fingerprints. But he denied leaving that bottle on her desk, or the note. And he passed a polygraph. Seems someone set her up."

Harry grinned. "Guilty as charged. She pushed me too hard. I warned her to walk away, but she wouldn't listen. So, what happens with her now?"

"We'll have to drop the arson charge against her. But we've got her for criminal incitement for the incident at the bakery. The idiots recorded themselves trashing the shop and posted it on the Internet. Some people just need attention, I suppose. Anyway, I'm recommending she gets charged for her part in tearing down Little Hawk's statue at the ballpark, too. It was a protected historical monument."

"Had a feeling she was in on that."

"Her and some friends. The idiots posted that stunt on the Internet, too," John said, shaking his head in bemusement.

"Throw the book at the assholes, John."

"I'm going to throw several books at Miss Ze and her minions. The charges may not all stick, but she's looking at some jail time if I have anything to say about it." John shuddered. "Damn, she's mean."

"I'll miss her," Harry said, trying to keep a straight face.

John chuckled. "I'm sure you will," he said. "What about the moderator at the C.A.T. who was arrested on child porn charges? Did you have anything to do with that?"

"Sure did. The guy's a bully and a douchebag, so I had someone hack into his computer. Now that I fessed up to framing him, they'll have to let him go, right?"

"They will. But the news media and a lot of social media sites have already crucified the guy. He can kiss his career and reputation goodbye."

"I can live with that," Harry said as he bent down and petted Rex, then stretched his legs. "I've learned there's a lot of small people out there, John. Especially on the Internet. And lots of them wanna believe the worst in others. Makes 'em feel better about themselves. You said yourself they'd turn on each other eventually. So, I figured I'd feed the assholes a few of their own."

"Remind me to never piss you off, Harry." The two men shared a brief laugh. "I didn't see your van or truck in the lot," John said.

"Gave the truck away and I sold the van. I'm driving a rental."

"That's smart. My guys and the A.T.F. are looking for both vehicles as we speak. And they're staking out your home. Steer clear."

"Figured that, but thanks for the heads-up." Harry handed John a manila envelope.

"What's this?" John said.

"Evidence. I got the boy idiot on video doing a drug deal. Nail the little bastard to the wall. And make him watch the video of me pissing on his car before I blew it up."

John grinned. "Will see what I can do. That was one helluva stunt. I've got something for you, too." John pulled a plane ticket from his jacket pocket and handed it to Harry, who looked it over. It was a one-way ticket to Palawan Island in the Philippines. "Go, Harry. Please."

Harry got up and stared at the sky. "I can't. Not without Patsy."

"I can't protect you anymore, my friend. You have to leave."

"I appreciate the gesture, but I'm not going anywhere."

John got up and turned Harry around to face him. "You'll go to prison, probably for the rest of your life. Do you understand that, Harry?"

"I'm not going to prison."

"Is there an option I'm missing here?"

"There is." Harry gave John a hearty hug and held on tightly. "Thanks for everything, John. You're a good friend. I'm sorry we lost touch for so long." Harry let go of John, grabbed Rex's leash and started to lead the dog away.

"I'm sorry if I started you down this road. When I suggested that you do some reading, I didn't know..."

Harry stopped and turned. "Don't blame yourself," he said. "I should be thanking you. You helped open my eyes. You gave me a purpose."

"Your town's proud of you, Harry. You fought the good fight."

"Did what I could, John. But it wasn't enough."

"What are you going to do now?" John said.

Harry didn't respond as he walked away.

***

Harry pulled his car into the parking lot of the Wayside Motel. He led Rex into his room, then locked the door behind him. He stared at a full bottle of bourbon sitting on the nightstand. He was tempted to crack it open right now and finish it off in one sitting, but he realized that he had the rest of the night to do that. He pulled back the blinds and checked the parking lot. All was quiet outside. He dug his laptop and ham radio out of a storage tote and plugged them in, then he took a nap. When Rex yelped, Harry patted the bed and the dog climbed in with him and nestled against his side.

Harry awoke just before nine that night. He grabbed the bottle of bourbon sitting on the nightstand, cracked it open and downed two gulps. Then he started up his laptop and ham radio, sat back, exhaled, and got on the air.

"Hey, Albrecht, how you feeling about your town today? We sure kicked the hell out of the C.A.T., huh? It was really great to see so many of you there. But it's time for all of you to keep the fight going against these bastards." Harry downed another shot of bourbon before going on.

"I love this town, and I've done what I can, but now I'm tired.... I'm really tired. Don't let these soulless bastards win, Albrecht. They want to tear this town and this country apart, and they will if you don't fight back. Walt Whitman said, 'There is no week nor day nor hour when tyranny may not enter upon this country, if the people lose their roughness and spirit of defiance.' Fight 'em any way you can, Albrecht, and fight 'em every way you have to."

Harry's voice trembled as he struggled to go on. "This'll be my last broadcast, folks. Fight the good fight. Make me proud. Make yourselves proud. Take back your town. Take back your country. Hoppin' Mad Harry, signing off." He flipped off the power on the ham radio, then he grabbed a legal pad and wrote three letters. After sealing the letters in envelopes, Harry plugged his video camera into the TV. He hit playback on the camera, then lay down on the bed next to Rex, setting the bottle of bourbon on the nightstand, easily within reach.

Harry spent hours downing bourbon and reliving the past on videotape: footage from his wedding reception, Patsy and Joey playing on the beach, and Joey smiling as he rode a pony on his tenth birthday. Harry smiled through his tears as the video montage rolled on. He, Patsy, Joey, Gertie and Charlie enjoying a summer day at a family barbeque in the backyard. Video of his daughter's wedding day, pictures of him and Patsy on their honeymoon, standing on a hotel balcony, overlooking the sea at sunset.

Harry choked up when he remembered promising his beloved wife that they would grow old together, not knowing then that life would deliver a cruel blow to his hopes and dreams. He continued to watch more happy memories until his vision was badly blurred and the bottle of bourbon was empty and toppled over. Harry buried his face in a pillow as the tears flowed freely. He cried until there were no more tears left. Then he fell into a drunken slumber.

***

Around noon the next day, Harry finally awoke. He sat up in bed, his brain throbbing against the walls of his skull. Rex lay at the foot of the bed staring at him, and Harry realized he hadn't fed the dog since early evening the night before. Every muscle in his body screamed as he dragged himself out of bed and poured food into Rex's bowl. "Sorry, boy." He petted the dog after setting down the food, and then went to the window and looked through the blinds. They hadn't found him yet.

He picked up his phone and called Charlie. "Hi, Sloan"

"Harry, is that you?"

"Yeah. Where's mom?"

"She's right here. The cops have been parked outside your house since yesterday. Where are you?"

"Not too far away. Can you and mom get a cab?"

Harry gave Charlie the address to the motel before hanging up his phone.

Fighting the worst hangover he could ever remember, he gulped down a couple of aspirin then took a shower. After dressing, he placed his video camera, the ham radio and Rex's food and toys into a box, and he stuffed the three sealed envelopes into the box as well. After eating and cleaning up the room, Harry sat on the bed, heaving a sigh.

He got off the bed when he heard a car's horn blaring in the parking lot. He stepped outside and saw a taxi. Charlie and Gertie were in the backseat. Harry handed the cabbie two hundred dollars. "Please wait for them," he said. "They won't be here long."

"You got it," the cabbie said.

Harry helped Gertie and Charlie out of the car. "What's going on, sonny boy?" Gertie said, grabbing Harry by the arm. "Why're you here? You need to come home."

"I can't right now, Ma. Wait here a minute."

Harry went back into his room. He returned carrying the box as he led Rex towards the taxi. He had the cabbie open the trunk and he set the box in it, then he packed Rex into the rear seat.

"Mister, I can't have pets in the cab," the cabbie said.

Harry handed him another hundred-dollar bill. "The dog won't be any trouble. Can you help me out here, buddy?"

The cabbie pocketed the bill. "Yeah, sure."

Gertie, who had seen Rex on more than one occasion, but didn't remember at the moment, stared at the dog, then at Harry. "When did you get a horse?" she said.

"He was Ronnie's. I need you guys to watch him for a while."

"What's going on, Harry?" Charlie said.

"I've got something to do."

"That's not much of an answer," Charlie said.

Gertie caressed Harry's face. "Come home, sonny boy. Please."

Harry was filled with profound sadness and joy. He was saying goodbye, but the fact that his mother recognized him at this moment meant everything to him. "I am going home, Ma." He tenderly kissed his mother's cheek, then hugged her nearly hard enough to break the frail, old woman in half. "I love you so much, Ma."

"More than the sun and the moon and the stars?" Gertie said.

"More than the sun and the moon and the stars."

"Me, too, sonny boy. Come home soon. I'll make us all dinner."

Harry took Gertie's arm and led her to the taxi, then gently tucked her into the rear seat. As if he sensed that this was the last time he'd ever see Harry, Charlie hung his head in sorrow. Harry placed his hands on Charlie's shoulders.

"I'll miss you, old timer."

"I - I don't want to say goodbye, Harry."

"Then I'll do it for both of us." Harry wrapped his arms around the old man and held on tightly.

Charlie whispered in his ear. "Whatever you're thinking of doing, don't do it, Harry. Please don't do it."

"Thank you for being so good to Mom and Joey, Charlie."

Charlie looked up and smiled. "You - you called me Charlie."

Harry smiled back at the old man. "It was on my bucket list."

"What are you going to do?"

"This town needs one more push in the right direction."

"Meaning what, Harry?"

Harry looked skyward. "It's…time."

Charlie grabbed Harry's arm. "No, it doesn't have to be. Please tell me you don't mean it. What about Joey?"

Harry started to choke up. "I – I screwed that up. He doesn't want me in his life anymore."

"That's not true. You just need to give him more time."

"He's not coming back. There's a letter in the box for him. Please make sure he gets it. And there's letters in there for Roy Patterson and Jessica, too."

"What about your mom and me?"

"You've got each other. Be happy."

Tears welled up in Charlie's eyes. "Harry…"

Harry smiled as he tenderly wiped tears off the old man's face. "I hope you and Mom live another hundred years, old timer. I'll see you again on the other side."

Harry gave the old man a gentle push in the direction of the cab. Charlie struggled to hold his ground, to no avail, as Harry pushed just a little harder. He then eased Charlie into the cab as Rex slid over and almost ended up in Gertie's lap.

"Sonny boy, what the hell are we supposed to do with this beast?" Gertie said.

"Love him, Ma, and he'll love you back." Harry tapped on the roof of the cab, and the cab pulled away.

"Come home soon, sonny boy," Gertie said, waving goodbye. Harry smiled through his sadness as he watched the taxi pull onto the highway.

***

When they returned home, Charlie left Gertie in the living room and locked himself in his bathroom. Using his Voiceover-enabled smartphone, he made a phone call.

"John Coleman."

"John, it's Charlie. Have you got a minute?"

"Of course. What's going on?"

"I just saw Harry. He – he scared me. I think he's going to do something drastic."

"Where is he?"

"The Wayside Motel off of Highway 18. Please hurry, John."

"I'm on my way."

53

John walked into the rental office of the Wayside Motel and showed his badge to the clerk. The clerk informed him that a man fitting Harry's description had just checked out fifteen minutes earlier. Stepping into the parking lot, John looked around, exasperated.

***

After driving for several miles on Highway 18, Harry pulled over and made a call. On the other end, Sheriff Roy picked up.

"What's going on, Harry?"

"Roy, tell 'em I'm at the ballpark, and I'm about to blow it to hell."

"Jesus, Harry, don't -"

"Gotta go, buddy." Harry ended the call knowing that Sheriff Roy would call the state police and the feds to alert them. He grinned, knowing that the Brownshirts, at that very moment, were busy wiring the ballpark with fake Semtex and defective detonators, and they would soon have company: a small army of well-armed men.

Harry had checked the town's website several days ago. The town council was off for the long Fourth of July weekend, so he hoped that any law enforcement officers guarding the building would take the bait and hightail it to Sioux Stadium, giving him the time he needed. He finished the two-mile trek up the highway to exit 17, then he cruised slowly down Division Street. He yanked hard on the wheel and pulled to the curb as a convoy of police cruisers blew past him, sirens screaming, heading for the highway. When the street was clear, Harry drove on. Seeing that the town hall's parking lot was now completely empty, he pulled into it.

He opened the car's trunk and pulled out a large duffel bag. He unzipped the bag and pulled out six bricks of putty that resembled Semtex in color and shape. He attached one putty brick to each of the building's four pillars which supported the second story balcony. Then he placed the remaining two bricks on the lower wall of the structure's two adjoining wings. Harry then grabbed a spool of detonation cord and unreeled it as he walked toward the eastern wing's wall. He connected one end of the cord to a brick of putty, then repeated the process on the western wing's wall.

Returning to the car, he connected the other end of the cord to the detonation box that sat on the ground. Getting on his phone again, he called the local television station and the Albrecht Gazette and told staffers at both media outlets that he was about to blow up the town hall building, knowing that the media would break land speed records in a race to be first on the scene.

Harry leaned against the car and pulled a photograph from his shirt pocket: a picture of Patsy and his daughter, Melissa, at the hospital on the day she was born. He smiled as he stared at it, remembering that it was one of the happiest days in his life. *I'm coming home, my loves.* He got on his phone and called Sheriff Roy again.

"Harry, what the hell's going on?! Where are you?!"

"When they're done rounding up the Brownshirts, tell 'em I'm at the town hall, and it's wired to blow. Please don't come, Roy."

"Harry—"

Just as Harry hung up, General Patton appeared. When Harry caught sight of him, he didn't even flinch; he expected the general to show up. Patton saw the picture that Harry held in his hand.

"Taking a stroll down memory lane, Blake?"

"Something like that."

"That's touching," Patton said. He looked around and saw nothing but an empty parking lot. "You promised me blood on this mission, soldier.”

Harry pocketed the picture as he sneered at the general. “You’ll get it, you bastard.”

Patton eyeballed Harry. “Did you just call me a bastard?”

Harry returned the general’s stare. “You heard me.”

The general snarled as he looked Harry up and down. When Patton realized he wasn’t intimidating the big man, he smiled. “You’ve got some stones on you, soldier. I’ll pretend I didn’t hear that. This time.” Patton sneered at Harry. “You think blowing up buildings makes you a hero?”

“I’m no hero. I’m just a guy who’s making a stand, is all.”

Hien appeared, and the general’s eyes nearly popped out of his head when he saw the little Asian man standing next to Harry. “Hot damn!” the general shouted. “It’s a Nip! Now we'll have blood!"

“Hello, Harry. I see the enemy is here,” Hien said.

Harry shook his head in a gesture of defeat. “I can’t… shake him, Hien,” he said.

“Try, my friend,” Hien said.

Patton stepped up to Hien. “‘The enemy’? What the hell’s that mean, Hirohito?” he said.

“He’s not Japanese, you asshole! He’s Vietnamese!” Harry barked.

Patton looked Hien over intently. Sensing an otherworldly power emanating from him, the general grimaced as he took a step away from him and pointed at Harry. “Get rid of him, soldier! That’s an order!”

“He feeds on shame, hate and guilt, Harry. Starve him. Let it go. Let it all go,” Hien said.

Harry began to sob. “I want to. I’m... so tired.”

Patton waved his riding crop in Harry’s face. “You remember what I do to crying soldiers?” he said. When Harry turned his back to the general, Patton morphed into Harry’s father. “Look at me, son.”

“That is not your father, Harry,” Hien said.

“I gave you an order. You don’t dare disobey me, son.” Patton said.

Harry turned to face the general, who still resembled Harry Blake, Sr. "Dad?"

Hien stood next to Harry. "That is not your father, Harry," Hien said. "Tell this abomination it's no longer welcome, my friend."

"You don't want to do that, son," Patton said.

"I do."

But Patton still stood there, defiantly.

"Let it all go," Hien said in a gentle tone.

Harry closed his eyes. He thought about his friends, the guys he fought with in Vietnam and the laughs he'd shared with them, and the tears. Harry thought about the people who had invaded his town and sought to destroy it from within, and how much he despised them for their arrogance and their hypocrisy. Then he thought about Patsy, his daughter, and Ronnie, and how much he missed them. And how much he yearned to join them. As a feeling of tranquility washed over Harry, the general started to fade away. But Harry's hatred for *them* still simmered in his heart, and the general reconstituted. Harry opened his eyes and saw the general still standing there, grinning.

"I - I can't do it, Hien."

"May I help, Harry? All you have to do is ask," Hien said.

"Please," Harry said.

Grinning smugly, Patton turned to face Hien. "Let me tell you a story, little man," the general said. "In May of 1916, my unit was in Mexico chasing down Pancho Villa. We didn't get the bastard that day, but we did kill Villa's second-in-command and two of his guards. You know what I did with their corpses? I had them strapped to the hoods of jeeps before we drove back to base."

Unfazed by the general's veiled threat, Hien smiled. "I know the story. Is there a point in telling it?"

Patton leaned in and whispered into Hien's ear. "I could do things to you if you don't fuck off right now. Bad things."

Hien stood firm. "Do your worst."

Patton swung his riding crop at Hien's midsection. It passed right through him. "What the hell? Who - what the hell are you?" Patton said.

"I'm about to become your worst nightmare," Hien said. He looked Heavenward. "May I?" Hien heard a voice - the Voice – give him permission. "You are hereby banished, fiend. Return to the abyss!"

General Patton pointed his riding crop at Harry. "I'm your superior officer, Blake. I own you! I order you to call this mongrel off!"

Trembling with rage, Harry jumped into Patton's face. "Fuck off!" he shouted. He then turned his back to the general and closed his eyes.

"Nooooo!" Patton bellowed as he vanished into nothingness.

Still shaking, Harry was unwilling to open his eyes. "Is he …gone?"

"He is," Hien replied.

When Harry opened his eyes and saw that the general was really gone, his trembling eased. "For good?"

"Yes, Harry. For good," Hien said. "You're free now."

Harry teared up. "I couldn't save my Patsy. I couldn't save my daughter. Or Ronnie. Or you."

"There was nothing you could do to save any of us, my friend. Absolutely nothing. It was just our time. Please believe and accept that. Please." Harry started to weep. "Harry, you don't know this, but Hans from the BOA was going to take his own life before he met you. You gave him a reason to go on. You saved him. You truly did."

"Really?"

"Yes, really, Harry."

Harry smiled through his tears. "Good for me, huh?"

Yes. Good for you," Hien said. "And if it were within my powers, I would stop you from doing what you're about to do."

"I know you would."

Hien looked towards the street. "They're coming, Harry," he said. "Please don't do it."

Sirens blared as a convoy of law enforcement vehicles, led by Sheriff Patterson, poured into the parking lot. Just behind them, media vans weaved through the bottleneck forming at the parking lot entrance as they jockeyed for parking spaces. A SWAT van barreled into the lot, then came to a screeching halt. Six men, armed with automatic weapons, jumped out of the van and took firing positions fifty feet from Harry. A.T.F. agents poured out of two more vans, crouching behind police cruisers and training their weapons on Harry, as well. Reporters and cameramen scrambled to set up as close to the action as they could get without getting pushed back by the police.

Harry had his audience. He knelt next to the detonation box and placed his hand on the plunger's handle as Sheriff Roy reached him.

"Harry. You don't need to do this."

"Wish you had stayed away, Roy."

John Coleman flashed his badge repeatedly as he navigated around the barricades set up near the parking lot's entrance. He slammed his car into park, got out, and surveyed the situation. When he caught sight of Harry and Sheriff Patterson, he pushed his way through a multitude of peace officers until he saw an F.B.I. negotiator, Stanley Belanger, standing behind a police van with a bullhorn in his hand. John grabbed the man's arm.

"I know him, Stan."

"You know this guy, John?"

"Yeah. Let me talk to him."

"You've got five minutes."

"Tell your boys to stand down!" John yelled as he walked away from Stan. He cautiously approached Harry, who was still kneeling with his hand on the plunger handle. John smiled at Harry, hoping to keep him calm despite the tension and noise that enveloped the men. "Did you hear the one about the parrot that waked into a bar?"

"Yeah. That's a good one, John. You already know Roy here," Harry said.

John waved half-heartedly in Roy's direction. "I do. Talk to us, Harry," John said.

"Not much to say at this point."

John stopped when he came within a few feet of the big man. "It doesn't have to end like this, Harry. Please give yourself up before it's too late."

"Told you I'm not going to prison, John. It's gonna end right here."

Frustrated, John ran his hand through his hair. "Why didn't you just take the damn airplane ticket?"

"A soldier doesn't run from a battle," Harry said.

A group of townsfolk gathered in the parking lot and tried to push their way past the barricades.

"Is that Harry?" a man said.

"It is," another said. "Give 'em hell, Harry!"

John pointed at the crowd. "Looks like you've got a fan club," he said.

"They're my people," Harry said.

"We can get you help, buddy."

Harry got to his feet, his hand still clutching the plunger's handle. He cradled the detonator box as if it were the Holy Grail. "You mean a padded room? And maybe a jacket that ties in the back? That what you'd have 'em do with me, John?"

"We'll get you a good lawyer. Hell, we'll get you an entire law firm if need be."

Harry stared at the sky. "We're way past that, buddy."

"You promised me the C.A.T. building would be the last time, Harry. You promised."

"I didn't lie to you, John." Harry pointed behind him. "Take a look."

John peered at the building's pillars, seeing what he thought were bricks of Semtex attached to each one. Sensing something was wrong, he took a few steps closer to get a better look. He realized there were no blasting caps attached to the bricks. He turned towards Harry. "There's no blasting caps, Harry. What's going on?"

Harry winked. "I must've forgot 'em," he said.

"What does he want?" Stan yelled, from thirty feet away.

Harry stared defiantly at the negotiator and shouted, "I'll tell you what we want! We want Little Hawk put back on his fuckin' pedestal at the ballpark! We want the name of the stadium to be Sioux Stadium again! We want the high school to be called the Chieftains again! We want those bastards to leave our kids to hell alone! We want all the assholes and bullies to fuck off and get the hell out of Albrecht, now!"

The crowd cheered. "Tell 'em, Harry!" a woman shouted.

"We want our town back!" Harry yelled.

"We want out town back!" the crowd chanted. "We want our town back!"

Harry faced the crowd and saluted them. "I do solemnly swear that I will support and defend the United States against all enemies, foreign and *domestic*; that I will bear true faith and allegiance to the same."

A trigger-happy SWAT sniper gripped the trigger of his rifle as Stan got on his bullhorn.

"Set the detonator down now!" Stan said.

"Or, what?" Harry yelled.

"Please, Harry, don't do this," Sheriff Roy said.

Harry looked at the F.B.I. negotiator and shouted, "I got the whole building rigged to blow! And I got hostages inside! I'll do it!"

John knew at that moment what Harry planned to do. "Oh, Jesus," he muttered. Panic gripped him as he turned and ran. When he neared the S.W.A.T. team phalanx, he waved his arms frantically. "Stand down!" he screamed. But the S.W.A.T. team ignored John. They were laser focused on Harry. The noise from the crowd reached another decibel level as they continued to chant, "We want out town back!"

John pushed on until he reached the F.B.I. negotiator. "He's bluffing, Stan! Tell your men to stand down!"

"You had your chance, John. It's my show now."

Sheriff Roy took a step towards Harry. "They'll kill you, Harry. Please…"

Harry raised his hand, and the sheriff came to a stop. "Left a letter for you with Charlie. Enjoy your retirement, Roy. You've been a good friend. Be happy." Then Harry whispered, "God, forgive me," before he pushed down on the plunger.

At the same moment, the trigger-happy SWAT sniper squeezed off a round. The bullet blew through Harry's chest and pierced his heart. John turned just in time to see Harry collapse to the ground. "Oh, Jesus, no..." The crowd fell silent as John ran to Harry, then went to a knee when he reached him. Sheriff Roy was already holding the big man's hand, and both men watched in horror as blood spurted from Harry's chest.

"Harry..." John murmured.

Harry smiled. "Hearts and minds, John. You gotta win..." Harry gasped for air, "...their hearts and minds."

"Paramedic!" John yelled. He gripped Harry's hand and held it tightly, watching in agony as blood oozed from Harry's mouth.

Harry turned towards Hien, who was standing over him with sorrowful eyes. "Forgive me, Hien?" John and Roy looked around, trying to figure out whom Harry was talking to. But they saw no one.

"There is nothing to forgive, Harry. Be at peace, my friend," Hien said.

"I'm coming home, Pats." Harry smiled as he drew his last earthly breath. When paramedics finally reached the men, John waved them off. He and Sheriff Roy bowed their heads as they continued to clutch Harry's lifeless hands.

54

Three days later, the longest procession of cars that the town had ever witnessed rolled slowly down Main Street. Residents of Albrecht and neighboring communities, from young children to the elderly, lined the street on both sides to pay their last respects to Harry Blake, Jr. as the hearse carrying his body crept its way toward Our Lady of Hope Cemetery. Mike Reardon and Ken Burton hung their heads as the hearse rolled by. Hans Wagner, standing across the street, saluted the hearse. The three men wiped away tears as the procession continued down the street.

Joey had gotten a call from his great-uncle James two days earlier telling him that his grandfather was dead, and James had nearly begged the boy to come home for the funeral. Joey agreed to return home. Now, Charlie, Gertie, James and Joey rode in a black sedan that trailed just behind the hearse. The boy stared out the window at a sea of faces lining both sides of the street while Gertie gazed at the crowd in confusion.

"There's a lot of people on the streets. Why are they here?" Gertie said.

"They're paying their final respects, Gert," Charlie said.

"Who passed?"

Charlie started to choke up. "A local man. A good man."

"Did I know him?"

"You knew him, and you liked him, dear. You liked him a great deal."

"What was his name?"

"Harry."

"Harry? That sounds familiar. How did he pass?"

"Fighting the good fight, like a soldier does."

"He was a soldier?"

"Right 'til the very end, dear. He loved this town. And the town loved him."

"Then we should pay our respects to the man."

"That's why we're here."

"I wish I remembered him," Gertie said.

Charlie wept quietly as he clutched Gertie's hand. The hearse continued down the street, and people hung their heads in deference and sadness as it passed by. Veterans saluted, and others solemnly waved goodbye. And many cried.

***

The service at the cemetery was a short one. A military honor guard team fired off three rifle volleys, and other service members saluted as Harry's casket was lowered into the ground into a plot next to his wife, Patsy, and his daughter, Melissa. A priest read from the Bible. "I am the resurrection and the life. He that believeth in me, though he were dead, yet shall he live."

***

Later that night, as Joey sat on his grandfather's bed, Charlie knocked on the bedroom door. "You here, Joey?"

"Yeah."

Charlie stepped into the room holding an envelope. He handed it to the boy. "It's from your grandpa."

"I don't want it," Joey said, tossing the letter on the bed.

"Your grandpa loved you, Joey. He tried to fix things between you, and you did nothing but ignore him. Your own grandfather. He's gone

379

now. Show him a little respect and read it."

Charlie left the room. Joey stared at the letter for a few moments, then he finally picked it up and began to read. ***Joey, I'm so sorry I had to leave you, but my fight was over. I took on those people the only way I knew how. They came to this town to bully us, and you can't reason with bullies or fanatics. You have to fight them. You have to expose them for the cowards they are. You have to expose them for the hypocrites they are. I fought for what I thought was right.***

Joey, don't ever let anyone tell you what to think or what to say. Don't ever let anyone silence you because you don't agree with them and their twisted beliefs. Your generation has to pick up the fight. Be your own man. And be happy. I'm going to be with your mom and grandmother now. I love you more than you'll ever know.

Joey dropped the letter on the bed and began to cry.

***

Just down the street, Jessica sat at her kitchen table and read a letter that Charlie had dropped off earlier that day.

Miss Jess, if you're reading this, I'm already gone. I'm sorry the last time we saw each other it ended so bad. That's not what I wanted, but maybe it was for the best. I was never good with long goodbyes. Thank you for giving an old coot some attention and companionship he probably didn't deserve. You're a good woman. Don't let them make you feel guilty for being just that. That's how they get power, power they didn't earn and power they don't deserve. Be happy, Miss Jess.

Jessica set the letter down and started to cry.

55

The people of Albrecht awoke. Two days after Harry was laid to rest, the town voted in a special referendum, and by an overwhelming margin, they ousted the four members of the town council who had voted to rename the town's baseball team. And the people expelled the council's chairman as well, the man who signed off on the school curricula that sought to teach the town's children critical race theory and attempted to sexualize them while hiding their agenda from the students' parents.

"They" Collins, the Pinetree County State's Attorney who couldn't decide what gender he/she/they were, who openly advocated for Albrecht's grade schools to host Drag Queen Story Hour, and who also campaigned for students as young as six- years old to demand to be called by personal pronouns, was removed from office in a recall referendum by an overwhelming margin.

Bitter about the outcome of the recall, Ms./Mr. Collins told the media that the people of Pinetree County were "unenlightened, stupid and just plain mean." Soon after, "They" decided to relocate to a more diverse, inclusive and equitable state. The people of Albrecht slept better the night he/she/they left for good. The new members of the council, along with the original two remaining members, unanimously voted to once again call the town's Double -A ballclub the War Chiefs, and the baseball stadium would once again be called Sioux Stadium, just as it had been for decades. And the high school got its team nickname, the Chieftains, back as well.

John passed along Harry's video evidence of Crash's drug deal to the D.E.A. Crash, his jaw still wired shut, lay in a hospital bed sipping his lunch through a straw when D.E.A. agents handcuffed him to his bed and assured him that they would return soon. They returned a few days later when Crash was able to talk again. And talk, the boy did. It was Crash's second offense for drug trafficking, and in a panic, he waived his Miranda rights, telling the feds everything he knew in the hope of receiving a lighter sentence.

Crash implicated his cousin, Fast Freddie, as the ringleader, and he gave up names and details faster than the court stenographer could type. Fast Freddie was arrested one hour later at the trailer that was his temporary office. After a brief trial, Crash was sentenced to twenty years in a federal prison. Fast Freddie received the same sentence, and he was permanently disbarred.

The members of the Brownshirts of America, except for Hans, were charged with domestic terrorism under the Patriot Act for attempted use of a weapon of mass destruction, despite the fact that no Semtex or any other explosive was found at the baseball stadium. Each man received a sentence of fifteen years in prison. The rec hall in Bremerhaven was reclaimed by the town, renovated, then reopened three months later to the public.

***

Before he and his wife left Albrecht for their retirement home down South, Sheriff Patterson tendered his resignation, effective at the end of the month. At dusk on the same day, he took a drive to Harry's home. Roy got out of his car and stopped when he saw a makeshift shrine of flowers and cards covering most of Harry's front lawn. He bowed his head in a moment of sadness and respect, then he made his way towards Harry's backyard.

He circled around to the rear of the utility shed and found a three-foot section of fresh dirt between the shed and the chain link fence that divided Harry's property from the neighbor's yard. Roy grabbed a shovel from the shed and began digging. When the shovel hit metal, Roy stopped digging and went to a knee. He pulled a heavy-duty, metal storage box from the hole and set it on the ground. The box held twenty pounds of Semtex, and step-by-step directions on how to detonate the explosive using a cell phone, blasting caps, and a serious set of testicles. In his goodbye letter to the sheriff, Harry had told Roy to let his conscience guide him. After refilling the hole and returning the shovel to the shed, Sheriff Roy hauled the crate to his car and placed it in the trunk. Before getting into his car, he took one last, mournful gaze at Harry's home. Then he looked Heavenward. "You're the man, Harry. Rest in peace."

***

Two weeks after Harry's death, the town of Albrecht witnessed several changes. The TID and BID organizations decided that they should relocate to a "safer space," a city more than a hundred miles from Albrecht. But the organizations that funded The Center for Alternative Thinking decided that they weren't going to be run out of town quite so easily. A building was leased on the northeastern edge of Albrecht. The day before it was scheduled to open, the new C.A.T. building was brought to the ground, and Semtex was once again the bomber's explosive of choice.

After what he called an "exhaustive investigation" that lasted two days, outgoing Sheriff Patterson stated in a press conference that his department had no leads regarding the "heat-related incident." The citizens of Albrecht were quite satisfied with that. And the feds got no cooperation from the town's residents when they descended on Albrecht in search of evidence pertaining to the latest bombing. It didn't matter to the townsfolk who destroyed the new building. They had a new hero, even if he remained anonymous.

Blowing up the new C.A.T. building was Sheriff Roy's parting gift to the town he had called home since he was a child. And if the organizations that funded the C.A.T. ever again decided to push their luck and try to establish yet another beachhead in Albrecht, the sheriff knew he could always return and set things right. He had more Semtex. And he knew more than a few of the townsfolk who would be glad to lend a hand, if need be.

***

John Coleman spent an afternoon with Charlie reminiscing about Harry, life, and their experiences in war. He promised Charlie that he would return to Albrecht someday soon to visit. And, if his wife agreed, John told Charlie that he was going to buy property in town and reside there permanently. That made Charlie very happy.

John did three more things before he left town; he officially tendered his resignation with the F.B.I., he called his wife and told her how much he loved her and that he'd be home soon, and he spearheaded a movement to have his friend, Harry Blake, immortalized. One month after Harry's death, the newly revamped town council voted unanimously to rename Higgins Park, Blake Park.

That same week, the town unveiled a bronze statue of a big man sitting on a park bench holding a cane in one hand. The other hand rested on the plunger of a detonation box. The statue sat at the edge of Blake Park, directly across the street from the defunct C.A.T. building. A memorial tablet adjacent to the statue read:

Harry Blake Jr.

Husband. Father. Friend.

Veteran. Patriot.